Book T

Douglas Niles is a ... writes books and d... and works at his home in the woods of southern Wisconsin. He and his wife, Christine, have two children, Alison and David, and are attempting to train an enthusiastic Bouvier named Kodiak.

Douglas Niles is the author or designer of over fifty titles, including his first three novels, the bestselling Moonshae Trilogy. His game design credits include numerous DRAGONLANCE® modules, the TOP SECRETS/S.I.™ game, and board games based on two Tom Clancy novels, *The Hunt for Red October* and *Red Storm Rising*.

FANTASY ADVENTURE

VIPER HAND

by Douglas Niles

Cover Art
FRED FIELDS

PENGUIN BOOKS
in association with TSR, Inc.

PENGUIN BOOKS

Published by the Penguin Group
Penguin Books Ltd, 27 Wrights Lane, London W8 5TZ, England
Viking Penguin, a division of Penguin Books USA Inc.
375 Hudson Street, New York, New York 10014, USA
Penguin Books Australia Ltd, Ringwood, Victoria, Australia
Penguin Books Canada Ltd, 2801 John Street, Markham, Ontario, Canada L3R 1B4
Penguin Books (NZ) Ltd, 182–190 Wairau Road, Auckland 10, New Zealand

Penguin Books Ltd, Registered Offices: Harmondsworth, Middlesex, England

First published in the USA by TSR, Inc. 1990
Distributed to the book trade in the USA by Random House, Inc.,
and in Canada by Random House of Canada Ltd
Distributed in the UK by TSR Ltd
Distributed to the toy and hobby trade by regional distributors
First published in Great Britain by Penguin Books 1991
1 3 5 7 9 10 8 6 4 2

Copyright © TSR, Inc. 1990
All rights reserved

FORGOTTEN REALMS, PRODUCTS OF YOUR IMAGINATION, AD&D,
TSR, DRAGONLANCE and the TSR logo are trademarks owned by TSR, Inc.

Printed in England by Clays Ltd, St Ives plc

Except in the United States of America,
this book is sold subject to the condition
that it shall not, by way of trade or otherwise,
be lent, re-sold, hired out, or otherwise circulated
without the publisher's prior consent in any form of
binding or cover other than that in which it is
published and without a similar condition
including this condition being imposed
on the subsequent purchaser

To Dirk Niles,
in memory of the Bighorns

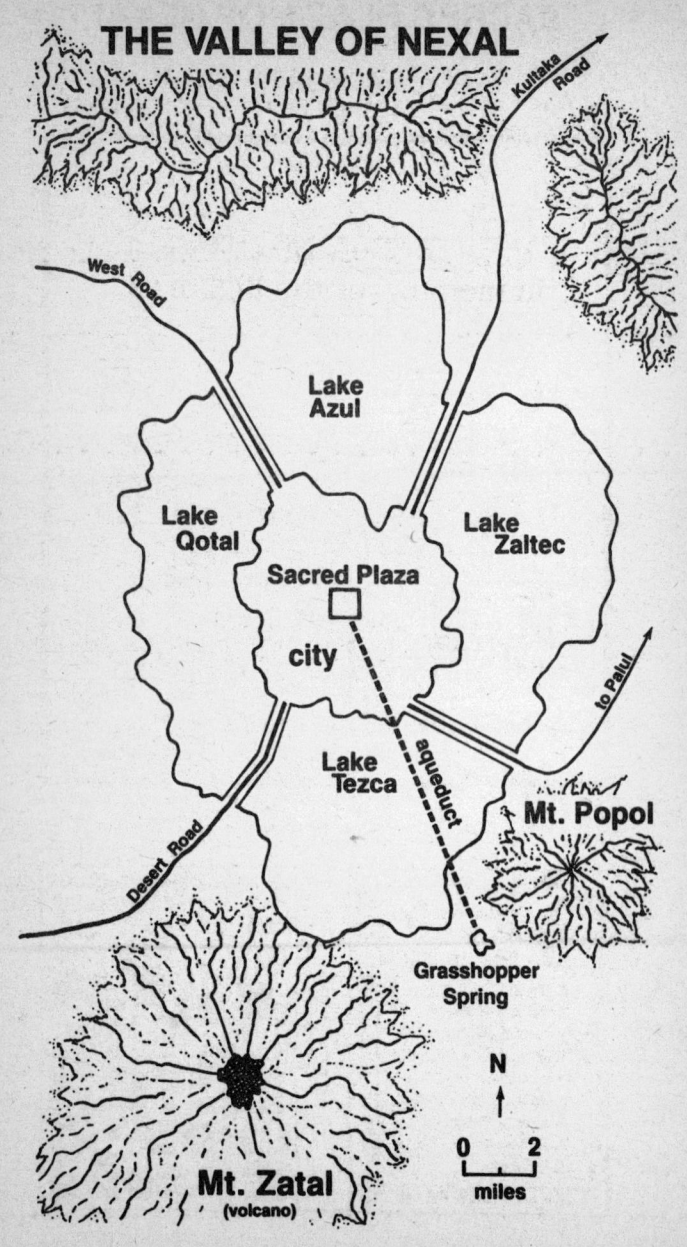

SACRED PLAZA OF NEXAL

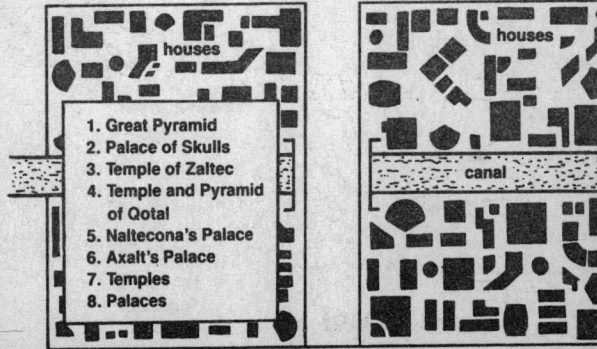

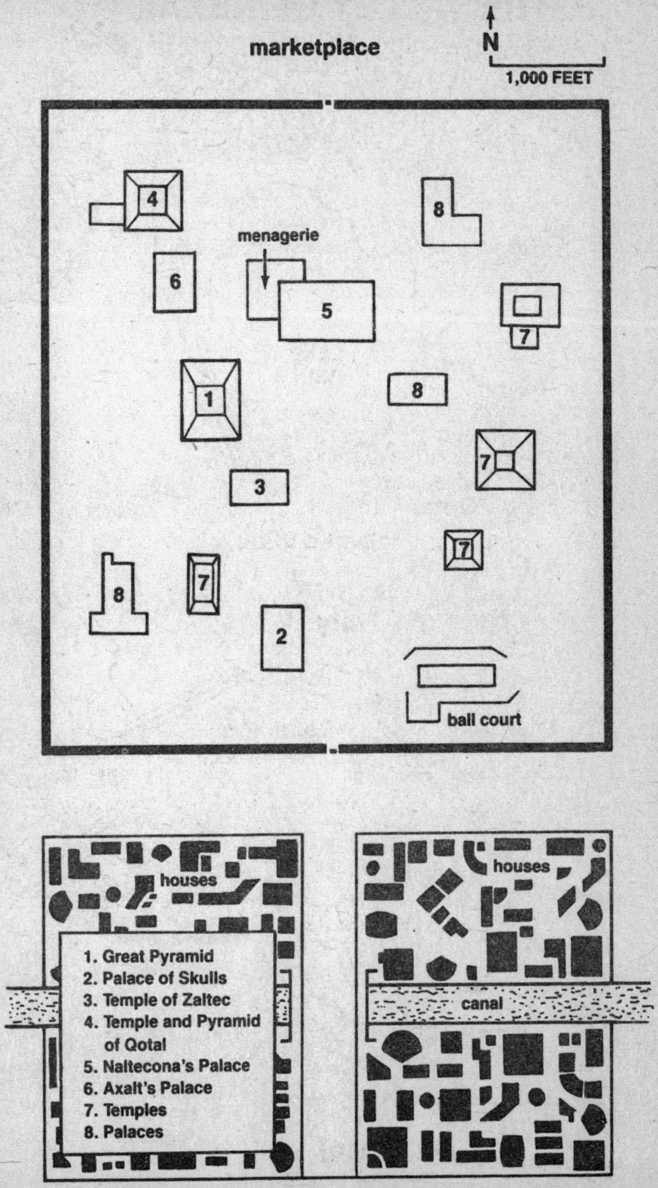

N
marketplace
1,000 FEET
menagerie
ball court
houses
canal
houses
1. Great Pyramid
2. Palace of Skulls
3. Temple of Zaltec
4. Temple and Pyramid of Qotal
5. Naltecona's Palace
6. Axalt's Palace
7. Temples
8. Palaces

Prologue

The gods grew complacent in the sameness of their immortal lives, content to accept the worship of mortals and to rule their lordly domains. Eternal, imperturbable, they passed the centuries in sublime disregard of the flesh-bound world below.

But occasionally the actions of a god's worshipers brought that deity into conflict with his fellows. Such a collision of godhood inevitably spelled chaos, even complete doom, for the peoples in the divine one's fold.

So it was with Helm the Vigilant, patron god of the Golden Legion. His faithful, the crusading soldiery of that legion, carried his banner forward into new lands—lands of great riches and beauty, but of dark savagery as well. Willingly, eagerly, Helm followed. Now he faced gods from beyond his ken—gods with an apparently unquenchable thirst for human hearts, human blood.

So, too, with Zaltec the Terrible, one of those thirsty lords. The ravenous god of war consumed the hearts offered by his priests with relish. Lordly master of Maztica, he faced the invading forces of Helm with a burning increase in his own hunger. Zaltec needed more hearts, more blood.

And with Qotal, once hailed as preeminent among the gods of Maztica. The Plumed One, however, had long since been banished from the True World by those who thought gods could only be worshiped with the shedding of blood and the taking of lives. Qotal sought to smooth the confluence of peoples and gods, but his power was weak, his presence all but unknown.

And also, below them all, seething with the darkness of her hatred and evil, so it was with another god—a god whose presence and interest the deities of Maztica did not even suspect. Lolth, the spidery essence of darkness and evil, dwelled far from the others, in the infernal reaches themselves. Queen of the dark elves—the drow—Lolth's hatred now focused against those of her children who no longer held her name in awe.

To Lolth, to them all, the land called Maztica was a gaming board, a table upon which lay the pieces of their immortal contest. It required but a thoughtless breath, or the casual flick of a limb, to sweep the board clean.

❧1❧
THE HOUSE OF TEZCA

Halloran felt certain they would die here in this miserable, waterless waste. The sun assaulted them from all sides, searing their skin, parching their dusty mouths, blinding their eyes with an unceasing glare.

His tongue swelling in his throat, Hal looked about, only dimly aware of the infernal surroundings. He and his two companions trudged wearily across the House of Tezca, the great desert named for Maztica's god of the sun. Harsh yellow shards of rock jutted from the sandy ground, and low, windswept ridges marked the horizon on all sides. In the far distance, purple mountains, capped with blinding snowfields, loomed against the skyline, taunting them with their unattainable promise of cool heights and rapid, icy streams.

Long since discarded, Halloran's steel helmet and breastplate were now lashed to the saddlebags of Storm, his once-proud war-horse. The sturdy charger plodded listlessly, sometimes tripping or stumbling. A few more hours without water, Halloran knew, and the steed would collapse.

Reluctantly, blinking against the pain, he looked to the man and the woman who were his companions. They, too, could last but a matter of hours unless they found water.

Poshtli, the Eagle Knight, seemed least affected. The proud warrior led the way, maintaining his steady stride across the rocky, undulating terrain of the desert. For days, Poshtli's strength had guided and propelled them. He had brought them to the desert—for good reasons, Hal understood—but now the torched landscape had become a trap. Burdened by this responsibility, the warrior drove himself mercilessly, leading the way without a backward look.

Douglas Niles

Erixitl, the beautiful young woman who had showed him so many wonders of her land, seemed but a distant memory to Hal now. It broke his heart to see her in this wasteland that must soon claim them all.

She looked at him now, her eyelids swollen by sun and dust. Her lips, cracked, sunburned, and bleeding, could no longer smile. She had not spoken since the merciless sun had risen uncounted hours earlier. If even her exuberant spirit had been broken, Halloran knew, their doom must be imminent.

For more countless hours, they marched, seeking shelter that could not be found. Their last water gone, consumed at the end of the previous day's march, they all understood that their only hope lay in continuous, desperate search.

"I have failed," Poshtli croaked finally as they crested yet another sharp, parched ridge. "It was a mistake to seek the desert dwarves. We would have done better to brave the lands of Pezelac and Nexal. There, at least, we would have found food and drink to sustain us."

Hal shook his head weakly. "But enemies, too. They would kill us before we could ever reach the city."

Erixitl stumbled past, as if she did not hear. But she did. She knew that she was the cause of their ill-chosen path, selected to avoid human habitation and the bloodthirsty priests who strived to place her lithe body across a gruesome sacrificial altar. Every tiny village had a temple devoted to this god of war, and any one of the priests to be found there would strive mightily for the chance to offer this girl's heart to Zaltec. She did not know why the priests of Zaltec sought her death so unceasingly, but she understood that their hatred was implacable.

Before entering the desert, they had slain one of these agents of death—not a priest, but rather one of the black-robed leaders of the cult of Zaltec known as the Ancient Ones. Even the priests of Zaltec looked to the Ancient Ones for leadership and direction. Halloran had told her that these beings were known as drow, or dark elves, in other parts of the world. Everywhere—on the Sword Coast, in Maztica, or beneath the surface of the land—they were hateful and malicious.

But the drow represented only one of the enemy's tentacles. The savage priests of Zaltec, the god of war, sought Erix's heart for their bloodstained altars. And unlike the dark elves, the priests of Zaltec would be encountered in every town, every small village, that lay in their path.

Another cause of their flight lay in Hal's former comrades, now his enemies, who fought under the golden banner of Captain-General Cordell. The mercenaries of the Golden Legion had sailed from the Sword Coast, the most populous shore on the continent of Faerun, in search of the gold and spices of Kara-Tur. They had found, instead, this land called Maztica, where gold aplenty awaited their depredations.

But his former swordmates now sought Hal as a fugitive and traitor. Betrayed by Bishou Domincus, the dour cleric who spoke for the legion's warlike god, Hal had fled into the interior of this strange land. Pursued by the frightening elf-wizard Darien, Halloran knew that either the wizard or the cleric would slay him at the first opportunity. He had only the company of these two loyal companions to keep him from a plight of complete solitude.

Their only hope of sanctuary, the trio had decided, lay in the great city of Nexal, the Heart of the True World. There they would seek the protection of the great Naltecona, Revered Counselor and ruler of all Nexal, and, perhaps more to the point, the uncle of the Eagle Knight Poshtli.

Hal and Poshtli looked across the bleak landscape from the crest of the low ridge. No trace of greenery gave the promise of water. The war-horse, Storm, hung his head listlessly. The faithful steed's eyes were glassy, his flanks covered with dust.

A sense of despair dropped over them like a black cloth. What could they hope for, besides a slow, parched death? Earlier, Poshtli's goal—to reach the desert dwarves that he knew dwelled somewhere in this rocky wasteland—had seemed like a hopeful alternative to death by magic or sacrifice. But now that hope faded, for they had seen no sign of any living creature for many days.

Suddenly Erix turned toward them, her face brightening with faint vitality. "Listen!" she croaked through her parched lips.

"What?" asked Poshtli, tensing.

"I don't hear anything," Hal said numbly.

"You *must!*" she snapped. "There! There it is again!"

"A cry . . . it sounds human," Poshtli whispered, his black eyes darting around the horizon. Halloran had still heard nothing.

"This way!" Erix declared, her voice full of sudden hope. She hastened down the sandy ridge, the men stumbling hurriedly behind her. Hal felt beyond hope, past depair, only noting dimly that they moved again. Erixitl's trail swung to the right, and they came around a rough shoulder of rock. "There!"

The woman pointed to a green splash of color against the brown rocks. At first, Hal thought she had found some succulent plant, but then the greenery took to the air with a beat of powerful wings, trailing its bright-plumed tail behind it.

"A macaw," breathed Poshtli. "A bird of the jungle! But here, in the desert?"

"He must have water nearby," Erix replied.

The bird flew upward and circled them for a moment. Then it dove away, coming to light on another ridge that lay beyond the low rise they had just traversed. Eagerly, with a desperate sense of hope, they started toward the bird.

It sat still, regarding them with bright, unblinking eyes as they shuffled forward as quickly as total exhaustion allowed. It squawked once, chopping its hooked beak. The macaw's large yellow claws shifted awkwardly on its stony perch, but still it stared at them.

Erix led the way. Suddenly she was no longer stumbling. Scrambling up the shallow slope, she almost reached the bird before, with a sudden flip of its wings, it again took to the air.

The macaw darted up and over the top of the slope, diving out of sight down the far side. Halloran shook off an irrational fear that Erix would fly away with the bird, disappearing from his life.

"Hurry!" Erix called excitedly, nearly sprinting to the top.

The others joined her at the rocky crest, gasping for breath. Even Storm lumbered along, almost trotting, until they all stopped and stared in amazement.

Before them lay a shallow valley, rocky, not as sand-covered as the surrounding desert. Steep shelves of crumbling stone plummeted to the floor of the depression, which resembled a great yellow bowl, perhaps half a mile across. It was so deep that they could not have seen inside it unless they were standing upon its rim as they now did.

At the bottom of the valley, a small blue pool, surrounded by green ferns, grass, and a few stunted palm trees, reflected the suddenly softened rays of the sun. A gentle wisp of wind formed ripples across its smooth surface, and from them, the sunlight glinted like cool diamond.

* * * * *

Shrouded in dark cloth, the Ancestor approached the caldron of the Darkfyre. The slender figure moved slowly, but with none of the stiffness common to an elderly human. In a sudden gesture, he threw back his hood, allowing the crimson light of that infernal blaze to wash over his stark, pinched face.

His dark features stretched taut over his narrow skull, and his white hair clung to his scalp, too thin to conceal the shiny black skin below. The Ancestor's nostrils flared with his breathing, and his thin lips parted slightly to reveal white teeth in red, clearly visible gums. His arms and legs seemed nothing more than bone, covered with tight skin. He was an image of death, a gaunt, skeletal figure propped up by some unseen force.

Except for his eyes. All of his energy seemed to focus in those wide, white orbs, reflecting the dim glow of the Darkfyre and amplifying it with heat of their own. He stared in relish at the unnatural blaze.

"The fire of true power!" hissed the ancient drow, his voice rasping like wind through dry leaves.

He watched the Harvesters now, as they fed hearts to the blaze. The Harvesters were young drow, not yet ready for the exalted order of the Ancient Ones, but dedicated to the attainment of that rank. Now they worked diligently, teleporting nightly across the land of Maztica to the sacrificial altars of bloody Zaltec, reaping the hearts torn from human victims in the sunset rites.

These grisly tokens of Zaltec's faith were brought here to feed the infernal appetite of the Darkfyre. The god's hunger, dictated to the priests by the Ancient Ones, brought an endless stream of captives, slaves, failed warriors—even faithful volunteers—to the altars. And as the hearts fed the fire, so did the power of Zaltec grow.

The caldron and the cavern itself, the central meeting chamber of the drow, actually lay far above the surface of most of Maztica, excavated and eroded into the towering summit of Mount Zatal. The volcanic peak dominated the valley of Nexal, overlooking that great city. Now the volcano rumbled, as if a giant belch signified Zaltec's pleasure with his meal. The sensation of power as the rock trembled beneath his feet pleased the Ancestor.

Finally the Harvesters finished, and the Ancestor took his seat, alone in the cavern. From his great throne, he studied the circular stone depression before him. Some twenty feet across, its lip even with the cavern floor, the caldron glowed with a crimson, evil flame. The fresh hearts gleamed like red coals, though they shed little heat. Most of their power seethed downward, into the heart of the mountain and the soul of Zaltec himself.

This is might, the Ancestor realized. *Zaltec is might! The worship of the god of war is a faith of true vibrancy and great power!* Known to the Mazticans even before the coming of the drow, Zaltec had not achieved his current influence until the Ancient Ones arrived. Spreading his cult of sacrifice, they had fed the war god as never before. Soon Zaltec's power would be supreme, unstoppable.

The Ancestor thought for a moment of Lolth, the spider goddess of the drow, deified by others of his folk, in other parts of the world. The personification of evil, Lolth was a cruel mistress, promising power to those who followed her faithfully.

Once the Ancient Ones had numbered among those faithful, devoting their strength and their lives to the spider goddess.

"Bah!" he exclaimed, sneering. The other drow were fools. Lolth had forsaken the drow of Maztica, had turned her back upon them when the Rockfire wracked the land. Splitting the very earth, tearing the bedrock itself asunder, that convulsion had cut off the Ancestors' tribe from the rest of the dark elf race. Now that tribe had become the Ancient Ones, spokesmen for the cult of Zaltec, revered by the peoples of Maztica. Lolth and her pathetic minions, separated from Maztica by vast stretches of land, counted for less than nothing here.

Zaltec alone became their life and their future.

The Ancestor stared again at the hot, crimson hearts, glowing like coals in their vast hollow. Zaltec would rule the land! The priests of that dark god, following the teachings of the Ancient Ones, worked to convert warriors to their cause, marking them with the snake's-head brand. The cult of the Viperhand had begun to flourish, and this was the perfect instrument for the drows' work.

Another perfect tool sat on the throne of Nexal itself, the venerable drow reflected. The great Naltecona, Revered Counselor of the Nexala and virtual emperor of Maztica, served nicely as a figure to be held in awe. The ruler himself didn't see how willingly he forwarded the cause of the Ancient Ones.

Yet Naltecona's death had long been foretold, and in his passing, he would create a void of power across the land. Maztica would require new masters. And the Ancient Ones, through the cult of the Viperhand, would be ready.

Two matters still caused the Ancestor some concern. One was the landing of the Golden Legion in Maztica. These warlike strangers threatened to destroy all the preparations of the Ancient Ones. With their steel and their magic, the invaders were a formidable foe. Still, the Ancestor had anticipated the invasion and had taken a precautionary step, some ten years ago, to counter it. That step had come to fruition, and it might be that it would turn the Golden Legion into a powerful, if unwitting, ally.

The other, more vexing, matter was that of the girl, Erixitl. She still, somehow, eluded them.

Recalling the vision that had chilled him decades ago, the Ancestor faced his grim knowledge. Zaltec had sent him a warning, in the form of a white, gleaming star. In the drow's vision, that star touched upon them just as Zaltec's mastery came to fruition. The resulting cataclysm wracked the dark elves, bringing the tribe to ruin. As an insignificant side effect, the continent of Maztica suffered horrible ravages from the force of the same convulsions.

After years of study, meditation, and sacrifice, the nature of the white star had become clear: A human girl held the seed of potential disaster. Not until much later had this girl been identified, again through the flaming picture of the Darkfyre, as Erixitl of Palul. She had been a mere decade old at the time, but orders for her death had instantly gone forth. Somehow she had escaped all his agents of murder—priests, Jaguar Knights, and finally even the drow Spirali, who had been slain by Poshtli and Halloran. Erixitl still lived, and while she lived the Ancient Ones' machinations remained in peril. She must die!

Then the mastery of Maztica would be assured.

* * * * *

Erixitl had never tasted anything sweeter than the water from the lonely desert pool. The macaw squawked, approvingly she thought, from one of the palm trees as the three humans and the horse slaked their thirst in the shallow, clear pond.

They collapsed in the shade of the palm trees and said nothing for a time as the sun sank toward the horizon and long shadows stretched across the little vale. The clear sky offered no sheltering cloud, and the desert heat still baked them. For now, it was enough to live, to know that their throats would not crack from lack of moisture, or their lungs parch from the dry air.

"We'll head north from here," Poshtli said after a while. "That should bring us into the south of Nexal, away from the surrounding cities. I'm sure we can carry enough water to make it that far."

"What then?" asked Halloran. Erix noted that his command of the Nexalan tongue grew with each passing day. Though she had learned his language—aided by magic—the trio conversed in Nexalan, which they all understood.

"We will see my uncle, Naltecona," explained the warrior.

"I expect that he will grant his protection, though there is no way to be certain of that. Some of his advisors will surely urge your harm. After Ulatos, bad blood will flow hot among the warriors."

The defeat of the nation of Payit by the forces of the Golden Legion had included a bloody rampage by the invading forces. The legion had attacked the Payit at their capital city of Ulatos. It had been the first, but probably not the last, violent conflict between the legion and the warriors from a nation of Maztica.

"But Halloran didn't aid his comrades at Ulatos!" objected Erix. "He saved me from them!"

"The great Naltecona will hear this, and we must have faith in his wisdom," answered Poshtli.

"I'll take that chance," said Hal. "For one thing, it seems we have few other choices—save constant flight. It runs against my nature to flee my enemies rather than to face them."

"Well said," Poshtli agreed. "Though we do well to choose a battle on our own terms."

"Agreed." Halloran nodded. "When it comes, it can't be any worse than some of the other fixes I've gotten myself into over the years. I've had battles against pirates and desert nomads, been surrounded by ogres . . ."

"Ogres?" asked Poshtli. "What are these 'ogres'?"

Halloran looked at him in surprise. "Well, they're fierce and huge—kind of like humans, but bigger and dumber, and very savage. They're monsters, of a type similar to orcs and trolls. Don't you have creatures like that in Maztica?"

Poshtli shook his head. "These monsters, manlike but savage, do not exist here. We have the *hakuna,* the fire lizard, and other dangers. But for a lack of ogres and orcs, it seems we should be grateful."

Erixitl listened to the men talk of monsters and warfare, feeling the weariness creeping over her even before the sky had completely darkened. She wished that these minutes of peace might last into hours, or days, though she feared this was impossible. Nevertheless, the prospects of future dangers could not overcome her present contentment.

In minutes, she slept. But sleep offered no peace on this night.

Erixitl became a bird, soaring above the expanse of Maztica. Or perhaps she was the wind itself, the warm embodiment of life-giving air, sweeping across the True World with a cleansing caress. She swirled above snowy peaks, whisked among green forests and heavy jungles. She knew a sense of freedom and power that had never been hers before.

Across Maztica she soared, over the lands of the Payit and the Kultakans, and finally, at the center of the continent, the realm of mighty Nexal. The twin volcanoes of Zatal and Popol barred her way, but the wind broke up and over the massif unchecked. She swept into the streets of the city of Nexal, and though she had never seen the great city, she recognized it—indeed, she knew it well. Beneath the cool wash of a full moon, hanging low against the eastern horizon, she darted around towering pyramids, along myriad canals, until finally she soared into the palace of Naltecona himself.

But here something was wrong.

Growing chill, she glided up the walls, onto the roof of the palace. There she saw the Revered Counselor, resplendent in a feathered headdress and his cape of many colors. Men of the Golden Legion surrounded Naltecona. In alarm, Erixitl coursed closer, noting the sharp shadows cast by the moon. The figures stood in a circle, a tableau for her inspection.

She saw a metal-helmed figure with steely hard black eyes, and she knew this was Cordell. With vague surprise, she noticed that Halloran, too, stood among them, though his former comrades did not desire his presence. She understood these things, even as she witnessed the frozen scene.

And around the palace, across the floor of a broad, enclosed plaza, glowered thousands of warriors. Upon the chests of many, Erix saw, was the pulsating crimson head of a living snake. The forked tongues of these vipers flickered forth, sensing blood in the air.

Then the stillness on the palace roof broke as, with slow but deliberate movements, the players came to life.

Under the glaring moon, slowly rising in the east, Naltecona fell dead. Erix swept forward, too late for aught but a final circle around the bleeding figure of the great ruler.

The men of the legion staggered back in consternation at the killing. The world turned dark, and chaos fell from the skies. The looming volcano rumbled.

And then black shadows spread across the face of Maztica. The land became a great, gaping sore, and poison poured forth. It spread in a growing circle, to the horizons of her vision, and it kept growing.

Erix knew that she was seeing the end of the world.

* * * * *

"It's called 'steel,'" Halloran explained, showing Poshtli the gleaming edge of his sword, Helmstooth. "It comes from a mixture of metals, combined under great heat. Mostly iron."

He enjoyed talking to the warrior, and during their journey had come to realize that he and Poshtli had much in common. At times, he almost forgot that this man was the product of a savage, bloodthirsty society.

"Iron? Steel?" Poshtli repeated the foreign words, lisping them off his tongue. He had seen Hal's weapons in action, had held and examined them before, but now he took advantage of Hal's growing command of the language to ask about them. "These must be metals of great power."

"Perhaps. They are strong materials, and hold a keen edge. You've seen them splinter wooden weapons and stone blades."

"These are metals that do not dwell in the True World," explained the warrior, a trifle wistfully.

"I think they do," Hal countered. "But you lack the tools—the 'powers'—to pull them from the earth."

"Metals. Silver and gold, these are the metals known to us. They are beautiful, even desirable. They have many uses—for art, for ornamentation. Lords wear lip plugs and earplugs of these metals, and the dust of gold is used for barter. It is easier to transport than a similar value of cocoa beans. Yet these metals do not cause a hunger in us such as they seem to among your own people. Tell me, Halloran, do you devour such metals?"

Hal laughed grimly. "No. We covet them, some of us, for they have come to represent wealth. And wealth represents power in our lands."

"We are of different worlds, different peoples," said Poshtli, with a slow shake of his head. He looked up, staring frankly at Hal. "Yet I am glad that our paths have crossed."

Hal nodded in agreement, surprised at the warmth of friendship he felt for this warrior. "Without you, Erix and I would surely have perished by now," he said sincerely. "I can only thank whatever gods watch over us that we have, the three of us, been brought together."

They both looked at Erixitl, who rolled restlessly in her sleep. Tossing her head, as if in sudden dismay, she threw a hand upward. Her long brown fingers rested across her forehead, and Halloran was struck, as he had been struck so many times before, by her serene beauty. The ravages of their march, soothed now by rest and water, seemed to melt away from her.

Soon the men, too, settled back quietly. Poshtli quickly slumbered, but Hal couldn't keep his eyes closed.

His mind was tormented by the confusing pictures of this land. He looked at Erix and Poshtli, recognizing their nobility of character, the depths of their friendship and loyalty. Each could certainly have fared better alone, rather than to remain with him, a giant, white-skinned stranger from another world. They showed him the strength, the fineness of Maztica.

Yet he also remembered the brutality of a cleric in Payit, a worshiper of Zaltec who had torn the heart from a helpless woman held prostrate across his vile altar while Halloran was restrained, helpless, scant feet away. He saw images of that grim, warlike god, and thought with a shudder of this culture that tolerated such a bestial religion. He wondered in amazement about such people, that they could accept as a god's due the gruesome sacrifice of so many of their own.

Now he journeyed to the city at the very heart of this world. Why? He asked himself the question that tore at him, but he couldn't be satisfied with the answer. True, he saw no other alternative. But he didn't belong here! Everything around him brought home the alien nature of this land. The barbarism of Maztican religion shocked and appalled him.

But where could he turn? Sitting up and shaking his head in frustration, he thought of his former companions in the

Golden Legion. Doubtless they all wanted him dead by now—certainly that was the desire of the dour Bishou Domincus and the quiet, menacing elven mage, Darien.

He thought of his escape from the legion's brig, where he had been sent by the Bishou in the man's grieving rage over his daughter's death. Hal escaped, seeking the chance to redeem himself on the field. There he had found Alvarro, ready to trample Erix into dust, consumed by bloodlust.

The choice then, as now, had been clear. He saved her and they fled, though the act must surely now have branded him a traitor.

So he remained with these true companions, accompanying them to Nexal, to this great city about which they both talked so reverently. He had, in truth, nowhere else to go. But there was more, much more, to it than that.

He remembered the Bishou's daughter, Martine, slain by the sacrificial knife. At one time, he had thought he loved her. Now he knew that her beauty, her smile, her pleasant attentions had been food for his vanity, nothing more. She had been a shallow, selfish girl and he a foolish knave. Though that thought relieved none of the pain of her death, it gave Halloran disturbing notions about his own life.

Once again his eyes fell upon Erixitl. She still tossed restlessly, and he longed to take her into his arms, to hold her. Yet he feared her reaction, and so he only watched, feeling more helpless than ever.

But he knew now that he loved her.

* * * * *

From the chronicles of Coton:

In silent worship of Qotal, the Plumed Father, I remain a faithful observer of doom.

Like the venom of a snakebite on the leg or on the hand or arm, the various seeds of catastrophe gather in the outlying realms of Maztica.

Already the Payit have been conquered, subjugated by the invading men and their brutal warrior god called Helm. The venom gathers in Payit, and of course it will flow through the blood of Maztica.

Douglas Niles

And the Ancient Ones work their wrack, leading the blind priests of Zaltec closer and closer to their own bleak destiny. The brand of the Viperhand becomes their symbol, and like the spreading inflammation of poison, it infiltrates and festers in the body of the True World.

Everywhere fractious differences divide the land. Kultakans strive against Nexal; Nexal strives to conquer all Maztica. This divisiveness, too, is toxic.

So grows the power of destruction, venom in the muscle and bloodstream of Maztica. And as is the way of such poison, it flows through the body of the land, until soon it will gather in the Heart of the True World.

♣ 2 ♣

THE CITY AT THE HEART OF THE TRUE WORLD

A small deer slipped between two encloaking ferns, silently pressing through the deep jungles of Far Payit. The creature hesitated a moment, then darted forward, sensing danger but unable to pinpoint the threat.

Suddenly a huge jaguar landed silently on the ground before it, fixing the deer with a sharp, penetrating gaze. The smaller creature froze in terror, staring into those unblinking yellow eyes. The only movement was the trembling of the deer's thin legs, the quivering of its heaving flanks.

For long moments, the jaguar held the deer spellbound. Then, with a slow, deliberate blink, the great cat dropped its lids over those bright eyes. Instantly the deer leaped away, springing through the brush in a desperate flight. So fast, so terrified was its escape that it failed to notice that the cat offered no pursuit.

"Well done, Gultec." The speaker, an old man with long white hair and brown, wrinkled skin, emerged from the brush and spoke to the jaguar.

Or to what had been the jaguar. Now, in the cat's place, stood a tall, muscular man. Both men were clad in spotted loincloths and otherwise were naked and unarmed.

"Thank you, Zochimaloc," said the younger man, bowing deeply to his companion. When Gultec looked up, his handsome face wrinkled slightly in confusion. "But tell me, Master, why do you bid me hunt thus, with no killing and no food?"

Zochimaloc sighed, sitting lightly on a moss-covered log. As he waited for a reply, Gultec pondered his own ease with this strange, wizened man. Weeks earlier, the concept of a "master" would have been one that the Jaguar Knight could never have accepted. Indeed, death would have been preferable to his own servitude and devotion. But now the old man who had become his teacher seemed the most important thing in the world to Gultec, and every day seemed to bring more evidence of how very little the warrior actually understood.

"Soon you will be ready to learn more," said the old man finally. "But not yet."

Gultec accepted the statement with a nod, not questioning his teacher's wisdom.

"Now let us return to Tulom-Itzi," said Zochimaloc. In a flash, the old man's form changed as he became a brilliant parrot. With a quick thrust of his wings, he took to the air, vanishing among the tree trunks and leaving Gultec to follow on foot.

The Jaguar Warrior pushed his way through the jungle patiently, though he couldn't help reflecting on the changes in his life that had brought him here. He remembered his despair when the metal-skinned strangers had destroyed his army and conquered the Payit—his nation. Then he recalled the freedom of his flight into the jungle as a wild, hunting jaguar.

His flight had ended with the humiliation of capture by men who served Zochimaloc; almost immediately his captivity gave way to the discipline of his teacher's long hours of training.

Never before had Gultec learned so much or asked so many questions. He had dwelled in the jungle lands all his life, yet Zochimaloc showed him how little he really knew about those jungles. Gultec studied animals and plants, he observed the patterns of the weather and the stars. Indeed, the pride of Tulom-Itzi was a building erected for no other purpose than the study of the heavens!

All of his studies, all the strength of his renewed discipline, his teacher often hinted, would soon focus in a great purpose—the reason Gultec had been brought to Tulom-Itzi. That purpose remained a mystery, but another trait the warrior had developed was patience.

And soon enough, Gultec knew, this purpose would be made clear.

* * * * *

They came around the shoulder of the great mountain and then stopped suddenly, all three of them frozen in awe. The blue waters of the lakes beneath them, far below on the valley floor, glittered like turquoise in the sunlight. On a flat island in the center of the largest lake lay the valley's gem: Nexal, the magnificent city at the Heart of the True World.

"See the four lakes?" said Poshtli, pride thrumming in his voice. "Named for the gods. Here before us, on the south, is broad Lake Tezca, for it lies along the tracks to the sun god's desert."

He pointed to the right. "To the east, the largest—Lake Zaltec, named for the war god. Largest, because war is man's grandest purpose, and no men are better at war than the Nexal!" The warrior suddenly cast a sideways glance at Halloran. He had recited, by rote, the lessons he had learned as a youth. Now he thought of Hal's countrymen in the Golden Legion and no longer felt so certain.

Quickly he pointed into the distance. "Lake Azul, deep and cold, named for the god of rain. And here, to the west, is Lake Qotal."

The latter was a brackish brown in color, obviously shallow, since tufts of grass and reeds extended far into the lake from its marshy shore. "The small stagnant one," Poshtli said, a hint of sadness in his voice. "Named for the absent god Qotal, who turned his back on his people and left them to the hunger of the younger gods."

Halloran tried to absorb the vista before him. His exhaustion vanished in the first moments of that stupendous view. The days of marching northward, finally leaving the desert behind, the fatigue of the long climb up this mountain, all disappeared in a sensation of reverent awe.

"Nothing you've said has prepared me for this," he noted haltingly, not looking at Poshtli as he spoke.

"It is the place I have dreamed about," Erix added quietly.

Hal looked at the three blue lakes, a rich deep blue, remembering that each was named for a bloodthirsty god of sacrifice. The fourth, the ugly brown one, they dedicated to the "Plumed God," the one who had disappeared. Still, he had learned that many Mazticans, including Erixitl, believed the tales that Qotal would one day return.

They lapsed into silence again, Halloran still staggered by the wonders below them: the city of white buildings and colorful plazas, covering many miles in breadth; the tall, terraced pyramids, gathered around and dwarfed by the mountainous massif the Nexalans called the Great Pyramid. He looked upon Nexal's sprawling palaces. He wondered at Nexal's great size, at the green fringes surrounding the buildings, extending into the lakes themselves. These floating gardens spread like a blanket of moss on the surface of the water, encircling the city in a belt of abundance.

The scope and scale of the city astounded him. He had seen Waterdeep, had lived in Calimshan and Amn, had traveled the length of the Sword Coast in the Realms. Yet none of those civilized lands could boast a city that compared to Nexal in size or grandeur. He estimated that a thousand or more canoes plied the waters of the lakes, while countless more maneuvered through the city's canals.

Erixtl of Palul saw the city for its beauty. She saw the profusion of flowers and their brilliant gardens, the glimmering blankets of feathers floating gracefully in the air above the markets. Fountains and pools reflected sunlight from a thousand large arboretums.

"My uncle is lord of it all," said Poshtli, his voice proud but surprisingly subdued. He had led them from the desert, into the high mountain pass, and now he seemed oddly overcome himself, though he had spent most of his life in the great metropolis below.

"It surpasses anything I have ever seen—the colors, the setting, the sheer *size* of the place! With no wall for defense, no bastions . . ." Hal's voice trailed away. For a moment, he even forgot about the savage rites that were the centerpiece of religion in this amazing place below them. The colors seemed to wink at them in the undying sunlight, beckoning them to descend, to enter.

"Did I not tell you it was truly the grandest place beneath the sight of the gods?" boasted Poshtli, beginning to lead them down the trail. "As for defense, no nation in Maztica would dare strike at Nexal. Even if they did, the lakes provide barrier enough. Now, come. We will reach my uncle's palace before dark!"

The path twisted down the mountainside, between looming Mount Zatal to the left, and another great peak, called Mount Popol, to the right. As they descended, the brush around them became thicker, soon towering into lush green trees that blocked for a time their view of the valley floor.

Soft breezes ruffled the trees, which reminded Hal of the tall cedars found along the Sword Coast. The steep descent passed easily, and they encountered no people along the forest trail.

After an hour, they reached a lush garden that surrounded a rock-walled spring. The trail circled the pool, and Halloran saw a stone-lined trench, filled with rapidly flowing clear water, leading away from the spring.

"An aqueduct!" he marveled, seeing the long span of stonework that carried water into the city.

"We have plenty of water in Nexal," explained Poshtli. "But this from the Cicada Spring is the sweetest to drink. It runs into the center of the city, where it can be sampled by all."

He led them from the garden, and the trail again emerged onto a cleared mountainside. Vast, terraced fields of mayz, the plump grain that, in Hal's experience, seemed to feed all of Maztica, surrounded them, and they could look over the softly waving fields to the city again. With Nexal noticeably closer now, Hal saw clearly the wide stone causeways that led from the shore to the city on its bright, lush island.

Erixitl looked over the city as Poshtli described to Halloran the construction of the aqueduct, which had occurred when the Nexalan warrior had been a boy. She saw an abrupt shadow fall across the sun, though no cloud appeared in the sky.

Suddenly Nexal looked to her as it had in her dream: a cool, barren city illuminated by white moonlight. She felt a flash of terror and, with a short gasp of fright, she tried to turn away.

But she could not. She saw the darkness linger over the plazas and the great market. It centered around the Great Pyramid, with its bloodstained altars. As she looked upon the place of those scenes of sacrifice, the shadows grew darker still, until finally she forced herself to look away. For a moment, she closed her eyes, shuddering.

Finally she turned back, and the city, with its intense, fragile beauty, glowed again with a sense of vibrant vitality. She saw it as it was now and relished its grandeur. But still the memory of the shadows remained, and as they neared Nexal, the frightening darkness lay heavy on her mind.

All too soon, she feared, the brightness and vitality before her could be gone.

* * * * *

Naltecona rested, dozing lightly in the soft *pluma* of his great feathered throne. The cushion of luxurious feather-magic held his body effortlessly, floating easily above the dais in the center of the great ceremonial chamber. The Revered Counselor, comfortable in a soft gown, bedecked with bright feathers on his head, at his shoulders, and knees, enjoyed a rare moment of peace.

Around him the priests, warriors, and sorcerers who made up his court stood in awkward silence. Their attendance was not required while the ruler napped, but none possessed the courage to leave and risk awakening the great man by his departure.

Stirring slightly, Naltecona felt his surroundings and even sensed the awkwardness of his courtiers. *Let them stand,* he told himself. *Let them learn some of the discipline that must guide my every move.* He felt a vague sense of scorn for these old men who fawned over him and followed him, yet seemed to offer no help in those matters where the counselor most desired advice and wisdom. Matters such as the puzzling strangers who had landed on the shores of the True World and conquered the Payit in a single, brutal battle.

Dozing again, Naltecona dreamed of the presence of his nephew, Poshtli. There was a true man! A warrior of courage, a man of wisdom and restraint. Too bad he could not replace a dozen of these fools around him with one more like Poshtli.

The doors to the throne room opened softly, yet the movement was enough to waken the Revered Counselor. He looked up in annoyance.

A priest hurried forward, pausing to bow obsequiously three times before he approached the feathered throne. The emaciated cleric, his frail limbs and face covered with the scars of self-inflicted penance, finally stood before his ruler. His hair stood tall above his head, a series of stiff spikes caked with the blood of the priest's sacrificial victims. He waited silently, his eyes downcast, as Naltecona blinked and stretched.

"Yes, Hoxitl?" inquired the ruler, recognizing the high priest of Zaltec before him. Zaltec was the patron god of the Nexala, and his patriarch, Hoxitl, claimed powerful rights of counsel.

"Most Revered One, we have word out of the desert of your nephew, Lord Poshtli. It is said that he returns with one of the strangers as his prisoner. This news is pleasing to Zaltec and the Ancient Ones."

"I have no doubt of that," said Naltecona ironically. He understood that any new prospect of sacrifice was pleasing to the god of Hoxitl. He looked at his other courtiers. "This is the proof for those who doubted Poshtli's eventual return. He left in search of a vision. I have no doubts that his visions have shown him more than most of you will ever know."

"Indeed," said Hoxitl, with another humble bow. "The wisdom of Zaltec has blessed him."

Naltecona's gaze penetrated the priest, though the still-bowing cleric seemed unaware of his ruler's stare. "There is more than one source of wisdom in the True World," he said sharply. "Do not let your faith blind you to this fact."

"Indeed," said Hoxitl, concealing his skepticism with another bow.

"Is that all?" asked the counselor, boredom creeping into his voice.

"There is another matter," replied the priest. "Should my lord counselor deem it his pleasure to attend, I inform you that we will consecrate more warriors into the cult of the Viperhand tonight, at the setting of the sun."

Viperhand. Naltecona felt a chill with the word. The cult of the Viperhand seemed to grow daily since the arrival in Maztica of the strangers from across the sea. It had always been the cult of Zaltec's faithful followers, but now warriors, priests, even common workers flocked to the temples to swear eternal allegiance to the god of war and to wear his bloody brand.

The mark was wielded by the high priest alone. Tonight that brand would be pressed forever into the flesh of more young Nexalans.

Naltecona sighed, ignoring the high priest's request. "Coton, come here," he called, turning to the rest of his retinue.

A white-robed priest bowed and stepped forward from the group. This one, in stark contrast to Hoxitl, appeared well fed, even to the point of a slight plumpness. His shock of white hair and his wrinkled brown skin were clean, unmarked by scars, blood, or dirt. Coton, high priest of Qotal, approached the counselor silently. Indeed, he did everything silently, in deference to a vow he had made to his immortal master, the Butterfly God.

"Leave us for a moment," Naltecona ordered Hoxitl. That priest scowled at Coton but stepped obediently away.

"One of the strangers comes to Nexal," explained the counselor. As always, he felt comfortable speaking to the unanswering Coton. "Hoxitl wishes to place his heart upon the altar of Zaltec.

"We know of the prowess of these strangers. Perhaps it would be good to have this one dead, no longer a threat. But I am curious about them, and how much of a threat can one man be to our city, our nation?"

Also in Naltecona's mind were the legends predicting the return of Qotal, the Butterfly God, to Maztica. He would return from the eastern ocean, it was said, in a great winged canoe. Some legends had even predicted that he would be pale of skin and bearded of face, just like most of these strangers!

These rumors lay heavy in the ruler's mind, but so, too, did the hunger of Zaltec. And now his cult, the cult of the Viperhand, spread more rapidly than ever before. With the coming of the strangers, the young warriors of Nexal seemed more eager than ever to make that sacred vow to Zaltec.

Coton, of course, made no reply, but the voicing of his

doubts propelled Naltecona into decision.

"I will not allow his death . . . not immediately," he explained to Coton. "I must allow him to live, even protect him, that I may learn more about him and his people." His mind made up, Naltecona turned back to Hoxitl.

"The stranger will be spared," he told the priest. Then he added, in deference to a vengeful god, "But I shall attend the consecration of the Viperhand at sunset."

* * * * *

Darien stretched languorously and arose from the bed, naked, crossing to the candlestick beside the door. Cordell held his breath, entranced by the pure whiteness of her form, the graceful curve of her albino skin. Squinting her tender eyes against the candle's brightness, Darien extinguished the flame with a quick puff of breath, plunging the cabin into darkness.

She returned to the bed, something Cordell smelled and felt but could not see. He silently cursed his lack of nightvision, so desperately did he want to look upon her. Whatever the nature of this burning feeling—was it need, desire, perhaps love?—he had felt it grow into a fire that consumed his heart. Now it burned as he welcomed her into his arms.

Finally she lay sleeping beside him. The gentle sounds of the city of Ulatos around them should have soothed Cordell into slumber as well. But instead he focused on the upcoming day, and on the march he would order his men to undertake at first light.

He prepared to lead the Golden Legion on a mission of unmatched audacity, and Cordell himself confessed to slight doubts as to the rationality of the plan. His force, five hundred steady veterans, would be augmented by perhaps five thousand warriors of the conquered Payit, whose capital city of Ulatos his legion now occupied.

From here, he would lead them to Nexal. Tales of that city's wealth, of the gold and power that lay there, drew him inexorably. These were the fruits of the expedition, the gold that had drawn them across the Trackless Sea. They would march to the heart of this savage continent!

He understood that the army awaiting him in Nexal was

greater—many times greater—than the force he had defeated here in Payit. His informant had also told him that another warlike nation, Kultaka, lay across his route of march to Nexal. They could be expected to resist the passage of Cordell's force.

Of course, there was no finer band of men than the iron-hard troops of the Golden Legion. Their accomplishments since the start of this voyage already guaranteed success. They had conquered a nation of warriors numbering more than a hundred thousand souls. They had gathered enough treasure to pay for the expedition ten times over.

Yet Cordell was prepared to risk it all for this audacious gamble. Indeed, he had made the stakes plain for all his men by sinking the fifteen ships that had carried them from the Sword Coast to this distant shore. The hulks of those vessels lay on the bottom of the shallow lagoon, beside the fortress called Helmsport just outside this city. The fleet gone, there could be no backing away from this challenge.

The captain-general rose and paced his sleeping chamber as the night hours ticked away. He thought of his captains—the steady Daggrande, the hot-tempered Alvarro, Garrant, all the others—men he could trust and rely upon, once he himself provided them with leadership.

The spiritual guidance of his men he trusted to the grim Bishou Domincus, now propelled by an implacable hatred for these savage people who had sacrificed his daughter Martine on their gruesome altar. And, too, he had the wizard Darien at his side. The albino elf was a force equal to a whole army.

Of the native warriors, he was not so certain. He would allow them to accompany him as guides, and also because their numbers would increase the impressiveness of his force. But he suspected that most of the fighting before them would be borne by his legionnaires.

"Can we do it?" he asked, half aloud, addressing the god Helm, lord protector of the legion. His mortal advisors, most of them, had counseled that his plan was madness—the legion would be cut off and surrounded halfway to their goal. Only Daggrande and Alvarro, perhaps because of the warlike challenge, had shown enthusiasm about the march. But that didn't alter the loyalty of the rest, he knew.

The Golden Legion would follow Cordell to Nexal. This he knew without a doubt. The question then became simple: Would they ever come out again?

* * * * *

Their view of the city grew before the trio with each step of the long descent from the garden and the spring. They passed through many villages of small straw huts, or buildings of shining whitewashed adobe, always drawing stares. Some of these villagers, intrigued by the tall stranger, or perhaps by his great black horse—a creature unique in their experience—followed the little party at a respectful distance as they drew ever closer to the shore of the gleaming blue lake.

Late afternoon brought no break to the summer's heat as they finally approached the water and the white stone causeway that led like an arrow to the colorful island city.

The Jaguar Warriors at the end of the causeway stared in astonishment as Halloran, Erix, and Poshtli approached. The guards' faces, framed by the open jaws of their jaguar-skull helmets, showed eyes widened in amazement. Spotted hides of tough *hishna*-enchanted catskin cloaked their bodies, and they half-raised their obsidian-studded clubs, called *macas*, as the strange party approached.

They stared not so much at the humans, as at the great black beast that ambled placidly behind them.

"Greetings, Jaguar Knights!" cried Poshtli in delight. He strode proudly ahead of his companions. The rivalry between the orders of Jaguar and Eagle Warriors was well known, and now the plumed warrior, resplendent in his cape of black and white eagle feathers, took great pleasure in the astonishment of the guards. Poshtli was also the easily recognized nephew of the great Naltecona himself, and thus was not casually challenged.

The Jaguars stared, mute, as the three humans and the horse marched up to the terminus of the causeway. Behind them, many villagers followed tentatively. The latter waited in anxious curiosity to see how the guards would react to the unusual trio.

"Have you lost your manners?" Poshtli demanded in mock indignation as the Jaguar Knights stared in silent awe. "A beautiful woman arrives at the causeway to Nexal, and you give her no welcome?"

Finally one Jaguar recovered his voice. "Wha-what is that creature?" he demanded.

Poshtli threw back his head and laughed, in what Hal judged to be a command performance. The guards stared at the horse, then at Hal, who again wore his steel breastplate and shiny helm.

"Storm?" Halloran asked Erix, trying to follow the conversation. He sensed Poshtli's joking manner but did not understand the complete exchange.

"Enough!" proclaimed Poshtli, gesturing the warriors aside. "We will explain everything to my uncle! Come, my friends—the palace awaits!" He gestured to Halloran and Erix to follow him onto the long causeway. The smoothly paved roadway, a full thirty feet wide, ran perfectly straight from the shore to the city, perhaps a mile and a half away, that beckoned them on the central island.

Hal saw the Jaguar Knights falling into file behind them, and as he looked backward, he saw that they had begun to lead quite a procession. Apparently every farmer, wife, curious child, or patrolling warrior had noticed their passage. More than a hundred Mazticans followed them toward the great city.

Halloran quickly forgot the growing crowd behind them as they neared the dazzling metropolis itself. The pyramids, brightly painted, decorated with feather plumes, almost alive in their brilliance, dominated the city and the entire valley with bright hues of green, red, blue, and purple. But colors dominated every structure, not just the pyramids. Bushes of bright crimson blossoms glowed on every street corner; the canals were lined with a profusion of hanging, flowery vines; bright feathers outlined many houses, while colored tapestries decorated balconies, walls, and doorways.

The causeway itself, Halloran saw, was guarded in several places by removable wooden planks that extended across gaps in the stonework. His soldier's eye took note of that defensive capability.

The lakes on either side were blue and crystalline, deep enough that he could barely make out the bottom, even through the clear water. He saw fish probing the weedy rocks that supported the causeway. Dozens of canoes drew near, carrying curious Maztican fishermen. Ahead, the pyramids and palaces loomed higher, even more magnificent in proximity than they had been in the distance.

Surrounded by this growing retinue, they passed from the end of the causeway onto the wide avenue leading to the heart of Nexal. Here young girls greeted them, spreading flower petals on the roadway in their path and leading them toward the palace. Now the white houses of the city surrounded them, though frequent canals, passing under stone bridges, reminded them that the lake could never be far away.

Poshtli strode proudly at the head of the procession, unnoticing of Erix and Hal. The latter walked slowly behind the Eagle Knight, looking to right and left, up and down, in complete, speechless awe. The wonders of Nexal overwhelmed them both, and they could only stumble along, mutely absorbing the spectacle. Halloran couldn't begin to estimate the number of Mazticans who gathered at the roadsides as word of their arrival spread. He was sure, very early on, that the crowds numbered in the thousands.

"Look—there's one of those priests!" barked Hal, warning Erix as he spotted a scarred, emaciated cleric in the crowd. The sight of the man's black hair, bristling in the bloodcaked spikes he had seen before, sent a tingle of apprehension down Hal's spine.

"A priest of Zaltec," said Erix warily. "There will be many of them here."

The black-robed cleric stared at them as they marched past, but he made no attempt to interfere with their progress. Indeed, his scarred face split into a smile as he saw them advance toward the temples that loomed at the heart of the city.

"It's hard to imagine such magnificence coupled with such savagery," Hal mumbled, half to himself.

Erix, however, heard him. "That is part of the wonder of

Maztica, and of Nexal," she replied in a matter-of-fact tone. "We can only stay close to Poshtli and hope for the best."

Hal decided not to admit that he already felt lost. He knew that he could never have made it this far without Erixitl's help, to translate and guide and explain things to him. Instead, he held his tongue, though he took her hand in his own. The cool, responsive grip of her fingers made him feel a little better. His tongue was tied by the emotion he felt, for it was more than just gratitude that drew him to Erixitl of Palul.

Finally they reached a closed gate in a wall no higher than Hal's head. The stone barrier ran for hundreds of yards to the right and left. Beyond it towered the grandest of the pyramids and palaces.

"This is the sacred plaza—the heart of the city," Poshtli explained. "All of the greatest pyramids are here, also the palaces and ceremonial centers. We will enter and I will find you quarters. Then I will see my uncle. I know he will wish to speak with you as soon as possible."

The gate swung open at some unseen command, and Halloran and Erixitl followed Poshtli into the sacred plaza of Nexal. There was no crowd here, just a smattering of curious warriors. Halloran nodded noncommittally as Poshtli led him toward a long, low building of whitewashed stone.

Behind them, with a dull thud, the gate in the wall slammed shut. None of them paid attention. Poshtli unconsciously accelerated his pace, pausing to greet some of the tall warriors who approached curiously at their entrance. He embraced a pair who wore the black and white feathered regalia of the order of Eagles.

Halloran and Erix lagged behind, overwhelmed by the grandeur of the sacred center. The huge area was mostly open plaza. It was surrounded by the long, low wall, and dominated by half a dozen pyramids—of which the most massive was the Great Pyramid itself, rising from the city's heart.

Several massive, low buildings sprawled across large areas here. In contrast to the brilliantly painted pyramids and the bright tile mosaics on the wall, these low structures gleamed brightly, their walls immaculate with fresh whitewash.

"That is the palace of Naltecona," said Poshtli, pointing to the largest of the white buildings. It stood on the far side of the plaza. "There is the palace of his father, Axalt, who died many years ago." Poshtli pointed out other buildings, each named for a previous counselor.

"Why does each ruler build a new palace?" asked Hal, stunned by the vast works of architecture. None of them was tall, but the smooth stone walls, wide doorways, roofs alternating between peaked thatch and flat, walled platforms, seemed to stretch for miles.

"The power of Nexal has grown with each, and so each must express that power with a dwelling more grand than his predecessor. Besides, the buildings have secrets. Each counselor constructs concealed passages known only to himself and his Lord Architect. The palaces are more than just grand houses; they are symbols of the growing might of the Nexala!"

Poshtli turned to Hal with a smile. "And you will see that the plaza allows room for even more."

Erixitl stopped in shock, suddenly recognizing the palace of Axalt. Her dream! It had been atop that palace that Naltecona had been slain! Her eyes fixed upon the building as she numbly followed the men across the plaza.

"Now, come. First we will find you quarters—a place where you can keep your horse, as well!" boomed Poshtli, gesturing them toward the large palace just beyond the Great Pyramid.

"Storm should stay outside," Hal countered. "Though I would like him nearby." He had forgotten that the Mazticans would have no familiarity with the quartering and tending of horses.

About then, Halloran noticed with surprise that long shadows, betokening the arrival of evening, stretched across the plaza. He hadn't noticed the day slip away, so distracted was he by their entrance into the city.

Hal's head involuntarily swiveled this way and that as he followed his friend. They passed a small pyramid that he thought was made of crumbling stone. But as they reached it, he saw with a chill of horror that the entire structure— perhaps sixty feet high—was made of human skulls, carefully arranged so that their unseeing eyesockets were all directed outward.

Erix, he saw, also stared at the grim monument.

Chilled, Halloran once again felt a sense of bleak despair. *What am I doing here?* he asked himself. He felt like a twig, swept along in the current of a raging river he could not dam or divert. Stealing a glance a Erix—his only anchor in this turbulence—he wondered if the evidence of Nexal's cruelty disturbed her in the slightest. She showed no reaction; after all, he thought, she had been raised among these people. Perhaps she was used to such architecture.

He looked up at the Great Pyramid as they passed in its shadow. The structure was too steep for him to see the platform at the top, but he could well imagine the regular scenes of murderous sacrifice that occurred up there. The shadow seemed to linger over him as they pressed forward, once again under the sun.

They were greeted at the wide doors by bowing warriors and several emaciated, scarred priests. The latter looked intently at Halloran and Erix, and the former legionnaire grew distinctly uncomfortable under the probing gaze.

"We must find them quarters—large, airy apartments where the stranger can keep his monster nearby!" Poshtli explained earnestly, with a subtle wink at Halloran.

Hal ignored the incongruity of the horse following them through the wide, palatial corridors. Other attendants and warriors joined them, keeping a respectful distance.

"Here," said Poshtli, sweeping aside a curtain of hanging beads with a flourish. "You will stay here as my guests. I go to find my uncle, but I will soon return."

Erix and Halloran stepped through the curtain to find themselves in a small, sun-drenched courtyard. A fountain spurted in the center of the area, which was filled with blooming flower bushes and small trees.

"Look at these rooms," breathed Erix, gesturing toward the shady chambers surrounding the garden.

Halloran stood mute with astonishment. He saw golden objects, depicting beasts, birds, and humans, hanging from the walls. One wall of a large room was decorated in a detailed tile mural, obviously depicting the valley of Nexal before it had been dominated by human settlements. Others held thick piles of sleeping mats, a small pool for bathing, and a barren room that Erix guessed was to provide guests with the proper setting for meditation.

Meanwhile, Halloran unloaded his pack, removing some of his valued possessions. There was the silver sword, Helmstooth, of course, which remained girded at his side. He also had an extra steel sword and a dagger—weapons of unique worth in this city of flint and obsidian blades.

Next he pulled out a heavy, leather-bound volume. He couldn't suppress a shudder of apprehension at the sight of the spellbook. It belonged to the wizard Darien, the albino elf who was lieutenant and lover to Captain-General Cordell, himself commander of the Golden Legion. Though Halloran had stolen the book inadvertently, he knew that the wizard's vengeance wouldn't stop short of his death should their paths ever cross again.

Still, he hadn't cast the book away. For one thing, he had been studying parts of it—simple, low-power spells such as he had once learned, when he had spent his youth in apprenticeship to a powerful wizard. Also, he felt that the book would be a powerful bargaining chip should a confrontation with the albino wizard ever arise.

Next he came upon the tightly wrapped bundle of leathery snakeskin that had given him his first experience with Maztican magic. This, Erixitl had explained, was *hishna*—the magic of talon and claw, not the *pluma*-magic of feathers and air. The snakeskin had bound him tightly upon the command of a cleric of Zaltec, and only the *pluma* of Erix's feathered token had released him. Neither of them knew how to use the snakeskin, but knowing its value, they had carried it with them.

Finally he found the two bottles of magical potions. One, he knew, contained the elixir of invisibility. The other one he had never examined. Erixitl deeply distrusted the magical liquids, and some of her nervousness had rubbed off on him. Thus he had never taken the sample sip that might have allowed him to identify the stuff.

"Come over here!" Erix cried, suddenly taking his hand and pulling him through the garden. "Look!" she cried, pointing to a small tree where several brilliant birds sat. They had small, hooked beaks, and glowed in shades of red and green.

Halloran saw the birds dimly, thrilling to the touch of her hand, breaking the contact reluctantly when they were interrupted by servants bearing plates of beans, mayzcakes, and venison. These were set upon a low table in the garden. Storm drank deeply from the pool and then began eating leaves from some of the flower bushes.

Erix and Hal sat on the ground beside the table and began to eat. Their eyes met and remained together. Halloran felt a whirlwind of emotions now that their journey was completed. He knew that he couldn't have made it without Erix, but that was only a small part of his internal turmoil.

Their entrance into the city, when they were surrounded by the people of Maztica, brought sharply home to Hal the extent of his *aloneness*. He couldn't forget that these barbarous folk might place him, without notice, on the evening's sacrificial altar. He had only the friendship of the Eagle Knight Poshtli to protect him—that, and his own wits, skill, and strength. It seemed a slim margin of safety when cast against the presence of tens of thousands of savage Mazticans.

Still, there was Erixitl. The beautiful woman sitting across from him had come to represent life and purpose to the former legionnaire. Now that they had reached this, their goal, he wanted to hold her at his side, to somehow make certain that she would never leave. But he didn't know how to articulate those feelings.

Erix looked at him, and he wondered if she understood his feelings. Perhaps she did, for at length she finally spoke.

"I feel," she admitted with a soft smile, "as though I have finally come home."

* * * * *

Naltecona reclined in the featherlift that slowly raised him to the top of the Great Pyramid. The setting sun cast a rosy glow across Nexal, filtered between the giant mountains that bordered the lush valley that was the Heart of the True World. One, Zatal, rumbled ominously. A cloud of steam hung above the summit, though the counselor took little note. The volcano had loomed overhead throughout the history of Nexal; often it had grumbled, but never had it roared.

Soon the lift reached the top of the structure, pausing as Naltecona slowly rose to his feet and stepped onto the stone platform that loomed high above his city. Hoxitl awaited him here, together with a group of his priests, the evening's sacrifices, and the new initiates to the Viperhand.

The temple of Zaltec was a large square building atop the pyramid. Here stood that hungry god's blood-caked altar, and beside it squatted the statue carved in Zaltec's image—a giant warrior armed with *maca* and javelins, with a beastlike, leering face. The statue's mouth gaped open, waiting for its imminent feast. Hoxitl went to the altar and turned to Naltecona.

"Zaltec's pleasure will be great now that the Revered Counselor again attends his rites," murmured Hoxitl. He gestured to his priests, and they hauled the first victim—a young Kultakan warrior—to the altar. The warrior's eyes were blank and he made no sound, though he fully understood his fate.

The priests drew him backward across the altar block, and Hoxitl raised his jagged obsidian blade. With one sharp cut, he slashed the warrior's chest and reached in to pull forth the still-beating heart.

Immediately one of the initiates rushed forward, stumbling to kneel before the high priest. Hoxitl raised the heart toward the now-vanished sun, then threw it into the mouth of the statue of Zaltec beside the altar.

The man kneeling before Hoxitl was a Jaguar Knight, who now tore his spotted breast cloak aside. Hoxitil lifted his voice in a shrill, angry chant. His face distorted into a mask of passion, twisted by the intensity of his prayer. Then the priest pressed his hand, still crimson with the blood of the sacrifice, against the warrior's chest.

A hiss of smoke and steam erupted from the Jaguar's brown skin, and the stench of burning flesh wafted through the air. Hoxitl's palm, flat against the man's chest, seared his skin in the diamond-shaped head of a viper. Aided by the arcane power of Zaltec himself, the brand scarred his skin and grasped his soul in a viselike grip. The scarring caused the warrior to grimace with pain, but the man made no sound. Finally Hoxitl pulled his hand away.

There, seared permanently into his chest, the warrior now wore the crimson brand, in the shape of the deadly snake's head. The wound glistened like an evil sore, seeming to give the snake a life of its own.

"Welcome," said Hoxitl, his voice a low hiss. "Welcome to the cult of the Viperhand."

* * * * *

From the chronicles of Coton:

At the bidding of the Plumed One, I continue the tale of Maztica's waning.

The True World cries for the presence of Qotal, but the Plumed One pays no heed—or at least he gives no sign. Perhaps, like his priests, he is bound by a vow of silence. He, too, feels the torment known to us.

To feel the need to speak, to correct wrongs, to teach and guide—that is the curse of our order. But to be bound by the vow, to only watch and wait and wonder—that is our discipline and our command.

And now I see in my dreams that the strangers come toward Nexal. They bring the shining light of their silver swords, their knowledge and magic. But behind them, and even, I sense, unknown to them, follow the shadows and the looming darkness.

♣3♣

DEATHSBLOOD

The crimson heat of the Darkfyre lit the cavern in a hellish glow. A dozen black-robed figures stood about the vast caldron, watching the seething mass of the blood-drenched blaze.

"*More!*" commanded the Ancestor, his voice a rasping hiss.

Another one of the Harvesters stepped forward, carrying the basketfull of his night's reaping. Reaching a bloodstained hand into the basket, the Harvester drew forth a lump of flesh that had, hours earlier, pumped life through the veins of a Nexalan captive.

But that heart had been ripped forth by Hoxitl, a bloody tribute to his brutal god. Then, when the priest and his attendants had left the pyramid, the Harvester had arrived. Each Harvester traveled the secret ways of the Ancient Ones, teleporting nightly from the Darkfyre to the sacrificial pyramids throughout the True World.

This one had claimed the hearts left atop the Great Pyramid of Nexal. It had taken him but moments to pull the still-warm hearts from the gaping mouth of the statue where Hoxitl had thrown them. Placing the grisly tributes in his basket, the Harvester had returned them to the Highcave in the space of a blink.

"*More—make it burn!*" hissed the black-robed Ancestor again, and the Harvester hurled the rest of his basket into the caldron. The Darkfyre hissed upward in greedy acceptance of the nourishment.

"We face a great challenge," the Ancestor finally said, speaking very slowly. "I do not need to remind you that we stand alone, forsaken by our kin, even by Lolth herself. Since the time of the Rockfire, we have been isolated, and yet we persevere.

"And so we must nurture our new god, feed the fires of our own power, and show our will to these savage humans. This is our task.

"Spirali set out to do this task, to work our will in the form of the girl's death. Though he was granted even the aid of the hellhounds, he failed. His death is just recompense for that failure."

"The girl has come here, to Nexal," said one of the robed drow after more than an hour had passed. The great city sprawled in the valley below them, for the Highcave was set high in the flank of the great volcano, Zatal, that overlooked the city.

"Indeed," replied the Ancestor. "Finally she comes to us, that she may be slain."

"It will not be easy," cautioned the drow. "It is said that she has the protection of Naltecona's nephew, Lord Poshtli."

There was no reply as the Ancient Ones absorbed this news. Poshtli was well known throughout Nexal as an intelligent, capable, and utterly fearless warrior-noble.

"Poshtli helped them to kill Spirali," said the Ancestor. "For this, he should be made to suffer. The girl's death may be just the beginning."

"Did they learn our nature when Spirali died?" asked another drow. The Ancient Ones took great pains to conceal their racial identity from the humans of Maztica.

"Who knows? And I do not care." The Ancestor wheezed as he continued. "Great events have occurred, and others are about to begin. A chain of destiny is unfolding, and the secret of our race will become insignificant as this chain advances."

"The cult of the Viperhand gains strength daily," offered another drow after further long pause.

"Good. Let the cult of violence grow like a weed, that it will be ready when we call upon it." The Ancestor nodded his satisfaction.

The ancient elf drew himself to his full height before continuing. "Remember the prophecy! Our destiny will be realized when we defeat the last obstacle, the one who is chosen by Qotal to be his champion. The chosen one is not a warrior or priest, as we had once supposed. No, it is this young woman!

"When she has been removed from our path, the death of Naltecona will open the way for us! When the Revered Counselor perishes, the cult of the Viperhand will see that we gain mastery over the True World!"

The Ancestor looked at the robed drow around him, his expression challenging each to dispute his words. Satisfied, he concluded with a voice grown suddenly firm.

"Nor does it matter whether or not she or her companions know who we are. What does matter is that she gives her heart to Zaltec soon! She must die!"

With a soft hiss, the Darkfyre rose and sparked in its caldron, then settled back with a rumble, as if it chuckled in gleeful agreement.

* * * * *

The inside of the lodge filled with smoke, steam, and sweat. The red glow of the low-banked fires cast the slick, bronze skin of the building's naked occupants in a crimson sheen. One of the warriors threw more water on the coals, and another cloud of steam hissed into the air.

This was the sweatlodge of the Order of Eagles, and the highest-ranking warriors of that avian banner had gathered to welcome Poshtli home in the cleansing ritual of the elite fraternity.

The returned warrior sat at the head of the lodge, between Chical and Atzil, two old veterans of the Eagle Knights. For the first time since their arrival in Nexal that day, Poshtli felt as though he had really come home.

After he arranged for quarters for Hal and Erix, he had spent a frustrating hour trying to arrange a meeting with his uncle, the great Naltecona. Finally, at sunset, he learned that the counselor had left the palace to attend the sacrifices on the Great Pyramid. Surprised and slightly worried, Poshtli, too, had departed the royal grounds to enter the city. He had come to this sturdy lodge, the headquarters of the Order of the Eagle Knighthood.

For a long time, the two dozen or so men who occupied the lodge sat in silence, letting the perspiration drip from their bodies, driving confusion and doubt from their minds. As the sweat trickled from their pores, they felt a purification that extended deep into their bodies, reaching even to their warrior souls. With the stoicism of their military fraternity, they sat uncomplaining as the heat intensified and the steam grew thicker and thicker, penetrating deep into their lungs with each deep, rhythmic breath.

"It is good to cleanse myself again," said Poshtli after a long silence.

"You have been gone a long time," Chical answered. "In the wilds, they tell me."

"Yes. I have not entered a lodge of Eagles since I left Nexal. But on this journey, I have seen many other things."

"They tell me you have met one of the strangers, a white man," said Chical.

Chical was old and bent at the waist, with a face covered with wrinkles. His long hair was pure white, and he kept it tied in a braid that reached his waist. Like most Mazticans, his body was virtually devoid of hair except for that on his head. He was the Honored Grandfather, the leader of the Eagle Knights—a proud warrior in his prime, whose wisdom and intelligence allowed him to lead the Eagles even though his physical peak was long past.

"Indeed I did, Father," replied Poshtli, using the honorary term for his teacher and mentor. He described Halloran to the others. "The invaders are strange men, and the monsters that they call 'horses' are fast and fearsome," he concluded. "But they are not gods or demons—they are undeniably men. Halloran is a courageous warrior, and his sword is sharper than any *maca* in Maztica."

He related what he had heard about the battle of Ulatos, where a small force of the strangers had routed a huge army of Maztican warriors.

"Pah!" uttered Atzil, the venerable warrior on Poshtli's other side. "How can you compare Payit warriors to the Nexal? Perhaps these white men did defeat the Payit, but it is inconceivable that their small numbers represent any threat to the Heart of the True World!"

Poshtli shook his head. "I mean no disrespect, but I counsel you to observe and study these strangers before taking action."

"Wise words, my son," said Chical, nodding. "An Eagle flies always with the army of the strangers. Our latest word is that they are preparing to march again. We do not know where they will go, however."

"They will come to Nexal," said Poshtli without a moment's hesitation.

"How can you be so sure?" demanded Atzil, the sudden tension in his voice belying his previous assertion of confidence.

"They are shrewd, and they hunger for gold. These are two things I have learned about the strangers. They will learn as much as they can about Maztica before they act. They are certain to discover that nowhere in the True World will they find as much gold as we have here."

"Certainly they would not think they could march to Nexal and take our gold," demanded Atzil indignantly.

"I do not know," replied Poshtli, shaking his head. "But I would not be surprised to see them try."

"My son, there has been much talk of these strangers during your absence," broke in Chical gently. Poshtli noticed, with surprise, that the other warriors had silently slipped from the lodge. Now just the three of them sat in the long, dark room. A slave entered quietly and threw more water on the heated rocks, sending another cloud of steam into the air. The mist hung heavy in the air of the lodge.

"This man who came with you, the one you call Halloran, has been expected," Chical explained. "There are some who wish to speak with him. But there are others who wish to see his heart given to Zaltec at the earliest possible time."

Poshtli sat up straight. "Is this the way we treat the guests of Naltecona?" he demanded.

"Silence!" Chical's voice grew momentarily harsh, then it softened. "It is not certain, but the cries for his heart come from the very highest authority! And, as yet, he is not Naltecona's guest—he is yours."

"But my uncle will welcome him!" protested the young Eagle. In truth, Poshtli grew suddenly concerned. He had been surprised when his uncle, the Revered Counselor, had been too busy to see him this afternoon, following his return to the city. Now he began to wonder if Naltecona had avoided him for a different reason.

"That is not certain," interjected Atzil, "for other voices may carry more weight."

"More weight? What higher authority can there be than the Revered Counselor?"

"Zaltec himself," said Chical simply. "Zaltec may desire his heart."

"Through the words of his Ancient Ones?" asked Poshtli, unable to keep the scorn from his voice. He remembered the death of the Ancient One called Spirali, slain by himself and Halloran. Hal had referred to the creature as a drow and had explained that there was nothing supernatural about them, though there was a great deal that was evil. The warrior knew that his comrades weren't ready for that tale yet.

"Do not underestimate the powers of Zaltec," warned Chical. "You are young and strong. We know of your bravery, and your recent accomplishment even suggests a capacity for wisdom." The venerable Eagle smiled slightly, taking the sting from his words. "But you are no match for the cult of Zaltec."

"The man comes to Nexal under my protection! Anyone who tries to take him will first have to deal with me!"

"You are a proud Eagle, my son." Chical met Poshtli's gaze squarely. "The order is also proud of you. Never has one so young proven himself of such worth. You have commanded the army on campaigns to gather many prisoners; you have fought and bested the bravest warriors of Kultaka and Pezelac. Now you have embarked on a quest for a vision and have gained that vision to return with this stranger.

"You are a great Eagle Warrior, Poshtli," Chical continued, his voice stern. "And you have sworn your obedience to the order. If you are told to leave the stranger in the hands of others, you will obey."

Chical rose suddenly, with the fluid motion of a much younger man. Atzil, too, stood.

"You have no choice," concluded Chical softly. He and Atzil turned and left the lodge.

Poshtli sat alone, dumbfounded. He stared into the air, seeking an answer. But all he saw was the smoke and the ash and the steam.

* * * * *

The white-skinned hand held the quill lightly, carefully scribing the symbols from the scroll into the leather-bound tome. As each symbol was copied, it flared briefly into bluish light before disappearing from the scroll. Finally the spell was reproduced in the book, and Darien tossed the now-useless parchment of the scroll aside.

Many blank pages remained in that volume, yet this was the last of the wizard's scrolls. The rest of her incantations would remain lost to her . . .

Until she recovered her spellbook.

Darien's tight lips curled into a sneer of hatred as she thought of the treacherous Halloran. His betrayal of the legion, his escape from imprisonment, these were only minor matters to the elfmage. But, she vowed as she had vowed many times before, for the theft of her spellbook, he would die.

Shaking her head, she saw with irritation that sunrise had begun to color the sky beyond the window of her room. Outside, she heard Cordell and his officers barking commands, preparing the legion for the march.

Unconsciously tightening her hood around her face, though the hateful sun would not crest the horizon for several more minutes, she pondered her own goals. Her hatred for Halloran simmered low as she considered more immediate concerns.

The march on Nexal would begin today. She sensed Cordell's passion for the mission and knew that she could do nothing to alter his aims. For a moment, she felt as though she was losing control of things, that events had started to move forward without her. Grimly she shook off the notion, standing and gathering her own possessions to herself. She couldn't allow that to happen, couldn't let the future plot its own course.

Control—*her* control—meant everything.

DOUGLAS NILES

* * * * *

"Poshtli didn't return here last night, did he?" asked Halloran. He had slept late and now wandered sleepily into the enclosed garden, where he found Erix.

"Nor this morning," she replied. She sat quietly, looking thoughtfully into the garden's fountain. Idly she picked up a peach and took a bite of the juicy fruit. Halloran noticed his own hunger and took a half melon from the bowl of fruit that had been delivered to their quarters.

He carried the leather-bound spellbook with him. At first he had intended to sit out here in the garden and study it. His early training as an apprentice magic-user lingered in his mind, at least enough so that he could understand some of the simpler portions of Darien's book.

But now such a pursuit seemed a dull way to start the day, and so he returned the tome to his knapsack. There he found the two potion bottles. One, he knew, caused invisibility, but the effects of the second were unknown. He picked up the second bottle, looking at the clear glass vial curiously.

"No!" Erixitl's scream almost caused him to drop the vial. Instead he set it back in the pack and looked at her in surprise. Her face had paled with fear.

"That one—it frightens me!" she said softly. "Throw it away!"

"That doesn't make any sense!" he argued. He resolved to sample the vial and learn its contents sometime when Erix wasn't watching.

"So there has been no word from Poshtli?" Hal ventured.

Erix seemed relieved at the new topic of discussion. "I wonder what he told his uncle," she mused. "How much do you think Naltecona has heard about your legion?"

"It's not 'my' legion anymore."

Hal vividly remembered his last view of his former comrades, the elite company of lancers. Under the command of the brutal Captain Alvarro, they had ridden amok, stampeding like animals among the Mazticans who had gathered to watch the battle at Ulatos. Uncounted hundreds had died simply to slake the man's thirst for blood. Indeed, it had been Alvarro's charge toward Erix that had forced Hal to take up arms against the legion.

"I'm certain Naltecona has heard enough to make him concerned." Halloran spoke, as did she, in Nexalan, now feeling quite comfortable with the tongue.

"Poshtli will make him understand!" exclaimed Erix enthusiastically. "I know he will. He seems terribly wise for one so young."

Halloran turned away, suddenly tense. He looked at the beauty around them, but all he could see was a strange, foreign world. What did Maztica know of wisdom? Of understanding? These people marched complacently up the steep pyramids, offering their lives and their hearts to a god!

What kind of god would ask such a price? And what kind of people would obey? Maztica remained a dark puzzle to Hal, a place that made him feel very much lost and alone.

Yet, despite his loneliness, there was Erix. Hal couldn't help but contrast the frightening aspect of Maztica with her. Even if he had another place to go, Hal wasn't certain that he could leave her.

"Do you remember that night, back in Payit, when we thought we had escaped?" he asked her. The warmth of that night, which they had spent sleeping—albeit chastely—in each other's arms was a memory that seemed to grow warmer with each reminiscence. It had been a time before their enemies surrounded them, when the land had seemed to beckon them with opportunity.

Also, it had been a night of closeness they had not repeated since. He studied her face as he asked the question.

"Yes—yes, of course," she said quickly. A flush crept over her features, and she looked away from him.

"I wish, somehow, that we could go back to that feeling of . . ."

Of . . . what? Simple love? He couldn't define even for himself what he was trying to say. He gritted his teeth in frustration. Why couldn't he tell her how he felt?

Erix stood and looked at him with understanding. "We can't go back to that. We have enemies now . . . the priests of Zaltec and the Ancient Ones certainly still seek us, though perhaps we have avoided them for a while. And the Golden

Douglas Niles

Legion—will your old comrades leave us in peace?"

As if to emphasize her remarks, at that moment they heard a call from beyond the reed curtain doorway to their apartments.

"Enter," called Erix.

A tall Maztican man entered and bowed stiffly. He wore a headdress of red feathers and a cape of feathers, golden, green, and white. Two large pendants of solid gold hung from his ears, and his lower lip bore a golden ornament. He was followed by two slaves dressed in clean white tunics.

The visitor's eyes met Halloran's. "The Revered Counselor, Naltecona, requires your presence in his throne room."

"Allow me a few minutes to prepare," replied Halloran after a moment's pause. The invitation wasn't a surprise, but it had caught him off guard. He wanted to polish his breastplate and carefully don his armor for this meeting. "We will be ready soon."

"You are to come alone," said the courtier. "Without the woman." His eyes never wavered from Halloran.

Out of the corner of his eye, Hal saw Erix clench her jaw. "I need her to translate," he objected.

"The counselor was most specific. Females are never allowed into his sight during the day, unless he specifically requests their presence."

Hal searched for another objection, feeling very vulnerable about the prospects of going on his own. He was surprised when Erix gestured, and he turned to look at her.

"Go!" she told him, in the common tongue. "You must not dispute the will of Naltecona."

"Very well," he agreed, watching as she stalked from the garden into her own sleeping chamber. Switching back to Nexalan, he told the richly garbed messenger that he wished to dress. The man stood silently as Hal donned his breastplate and boots and set his helmet on his brow. Girding his sword to his belt, he followed the man from the apartment, cursing the haste that had given him no time for spit and polish.

They marched silently down several long corridors, then stopped before a pair of massive doors. Here, to Hal's surprise, the courtier doffed his feathered accoutrements, handing them to an attendant who gave him in return a tattered leather shawl. The nobleman placed this shawl over his shoulders.

The attendant lifted another of these ragged cloaks, looking meaningfully at Halloran. But the noblemen shook his head slightly, leading the former legionnaire into the throne room as the slave looked after them in surprise.

Halloran's steps slowed as awe overwhelmed him. The inside of the chamber was huge, with a high ceiling of thatched leaves supported by heavy beams. Gaps between the ceiling and the top of the wall allowed natural light into the room.

Perhaps two dozen people stood in the chamber, Hal saw. With one exception, they wore the tattered leather cloaks and torn rags such as the messenger had just donned.

The exception, Halloran knew, was Naltecona.

The Revered Counselor of Nexal reclined on a floating litter of brilliant feathers. The litter hovered over a platform several feet above the floor of the room. The attendants, Hal noted, all stood on the floor.

He was surprised when Naltecona rose to his feet as Hal approached the throne. The ruler wore a headdress of emerald feathers, long plumes of iridescent green that waved regally high over his head. Gold chains encircled his neck, and golden ornaments weighted his wrists, ankles, ears, and lip.

As the counselor rose, a great cape of feathers spread behind him, floating weightlessly in the air and trailing after Naltecona as he moved forward.

"Greetings, stranger," said the Revered Counselor, approaching Hal and then stopping two paces away to look him up and down.

"Thank you, Your . . . Reverence," replied Halloran, uncertain of the correct title. His Nexalan, which had begun to flow so smoothly with Erixitl, all of a sudden felt like a clunky foreign tongue, something he would never master.

Naltecona clapped his hands, and several slaves brought forward bundles to lay at Halloran's feet. "Please accept these presents as a token of welcome to our land," offered the ruler.

DOUGLAS NILES

Halloran looked down at the array, suddenly dizzy. He glanced quickly past the feathered cloak and thick bolts of cloth, instead focusing on two bowls that had been placed with the treasure. He wanted to kneel down and scoop up those bowls, one of which contained a pile of metallic yellow dust and the other a pile of smooth, cream-colored pebbles, but he managed to marshal his restraint. Instead, he bowed formally, studying the treasures surreptitiously as he bent over them. Gold! And pearls! His heart leaped in excitement.

"Your generosity overwhelms me, Excellency," he said haltingly. "I regret that my poor traveler's lot does not allow me to repay you in kind."

Naltecona held up a hand, dismissing the apology. He obviously relished the role of the beneficent one. "Are you an emissary—a speaker—for your people?" inquired the ruler.

Halloran phrased his answer carefully. "No. I am a solitary warrior, one who travels the land such as your nephew, Poshtli. I seek a destiny that is mine alone."

He didn't want to admit that he was a fugitive from the legion, a man who undoubtedly had a price on his head by now. But neither could he misrepresent himself as Cordell's agent.

Naltecona nodded thoughtfully at the explanation, scrutinizing Hal as he spoke of a search for destiny. Obviously the ruler was a man who believed in destiny.

"Hoxitl, Coton . . . come here," ordered Naltecona. Hal saw two elderly men—one filthy, scarred, and emaciated, wearing a robe of stained dark cloth; the other clean and well fed, dressed in a white tunic—step forward from the crowd of attendants behind the counselor. The clean one, Coton, reminded Halloran of Kachin, a cleric of the god Qotal who had died defending Erix from the drow elf Spirali. Naltecona confirmed this connection with his next words.

"These are my high priests, Hoxitl of bloody Zaltec, Coton of the Butterfly God, Qotal. I wish for them to hear your answers to my questions. Now, tell me . . . who is your god?"

Halloran looked up, startled by the question. Gods had never played much of a role in his life. Still, it seemed to be a question that required an answer.

"Almighty Helm, the Eternally Vigilant," he said. That warlike god, patron deity of the Golden Legion, was as much of a spiritual light as Hal could claim.

"We have many gods in Maztica," explained Naltecona. "Zaltec and Qotal, of course, but there are also Azul, who brings us rain, and Tezca, god of the sun, and many more."

"Many, and enough," added Hoxitl quietly. That cleric, his face smeared with dirt, ashes, and dried blood, regarded Halloran with hate-filled, burning eyes. "We have no room for a new god in Maztica!"

Halloran met Hoxitl's gaze with a challenge of his own. Though no great devotee of Helm, he would not yield to the cleric's implicit assertion of Zaltec's sovereignty.

"You must learn more of our gods," continued Naltecona. "Tonight it will please me to have you attend our rituals. You may accompany me to the Great Pyramid, for the sunset rites of Zaltec."

Hoxitl leered at him as Hal's heart pounded and his mind reeled with horror. He recalled the rituals of Zaltec, the hearts torn from captives and offered to sate the hunger of the bloodthirsty god. Halloran did not fear for himself, but his revulsion was so strong that the thought of the rite almost sent him lunging for the depraved Hoxitl, his hands clawing for the priest's throat.

He called upon all of his restraint, keeping his voice dispassionate as he addressed Naltecona.

"I am grateful for your invitation," he said quietly. "But I cannot attend your ritual. My god will not permit it."

Naltecona took a sudden step backward, almost as if he had been struck. His eyes narrowed. Over his shoulder, Hal saw Hoxitl's smoldering gaze break into a raging fire of hatred. Coton, on the other hand, looked mildly amused. Time seemed to come to a halt as Naltecona stared at Halloran.

"Very well," said the counselor abruptly, whirling around and stalking back to his throne, the feathered cape floating dreamily through the air behind him. For a moment, Hal stood still, wondering if he should leave. Then Naltecona stopped and turned back to his guest. The Revered Counselor's eyes gleamed like cold, black ice.

"Take his gifts to his apartments," he barked at the two

slaves who had brought the parcels forward. Then he turned back to Hal.

"You are dismissed," he said shortly.

* * * * *

Erixitl paced around the luxurious apartment. The lush garden, the splashing pool, the fabulous ornaments, everything seemed suddenly like a metal cage that imprisoned her spirit and sealed away her future.

Something about the pool reminded her of a stream she remembered from her childhood—a crystalline brook that splashed through the town of Palul, her native village.

Palul. The town that she knew was a bare two days' journey away, now that she had reached Nexal. She had been stolen from her home ten years ago by a Kultakan Jaguar Knight who had sold her into slavery. From there, she had been traded to a priest from distant Payit, where she had been taken just before the strangers' arrival.

But now she had come back to the land of Nexala, to the city of Nexal. She wondered if her father still lived, if he still worked his colorful *pluma*. Unconsciously she touched the amulet at her throat, her father's gift to her. The feathered token had power, she knew—power that had saved her life more than once.

Lotil the featherworker had been a good father, a simple man who worked with his hands and loved color. Indeed, he used varieties of hues and shades in ways Erixitl had never seen elsewhere.

She remembered, too, her brother, Shatil, who was just beginning his apprenticeship to the priesthood of Zaltec at the time of her capture. Had he been accepted into the order? Or had his heart been given to that bloody god in ultimate atonement, a common end for apprentices who failed?

She had always assumed that she would return to visit her village once the journey to Nexal had been accomplished. Now they were here, and Palul seemed to beckon. Halloran, who had once been so lost in Maztica, now seemed self-assured and at least moderately fluent in the Nexalan tongue. Still, she knew that she didn't want to leave him. Indeed, her thoughts about Halloran had grown increasingly, disturbingly warm. She wanted him to need her.

And Poshtli—what had happened to Poshtli, anyway? The Eagle Knight certainly didn't require her presence. Let both of those men get along without her, she decided suddenly. Turning toward the door, she momentarily considered marching straight out of the city and striking out on the road to Palul.

But she stopped when she saw the tall figure at the door. Poshtli nodded once and stepped into the apartment. Though he didn't wear his helmet, his cloak of black and white feathers made his shoulders broad, and his eagle-claw boots seemed to add authority to his step.

The knight looked around, apparently to see if Hal was present. Then he stepped toward her.

For a moment, she saw him as a magnificent man. He was such a grand warrior, so tall, so proud, so handsome! He reached his hands out to her shoulders, and the look in his dark brown eyes was warm with smoldering heat. Not fully understanding why, she shyly removed his hands and turned away from him.

"Has anyone bothered you here?" he asked, his voice strangely intense.

"Bothered us?" She turned back to him in surprise. "No, of course not. What do you mean?"

Again he fixed her eyes with that look of intensity, and she squirmed under his gaze. "There may be danger," he said, suddenly looking away, as if distracted. "More than I anticipated." He looked back at her, and she heard the deadly seriousness of his voice. "Erixitl, please call me if you see anything that frightens you—anything at all!"

Erix suddenly felt alarmed. "What is it? Why should we worry?"

"It's nothing," the warrior scoffed, abruptly casual. "I want to make sure the palace slaves are treating you well. And Halloran? He . . . is well?"

"Of course he's well!" Erix detected a strain in Poshtli's voice as he mentioned the other man's name, and she felt a little thrill. "He's gone to speak with your uncle. Naltecona didn't desire to see me, however. I suppose I . . . What is it?" She noted, with annoyance and then alarm, that Poshtli had ceased to listen to her.

"Remember, I shall be nearby," said the knight. "Do not hesitate!" Once again that smoldering heat flushed his eyes.

"If you need help, call me." Then, with a swirl of black and white feathers, Poshtli was gone.

* * * * *

The long road inland twisted back and forth across the face of the mountain. Like a long snake, part feathered and part armored, the column wound along the turns of the trail, slowly creeping away from the coast.

The Golden Legion marched at the head of the column, the mercenaries setting a brisk pace even over the rough ground. The companies of footmen marched two or three abreast on the winding trail, armor-plated swordsmen leading the way. Helmeted crossbowmen, led by the redoubtable Daggrande, followed, and then marched the spearmen, the cavalry—resplendent in shiny breastplates on their prancing, eager mounts—and the ranks of lightly armored swordsmen.

Several dozen large, shaggy greyhounds bounded beside the column, obviously delighted in the return to the march. Cordell watched the dogs with mild amusement, remembering the shocking effect they had had upon the Payit, who had never seen a dog bigger than a rabbit before.

Behind the Golden Legion trailed the colorful spectacle of five of the huge regiments, called "thousandmen," of the Payit. That nation, conquered by these strangers from across the sea, had now thrown its military weight behind that of the metal-shelled invaders.

The azure waters of the Ocean of the East, known to the legion as the Trackless Sea, slowly slipped from sight, now barely visible through a notch in the hills behind them. The trail they followed worked its way up to a high, saddle-shaped pass between two snow-capped summits. This, their Payit scouts had told them, marked the border to the lands of the warlike Kultaka.

Cordell, at the head of the column, dismounted when he reached the pass. He tethered his horse beside the trail as his troops marched past. Climbing several dozen feet to one side of the pass, the captain-general looked from the ocean to the east, past the column of his troops, into the green bowl of the Kultakan farmland to the west.

For a time, his eyes lingered on the ocean. He remembered the turquoise purity of those coastal shallows, a deeper, richer blue—or so it had seemed—than any shore along the Sword Coast. He blinked, momentarily melancholy, for he knew that he would not see his homeland again for a long time. Some of his men, he suspected, had laid eyes upon it for the last time. Shaking his head, he quickly banished the morbid thought.

"They're watching us, you know."

Cordell turned to regard Captain Daggrande. The dwarven crossbowman had clumped to his side and now stood looking over Kultaka.

"Of course they are," agreed the commander. "I want them to see us, and wonder."

Daggrande nodded approvingly. Payit informants had told them that the Kultakan army was large and fierce, second only to Nexal in the military heirarchy of Maztica. Still, none of the legion's officers shrank from the inevitable clash that their march was certain to provoke.

"Darien is observing Kultaka even as we march," explained Cordell as Bishou Domincus joined them.

"May the vigilance of Helm open her eyes wide." The tall, dour cleric scowled at the green valley, willing the enemies of the legion into view.

"She will find them," assured the general.

"Yeah," said Daggrande, with a spit to the side. "That she will." The elven mage Darien, with her white skin and albino's bleached hair, had always unsettled the dwarf. Her abilities would inarguably prove useful, perhaps even decisive. By now, she no doubt flew over the Kultakan cities, invisible. Nevertheless, something about her never failed to arouse Daggrande's ire. He buried his feelings forcibly, knowing that his commander loved the elven woman with a passion as consuming as it was mysterious.

"Helm curse all these devils!" snarled the Bishou, though there was still no sign of movement in the Kultakan valley. Since the death of his daughter on a sacrificial altar in Payit,

Douglas Niles

the Bishou had sworn a grim vendetta against all of Maztica.

A red-haired horseman rode up to them, reining in his steed but not dismounting. He flashed a grin at the others, displaying many gaps in the teeth that showed through his thick, orange beard. "I hoped they'd be here to meet us," he laughed, with a contemptuous look at the valley before them. Still laughing, he kicked the flanks of his horse and galloped on, riding beside the column that twisted its way down the far side of the pass.

Cordell shook his head, trying to conceal his concern. "Captain Alvarro has always been a little too eager to fight," he said so that only Daggrande could hear. "I hope he's ready when the time comes."

Now their allies, the Payit warriors, passed before them. These tall spearmen wore headdresses of multicolored feathers. They marched proudly, brandishing their weapons for their new commander's benefit.

"They've recovered well from their defeat," observed Cordell. Barely a month had passed since the legion had dealt these warriors the stunning battlefield defeat at Ulatos.

"They're looking forward to giving some of the same to their neighbors," remarked the dwarf. "They've never cared much for the Kultakans." Daggrande had helped to train the Payit, and had come to understand a little about the Maztican mind—not a great deal, but certainly more than any of his comrades.

One more man came to join them as the warriors filed past. This one dismounted awkwardly and wheezed as he took the few steps upward to join them. The others ignored his arrival until he spoke.

"This is crazy!" exclaimed Kardann. The High Assessor of Amn, he accompanied the expedition in order to tally the and treasure they gained. He had never imagined himself marching with a small column of soldiers into the heart of an enemy-held continent. "We'll all be killed!"

"Thanks for sparing my men from the insight of your prescience," said Cordell wryly. "In the future, I expect you to keep such outbursts to yourself."

Kardann bit his lip, scowling at the general. He feared Cordell, but it was not the fear of the soldier for the harsh commander. Kardann feared Cordell the way the sane man fears the mad. The accountant suppressed a shudder as he recalled the outcome of their last disagreement. Cordell had ordered his entire fleet of ships sunk, simply to convince his men that they were here to stay.

Now Kardann wanted to point out the folly of their venture, but he was afraid to speak. He hated the thought of this expedition into the unknown, but he hated even more the thought of being left behind. Besides, he knew that Cordell didn't take his warnings seriously.

The captain-general slapped his gloved hand against his thigh, reinvigorated by the sight of his troops. The land before them looked smooth, rich, and inviting.

"Come, my good men!" he commanded, including Kardann in his expansive gesture. "On to Kultaka—the first step on the road to Nexal!"

* * * * *

Far from Maztica, deep in the nether regions, dwelled Lolth, spider goddess of the drow. Her presence on the continent of Faerun lay far to the east, and far beneath the lands washed by the sun. Those of her dark elves who lived to the west, beneath the place called the True World, formed a small tribe, insignificant among the vibrant, savage nations of the drow.

Yet Lolth was a jealous goddess—a deity who would brook no faithlessness. Now she heard the words of the Ancestor. She heard them and seethed.

Forsaken by their god? So they claimed now. They worshiped Zaltec, they fed him and used his priests like puppets. Now they worked his people into a frenzy, using their power—seated in the Darkfyre—to form this cult called the Viperhand.

So the Ancient Ones despaired of Lolth? Indeed.

Before she finished with them, the black spider goddess vowed, they would learn the true depths of despair.

4

KULTAKA

Takamal, war chief and Revered Counselor of Kultaka, was widely known as the wisest man in the True World. Had he not defended his homeland against Nexalan depredations throughout his lifetime of more than seven decades? True, the Kultakans were a fierce and warlike people with a fine warrior tradition, but their numbers were only a quarter or less of the equally warlike Nexalans.

Only once, when the forces of Nexal had been commanded by the young but highly accomplished Eagle Warrior, Lord Poshtli, had the two sides exchanged equal numbers of prisoners. Always before and since, the Kultakan forces left the field with two or three Nexalan captives for every one they lost.

But now Takamal confronted a problem for which his long rivalry with his inland neighbor had not prepared him. He was an old man, but still spry, and so he stalked about his throne room in Kultaka, loudly demanding answers from the empty room. For this was the way Takamal pondered.

"Are they truly mighty? They defeated the Payit in a great battle at Ulatos—so? Does this mean they can defeat the Kultaka? Can they beat *me?*"

Takamal pounded his fist into his palm, seething. Just this once, he wished that the gods would answer! He heard the clatter of javelins in the courtyard outside as young tribesmen trained under the strict eyes of older warriors.

Perhaps that was his answer. In truth, he knew that it was. He would face this problem as he faced every other threat to his domain.

"My observers say they bring five thousandmen of the Payit—bah! They do not concern me. And the tale of their battle against the strangers, fighting them in an open field!

This is foolish, when the gods have provided them with ground to conceal them!"

Now, Takamal sensed, the gods listened. One god, in particular, he wanted to take heed.

"Zaltec, your shining spear shall precede us to war! I will meet these strangers and their fawning Payit slaves—but I will choose my ground with care."

He scowled, nodding his head so that his feathered headdress bobbed in the air. He stood tall and crossed his arms across his breast, addressing the image of Zaltec, god of war, in his mind. Takamal reached a decision, and as always the deciding lightened his spiritual burden.

"The entire might of Kultaka shall gather, a league of thirty thousandmen! Our Jaguars will rend, our Eagles pursue, and we will send these foreigners back to the sea!"

* * * * *

The coals lay cold in the firepit. Dank humidity lingered in the air of the lodge, a reminder of the steam that had permeated the low house many hours earlier. Poshtli sat alone, as he had sat throughout the long hours of the night, long since the other Eagles had departed for their homes and beds and women.

Faint outlines of sunlight cracked through the door, telling him that the new day had dawned. But still he could not bring himself to leave.

What was there for him, beyond the sanctuary of this hallowed lodge? Though his face remained an expressionless mask, Poshtli's soul writhed in an agony of torment. Never had he felt so powerless.

Once again, on the previous night, Chical had warned him against interfering in the fate of the two he had brought to Nexal. Poshtli regretted their decision to come here, for he felt he had done nothing but lead his friends into a great trap.

True, Halloran seemed safe enough for the time being. Naltecona had seemed to take a liking to the soldier, spending many hours each day talking to Hal about the world across the Eastern Sea. Certainly his uncle would not order harm to his guest.

But other, darker forces seethed below the surface, and these were the powers against which Chical had warned him. The priests of Zaltec clamored softly, but with increasing agitation, for the heart of the intruder. Of the woman, Erixitl, they said nothing, but the Eagle Warrior had seen the glint in Hoxitl's eye as the high priest had observed her in the sacred plaza. It was a look he imagined upon the face of a great hunting cat before it sank its fangs into the flesh of its gentle, unsuspecting prey.

And so the agony of his own helplessness tore at him, aggravated by the sense that it was he who had brought his companions into this danger. For Hal, he could do little—indeed, he could do nothing, without renouncing the sacred vow he had taken to his order.

Finally Poshtli rose to his feet with liquid smoothness, despite the long hours of immobility. Perhaps, for Hal, he could do nothing.

But he decided upon a plan to protect Erixitl.

* * * * *

The days in Nexal passed quickly for Halloran, but not so for Erixitl. Every day the soldier was summoned to another audience with Naltecona. The Revered Counselor pressed him for details about Hal's world, about the lands of Faerun, the gods that were worshiped there, the magic that was practiced there.

Hal grew more and more torn between fascination with this beautiful, ornate culture, and horror at the underlying butchery required by these peoples' gods. He felt a genuine respect for Naltecona, perceiving the counselor as a man of wisdom and pride, not afraid to admit that he didn't understand everything about the world.

And the wonders of Nexal! He saw little of the city beyond the walls of the sacred plaza, yet even within that small area, there towered structures of dazzling height. Around him, painted on the sides of the pyramids, a myriad of bright patterns and colorful murals caught his eyes. The gardens and fountains were clean and fresh, more serene than any he had known in his homeland.

But atop the pyramids, he knew that a steady, routine

slaughter occurred night after night. The priests of Zaltec were everywhere, with their blood-caked hair and filthy, scarred bodies. They looked at him hungrily, and he met their gazes with a harsh, disdaining stare of his own. So far, neither he nor the priests had blinked.

Never after that first day did Naltecona again suggest that Hal accompany him to a sacrifice. Often he asked him about Helm, and Naltecona seemed interested to note that Cordell, the leader of the strangers, also worshiped this god.

Meanwhile, for Erix, there were hours of solitude in the peaceful garden, which felt every bit as much a cage as ever. She wanted to see the city with Halloran, or Poshtli, but instead she found herself walking about with an escort of palace slaves. Somehow the sights that she had always expected to dazzle her seemed disappointingly mundane.

At other times, the strange shadows surrounded her, threatening to block out the sun, even the world itself. They became so dark, occasionally, that she couldn't see the ground beneath her feet—though full, cloudless daylight reigned overhead. She grew hesitant to raise her eyes upward, for always she saw the looming presence of Mount Zatal. It seemed, to her suddenly keen vision, that the mountain swelled like a festering sore, ready to explode its putrescence across the True World. Often she felt the earth rumbling beneath her feet, though others around her seemed to take little note of the tremors.

She began to wonder if she was losing her mind.

She found occasional moments of pleasure in the great marketplace. Among the presents that had been placed in their room were sacks of cocoa beans, and feathered quills filled with gold dust—the two principal forms of currency in the great city. For the first time in her life, Erixitl had her own money to spend. She also had the most elaborate marketplace in the True World to spend it in.

There, vendors from all the lands of Maztica—except, of course, for Kultaka—offered their goods for sale or barter. The most common means of exchange was the cocoa bean, which she had seen in the abundance of its harvest in Payit. It amused her now to see peddlers counting the brown nuggets, one by one, in order to conclude a sale.

Douglas Niles

They traded for fine bolts of cloth, for bright shells and long quills filled with gold dust. Carvers offered tiny replicas, in wood or stone, of the gods. Stonechippers presented sharp-edged *macas* and knives, and obsidian-tipped javelins and arrows. Bowyers sold their weapons, hewn from the most resilient willow or the hardy cedar.

She stopped once, momentarily enthralled by the *pluma* offered by a humble featherworker. The craftsman, a wrinkled old man whose nimble fingers belied his otherwise arthritic appearance, held up a cape for her inspection. The garment was a fine mesh, interwoven with tiny tufts of the most brilliant feathers she had ever seen.

Almost ever seen, she reminded herself, unconsciously touching the token at her throat. That gift from her father was more than a decade old, yet though its feathered fringes were single, delicate strands of color, the amulet hadn't lost a single plume over the years.

"I see you know of *pluma*," said the old man sagely. He let go of the cape, and it hung motionless in the air. The man made a curt gesture, and the cape swirled around Erix to settle softly about her shoulders.

"Take the mantle," offered the featherworker. "May it protect your skin as the amulet protects your spirit."

Erix was about to protest, to offer the man some payment for the cape. Indeed, it was the first thing she had seen in the market that really attracted her attention. Yet the featherworker was suddenly engaged in an earnest sales talk with a tall Eagle Knight. Though Erix came past this spot a little later, she saw no sign of the old man nor his blanket of goods. Strangely, none of the other vendors nearby seemed to remember him.

But the cloak was soft and warm on her shoulders and seemed to lighten her spirits somewhat as she returned to the palace, to the apartments around the garden. And as she expected, there was no one there.

This time her solitude was short-lived, however. The rattle of the doorway curtains told her that someone stood without, and she looked up to see Poshtli, silently awaiting her permission to enter.

"Come in," she said, delighted to see the warrior. His face, which had been unusually taut since they had arrived in Nexal, seemed once again smooth and untroubled.

Erix spun, allowing the feathered cloak to rise from her shoulders and circle her in the air, a brilliantly colorful frame for her own brown skin and swirling black hair. "Do you like it?"

"It's beautiful," he said, and he meant it. "But not as beautiful as the woman it warms."

Erix stopped suddenly, looking at Poshtli in surprise. Suddenly she blushed and looked down, pleased but taken aback by his remark. He stepped to her side, and she looked up at him again.

"Erixitl . . . I've wanted to speak to you for weeks, since the day we met, to tell you what's been in my heart. Always something seemed to stop me. We haven't been alone, or my tongue would become tied into a knot in my mouth and I could not speak.

"But no more!" He held her shoulders and looked into her eyes, noting the flecks of green there. "You are the most entrancing woman I have ever known. Your beauty leaves me without words. No other woman has done this to me!"

"My lord!" she blurted, stunned by his words. A turbulent flash of excitement grew in her stomach, but it was a tense, nerve-wracking feeling.

"Erixitl of Palul, will you become my wife?"

For a moment, she froze. Her excitement turned into fright, or at least a certain breathless nervousness.

But then suddenly his lips were pressed to hers. His kiss was hot, and she welcomed it with warmth of her own. She felt him holding her, and she wasn't at all sure she wanted it to end.

* * * * *

Halloran's step was light as he hurried back to the apartment. Naltecona had just offered him a house of his own, as repayment for Hal's teaching the Revered Counselor more of the ways of the strangers.

The soldier had made it clear, and the ruler had accepted, that these lessons did not include teaching Maztican warriors how to fight against the legionnaires. A fugitive from the legion he might be, but he couldn't bring himself to help prepare for the deaths of his former comrades-in-arms.

But it was not the men of the Golden Legion that Hal thought of right now. The one who mattered awaited him in the quarters around the garden.

For a moment, he winced inwardly as he thought of how little time he had spent with Erixitl since they had reached Nexal. Appointments with Naltecona, visits to the lodges of the Eagle and Jaguar Knights, long discussions with Maztican alchemists and sorcerers—all of these had kept him busy. He had allowed his fascination for the newness of Nexal to deprive him of the company of the one with whom he most wanted to share his life.

But no more. Now, with the secure offer of a house, he was no longer a wandering fugitive. He had grown to love this magnificent city. More importantly, he realized that he loved the woman who had brought him safely here.

His step increased in urgency as he turned the last corner. He reached for the beaded curtains, his heart singing. Then he heard voices from inside, and unconsciously he froze.

". . . become my wife?" The words were Poshtli's, Halloran sensed with a cold stone sinking into his stomach. *What would she say?*

Then, through the beads of the doorway, he saw Poshtli scoop Erix into his arms. Her own arms went around his shoulders, pulling him closer.

Stunned as if he had been struck on the head, Halloran lowered his hand from the doorway. Stumbling slightly, he turned and walked away.

* * * * *

Fire surged upward, illuminating the inside of the long building. Apprentices threw more wood on the flames, and now bright, yellow light surrounded the great statue of leering, bloodthirsty Zaltec.

Hoxitl entered the room, shedding his dirty robe and approaching the statue naked but for his breechclout. His hands were red, caked with the blood of the Viperhand ceremony. Tonight, as upon so many nights since the strangers had come to the True World, he had branded many of the faithful with the sign of the hand.

Like all the others, they took the vow, pledging hearts and minds, bodies and souls—their lives themselves—to Zaltec. In this age when strangers from across the sea marched in their land, they found their only comfort in this cult of hatred, and only Zaltec offered hope of successful resistance. The cult flourished, and this pleased Hoxitl. He suspected that the cult of the Viperhand would be the only force that could truly stem the tide when war swept the land as it inevitably must.

But now he had other, more immediate concerns.

"What is the word?" he inquired of a priest who emerged from the shadows to stand beside him, looking up at the statue.

"It will have to be done in the palace," said the newcomer, Kallict. A young, vigorous priest, Kallict had shown great skill with the sacrificial blade and possessed a keen wisdom for one of his age. Many priests thought he might one day succeed Hoxitl to the rank of patriarch.

The current high priest scowled at the news. "Does she not venture into the city?" he demanded.

"Rarely," replied Kallict. "She has gone to the market several times, but always with an escort of palace slaves—and always during the day."

"Taking her from the palace will be difficult," said the high priest.

Kallict removed a stone knife from his belt. Facing the older priest squarely, he extended his arm, which was covered with long, straight scars. Laying the blade against his own skin, Kallict drew the knife sharply toward himself. Red blood welled from the wound and dripped, unheeded, to the floor as the young priest looked at his patriarch.

"By Zaltec, I will find a way to do it." They both knew that his vow was as good as the blood that now collected into a small pool on the floor.

* * * * *

"They await us on the slopes," reported Darien. "Beyond the next pass lies their city, so I am certain they will fight us here."

DOUGLAS NILES

Cordell took the elfwoman's hand in gratitude for the warning. Without it, his legion would almost certainly have marched into ambush.

"Deploy to meet them," barked the captain-general to his assembled officers. The legion's march had taken it westward down a wide valley. Now they neared the higher ground, where the valley rose to this saddle-like pass, many miles inland from the border of Kultaka.

"Daggrande, deploy your crossbows across the front. Garrand, advance up the slope in a diversion. See if you can lure them into a charge. Alvarro, keep the lancers hidden, in reserve."

With the efficiency of long practice, the Golden Legion deployed for battle. The light foot soldiers of Garrand's company spread into a skirmish line. The heavy crossbowmen of Daggrande's units took station behind them, while Alvarro held his horsemen out of sight. The warriors of the Payit Cordell sent in two great wings to the right and left, using his Maztican allies to insure that his legion wasn't caught in a flank attack.

An overcast sky hung heavily over the valley, almost touching the highest of the surrounding peaks. All morning long the gray blanket had pressed close, darkening the landscape, threatening and rumbling, but yielding no moisture.

* * * * *

A shower of arrows, as thick as a summer downpour, soared outward from the slopes, arcing down to spray the assembled footmen of Cordell's legion.

"Shields up!" shouted Daggrande, nervously eyeing the heights.

With a clatter of stone against steel, the arrows shattered against the metal bucklers and helmets of the legionnaires. One or two found a chink, driving into a bicep or painfully pricking a shoulder, but most of the missiles bounced harmlessly from the protected troops.

Again and again the arrows flew into the air, like a streaking cloud of locusts, but always the metal shields of the legionnaires saved them from catastrophe.

"Move up, now—look lively!" Daggrande raised his steel

crossbow, searching the brushy slope before them for some sign of the enemy. He saw the Kultakan archers backing up the hill, away from his slowly marching company. The temptation to charge them was great, but the dwarven veteran shrugged it away. The nimble warriors would have no difficulty slipping away from his heavily encumbered troops.

Instead, the company marched to the measured cadence of the drummer, maintaining a straight line even as a portion scrambled through a ditch or another section forced its way through a dense thicket.

"Halt!" he cried, as they reached a steeper, rockier portion of the slope. "Shields!"

Again arrows showered them, as thick as a cloud of stinging insects, but fortunately with not much greater damaging effect. The dwarf saw with satisfaction that, though several of his men bled from fresh and obviously painful wounds, not one of them had broken ranks or fallen.

Now a shrieking din of whistles, horns, and shrill yells suddenly broke from the ground above them. Where Daggrande had seen a broken slope with occasional flashes of movement, now he beheld a horde of many thousands of feathered, painted Kultakans. The natives leaped to their feet from countless holes in the earth, as if they had appeared by magic.

Another shower of arrows erupted, and even before the missiles fell to earth, the Mazticans broke into a howling downhill charge.

* * * * *

"Fly, my feathered ones! Fly to victory!"

Just beneath the top of the ridge, Takamal sprang to his feet. The war chief of Kultaka turned his face to the sun, raising his voice in a long, ululating howl, letting the exultation of his own spirit lift the hearts of his charging warriors.

Behind him, a rank of warriors stood, each holding a long pole. Atop each shaft fluttered a different banner of brilliant feathers. When raised alone or in combination, they served to communicate orders to the Kultakan army.

Along the ridgetop, the Eagle Knights stood above a steep

embankment. The black-and-white-cloaked warriors hurled themselves into space, changing to the forms of diving birds and soaring free before they crashed to the rocks below.

"See the strangers recoil!" cried Naloc, high priest of Zaltec and Takamal's lifelong advisor.

Indeed, the feathered swarm of the Kultakan charge had swept fully around the silver figures of the enemy. Virtually immobile in comparison to the fleet Kultakans, the strangers could only tighten their ranks and form a rough circle against the all-around assault.

"Still, they fight well," admitted Takamal as his flash of joy settled back to grim determination. "Very few of them have been slain."

Below them, the Eagles settled to earth. Quickly they became humans again, raising the wooden *macas* and whooping as they hurled themselves into the attack. Against them stood a single line of the strangers, wielding their silver shields and those long, metal knives. As the two lines clashed, dozens of Eagles fell, but only one or two of the enemy.

The chief knew that his encirclement would have meant the annihilation of any Maztican foe. Many of his warriors had fallen to the silver knives and metal-tipped arrows of the soldiers, and he knew there would be much grieving after this fight.

"Even the Payit serve them well," observed Naloc. Takamal had ordered small, sharp attacks against each side of the enemy position. The strangers' Maztican allies held both flanks of the position without faltering.

"Bah! We send only a diversion against them." Takamal barely took notice of the natives among the enemy. "It is the foreigners we must beat—and look, we press them back!"

"And still no sign of their monsters." Naloc looked anxiously about the field. Neither of them knew fully what to make of the tale of the half-man, half-deer creatures that reputedly helped the strangers to rout the Payit. The stories had seemed fantastic, yet the defeat of the Payit couldn't be questioned.

"If they appear, so be it. We are ready."

As if in reply to Takamal's challenge, they saw the objects of their curiosity erupt from a narrow draw with shocking speed.

"By Zaltec, it's true!" whispered Naloc in awe.

Takamal did not answer. He stared in amazement, but without fear, at the thundering creatures. The man-forms grew right out of their backs, he could see. They came in four waves, about ten of the monsters in each. Around them dashed shaggy, slavering beasts with long white fangs and bristling spiked collars. They reminded Takamal of coyotes, but they were much larger and more savage of aspect. Also, these beasts fought with every bit as much bravery as the soldiers, leaping against the warriors and tearing with their savage jaws.

The great beasts and their smaller companions raced forward, up the smoothest ground in the center of the pass. Each of the monsters carried a long spear—the longest spears Takamal had ever seen—and the force of their charge carried them like a landslide into the first ranks of the Kultakan warriors.

The warriors didn't even slow them down. Takamal saw with grudging admiration how the beasts tore a swath of death through his beautiful feathered ranks. Later, he knew, he would suffer for the broken bodies left in the wake of the attack, but now his mind worked rapidly, searching for the proper counterstroke.

"There!" he said, pointing along the route of the charge. "They come as we had hoped."

"Your wisdom once again shows the blessings of Zaltec," marveled Naloc, with an awestruck look at his chief. It had been Takamal who had guessed that the monsters, if they appeared, would attack along the stretch of smooth ground.

And it was here that the Kultakan leader had laid his trap.

* * * * *

Alvarro grinned as his lance tore through the feathered shield of a Kultakan warrior. His horse thundered forward, eagerly trampling the panicking spearmen before them. Beside him, the ranks of the lancers spread apart. Now they advanced in a line that meant death for any native warrior unfortunate enough to stand in its path.

The captain rode at the fore, urging his charger to keep just a neck ahead of the rest of the line. His black armor distinguished him, but his helmet also trailed a black streamer, insuring that his men could see him anywhere on the field—his men, and the enemy, too, Alvarro thought with a look at the fleeing natives before him.

The savages were breaking! His heart pounded with excitement as he saw that his riders would carry the battle. He struck again, and this time the lance was torn from his hand, stuck in the body of its victim. The rider pulled his longsword, as most of the horsemen around him had also done.

The charge carried the riders onto the lower slopes of the ridge. Soon they would reach the warriors surrounding Daggrande's company, relieving the encircled legionnaires.

The horseman didn't see the tall pole, with its banners of bright feathers, dip and wave atop the ridge. He wouldn't have understood the command that the gesture issued, in any event.

But he saw its results.

The charge continued, though the smooth ground gave way to rougher terrain. Sheer momentum carried them onward, until suddenly Alvarro found himself among rocks and brush instead of the open field. From behind this cover swarmed a nightmare attack that stopped the cavalry charge cold.

Alvarro gaped in astonishment as a huge spotted cat, bigger than any leopard, leaped onto a rock. With a shrill cry of rage, the beast exposed long fangs and curved, wicked claws. Still snarling, the cat leaped.

Instinctively Alvarro brought his sword up, but it was the equally instinctive reaction of his horse that saved him. The steed reared backward in panic, and with its front hooves, it struck the feline to earth. The cat crouched, snarling, and Alvarro saw to his horror that more and more of the creatures were emerging from cover to spring on his unsuspecting riders.

"Back!" Captain Alvarro howled, his voice shrill. "Away from these devils!" He struck one of the creatures on its skull, killing it. At the same time, he saw a horse stumble and fall to the earth under the weight of several cats. The rider, screaming in terror, was torn from the saddle and quickly disappeared beneath a nightmarish tangle of claws and fangs.

The horsemen desperately pulled away, and in moments, the line thundered backward in full retreat. Not a steed escaped without raked, bleeding flanks and legs.

Once again Alvarro led his riders, this time in terrified flight. Flecks of spit drooled from his lips as he choked back the inarticulate fear. But he could not pull his reins.

* * * * *

"Helm curse him!" snarled Cordell, his stomach turning to a knot as Alvarro turned away from the jaguars. "The worthless dog!"

"Who could stand against those devils?" challenged Bishou Domincus. "They are clearly the work of their foul gods!"

"Did either of you see that?" asked Darien coldly. Her voice got the men's attention abruptly.

The trio stood on a small rise, below the slope where the battle raged. Cordell, knowing that the survival of Daggrande's company itself was at stake, turned to her in annoyance.

"See what? What are you talking about?"

"Up there," the wizard said, pointing coolly. Darien's shocking white skin showed as she raised her hand to point toward the ridgetop. Normally she disliked exposing any patch of her skin to the sun, but the heavy overcast of the day spared her discomfort.

"That feathered pole?" asked Cordell, his mind quickly grasping Darien's meaning, if not her intent. "That must be the war chief. The Payit did the same thing."

"A great chief," mused the wizard. "That was a clever trap, and it was his pole that signaled the attack."

Cordell looked skyward again, his black eyes flashing. "I see what you mean," he breathed softly.

* * * * *

"Of course!" Takamal, carefully watching the battle, saw

the horseman fall and instantly understood the monsters. "They are only beasts that carry men into battle!"

His heart surged, full of pride at the noble attack of his Jaguar Knights. Dozens had been slain beneath the feet of the lumbering beasts, but still they pressed their attack. And now the riders had been pushed back!

"Magnificent!" whispered Naloc. "Zaltec has smiled upon us this day."

"Perhaps he *will* smile upon us," cautioned the chief. "But the attack isn't broken yet. Witness how the silver soldiers resist, even when surrounded." He gestured toward the field below, where the circle of swordsmen still stood amid the howling mass of Kultakan warriors. For many minutes, they had been cut off from the rest of the legion, yet no more than a dozen had fallen—and at the cost of many hundreds of Kultakan dead.

"Now! Signal the advance!" barked Takamal.

Two of his signalmen raised banners, each of which glowed bright crimson under the heavy gray sky. The pennants streamed in the slight wind, stretching weightlessly into the air. For a moment, the battle paused as the Mazticans took note of the command fluttering from the knoll atop the ridge.

But then they saw something else up there. Naloc, and Takamal himself, whirled in astonishment as a figure suddenly appeared on the ridgetop, barely thirty feet away.

The newcomer was a woman, Takamal saw—a woman with shockingly pale skin, and hair the color of snow. She wore a dark robe, but now the wind whipped that robe away from her body and he saw the bleached skin on her arms, her legs, her torso.

He saw, too, that she was very beautiful, in an icy sort of way. A golden circlet surrounded her brow, and her high cheekbones suggested nobility. Her eyes were wide, pale . . . and empty.

"By Zaltec!" gasped Naloc. The cleric seized his sacrificial dagger and held the stone blade over his head, lunging toward the woman. She seemed to be unarmed, though Takamal noticed a slender stick thrust through her belt.

She raised a hand and spat a word at Naloc—a *word*—and

the cleric grasped his chest with a dull moan and collapsed to the ground. He kicked his feet reflexively, as does a sacrifice sometimes even when his heart has been torn away. Takamal knew that Naloc was dead.

The war chief of Kultaka stood tall, unbent even after his seventy years. He looked up at this slender female, who now turned those icy eyes on him. Takamal stood and watched. So, too, did the warriors of Kultaka, gathered on the field below.

A bolt of yellow energy, like a shot of lightning from the clouds, exploded from the woman's hand. She pointed her finger, and the power surged forth with a hiss and a crackle, faster than the eye could follow.

The magic drove into Takamal, for a moment outlining his body in sizzling blue flame. The smell of burned flesh wafted through the air. Still the great chief of the Kultakans made no sound, no movement. The energy of the lightning bolt exploded past, striking two of his flag-bearers dead behind him.

Then Takamal toppled, his life burned away by sorcery. Rigid and scarred in death, the war chief's body fell forward, tumbling from the ridge to spill down the long slope, finally crashing to a halt among the still, stunned members of his army.

A few feathers from his singed headdress floated through the air, coming to rest on the ground atop the ridge, far above the Revered Counselor's shattered corpse. Those feathers, and two footprints outlined in black soot, were all that remained to show where Takamal had been.

* * * * *

From the chronicles of Coton:

The legend of the Plumed One's departure includes the promise of his return.

Qotal journeyed to Payit and climbed aboard a great feathered canoe, to sail onto the Eastern Ocean. He turned his back upon Maztica, for everywhere the people followed gods of lust and blood. Zaltec smiled, to see the Feathered Serpent sail away.

DOUGLAS NILES

But Qotal promised that one day he would return. He told of three signs that would preface his arrival and bade the folk of Maztica to watch and to wait.

First would come the couatl, messenger of Qotal and harbinger of his return.

Second would be granted the Cloak of One Plume, to be worn by Qotal's chosen one, offering protection and beauty so that all may learn the glory of his name.

Third, and most mysterious, would come the Summer Ice.

But for now, these tales are mere legends. Even the couatl, who tantalizes me, I see only in my dreams.

♣ 5 ♣

DANCE OF THE JAGUARS

Tulom-Itzi sprawled across the jungle hills of Far Payit, a large city that looked like no city at all. Several stone pyramids jutted steeply above the treetops, and the great dome of the observatory squatted atop the highest hill. Wide grassy paths twisted among trunks and vines of forest, and several large green expanses of land had been cleared of trees altogether.

But the overwhelming presence of the forest ruled the land. The structures of men, such as they were, became a part of the jungle rather than its conqueror.

"Of course," Zochimaloc had explained to Gultec, "at one time the city housed tens of thousands of people." Now a mere fraction of that number dwelled there, the descendants of Tulom-Itzi's long-forgotten founders.

The people of Far Payit differed little from his own in appearance, Gultec realized. Short and well-muscled, deep brown of skin, they were an industrious, inventive folk. Their culture, however, seemed very foreign to the Jaguar Knight.

Never had he seen people of such gentleness. They knew nothing of war, save that it was a scourge known in their distant past. Yet their knowledge in other areas astounded him.

The surgeons of Tulom-Itzi knew cures for the poison-that-sickens-blood, for the disease of body rot, and for other horrors that would result in sure fatality for a Payit or other Maztican. Astronomers studied the skies, predicting even such things as the irregular passage of the Wandering Stars. Here musicians created lyrical ballads of legend and romance.

Gultec had come to know and love these folk, but none did

he revere so much as his teacher. He thrilled to each minute with Zochimaloc, and each day seemed to open the door to new wonders of knowledge and understanding. Today, Zochimaloc walked with him to the *cetay*, the great well that lay to the north of the jungle city. It was, Zochi promised, to be an important lesson.

"Once the *cetay* was used for sacrifice," explained the wizened teacher as they reached the lip of the depression. "But now it serves best as a source of wisdom. Come, sit with me here."

The *cetay* was a circular hole several hundred paces across. Stone walls plummeted, with many jagged outcrops, to a clear surface of water hundreds of feet below them. Zochimaloc, who walked with a long wooden staff today, settled easily onto a benchlike boulder at the very lip of the well. Gultec sat beside him.

For a long time—more than an hour—the two sat in silence. Gultec studied the smooth, blue water so far below him. He saw slight swirls in its surface, as if a hidden current agitated its depths. Gradually, unconsciously, his mind emptied of its external concerns.

After his months of study, Gultec recognized the plants of the jungle for all their beneficent or dangerous qualities. He understood the arrangement of the stars in the heavens and their influence upon earthly concerns. He could now freeze any animal with the force of his gaze, and he suspected that this mastery extended to humans as well.

Zochimaloc did not allow him to test the latter ability, however, on the free peoples of Tulom-Itzi. And unlike any other land Gultec knew, these folk of Far Payit kept no slaves.

An overwhelming sense of peace flowed through Gultec. He felt a contentment he had not previously imagined, and his mind floated freely with the relaxing pace of his meditation. Slowly, then, the gentle tapping of Zochimaloc's staff penetrated his awareness, and he looked up at his teacher.

"What thoughts are in your mind, Gultec?" asked the old man in a kindly tone.

Gultec smiled softly. "I feel that this is a haven for me, a calm eye in the storms of the True World. Knowledge of

Tulom-Itzi must be kept from the rest of the world, or I fear your fragile peace will vanish."

"Know this, Gultec," Zochimaloc replied with a deep sigh. "Our peace will indeed disappear. It will not be terribly long before it does, though perhaps we have a little more time than Nexal."

The Jaguar Knight looked around sadly, trying to imagine Tulom-Itzi suffering the ravages of war. It never occurred to him to question his teacher's knowledge. If Zochimaloc said this, it must be true.

"This is why you have been brought here, Gultec. Our people know nothing of war. You do."

Now he turned to the old man in shock. "What can I possibly teach you? The wisdom of your people shows me to be a mere jungle barbarian in contrast! And the only important war I ever fought, I lost!"

"Show more faith in yourself," Zochimaloc chided gently.

"But I have so much more to learn!"

Smiling, the teacher climbed to his feet, without the aid of his staff. "You know more than you think. The forms and shapes of your body, for instance. Which do you know?"

"I am a man and a jaguar," said Gultec, surprised at the readily answerable question. He rose to stand beside his teacher at the lip of the deep *cetay*.

"A bird?" asked Zochi ironically. "A parrot, perhaps?"

"No, of course not!"

"But think of the parrot, Gultec. Think of the bright feathers, the strong wings, the sharp, hooked beak, the powerful claws. Think of these things!"

Surprised by the sudden sharpness in his teacher's tone, the warrior's mind pictured the jungle bird. He didn't see the sudden, quick lash of Zochimaloc's staff. His teacher pushed him sharply, his frail frame striking with surprising power.

Gultec tumbled from the rock, dropping into the rocky pit of the *cetay*. Shocked, his arms reached out reflexively, but the attack had been too sudden, too unexpected. He grabbed nothing but air.

But he grabbed the air, *and it held him*. With a soaring dive, his bright green tailfeathers instinctively steering his flight, he flashed across the surface of the water.

And then he spread his wings and he flew.

* * * * *

Erix rose and paced the garden again, confused and nervous. Where was Hal? This was his longest absence since their arrival in Nexal a week earlier. The long shadows in the courtyard told her that sunset approached, and Hal's audiences with Naltecona had never before lasted much beyond noon.

Then the shadows darkened. She turned away, suddenly frightened, until she realized that it was only a cloud passing over the sun. Still, those black images continued to dance around the corners of her vision, filling the spaces around her with shadows.

A vague shudder passed through her body. She recalled the dream that had come to her in the desert, of Naltecona slain among the men of Cordell's legion. The shadows around her darkened the palace, darkened it even more than had the moonlight in her dream.

She thought again, wistfully, of Poshtli's visit earlier in the day. He had been so noble! His proposal had fallen on her like a shock, and she knew it offered a life such as, weeks earlier, she could never have imagined. A life of luxury and comfort, with slaves for every need, among the society of the grandest folk in all Nexal.

Why then had she rebuffed him? She was still not sure. She only knew that, after moments in his arms, her lips pressed to his, she sensed that he did not love her. Erix also knew that, though she was dazzled by his prowess and presence, her affections did not extend to love.

So, gently and quietly, she had told him so. He had accepted her decision with surprise, but not anger. Poshtli had bowed formally and left. The Eagle Knight had no sooner departed than she found herself anxiously awaiting Halloran's return.

But that had been hours ago. Her eagerness had turned to anxiousness, unease, and now it threatened to become fear. Surely the Revered Counselor wouldn't harm a visitor under his own roof, would he?

She looked out in the courtyard, where the gay splashing of the fountain seemed to mock her. Storm raised his head, as if the horse sensed her eyes upon it. Then the mare ambled to the fresh pile of clover and grass that the slaves had brought that morning.

Suddenly the horse, the whole scene, fell into darkness, as if something huge blotted out the sun. Again that terrible sense of a doom-filled destiny seized her. Involuntarily she clapped her hands to her eyes and moaned, willing the shadow away.

"What is it? Erix, what's the matter?" She felt the touch of strong hands on her shoulders and spun to grasp Halloran in a fearful embrace. He held her, soothing her gently, until finally she risked another look at the courtyard. Once again the slanting rays of the low sun cast bright illumination on the dancing fountain and its framework of blossoms.

She saw Hal looking around in alarm. "It was . . . nothing," she explained quickly. "Just a sudden chill."

He sensed that she wasn't telling him everything, but he didn't press the issue. He had noticed her sudden, brief distractions before, on their journey to Nexal, but she had never offered him any explanation.

Let Poshtli worry about it, he thought, almost savagely. Abruptly he dropped his arms to his sides and turned away.

Erix, surprised by his sudden shift, spoke tentatively. "What happened? I—I was worried about you."

He turned to her and she drew back, frightened by the look of anger on his face. "I went for a walk. Through the market, to the floating gardens. I wanted to see the city."

"But we were going to do that together when you had time!" Erix's objection came more from surprise than annoyance.

"Together? I hardly think that would be appropriate, anymore, do you?" The picture of Poshtli wrapping this woman in his arms flashed again through Hal's mind, and he winced at the painful memory.

"But . . ." Erix couldn't understand his anger. "Why are you talking like this? What's the matter?"

Halloran whirled away, pacing across the garden. Words of anger and jealousy surged through him. Only with the greatest effort could he hold them back. In his heart, he knew that Poshtli had been too true a friend to deserve the vitriol that Hal wanted to spew.

Finally he turned back, speaking to her from several paces away. "Naltecona has offered me a house. I can no longer stay here, for obvious reasons. I will move there as soon as it can be arranged. Until then, I will try to leave you your privacy."

"What do you mean?" Erix felt a brief flash of panic.

But then her own anger took over. How could he treat her like this? She had been worried about him, relieved to see him. Suddenly the mere sight of him inflamed her. She had to get away from him or her anger would not be contained. In that moment, she knew that she would take the journey she had thus far delayed, to the one place in the world she could go.

"Never mind! I don't need this place either! I'm going home—home to Palul, to my father and brother! Take your house and live like a great, wise man!"

For a moment, Halloran stared at her, dumb with shock. He thought of Poshtli, wondering if the noble warrior knew his betrothed planned to suddenly depart Nexal. "Home? But what about—"

"You can stay in Nexal—see the city all you want!" she shot at him, cutting him off. Suddenly she shivered as that shadowy presence crept into the room, against the walls and floor, muffling her sight. Darkness welled around her, casting the shadows across the garden, even blocking out the sun. Only Halloran stood out before her, in the light.

But she turned her back on that light, and then she was out the door.

* * * * *

"The cult of the Viperhand spreads quickly," hissed the drow, his hood thrown back so that the crimson blush of the Darkfyre washed over his black face and white hair. "But we control it well, for it lies under the thumb of the priests."

The drow spoke to a circle of his equals, and to the Ancestor. The Harvesters had yet to begin their grisly night's work. For long moments, the group remained silent as the Ancient Ones meditated.

"The Viperhand does well. When our need arises, it will be ready." The words came from the Ancestor, his voice rasping through the cavern. "Let the humans spread their cult of Zaltec and let it further our own ends."

"The priests want to give the white stranger's heart to their god," said the drow, persisting.

"We require that the girl be slain. She alone, by the prophecy, carries the threat to us of ultimate failure. Yet this man helped to kill Spirali. He has protected her from Payit to Nexal, and still they remain together. Let the priests and their agents kill them both. It will serve as a useful warning to the strangers."

"We cannot expect a single death to frighten them off!" objected another of the Ancient Ones.

"Of course not. But our vengeance will be exacted for Spirali. And the only one of the invaders to see Nexal thus far will be destroyed. The others will take some time to reach here.

"During that time, the cult of the Viperhand can grow stronger still, so that when the invaders arrive, we will be able to meet them with strength." The venerable drow looked at his companions. His eyes, stark white and very wide against the midnight skin of his face, gleamed.

"Let the word be sent to Hoxitl," said the Ancestor, his voice suddenly firm. He leaned forward in his thronelike chair. The cherry glow of the caldron disappeared, lost in the greater darkness that was the Ancestor.

"The girl and the man shall die tonight!"

* * * * *

"These are the sons of Takamal."

Darien emotionlessly gestured at five warriors. The elven wizard had used her magic to learn the Kultakan tongue, speaking to the natives who had been summoned to their city square. Now she awaited Cordell's instructions. The once proud men now stood, almost naked, before their conquerors. The meeting took place in the center of the city of Kultaka, in the very shadow of Zaltec's pyramid.

Around the leaders stood the trim ranks of the Golden Legion and its Payit allies, surrounded by the silent masses of Kultaka.

"Why have they doffed their clothes?" asked the general. "Tell them to put them on."

"They say that their defeat has left them unworthy to wear the garb of warriors."

"Nonsense!" Cordell smiled at the Kultakans—the full, ingratiating smile that helped him command, to the death, the loyalty of his men. "Tell them that we have not conquered them, that we are in fact very sorry so many of their brave warriors have died in battle against us."

Darien turned and translated as Cordell looked around at Kultaka. The city showed far less opulence than had Ulatos. Unlike the capital of the Payit, many of the structures here had been built for defense. The flat housetops were surrounded by waist-high walls. Windows were small. The streets were still lined with flowers, but the profusion of feathermagic that was so extensive in Ulatos was completely absent here.

It had taken only hours to discover that the Kultakans were much poorer in gold than either their jungle neighbors to the east, or, reputedly, the Nexalans to the west. What few treasures they had were stacked here, willingly offered by the abject sons of the slain war chief.

"The oldest, this one called Tokol, asks why you show such kindness. Is this how you prepare your captives for sacrifice?" Darien pulled Cordell's attention back to these men. And now his plan for them was complete.

"You are not our enemies! We did not want to attack you. We merely sought passage through your lands, and some food. We are on our way to attack the treacherous Nexalans, whose land lies beyond your own."

Cordell saw, without surprise, that the Kultakans were intrigued by his reply. Tokol spoke again. "Surely it is a great tragedy that we did not know this, for the Nexalans are our greatest enemies! It is good that you attack them."

"And truly, we shall beat them," replied the captain-general. "For we have been tested this day against the finest warriors in Maztica!"

Now he saw the heads come up, some measure of pride returning to the sharp-featured faces. Tokol spoke again. "We offer you what food you desire, and ourselves as slaves. May your march be a success." Tokol, mimicked by the others, bowed deeply.

"I could never see such men as you reduced to slaves," objected Cordell, raising his voice. "No! Indeed, I can only see you as warriors! Proud, strong men, marching against Nexal!"

He had seen the worth of the Payit in battle, and now he found a force of warriors that showed far greater skill, and larger numbers, than the legion of his Payit allies. As he continued, he saw in the faces of Takamal's sons surprise at his words. A faint look of hope in their eyes convinced him that he took the right tack; he sensed that these warriors would do anything to regain their own manliness.

"Will you not join me? Your hosts, added to my legion, will make a splendid spectacle for the march on Nexal!"

Tokol saw no need for hesitation or consultation before he replied.

"We are eternally grateful for the kindness of our conqueror. We offer you whatever captives you need to celebrate your victory. The rest of us shall be proud to march with you to Nexal!"

"Captives?" Cordell suddenly saw their meaning. "No! We do not slay our enemies to feed our god. Instead, there will be this decree, the one law I will place upon you."

Now the general's eyes flashed as Darien translated. The Kultakans stood as if spellbound, awaiting his command. "There is to be no sacrifice among you! Hold your captives as slaves or let them go as you wish. But you may not offer their hearts to your pagan gods!"

Tokol recoiled as if struck. Instinctively he looked up at the nearby temple, as if expecting a bolt to issue forth and strike Cordell dead. But nothing happened.

"Do you understand?" barked the legion's commander.

"It shall be as you command," said Tokol, with another low bow.

* * * * *

Douglas Niles

The four Jaguar Knights stood stiffly before Kallict as the priest performed ritual cuts, scarring their earlobes, forearms, and cheeks with short chops of his sharp obsidian dagger. None of the men cried out, of course, for to do so would have betrayed the trust of their vow.

The vow of the Viperhand.

After the ritual scarring, each of them stepped before Hoxitl and knelt. The only sound was the high priest's chant as he pressed his freshly bloodied hand to the chest of each supplicant.

Finally the four stood branded, their spotted cloaks thrown open so that the raw wounds on their chests stood proudly forth.

"You Jaguars have been selected by Kallict for your bravery and your devotion to Zaltec," said Hoxitl, fastening each in turn with the burning glare of his passionate gaze. "Your task is simple and direct, and your service will be in the name of Zaltec himself!"

The Jaguar Knights bowed their heads humbly, but the high priest smiled to himself as he saw their bodies tense with excitement.

"There are two people—a woman of Maztica, and a man from the strangers—dwelling in the palace of Naltecona. Zaltec hungers for the man's heart. He wishes to taste of the stranger's blood. The woman, too, must be slain, though she can die in her chambers.

"You are to enter the palace tonight. Kill the woman and bring the man to us. And know that Zaltec shall remember and reward."

* * * * *

The horse whinnied nervously, and Halloran came instantly awake. Storm had grown fat and lazy on the easy life in the palace, and the horse rarely made any sound of distress or displeasure.

But again that whinny, and this time the alarm in the sound was clear. Indeed, the horse sounded close to panic. Hal felt pressure against his chest and realized he had fallen asleep with the heavy spellbook on top of him. He had been studying it, trying to master a few more of its secrets, when sleep had claimed him.

Then he remembered. Erixitl was gone! All the loneliness and despair came back to him, a wave of hopelessness that left him weak and paralyzed on his bed. Never in his life had he felt so alone, so useless. Roughly he forced the emotion aside, fixing his attention on the disturbance that had awakened him.

Sliding Helmstooth from its scabbard beside his bed, Halloran extended the longsword before him and silently stood. The dim glow of the enchanted longsword's blade barely illuminated the chamber.

A sudden stench assailed his nostrils, reminding him of an inn he had frequented back in Murann. The place had been surrounded by alleycats, and the odor reminded him of the tomcats who sometimes yowled on the fence outside.

A low growl rumbled in the darkness, confirming his suspicions.

"*Kirisha!*" he cried, and instantly the room was awash in cool, white light. The magic spell allowed him to see and also startled and frightened the intruders.

These, he saw, were a pair of monstrous jaguars. Halloran gaped in shock for a moment, but then his fighting instincts took over. The cats crouched in the doorway to his room, blinking at the light and uttering their deep, rumbling growls. One spread his jaws in a snarl, and Hal grimaced at the huge fangs he saw there.

Storm, in the garden, whinnied in terror, and Hal didn't stop to think. Instead, he charged into combat with an almost welcome sense of release.

Helmstooth pricked one of the jaguars in the shoulder, but then Hal grunted in pain as the other sprang at him, raking his thigh with long, curving claws. "Damn!" he hissed, limping backward. He lunged into another attack, but both the cats leaped nimbly out of the way.

He heard another sound in the large room beyond his own. More of them! For a moment, his heart filled with panic as he saw two jaguars slinking toward Erix's room. It was with a great sense of relief that he remembered she was gone, safe on the road to Palul.

But that same relief quickly turned to anger. His frustra-

Douglas Niles

tion with her departure, and now a growing sense of outrage at this invasion, galvanized him into action. He feinted at one of the cats and then, as the other lunged toward him, turned to sink the point of his blade into the second cat's well-muscled chest.

As quickly as Hal struck, the first jaguar leaped toward him, and he scrambled desperately backward, barely avoiding a potentially disemboweling slash at his gut. He felt acutely aware of his vulnerability. His steel breastplate hung beside his bed, but he had no chance to don it.

Suddenly the unwounded jaguar sprang into the air, in a powerful leap that drove toward Hal's face. The man twisted out of the way but heard the cat land behind him while the other one crouched, still menacing him from the door.

Hal's reaction was as instantaneous as it was desperate. Knowing the two-sided attack meant certain death if he let them spring, Halloran struck first, driving savagely at the wounded jaguar in the doorway. He slashed at the creature's face and then, as it twisted aside, drove his sword into the unprotected flank. Helmstooth lunged forward almost of its own will, as if the steel blade somehow sought the blood of this feline victim. The sharp tip penetrated fur, skin, and muscle, finally puncturing the savage heart.

With a yowl of pain and dying rage, the animal fell to the ground, kicking helplessly. Hal gaped, watching the fur-covered limbs slowly stretch and twitch. A paw distorted grotesquely, the claws extending and straightening. Then the claws became fingers, the fingers of a human hand that lay limp in death. The body of the beast, as it perished, returned to the form of the man that was its soul.

His fascination with the gruesome transformation almost cost Hal his life. A premonition of danger warned him to roll to the side, and he barely dodged the leaping attack of the jaguar that now sprang out of his room. This cat, and the other two that darted out of Erix's empty room, now faced Halloran. In the courtyard, the horse cried again, a whinny shrill with panic. At least Storm still lived, Hal thought.

But the three cats crept closer, jaws wide. Their yellow eyes gleamed at him, reflecting the glow of his light spell, mocking him with their advantage in numbers.

Behind him, Hal felt the corner of the room blocking him in. He knew that he was trapped.

* * * * *

"Can you listen to me, Grandfather?" asked Poshtli, bowing humbly outside the door to Coton's cramped quarters.

The high priest was the only person the warrior could turn to, the only one upon whom he would confer the honorary title of "Grandfather." Coton had always been his trusted adviser, and even after the cleric took his vow of silence, Poshtli had found these one-sided discussions very useful. And Coton, too, seemed to enjoy the companionship.

The cleric of Qotal smiled gently, waving a piece of *copal* incense around his small painting chamber, leaving a trail of sweet smoke in the air. He gestured for the Eagle Knight to enter and sit.

"I feel as if I am in the grip of a giant's hand," said Poshtli, clasping his hands together and staring into Coton's deep, unfathomable eyes. "I have answered what I thought was the will of the gods. I have brought the stranger to Nexal because that was the hope of the city. Him and the woman, Erixitl." For some reason, it was difficult to say her name. He told Coton of his proposal, her gentle rebuff. "Perhaps she doubted the depth of my devotion. Truly, I offered my hand out of fear for her, though indeed she is strong, smart, and very beautiful. She would be a fine wife.

"And her life is in danger! I have brought this trouble upon her! By marrying her, I hoped to protect her!"

Coton stood and stepped to the door of the small chamber. The sun had long since set, and he saw the dying torches on top of the great pyramid, left there by the priests of Zaltec hours earlier, before they had descended from their grim evening rituals. Poshtli turned to follow the cleric with his eyes.

"I have seen the destiny of Nexal, Grandfather! It is to lie in ruins—in black, smoking wreckage!" The Eagle Knight stood. "My visions have shown me that this stranger offers some hope of salvation, but now he, too, is seized by events beyond his control!"

Poshtli abruptly reached his hand to his shoulder and plucked one black, white-tipped eagle feather from his cloak. He offered the plume to Coton, and the old cleric reached out to take it.

"If I aid Halloran, I shall break the vow to my order, for this I have been forbidden to do." Now the knight's pain was mirrored in the cleric's eyes.

"I have spent my life striving to be the finest Eagle Warrior the True World has ever known. Now the life of a man from another world can snatch that away from me. For I know this, Grandfather: I cannot let him die."

Coton nodded, his face expressionless. As always, however, the silent cleric had helped Poshtli in some mysterious way to clarify what was in his own mind. Now the warrior nodded respectfully and thanked the cleric for listening. Then he stepped quickly from Coton's temple.

Some unconscious sense of urgency propelled Poshtli's step as he started into the palace, toward the apartments Naltecona had provided for his friends. As he drew closer, his hurried gait broke into a trot, and then a run.

Poshtli dashed around the corner before the apartments, somehow certain that danger loomed. He saw a group of slaves huddled outside the door, listening in terror but not daring to peer inside.

"Move, damn you!" he cursed, knocking the slower ones aside.

He sprang through the door and immediately saw the dead Jaguar Knight illuminated in the strange pale glow that emerged from Halloran's room. A growl in the corner called his attention to the shadows, where he saw Halloran backed into a corner, facing three monstrous felines.

Poshtli barked a sharp sound, the shrill, keening cry of the hunting eagle. Instantly two of the jaguars spun to face this new threat, while the third crouched before Hal, its tail twitching tautly from side to side.

For a moment, the Eagle Knight froze. His *maca* felt light in his hand, eager for blood. But suddenly the memory of his vow, the clear orders from the leaders of his order, came back to him. He was prohibited, by the terms of that vow, from aiding Halloran against the forces of Zaltec.

The great cats crept forward, threatening growls rumbling from their deep chests.

Poshtli ignored the feline attackers for a moment. Then slowly, deliberately, he lifted his Eagle helmet off his head and tossed it aside, shrugged his cloak of feathers from his shoulders, and let it settle to the ground around his feet.

Now he crouched into a fighting stance with his *maca* raised toward the cats. "Tell me when," hissed Hal, lifting the silver shaft of his longsword.

Poshtli nodded. "Now!"

Slashing downward with the wooden club, Poshtli leaped forward. The blade, studded with razor-sharp bits of obsidian, chopped into the back of one of the jaguars. The creature howled in agony, trying to twist away, but Poshtli circled with the creature's turn, using it to block him from the attack of the other enraged feline.

Meanwhile, Halloran darted at the third cat. The animal reared up, slashing toward the man's face, but Hal ducked under the attack and drove his blade into the beast's heart. Before it had stopped twitching, he leaped across its fallen body and drove his blade into the last of the jaguars.

For a few moments, they stood panting among the four bleeding bodies. The last three shifted back to human form as they died, feet and arms and legs and hands growing from the spotted feline limbs.

"Erixitl?" asked Poshtli, slowly and fearfully.

"She's . . . safe. She's gone," Hal answered.

"Gone?" The Eagle Knight didn't hide his surprise.

"Back to Palul, to her home." Hal explained Erix's sudden decision to the knight, omitting the details of their argument. He found it hard to rekindle his jealous anger, much of which had previously focused on Poshtli. While he missed Erixitl already, he was grateful that she had been gone on this night.

To Hal's surprise, Poshtli seemed pleased to hear of her departure. Indeed, Hal couldn't figure out why the warrior wasn't more distraught at the sudden absence of his bride-to-be.

"That could be the safest thing," he replied. "Who else knows where she's gone?"

"No one, so far as I know. Just you and me."

"Let's keep it that way. I think it is best for her if Erixitl of Palul disappears for a while."

* * * * *

From the chronicles of Coton:

Seeking the light among the deepening shadows . . .

The darkness haunts my dreams nightly, this same blackness of which Poshtli speaks. It is a vision of a wasteland, a place of death and decay, of monstrous deformity and perversion. It is a ruined expanse of ash and grime, and it is called Nexal.

I fear this vision more than I have feared any other thing in my life. It is a grim destiny that may be greater than any of the humans who hope to stand against it.

And if it prevails, I fear that we of Maztica—our city, our nation, our people—I fear that we will soon be but a memory, a distant vision that will vanish forever with the lives of our children.

🟣 6 🟣
PALUL

"That light—what is its source?" Poshtli gestured to the milky glow that still emanated from Halloran's room.

"It's . . . sorcery. Something like your *pluma*." Hal pointed to the glowing aperture. "*Kirishone*," he said, and instantly darkness cloaked the rooms.

"*Kirisha!*" He repowered the spell, enjoying the look of surprise on Poshtli's face.

"Can all of your people do this . . . sorcery?"

"No. I studied this craft when I was much younger, but I know very little of real power. I can illuminate a room, shoot a bolt of magic, maybe make someone fall asleep if I try hard—that's about all. But there are those who devote a lifetime to the practice of magic—they are to be feared greatly." The picture of the elfmage Darien came vividly to mind. It was a picture he hoped he would never have to face in the flesh.

The knowledge that he held her spellbook intruded itself once more, uneasily, into Hal's mind. Often he wished that he could simply return the tome to her, but that was impossible. Undoubtedly, however, she was very much interested in regaining it.

"You come from a wondrous and frightening people, Halloran. My only hope is that you are not to be the ruin of Maztica."

Poshtli fixed him with a level gaze, and Hal squirmed, finally looking down in discomfort. His eyes fell on Poshtli's cloak, now stained with the blood of a dead Jaguar Knight, on the floor.

"Why did you take your cloak off?"

The immediate pain in Poshtli's face shocked Hal, all the more so since it was the first such emotion he had ever seen the stoic warrior express. He regretted the question as soon as he uttered it.

Poshtli took a deep breath. He knelt, wiping the blood from his weapon on the spotted cloak of one of the slain men. When he rose and looked at Hal again, his face was lined with strain. "I cannot tell you. But I have no regrets, and I am no longer an Eagle Knight."

The inference was not difficult: By aiding Hal, the knight had violated some trust of his order. He had shed his cloak and helmet before the fight deliberately. And yet it was a decision he had made resolutely.

"Thank you," said Hal, suddenly finding it difficult to speak.

Poshtli nodded, a half-smile on his face. He held up his weapon, and Halloran saw that several of the obsidian teeth were chipped. "Hard skin," the Maztican grunted, indicating the corpse at his feet.

"Just a minute." Turning to his saddlebag, neatly stowed in a corner, Hal withdrew a weapon from within a rolled-up blanket. It was a straight, slender longsword, with a double edge of razor-sharp steel. Halloran had kept it even after he had regained his lost Helmstooth, knowing that the weapon was priceless in the True World.

"Will you take this?" he asked, extending the hilt to the former Eagle Knight. "Now that you don't have your order behind you, perhaps you'll need a good weapon in front of you."

Poshtli took the weapon and hefted it, surprised by its lightness. He knew, having seen Hal use his blade in combat, that it could cut through any weapon wielded by his countrymen and render their cotton armor useless.

"Thank you," said the Maztican sincerely. "It may not replace my feathers, but it gives me an effective claw."

"Perhaps we'll need it. I've left my legion, and now you have departed your order. It looks like it's you and me against Maztica, friend."

Hal felt his comradeship with this brave man deepen. He regretted his earlier jealousy, though the memory of Erixitl in Poshtli's arms still gave him a sharp jab of pain. Still, the terrible sense of loneliness he had felt at her departure began to lessen. Was there any real purpose in his being here? Could he in fact make some kind of difference? Halloran resolved to find out.

Poshtli laughed, but there was a serious edge to the sound. "We're both lone wolves, Halloran of the Sword Coast. But perhaps not so alone as we might think."

"What do you mean?"

"At first light, I suggest we seek an audience with my uncle. We'll see what the great Naltecona has to say about an attack under his own roof."

* * * * * *

Her first night out of Nexal, Erix had barely enough time to cross the causeway to the mainland before sunset brought a temporary end to her journey. She sought shelter for the night in one of the travelers' inns that commonly dotted the landscape near Nexal.

These simple hostels offered a straw mat for sleeping and a bowl of beans or mayz, for a few cocoa beans or other barter goods. Fortunately, she had brought a small pouch of beans with her when she left the palace. The beans, her new feathered cloak, the *pluma* token from her father, and her dress were the only things she had taken with her.

She paused outside the inn and looked back at the valley, sharply etched as it was in the slanting rays of sunset. Shadows wisped like black smoke through the streets and across the lake, and she could no longer tell if they were the products of her disturbing premonitions or the actual descent of evening.

Beyond the city, she saw Mount Zatal clearly outlined against the sky. The mountain seemed ready to burst, swollen as it was from the volcanic pressure within. She imagined the folk of Nexal, busily going about their evening tasks. *Can't they see it? Don't they understand the danger?* With a deep sigh, she tried to accept the fact that they could not.

One person down in that city she thought about in particular. How could Halloran have hurt her so? He hadn't tried to stop her from leaving, hadn't offered to come along. A lump caught painfully in Erix's throat, and she roughly tossed her head, looking away. So be it, she decided, though the decision of her mind did not extend to her heart.

A file of slaves entered the yard of the inn, followed by a plump merchant. Erix saw them set down great bundles of brightly colored cloth while the merchant, with a curious look at her, passed inside. Her sense of melancholy grew as she looked at the bright materials.

The colors brought back memories of her father. How he had loved his colors! The way his fingers could work a single delicate plume into a work of art had always amazed and thrilled Erix. She wondered if he still worked at his art, or even if he still lived. Would he know her, this woman who had been a girl when last he saw her?

Sighing, impatient with the journey before her and depressed by the man and the city behind, she turned to the door and entered the low building. She drew immediate stares at the inn, for a woman traveling alone was an unusual visitor. She shrugged off the looks, and also the attentions of several young Jaguar Knights who were on the road to Nexal. After sleeping lightly, Erixitl left at first light.

The next day took her out of the valley of Nexal, into the high country that began to look very familiar. She spent that night in the village of Cordotl. From there, she could see the glorious city behind her.

But also from there Erix could look into a rich, green valley to the east. At the far side, she could barely make out the squat bulk that was the pyramid in Palul. The tiny glimpse made her heart pound, and she could sleep but little that night, leaving early again the next day. By walking fast, she hoped to reach Palul while there was still time left in the day.

Her pace accelerated even more as, shortly past noon, she reached the mayzfields below Palul itself. The steeply climbing trail was no deterrent. She even imagined she could see the tiny dot of her father's house high on the ridge above the town.

Erixitl entered the town and paused, looking around at the whitewashed, flat-roofed buildings. The pyramid still stood in the center of the plaza. Once it had seemed huge, but now it looked like a cheap imitation of the grand edifices in Nexal. The trees looked somewhat bigger, and she didn't see anybody that she recognized, but it wasn't hard to remember that this was the town where she had spent her first ten years.

Erix started through the square, toward the trail that led up the ridge to her father's house. Suddenly she stopped, appalled. The whole plaza had gone dark around her. A terrible sense of foreboding gripped her soul, weakening her knees. Erix couldn't lift the shadows by rubbing her eyes, so she kept her gaze directed downward. Frightened, she hurried through the town as quickly as she could.

Past the pyramid, she saw the low stone building that housed the priests of Zaltec. A pair of statues, depicting squatting, fierce jaguars, stood to either side of the dark doorway. For a moment, she considered stopping at the temple and inquiring about her brother, Shatil. But she discarded the idea, since the priests had little time for women, and, in any event, the news might be bad. Erix well knew that only about half of the apprentices actually advanced to the priesthood of that grisly order. The others usually made the ultimate payment for their failure.

And in truth, it was her father that she truly longed to see again. She wondered about stopping to ask someone if Lotil the featherworker was well, if he still lived in the white house on the ridge, but this knowledge, too, she preferred to gain for herself. Through the town, she nearly ran up the trail that cut steeply back and forth as it ascended toward the house.

Finally she stood before it. The whitewash had fallen away, she saw with surprise, leaving the walls cracked and in need of repair. Nor did the flower beds around the house show the life they had once exhibited. Her father had planted and tended them, for he loved to be surrounded by color.

Hesitantly she advanced to the door. There she saw the familiar figure, hunched over his featherloom. Perhaps a little more bent, more frail than she remembered, but it was him. She felt her breath catch in her throat, and for a moment she choked, speechless. Then she found her tongue.

"Father!" she cried, bursting through the door. Lotil looked up quickly in surprise. His expression crinkled into a

Douglas Niles

grimace of disbelief as he stared past her, climbing to his feet.

"Father—it's me! Erixitl!" She sprang toward him and swept him into her arms, feeling his thin body beneath her skin. Still his eyes looked past her, though he embraced her warmly and sobbed with joy. He leaned back, and she saw his wrinkled face, his thin white hair, and finally she understood.

In a gesture of monstrous cruelty, the gods had taken his sight, leaving this man who so loved his colors completely blind.

* * * * *

"Why must you see me so early? What is wrong?" inquired Naltecona, looking up at Poshtli and Halloran from a plate of half-eaten mayzcakes. Around him, on the floor of his dining chamber, were arrayed more than a hundred other dishes, for it was the Revered Counselor's habit to choose his meals only after a multiplicity of alternatives had been offered.

"And where is your helmet? And your cloak?" Naltecona suddenly demanded, studying Poshtli curiously. The warrior wore a clean white tunic, with his long black hair tied behind his head. It was the garb characteristic of a common warrior.

"That is part of our tale," explained Poshtli. "Can we walk elsewhere, away from the ears around us?"

Naltecona looked around questioningly. There were only slaves moving about the dining chamber now, though often other nobles or priests called upon him here.

"Very well. Let us go to the menagerie."

Without a further word, the ruler led them through back passages of the palace, places Hal had never been before. He had heard of the counselor's garden of caged beasts, but he hadn't yet seen it. From what he had been told, he knew it was a private spot, reserved for Naltecona and his most influential confidants.

Finally they emerged from a wide doorway into an enclosed courtyard. Open to the sky, the area contained a profusion of flowers and trees. It was only as they stepped along the graveled path among the foliage that Hal saw cleverly concealed cages.

The first of these—small and carefully built into the shrubbery—contained birds. Hal stared, distracted, at green, red, and gold parrots and macaws such as he remembered from Payit, but also elegant geese, a colorful array of ducks quacking around a small pond, peacocks, herons, and hawks.

One of the macaws squawked, a familiar sound. With a pang, Hal remembered the macaw that had led them to water in the desert, for the bird caused him to think of Erixitl.

A little farther on, they reached a cage that Hal at first thought was empty. In the shadows beneath a spreading tree, however, he saw stealthy movement. In seconds, a slick black feline came into view. The creature looked like a jaguar except for its inky pelt, and as it slinked along the fence, it growled, a sound identical to that great spotted cat's menacing snarl.

"Yes," replied Naltecona in response to Hal's quizzical look. "It is a jaguar. These black ones are very rare, and thus very precious."

"A creature of the night, the jaguar," said Poshtli, slowly and carefully. His uncle looked at him curiously, and the warrior quickly explained the attack on Hal the night before. He added the reason for his doffing of the Eagle regalia.

"This you would do for the stranger?" asked Naltecona, as if Halloran were not there. The question needed no reply. Both Hal and Poshtli noted that the ruler had shown no surprise when told of the attack. Now he looked at his nephew appraisingly.

"The loss is to the order of the Eagles. I am proud of you, my nephew. The stranger shall be safe under my roof. I shall make the decree myself. As to punishment of the transgressors, your weapons have seen to that."

Hal was about to point out that the Jaguars must have received their orders from somewhere, but he caught Poshtli's warning glance. Instead, he nodded and sensed Naltecona's relief as the counselor led them farther along the walkway.

The beast in the next cage caused Hal's pulse to race. The

Douglas Niles

largest creature in the menagerie, it sprang at the bars as the humans passed. Its lionlike face contorted into a mask of hatred as it slashed with huge paws. A pair of great, leathery wings flapped fruitlessly from the creature's shoulders. Barely visible beneath the creature's flowing mane was a ring of brilliant feathers encircling the beast's neck. It opened its mouth wide, and Hal clapped his hands over his ears.

"You know of the *hakuna*," said Naltecona, noting Hal's protective gesture. The soldier was embarassed when the creature spouted an incongruously mild squeak. "This one has been altered. Its roar has been muffled by that collar of *pluma*."

"Good idea," grunted Halloran sheepishly. "The one time I met one of those things, it knocked me flat on my back with its roar."

"Rare is the man who gets up to tell that tale," observed Poshtli as they reached the next cage.

This one was empty, but also unique in that its cage was a screen of thin saplings, not the heavier but wider-spaced poles that enclosed most of the other cages. On the wall at the back of the cage, outlined in brilliant mosaics of turquoise, jade, and obsidian, was the figure of a long snake. It was unusual, both for the pair of wings that sprouted from its body and for the feathers that appeared to cover it in lieu of scales.

"The couatl." Hal identified the creature before the others could speak.

"You are also familiar with the feathered snake?" inquired Naltecona, surprised.

"Indeed. It was a couatl that brought Erix and I together. It gave her the gift of tongues. That's how she learned to speak the language of Faerun."

He noticed Poshtli looking at him in shock, Naltecona with frank disbelief.

"You never mentioned this!" accused the warrior.

"I'm sorry!" Hal was taken aback. "Should I have?"

"The couatl is the harbinger of Qotal." Naltecona explained. "It has not been seen in these lands since the Butterfly God departed for the east, long centuries ago. You have been granted an experience that the patriarchs of Qotal would give their lives for!"

"We encountered the creature in Payit. In fact, it saved me from certain death. It talked a lot, and it didn't seem to like me very much."

Poshtli and his uncle exchanged looks of amazement. The ruler turned back to Hal and stared into his eyes with a look of penetrating scrutiny.

"I must ask you some questions. This man, Cordell . . . he is indeed a man?"

"Of course. A great man, but—as I have said before—nothing more than a man."

"Tell me, have you seen him wounded?"

"Many times," replied Halloran, wondering at the ruler's line of questioning. "During a battle, years ago, with the Northmen of Moonshae, Cordell was almost killed. One of the raiders cut him from his horse with a blow of his axe. The edge of the weapon split his breastplate and laid open his chest from here to here." Halloran gestured from his collarbone to his navel.

"And he lived?"

"Only because the Bishou—that's our priest—used every power at his command. It was the mercy of Helm that saved his life." *Or something*, Hal thought, still ambiguous about the role of the gods in all this.

"And Cordell . . . he, too, worships this god?"

"As I've said, yes. I don't understand what you're getting at."

Naltecona stepped away and then turned suddenly back, his *pluma* cloak circling around him. "Is it possible that Cordell is a god? Can he be Qotal, returning to the True World to claim his rightful throne?"

Hal's jaw dropped. "Cordell, a god? No. He's a man like you and me—a man who breathes like us, who loves women and food and drink. He's a leader of men, but he's unquestionably a man himself!"

Halloran didn't see Naltecona's face, for the ruler once again turned away. Perhaps the soldier wouldn't have understood the sly smile playing across those regal features, but he would have understood the words the counselor mouthed, which is why Naltecona said them silently.

A man who lives, and thus a man who can be killed.

* * * * *

Hoxitl trembled as he entered the Highcave. Never had he so feared the result of a visit to the Ancient Ones as he did now. Two young priests, promising apprentices, accompanied him. He bade them to follow him into the cave instead of taking the usual apprentices' role of waiting outside. The high priest couldn't bear to face the drow alone.

A flash of smoke puffed from the caldron of the Darkfyre, and then he saw them: a dozen black-robed figures standing immobile around the huge, seething mass of crimson heat.

"Why do you come to us?" hissed one, the Ancestor.

"The girl—the girl has disappeared again. She departed Nexal before we struck. We are searching for her, but we do not know where she is—yet. But soon—"

"Silence!" The Ancestor raised a black-cloaked hand. For a moment, Hoxitl stood frozen in terror, wondering if the gesture meant his death.

Instead, the Ancient One flicked his hand toward one apprentice. The young man gasped, and then moaned in deep, wracking pain. He staggered and stumbled, then stiffened spasmodically and toppled forward into the caldron. The other young priest turned to flee, but the Ancestor moved his hand slightly and this one, too, gasped and choked, then fell into the crimson coals.

The apprentices writhed and twitched, slowly sinking into the horridly pulsing fuel of the Darkfyre. Soundless screams twisted their mouths. One turned desperately to face Hoxitl, and the high priest flinched at the look of hopeless agony on the man's face. Then he disappeared into the gory mess. In seconds, his companion followed.

Nearly gagging, Hoxitl stumbled back on weak knees. For moments, he feared to raise his eyes, but the Ancestor did nothing to him. Finally he took a breath, beginning to believe that he would be allowed to live.

Weak with relief, Hoxitl mentally congratulated himself on bringing the two others. Had he been alone, he felt certain that the Ancestor would have punished him directly.

"Do not fail me again—or *I* shall come to *you*!" The Ancestor's white eyes burned forth from the darkened depths of his hood.

Hoxitl bowed silently and then scuttled away.

* * * * *

"That cloak," said Lotil. "Where did you get it?"

Erix looked at her father in surprise. Her cape from the featherworker in Nexal lay beside the door. She knew that Lotil hadn't touched it, and yet his blind eyes were now directed toward the garment with the first hint of focus she had detected.

"Can you see it?" she asked in wonder. She felt a confusing mixture of emotions, now that the initial shock of their meeting was beginning to fade. An overriding sense of happiness warmed her, to know that her father was alive and that they were together again. Still, he looked so very much older—as if he had aged far more than the ten years she had been gone—and this truth she found heartbreaking.

Lotil shook his head sadly. "I can sense the *pluma*, that's all. Tell me, child, where did it come from?"

She told him of the craftsman in the market, of his insistence that she take it, and her inability to find him later. She was surprised when Lotil smiled knowingly. "Do you know someone like this?" Her father, a renowned worker of *pluma* for many decades, was familiar with most of the masters of his craft.

"No," he said with a chuckle. "But you do. The cloak goes very well with your amulet, don't you agree?"

Erix nodded, laughing and crying at the same time. "Your eyes," she said hesitantly. "When—"

Lotil held up his hand, brushing off the sympathy in her voice. "They left me as I aged—but age cannot take my fingers! See?"

Erixitl looked at his featherloom and saw an elaborate mantle of brilliant pluma taking shape there. Lotil had placed the colors carefully, so that the cape depicted a golden hawk with its wings spread wide. "It's beautiful," she whispered reverently.

"My fingers can see to weave the *pluma*," he said. "And

Douglas Niles

now the daughter I thought was dead has returned to me. What more could an old man ask for?"

Erix told her father of her life since, ten years ago, the Kultakan Jaguar Knight had snatched her from the ridge above this very house, of her slavery in Kultaka, and then her sale to the Payit priest of Qotal, who had taken her to his distant jungle land. And how she had met the stranger, Halloran, and been visited by the feathered serpent, the couatl.

Her father listened silently, only remarking about the couatl. "Nobody has seen one for many centuries," he had announced, impressed.

"What of Shatil?" Erix asked hesitantly after concluding her tale. "Is my brother well?"

Lotil sighed. "As a priest, he does very well. He is already the first assistant to the high priest here in Palul."

Erix understood her father's mixed feelings. While she and her brother had been raised, as all Maztican children, to understand the necessity of the blood rituals demanded by Zaltec and many of the other gods, she knew that her father had never approved of those rites. Although he had never told her bluntly, she had always suspected that he despised the bloodthirsty practices of the priests.

Yet now, as first assistant, her own brother was a main practitioner of those rites. Palul, a much smaller community than Nexal, offered but an occasional sacrifice at dawn or at sunset. Shatil undoubtedly performed a significant number of those rituals himself.

"He is an important man in the town," continued her father, "but he listens only to those who say what he wants to hear, who echo the chants of Zaltec and his ilk. He has even told me he intends to journey to Nexal to take the vow of the Viperhand."

Erix took her father's shoulders in her own hands, surprised at his frailty. The thought of the Viperhand emblazoned on Shatil's chest caused her sharp panic. She knew little about the cult, except that its members espoused hatred and warfare against the approaching strangers from the Realms.

"Father, who is this?" The voice from the door spun them both around.

"Shatil?" asked Erix hesitantly.

"Erixtl? Can it be you?" Her brother stepped into the house, then swept her in his arms. "Zaltec has been kind to bring you home!"

She clung to him, for a second remembering the youth she had admired so much in her childhood. Then they separated, and when Erix looked at her brother, her memories vanished. Shatil's head bristled with the customary spikes of hair worn by the priests of Zaltec. Scars covered his arms and his ears and cheeks, where he had marked himself in ritual penance.

"You have become a woman," Shatil said approvingly.

"And you are . . . a priest," she replied.

She looked from the young man to the old, wondering if the sun had suddenly set. Then, with a shudder, she knew that she saw that darkening premonition again, settling across the men and the room.

All through the house, everything was shadows.

* * * * *

"Captain Daggrande." Cordell looked up from the table, which was covered with maps and rosters on parchment sheets.

"General?" The dwarf stood before his commander, carrying a padded cotton tunic such as the Maztican warriors wore as armor.

"Have you tested the stuff?" The captain-general indicated the armor.

"Yessir. It seems to stop the arrows and darts pretty well. It also takes the sting from a chop with one of those swords—*macas*, they call 'em. With a buckler, a fellow could protect himself pretty well."

"And comfort? Encumbrance?"

"Sir, in this heat, these cotton things put a steel breastplate to shame. The men who wore 'em moved faster and farther than those who wore steel." The dwarf reported on a series of tests he had conducted outside Kultaka while the legion refitted for its next great march.

"Excellent!" Cordell stood up and came around the table to clap Daggrande on the back. "Have the men outfitted in them. Those that want can keep their steel, but tell them the pace of our marching will pick up."

"Very well, sir!" Daggrande turned to go as another man entered Cordell's headquarters, which was located in Takamal's palace in the city of Kultaka.

"What is it?" asked the commander, seeing that the newcomer was Kardann.

"I—I wanted to tell you that perhaps I might have been wrong," offered the assessor tentatively. "There must be ten thousand Kultakans out there ready to march with us!"

"In fact, there are twice that many."

"Perhaps—perhaps this is not madness, after all. If the gold of Nexal proves as plentiful as we have been told. . . ." The assessor trailed off, his mind already working the imaginary figures.

"I appreciate the vote of confidence," said Cordell wryly. "Now, if you please, I have work to do."

The next to enter was Darien. She had taken to studying her new spellbook and performing her meditations at night since they had reached Kultaka, so Cordell had seen little of her lately. The sight of her brightened his heart, but she didn't respond to his welcoming smile.

"Have you spoken to Alvarro?" the elfwoman asked.

Cordell sighed. "Yes. I warned him that a repeat of his flight would cost him his command. He blustered and made excuses. The damnable thing is, I think he knows I don't have anyone who could replace him!"

"It seems he only enjoys the killing when the victim does not fight back," Darien said scornfully. "Perhaps you should make an example of him."

"The Bishou argued against that . . . hard. He thinks too highly of our captain of horse. By Helm, what I wouldn't give for another Halloran!"

"A loyal one, you mean," said the elf wryly.

Cordell shrugged. "I never questioned his loyalty until the Bishou gave him no alternative but flight."

Darien's eyes flashed. No matter Cordell's opinion, she hated the fugitive rider with a vengeance. He would die for the theft of her spellbook! For now, she, too, shrugged. "That chief, Tokol, is here," she noted.

"Send him in."

The son of Takamal, who had assumed command of the Kultakan forces, entered what had once been his father's palace. "Welcome, my ally!" boomed Cordell, ushering the warrior forward even as Darien translated.

"We are ready to march with you." Tokol bowed deeply.

"Splendid. We have but to decide on our route. We shall leave in the morning." Cordell gestured to the maps. "Your men tell me that there are two routes to Nexal. One, the longer one, winds across flat country, I'm told. Do you know of these routes?"

"Yes, Captain-General Cordell. But that route is overly fatiguing, with little water. It is unnecessarily long. Instead, I recommend that we take the high trail."

"This one, here?" On the map, Cordell gestured to a trail that seemed to climb into the mountains west of Kultaka and wind tortuously through high country before emerging in a small valley east of Nexal.

"Yes. We will find water on that road and can cross it in a week of marching. Then, when we come down to this town, we can gather our strength for the approach to Nexal."

"This town?" Cordell pointed. "What will we find there? What is it like?"

"It is a little place of no consequence," explained the chief. "It is called Palul."

* * * * *

From the chronicles of Coton:

Below the rising storm clouds, the wind begins to howl.

Naltecona comes to me in the morning, his face haggard and his eyes wide. An unaccustomed tremor creeps into his voice as he speaks.

It seems that he has been given a dream. He speaks of shadows and despair, of the ruin of the True World. Almost as an afterthought, he sees his own death.

But he has decided to strike first. The great Naltecona will administer a blow to crush the invaders before they can reach Nexal. No longer does he fear the man, Cordell, as a god.

Douglas Niles

He has the twin examples of Kultaka and Payit before him now, and he will not repeat their mistakes. He will plan carefully, inventing a shrewd strategem to lure the strangers into an inescapable trap.

I cannot speak, or I would warn him that a trap may sometimes ensnare the trapper.

⚜ 7 ⚜
TREACHERY AND DEFIANCE

"What is the meaning of this?" demanded Chical, gesturing to the cloak, boots, and helmet that Poshtli laid on the floor before him.

"I am here to inform you of my withdrawal from the Order of Eagle Knighthood," explained the warrior stiffly. He and his venerable mentor stood alone in the darkened sweat lodge. Though it was a hot and sunny day, the heavy log building remained cool and lightless.

Chical stood still, staring at Poshtli for several minutes. The younger man met the gaze with a challenging glare of his own.

"I know that you cannot renounce your order lightly," Chical said eventually. "And this makes me fear that the stranger has placed some sorcery over you."

"No. It is a question of honor. I brought him here, in safety and with good intent. I can no more turn my back on that than you could renounce your responsibilities as leader of the order."

"Are you aware that his companions, his army, are even now marching on Nexal? They have conquered Kultaka and enlisted the defeated warriors of our ancient enemy in their cause against us."

Poshtli's look of surprise showed that he had been unaware of this fact. Still, his reply came quickly. "That is not Halloran's army any more than the Eagle Knights are mine. If the strangers attack Nexal, I will fight in the defense of my homeland—as a common warrior, if I must."

"Your departure means more than simply leaving the order, you understand," said Chical sadly, gesturing toward the garments at his feet. "We are not mere strangers now."

"I understand," agreed Poshtli. "Now we are enemies."

* * * * *

"Summon Hoxitl, Kalnak, and Chical," ordered Naltecona. Slaves hastened to obey. "The rest of you, leave!" A dozen raggedly dressed courtiers scurried from the room, relieved at the opportunity to reclothe themselves in their accustomed finery.

The high priest of Zaltec was the first to arrive, though Hoxitl was closely followed by Chical, captain of the Eagle Knights. Shortly thereafter Kalnak, captain of Nexal's Jaguar Knights, arrived.

The two knights had placed tattered shawls across their resplendent armor. Hoxitl, already dirty, blood-caked, and emaciated, didn't need to do so, since his appearance created no risk of diverting attention from Naltecona's splendor.

"Have you reached a decision about the strangers?" asked Kalnak hopefully. He had been one of the most adamant in advocating an attack against the legion before it reached Nexal.

"Indeed," said the ruler. "The knowledge has come to me—in a dream—that their leader is indeed a man and not a god. He is not Qotal returned to the True World to claim his throne. He is an invader who must be stopped!"

Kalnak's face split into a wide grin, framed grotesquely by the widespread jaws of his jaguar-skull helm. Hoxitl, too, smiled in anticipation of the many captives such a campaign would gain for Zaltec. Only Chical showed less than delight.

"Have you decided where and when this attack will take place?" inquired the Eagle Knight.

"Yes. My spies have reported to me the route of their march. I have selected the perfect place and formed a plan."

"Where?" inquired Kalnak. "Can we strike soon?"

"We place the plan in motion today. The march of the strangers takes them toward Palul, and this is where we will meet them." Palul, although a village under the control and governorship of Nexal, was still safely removed from the great city itself. It seemed to them all a good choice.

"Splendid!" agreed the Jaguar Knight. "We can destroy them in the high pass before they reach the town!"

"No," Naltecona disagreed. "That is not the plan. I want each of you to gather your most trusted knights. Take many thousandmen of warriors, too. But you are not to array for battle before Palul."

The others looked at him in confusion, and Naltecona enjoyed their curiosity. He paused for a few moments to let his listeners wonder.

"Instead, we will invite the strangers into Palul. There a great feast will be held, with much dancing and drinking of *octal*. Their Kultakan allies, we will insist, must remain outside the town."

"But we, with our men, will be in the town?" guessed Kalnak.

"Yes! And you, my chief of Jaguars, will give the signal. When the feast progresses, and the invaders have had much to drink, you will fall upon them from all sides. In one short battle, the strangers will be annihilated!"

"An excellent plan!" cried Hoxitl. "We shall take many captives—perhaps the majority of the invading army—in such an entrapment."

"And you, Chical? You have said nothing." Naltecona fixed his chief of Eagles with a scrutinizing eye.

"There is a thing that troubles me, Most Revered One. Always the warriors of Nexal have met their foes on the field, striving through courage and strength to prevail. It does not seem right, this masquerade of celebration and then slaughter."

"Would you have us face the magic and monsters of this legion in battle, so that we may all be killed?" challenged Kalnak before Naltecona could reply. The ruler smiled, pleased that the argument was between his underlings and did not involve himself.

"Until we know that they cannot be defeated this way, I would. I am not afraid," Chical replied.

Kalnak bristled, and only the upraised palm of the counselor prevented him from drawing his *maca*. "Nor am I afraid, but neither am I a fool," he sneered.

"These strangers have already bewitched the men of Kultaka," observed Hoxitl. "*After* they killed Takamal, something our bravest warriors have been unable to do, though not for want of trying, for many years!"

Chical bowed to Naltecona, ignoring the other two. "As

my lord wishes, so it shall be. When will the strangers arrive in Palul?"

"They departed from Kultaka two days ago, and they march quickly. They could reach Palul in four more days—six at the most—so we must move quickly and quietly. We will send ambassadors to greet them, to offer presents, and to prepare the banquet. In the meantime, I want you to gather the force I have described.

"You are to march for Palul no later than tomorrow morning."

* * * * *

"Did you find out what all the excitement was about?" asked Halloran, when Poshtli returned to the house just after noon.

Two days earlier, they had both seen long columns of warriors filing out of the sacred plaza. They deduced that the march had something to do with Cordell, but Poshtli had been frustrated in his constant efforts to learn more. Now he returned to the house on the third day, and Hal feared that he wouldn't learn anything until it was too late.

The former knight had accepted Hal's offer to share his dwelling, since the lodge of the Eagles was no longer his home. Neither of them had wanted to remain in the palace, despite Naltecona's assurances of their safety.

The Revered Counselor, however, had been as good as his word in providing a residence for Hal. Indeed, the house was a dwelling that might have sheltered a high nobleman or esteemed sage in Faerun, so sumptuous were its appointments.

The structure stood near the sacred plaza, at the intersection of two streets and a canal. Adobe bricks, whitewashed to a gleaming brightness on the outside, formed the wall around the rooms and large courtyard of the dwelling. The house was two stories high, with three large rooms on the first floor surrounding the open courtyard.

Halloran hadn't yet been comfortable in the house, however. His mind whirled with anxiety for Erixitl. He hoped that she had reached Palul safely, that she would remain safe from the likes of the Jaguar Knights who had struck in the palace. He couldn't understand why Poshtli didn't show more concern, why he didn't go to her.

Yet Hal couldn't ask Poshtli such a question, with its implications of dishonor. He had thought about going to her himself, but then he remembered the eagerness with which she had left him. He felt certain he wouldn't be welcomed by her now.

At times, in the depths of his despair, he even considered returning to the legion. Perhaps he could return Darien's spellbook to the wizard, and everything . . . He quickly dismissed such thoughts, remembering the hatred of wizard and cleric both. No, the legion meant death for him.

So he tried to study the spellbook. He exercised Storm, polished his weapons and armor, or stalked through the rooms of his house, wasting time while he waited for Poshtli to find out what was happening.

These rooms included a small anteroom, with brilliant frescoes on the walls depicting birds, snakes, and jaguars in a tropical setting. The anteroom led into the flower- and tree-filled courtyard, where a turn to the left took one into a large chamber with a fireplace and many thick straw mats on the floor. Halloran finally found himself growing used to the Maztican custom of sitting on these mats, though he had resolved to make himself a chair sometime soon.

The other room on the first floor was a cooking room, with a firepit and several bins for storing mayz, beans, and fruit. The upstairs rooms were four sleeping chambers, a pair of small rooms for slaves, and a wide balcony overlooking the canal. The landward sides of the house and courtyard were surrounded by its outer walls. The courtyard met the canal with no barrier, however, and Hal had soon purchased a canoe that he kept tied up there.

Storm, meanwhile, lived in the courtyard. Hal rode the mare frequently, since the Mazticans thrilled to the sight of the great horse. He often rode him about the sacred plaza or the city streets.

Naltecona had assigned several slaves to Halloran, to perform his cooking and whatever other tasks he desired. His slaves included an old man, Gankak; the fellow's hardworking wife, Jaria; and a pair of young women, Horo and Chantil.

Since Hal was uncomfortable with the notion of owning another human being, he resolved to treat the slaves as servants. He tried to grant them privileges, such as a day of no work, and a few cocoa beans to spend in the market. To his surprise, he found that the slaves purchased items for *him* with the beans. As to the day off, they only stopped working when he ordered them to do so.

Then, after a week in the house, they had seen the massive columns of warriors filing from the sacred plaza, leaving the city by its southeast causeway.

"What's going on? It must be Cordell they're marching against! Did you learn anything?" Halloran bombarded Poshtli with questions.

"That's why I'm late. I finally had some luck," explained the Maztican. "All the captains of the Eagles were gone, and the apprentices didn't know much. They got called to arms in a hurry, by the order of Naltecona. It's very secret, and at first I thought I wouldn't learn anything."

"But?"

"One of the young fellows—he's always been a favorite of mine—talked to me after the exercise. I came here as soon as I could after he told me."

"Told you what? Tell me, man!" Halloran grew cold with apprehension, his fear centering around Erixitl. "Where are they going?"

"They go to ambush the legion," said Poshtli, taking a deep breath. "At Palul!"

The sound of his words still echoed through the house as Hal's face whitened in alarm. Erix! She was in Palul! "I'm going to get her," he blurted. In seconds, he gathered his arms, armor, and saddle. As he started toward the courtyard, he saw the warrior standing at the door, holding his own steel sword.

"I'm going with you," said Poshtli.

* * * * *

"Excellent!" hissed Zilti, high priest in the temple of Zaltec of Palul.

"The slaughter will be complete," agreed his first assistant, Shatil. They met with Hoxitl in the darkened temple in

Palul. The evening rites were done, and the patriarch of their order had paid them the high honor of a personal visit. There he had outlined Naltecona's ambush.

"You, the priests, must be ready to move in quickly," continued Hoxitl. "As soon as we have any of the strangers in captivity, we will open their bodies and take their hearts. Zaltec will be fed immediately, that he may smile upon our endeavors. We will continue to feed him until the fight is long over and all of the strangers have given their lives to him."

"The warriors will conceal themselves in the buildings around the plaza?" asked Zilti.

"Yes. The festival will be for the people of Palul, with much food and drink. The hunters have slain many deer, for it is said that the strangers are over-fond of meat."

"How do we know they will attend the festival?" inquired Zilti, pressing for further details. "Perhaps they are not like us. They may not like celebrations."

Hoxitl shrugged. He had bigger problems to worry about than the objections of the priest of this minor town—problems such as the location of the woman, Erixitl. Inwardly he blanched as he recalled the fates of his two apprentices.

"We will do the best we can," he said. "We know little—nothing, really—about these strangers. I have had the chance to observe one of them in Nexal, and he seems human in most respects."

"I know someone who knows these strangers. She even speaks their tongue!" offered Shatil.

"Who?" demanded the two priests together.

"My sister! She met the white men when they first landed in Payit, even learning to speak their lanuage!" Shatil said eagerly.

"Splendid!" said Hoxitl. "Send her to the village before the invaders get here. She will be very useful for translating."

"I shall summon her immediately," said Shatil, flattered by Hoxitl's attention. "I know Erixitl will be proud at the honor we do her."

"What is it?" asked Zilti in alarm. He had watched, astonished, as the patriarch's face flushed. Hoxitl shook his head as if he had been struck dumb and needed to clear his mind.

"It's . . . nothing," said Hoxitl, struggling to contain his glee. "Your plan is a splendid one," he told Shatil. "Very good indeed."

* * * * *

The long column snaked over the green ridgetops and back down into the lush valleys. Water and food, as Tokol had promised, were plentiful. Also, garbed in the lighter cotton armor, the legion moved at a brisk pace. A bright sun shone from a clear sky overhead, as it had throughout their march from Kultaka.

"By tomorrow we shall reach Palul," explained Tokol, standing beside Cordell atop the crest of a ridge.

"Darien is observing the village even now," said the commander, gesturing toward the ridges before them. The Kultakan had told him that Palul was still two or three valleys away. With a shudder, the young chief looked to the west, trying to understand the power of this woman who could fly, disappear from sight, or slay a great man like his father simply by raising her hand.

Behind them, the column extended to the bottom of the valley they had just passed through. The five hundred men of the Golden Legion marched in the fore, followed by twenty thousand Kultakan warriors and the five thousand warriors of the Payit. Cordell reflected, with quiet pride, that never had he had so many men under his command.

And never had such a tempting objective loomed before him. The images of gold and silver danced through his mind, enlivened by the many tales he had heard of the wealth of storied Nexal. The tales of the pyramids, of the size of the city, and the wealth that had been collected there after many years of taxing their subjects made his pulse pound.

Tokol gasped and stepped suddenly backward. Cordell looked up to see Darien. The elven mage had appeared on the ridge beside them. She was completely muffled in her robe today, for the sun was very bright.

"I have seen the village," she explained. "Actually, it is more like a city by the standards of Faerun. It seems to have nearly a thousand houses in the community itself, and many more spread across the surrounding hills and valley."

"Any activity there?"

"Yes. In fact, they seem to be preparing a feast. The women were placing flowers and feathered blankets all around their square. My guess is that they are preparing to welcome us."

The news was eminently pleasing to Cordell. "Perhaps we won't have to fight a battle at every stop after all," he observed. "If they're planning a feast, let's not keep them waiting."

* * * * *

"No! I don't want to talk to the invaders!" Erix tried to keep her voice down, but she couldn't hide her tension.

"You have to. It's important, more important than you can imagine," argued Shatil. The two of them stood in the small yard before their father's house. Lotil was inside, working at his loom.

"You are the only one here who can understand them!" persisted her brother.

Erix avoided looking over her shoulder at the town. In her vision, it had grown darker every day, every time she looked at it. Now all she saw of the great plaza in Palul was a black void, shadows impenetrable but terribly ominous.

But when her eyes fell on the looming ridgetop behind her father's house, she saw another view she found unsettling. Not because of any dark shadows she saw there, but because of the memories of her last climb up to the top, when she had been snatched into slavery by a Jaguar Knight. In the days she had been home, she had not been able to bring herself to climb that ridge.

Shatil turned away in frustration. His sister's resistance to his suggestion surprised him. In view of her reluctance, he had decided not to tell her of the true purpose behind the feast. Not knowing how she would react, if he told her the truth, he ran the risk of causing her complete refusal.

"You have told me of the battle at Ulatos," said Shatil, trying a different approach. "Perhaps if you are there to speak with the strangers, to reason with them, such an outcome can be avoided."

"How could I do this?" she demanded. But that argument of her brother's had struck home. Perhaps there was nothing she could do—a glance at the plaza showed the darkness as thick as ever—but she was indeed the only one in Palul who had any chance of talking with the strangers.

"Come to the village in the morning," Shatil urged. "Our scouts have told us that the hairy men camp just to the east tonight. "They will reach Palul by midday—for the feast! Please, you must be there, too!"

Erixitl remembered her vision the night they found the pool in the desert. The image of Nexal in ruins came back to her now as freshly as when she awakened from the nightmare. But she had seen no indication of disaster in Palul. Perhaps her presence could in fact prove beneficial.

"All right. I will come and see if they will talk."

"You are doing the right thing," said Shatil, embracing her. "I must go back down to the temple for the evening rites. I will stay there tonight and see you when you arrive."

Shatil hastened down the mountain, and Erix watched him go. It seemed that her brother's black robe became a blur with the darkness below, and soon he disappeared from sight. Finally she recognized the shadows of sunset growing around her and turned toward the house, grateful that darkness would bring a respite from her own personal shades.

"What is wrong, my daughter?" inquired Lotil as she entered.

"I'm fearful of what will happen, tomorrow and beyond," Erix admitted. She told him of Shatil's request for the morrow.

"But, Father, you must promise me something," she continued. "Tomorrow, do not come to the village. Stay here and wait for me to come to you in the evening."

"What's this?" objected the old man, sitting taller at his featherloom. "My daughter gives me orders?"

"Please, Father. It's very important!"

"You can see things, my daughter, can you not?" asked her father suddenly. "Tell me, Erixitl, can you see tomorrow?" He fixed his sightless eyes upon her face, and Erix felt as if he could see to the depths of her soul. She squirmed uncomfortably.

Erixitl had told her father nothing of the dark images she saw. She knew that the tale of darkness, with its suggestion of impending doom, would weigh heavily upon him as well as her. Better, she thought, to bear her load in silence.

But somehow he knew, and this knowledge was a great and sudden relief to Erix. All at once, in a torrent of words, she told him of the shadows she had seen across Nexal, and of the greater darkness that lay on the town of Palul.

"This is the working of the gods, child," Lotil said finally, holding her hands as she sat beside him. "And in this you see the balance of all things. My sight has been taken from me, but your eyes have been opened in a way that few ever know. You have been granted a window to look into the future. And through that window, perhaps you will see enough to work important changes. Your brother is right, Erixitl. It is important that you go to the town tomorrow.

"Just as my loss is not so bad a thing as you might think—I have heard bird songs I never imagined before, and it is as though my nostrils have opened to a whole world of new scents—so is your gift, in some ways, a curse.

"But you can speak to these strangers. Perhaps more important, you can understand them. This gift from the couatl can be a burden, but there is certain to be a reason it was given to you. You must not be afraid to face your destiny.

"Bear it well, Erixitl, daughter of Lotil. Bear it well and make me proud.

"And, yes," the old man concluded. "I shall do as you request and stay home tomorrow."

* * * * *

The Golden Legion marched into Palul in perfect order, the beat of drums setting the cadence for the marching men-at-arms. A great throng of people had gathered at the outskirts of town. The Mazticans stood at both sides of the column and watched and wondered as the strange procession passed.

Erix stood in the square, with Shatil, Zilti, and some eminent Eagle and Jaguar Knights who had arrived from Nexal

Douglas Niles

to greet the strangers. She wore the bright feathered cloak from the market, and its brilliant colors complemented her dusky skin and long, black hair. The legionnaires who marched past stared, captivated by her beauty. Standing with the village luminaries, Erix didn't realize that they stared at her.

Together they greeted the legionnaires as more and more of the men entered the plaza. The square was all in natural light, and Erix felt tremendous relief that, for now at least, the shadows were absent.

The riders, all forty of them, followed the first company of footmen. They wheeled and bucked their horses, frightening, amazing, and thrilling the Mazticans with the show. The greyhounds growled and snapped, sending the watchers reeling back.

The leader of the horsemen pranced up to the group gathered around Erix, whereupon the mount did a tight, circling whirl. The black streamers on the man's helmet floated into a ring around him as a murmur of approval arose from the watching villagers.

Suddenly those streamers brought a jolt of recognition to Erix. She studied the rider and knew with a certainty that this was the same man.

Her mind flashed to the battlefield at Ulatos, with dead and dying Mazticans everywhere. The legion's riders thundered at will about the field, trampling, stabbing, slashing their way through the enemy wherever the Payit tried to stand. This one, with the black streamers, saw her and raced forward. She had stood still, expecting to die, and then Halloran had appeared to save her life.

The rider's eyes met Erix's once, and she quickly looked down. She felt his gaze linger on her a moment longer, but then the red-bearded captain moved away. More and more legionnaires marched into the plaza behind him.

Soon came the imposing presence of Cordell himself. They had no difficulty identifying the man atop his prancing black charger. He held his piercing black eyes high, looking over the heads of the crowd. His steel breastplate gleamed, but it was his supremely confident, even arrogant posture that clearly marked him as the commander.

Behind Cordell came two more of whom Erixitl had heard much: the elven mage Darien, completely masked by her dark robe, and the tall, scowling Bishou Domincus.

Then row upon row of footmen marched forward, until nearly all of the strangers had entered the square. The file of their Kultakan and Payit allies approached the outskirts of the town.

Kalnak and Chical advanced and stood nearby, bowing deeply, as Cordell dismounted. They clapped their hands, and slaves hurried forward, placing bundles of presents on the ground and unwrapping them before the delighted captain-general.

They unwrapped large packages of brilliant feathers, capes of *pluma*, beautiful shells, and tokens of jade and coral. All was greeted with polite interest. Then finally a cloak was removed from atop a pair of large circular bowls, revealing in one a pile of fine gold dust. The other contained an equal pile of silver.

These, Erixitl saw without surprise, caused Cordell's eyes to flash. The captain-general involuntarily licked his lips, looking back and forth from the gold to the silver.

"These gifts are a token of love and friendship from Naltecona, Revered Counselor of Nexal," said Erix, in the common tongue of the strangers.

Instantly the legionnaires within earshot fell silent. She saw Cordell staring at her, his piercing black eyes narrowed suspiciously. "Where did you learn our speech?" he asked.

"It—it was a gift, bestowed upon me by Chitikas Couatl," she explained. "You would call it magic."

Cordell looked to Darien, invisible within her deeply cowled hood. The hood nodded, barely perceptibly. "Splendid!" boomed Cordell. "Please continue!"

"We are preparing a feast in your honor. We would be joyful if you would join our celebration."

"Of course we will!" Cordell threw back his head and laughed, in fine spirits. Erix wished she could stop there, but her instructions from Kalnak had been clear.

"We must please ask that your allies from Kultaka camp outside of the village. You see, they are the hereditary enemies of our people. There would certainly be trouble if they were allowed into the town."

Once again Cordell's eyes narrowed suspiciously, and he looked at the warriors arrayed behind Erix. Nearly a thousand men were visible around the village, but they were not carrying weapons, nor did they seem to be deployed for an attack. Neither he, nor Erix, knew of the thousands more concealed inside the houses or behind garden walls. Also unsuspected, another ten thousand men lurked in the brushy cover around the village.

Apparently the captain-general's suspicions remained slumbering, for after a moment's thought, he nodded. "That seems to make sense. All right, consider it ordered! Bishou Domincus, tell Tokol he'll have to keep his men outside—on my orders."

"Yes, General," said the dour cleric, bowing and departing with a distasteful look at Erixitl and the warriors. As he left, Erix saw Cordell lean toward Darien and whisper something. The elven wizard nodded and turned away. She melted into the crowd of legionnaires and Mazticans as Cordell turned back to Erix.

The red-bearded captain, now on foot, clumped up to Cordell, his heavy horseman's boots scuffing across the pavement. Erixitl remembered that Halloran had told her his name was Alvarro. He stared at Erix again, and she squirmed under the pressure of his gaze. Surely he couldn't remember her. His mouth opened in a wide grin as he turned away, but she saw no sign in his eyes that he recognized her from the Payit battlefield.

"Now, what's this about a feast?" he asked.

* * * * *

Darien stepped carefully among the throng that had gathered in the plaza. The legionnaires, from long experience, moved quickly out of her path. Perhaps because of the troops' example, or else because her slight, muffled figure seemed mysterious and thus frightening, the villagers also moved aside to give her a wide berth.

Soon she found the type of place she sought—a shady path between two buildings, where several towering trees served to block out the sun. Also important, several warriors relaxed here, enjoying the respite from the hot sun in the plaza. With relief, she threw back her hood. Even in the shade, the brightness was uncomfortable, but at last she could bare her head. And she must be unmasked in order to perform her assigned task.

Several Maztican warriors stood back as the elf walked among them. She smiled, passing her milky eyes over the men. When Darien smiled, she was a very beautiful woman indeed, and her beauty was not lost on these warriors.

"Come," she said to one, speaking the language of Nexal, which she had learned earlier through the casting of a simple spell.

The fellow, a tall, lanky spearman with a shirt of padded cotton and a headdress of green feathers, stepped quickly forward.

Darien led him down the pathway until they were out of earshot of his companions. Though these had started to follow Darien and the spearmen, another look from the mage—this one was not a smile—had quickly backed them off.

Darien reached her long white fingers to her ear and started playing with a strand of white hair. Her eyes stared into the warrior's, and then she passed a hand before her face.

"*Ghirrina*" she said, whispering the charm spell softly. Instantly the warrior's face relaxed into an expression of complete trust, and Darien knew the spell had been successful. The warrior now regarded her as a faithful friend and confidant.

She began to ask him questions, and he began to answer.

* * * * *

From the chronicles of Coton:

Seeking a worthy lord among a seething nest of godhood. Zaltec's presence, always here, always hungry, is growing into a force to wrack the True World. The cult of the Viperhand, whereby young warriors—even some women and untrained youths—vow their hearts and souls and bodies to the god of war, has grown like a tumor in Nexal.

The god of the strangers, Helm, is also a presence I can feel. Eternally vigilant and watchful, he stakes his claim to Maztica boldly, a clear challenge to Zaltec.

Now, too, I have sensed a new and spidery essence, a goddess of darkness and evil such to make even Zaltec appear playful and benign. Her name is Lolth. This being is tied to the Ancient Ones, I know. She watches from a great distance, but her interest grows intense.

But she is also tied somehow to the strangers. This is a connection I cannot identify, but I sense that it is very real. And this frightens me deeply.

A connection between the True World and the land of these strangers that goes beyond the bounds of the human cultures is dangerous enough. A connection that is personified in the blackness of this spider queen has the potential for menace and disaster beyond belief.

⚜ 8 ⚜
A FEAST FOR VULTURES

Halloran and Poshtli clung to the horse and gave the powerful mare her head. Rejoicing in the countryside after weeks in the city, Storm galloped with the exaltation of a wild beast escaping to freedom from a cage.

The two men bore their steel swords. Halloran wore his breastplate, Poshtli the padded cotton armor of the Maztican warrior. Hal's other possessions—the potions, the spellbook, the leather snakeskin bond—these he had buried in the garden of his house back in Nexal.

They rode in grim silence, out of the valley of Nexal, past Cordotl, and along the mountain road. Their faces—one pale and bearded, framed in brown hair; the other brown, smooth, noble-featured beneath hair of black—reflected their inner turmoil.

Both of them were sick with fear for Erixitl.

Palul lay a mere two days' march by foot from Nexal, so they knew that the warriors of Naltecona's ambush had already arrived at their destination. The question was whether or not the two of them could get there before Cordell.

Halloran spent every moment of silence cursing himself, an unrelenting stream of rebuke that slashed mercilessly from all sides. How could he have let her go? Wallowing in his self-pity, he had committed a criminal act of neglect against the woman he loved.

And by Helm, how he loved her! The feeling burned like never before, brought home by his acute fear.

"I asked her if she would become my wife," said Poshtli after Storm slowed to a brisk walk. Hal jerked upright. He felt suddenly embarrassed about his unnoticed presence at that meeting.

"You are a very lucky man."

"She refused me," the warrior said frankly. He chuckled, a forced good humor. "An honor any family in Nexal would hail, but she said no."

Stunned, Hal didn't dare speak. His embarrassment turned to shame over the blind assumption he had made. Slowly he realized that his stupidity had driven Erix from him in Nexal, sending her, all unwittingly, to the center of a vast and growing storm.

Angrily he kicked Storm's flanks, and the mare broke into a fast trot. Despite the load of two men, she held the pace for hour after hour.

"It will be evening before we reach the village," said Poshtli, observing their progress.

"We'll get there in time—before Cordell." Halloran spoke with a forced confidence he didn't feel. In truth, he did not know when the legion would arrive in Palul, or how much delay would follow before the ambush.

Neither of them wanted to think about the other possibility, the thought that battle could be raging in Palul even now. But they couldn't avoid thinking about it. The question kept coming back, rearing up and taunting them in their imaginations.

What if they were too late?

* * * * *

To Erixitl, the feast seemed a grand success. They ate melons and citrus and venison and mayz and beans and chocolate. The foreigners seemed to enjoy the food. They made a great deal of noise when they ate, talking and joking and laughing. She saw the square in its natural sunshine, without the ominous cloak of shadows that had been so often here before. Still, she found that she couldn't entirely forget the sense of dire portent that had come with that darkness.

Erix sat on a huge feathered blanket with Cordell and Bishou Domincus, and also the Jaguar Knight Kalnak and the Eagle Knight Chical. The dour cleric of Helm remained silent, but the three men of war seemed to greatly enjoy exchanging tales of battles through Erixitl's translation. The Mazticans expressed great interest in Cordell's equipment, and the general allowed them to examine the blade of his sword.

Some time shortly after the feast began, the robed elf-mage joined them. Looking at her slight figure—Darien was shorter than Erix, and far more petite than the human legionnaires—the Maztican woman found herself wondering what lay behind that deep, cowled hood. Erixitl easily understood why Halloran had always found the elven wizard's presence unsettling.

Darien sat beside Cordell. She leaned toward the captain-general and, though Erix could hear nothing, it seemed as though a silent message was passed from the wizard to the commander. Indeed, Cordell suddenly stiffened. His black eyes narrowed to dark spots, and below hooded lids, he shifted his gaze from Kalnak to Chical, and then to Erix. She squirmed under that penetrating stare, feeling an anger and menace there that had previously been absent.

But she had little time for musing or pondering. Kalnak and Chical had many words for the foreigners, and Erix was required to translate each statement.

"The Kultakans are old women," Kalnak was explaining. "It is no wonder you defeated them. Do they serve you well as slaves?"

"They are my allies, not my slaves," said Cordell pointedly. His voice had a new edge to it. "And in truth, they fought like men—on a battlefield, in a fight between armies."

Chical twisted uncomfortably beside Erix. She sensed that the Eagle Knight wished he were somewhere else. The Jaguar Knight Kalnak took no note, however.

"Perhaps the Kultakans fight well," Kalnak grudgingly admitted. His voice then became nearly a sneer. "But they are savages and barbarians when compared to the high culture of Nexal."

Erix translated loosely, trying to smooth the arrogance of the Jaguar Knight. It was a great breach of manners to talk so rudely to a guest, and she didn't understand why Kalnak was doing so. At least Cordell didn't seem to take particular offense. In fact, the bearded general seemed mildly distracted.

"If you'll excuse me, I have to tend to the comfort of my

men. I'll be back presently. Bishou, Darien, come with me please." Cordell stood up and, with a deep bow, left them to move among his feasting troops.

The plaza of Palul was crowded with humanity. The five hundred men of the Golden Legion were gathered in several large groups, each surrounded by Mazticans who fed them and offered jugs of the mildy alcoholic *octal*. Thousands of natives feasted here, too, while children dashed about and mothers tried to keep track of their offspring.

The horses, in particular, proved magnetic to the little ones, who gathered around the steeds. With the permission of the riders, some of the bolder children stepped forward to offer carrots, ears of mayz, and other treats to the mounts. Erix saw one tall, gangly youth who wore a headband decorated with macaw feathers in imitation of a warrior. This one actually stroked the muzzle of one of the chargers.

Beside the mounts, great war hounds lolled on the stones. Their long tongues hung from their loose jaws, and they drooled, panting in the heat.

Erix saw Bishou Domincus go over to the horsemen and talk to them. Alvarro, staggering slightly and holding a jug of *octal*, heard the cleric speak and scowled in reply. Cordell circulated among his men, stopping at each group in the plaza. Darien had disappeared again, and Erixitl found the mage's vanishing act as unsettling as her appearance. Meanwhile, Kalnak and Chical had huddled together in conversation behind her.

Then, as she looked around at the flowers and feathers, at the food and the gaiety, a black cloud seemed to descend across her eyes.

Once again the plaza lay concealed beneath a monstrous shadow.

* * * * *

"It is almost time," Zilti hissed, finding Shatil near the base of the pyramid. That structure, dominating the great square, was to be the focal point of the attack.

"All is ready," replied the younger priest. "What about the Kultakans?"

VIPERHAND

"There are ten thousand Nexalan warriors hidden on the slopes above them. As soon as the attack begins, they will fall on our ancient enemies and keep them busy. Then, when the battle in the town is won, our warriors will go into the field to complete the destruction of the Kultakans." Zilti turned around nervously, his fingers absently scraping at one of the many fresh scars on his forearm.

"Where did their leader go?" Shatil asked suddenly. He had looked over toward Erixitl and saw that his sister still sat on the feathered blanket with Kalnak and Chical. But Cordell and the other two strangers—the sorcerer and the priest—had disappeared.

"There he is." Zilti pointed, relieved.

Cordell had just spoken to a short, stocky man with a bristling beard. Erix had referred to these smaller strangers as "dwarves." Shatil's sister had explained that their small size in no way diminished their fighting prowess, but this was a fact of which they were frankly skeptical. Now this dwarf walked among his men, stopping after to nod and talk with them.

The captain-general finally returned to the blanket where he had been feasting. The knights and Erix stood up at his approach, and for a moment, they all stood there, as if reluctant to sit back down.

"Any moment now," said Zilti, barely able to contain his excitement, "Kalnak will give the signal. Then the battle will begin!"

* * * * *

"You referred to the Kultakans as old women," charged Cordell. This time his elven mage translated before Erix could begin to speak. Darien placed all the accusatory inflection that had been in the captain's voice in her own version of the words.

"They are our lifelong enemies!" insisted Kalnak, taken aback by the guest's sudden aggressiveness.

"I say that the old women are those who fight their battles disguised behind women and children, behind feasts and presents!"

As Kalnak stared in shock, Cordell whisked his sword

from its scabbard and raised the blade high. "This is the reward for treachery!" he cried.

The blade dropped, arcing through a silvery circle in the sun. Its passage caused a whistle of air, so quickly did the captain-general strike. The keen edge met Kalnak's neck as the Jaguar Knight still stared, and the steel didn't lose momentum. Instead, it passed cleanly through the neck and emerged in a shower of blood from the other side of his body.

The head of Kalnak, still wearing its jaguar-skull helmet, toppled to the side. Red blood spurted from the stump of his neck, and the headless body staggered forward for a step or two, almost as if it would mindlessly attack its killer. But then the corpse sprawled forward and pumped the rest of its life onto the paving stones of the plaza.

Erix saw the blade as a streak of thick blackness through the gray shadows that masked her eyes. She stood frozen in shock, stunned by the monstrous evil of their guest. The entire square fell silent for a moment.

Suddenly a flash of blue-white light cut through the air, penetrating even the heavy shadows across Erix's vision. She saw the wizard Darien standing off to the side. In her hand was a small stick, and it seemed that the stick was the source of the flash. Erix remembered Hal telling her of something like this—what had he called it?

Screams of pain and shock erupted from the plaza. Erix saw that, where the pale light had flashed, all those who had been feasting and talking and laughing were suddenly still. Some of them had toppled over, while others remained frozen in the positions of sitting, eating, even standing.

Frozen in position? *Icetongue*. She remembered the tale of that stick now. Hal had called it a wand of frost and explained that it slayed quickly and magically, killing many at a time.

There was no doubt in Erixitl's mind that most of these victims had perished—a hundred or more Mazticans, slain in one silent attack! Only around the edges of the afflicted area did she see the wriggling, crawling figures of wounded. These miserable souls desperately crawled away from the stiff corpses behind them, and Erix saw that many of them dragged useless legs or showed ugly patches of scarred, frostbitten flesh.

Later Erix would realize that the pause had only lasted seconds, but at the time, it seemed as though many minutes ticked by while they all stood motionless in the plaza. The attack of Icetongue finally broke the paralysis. Again the wand flashed its chilling blast, and the pale white light illuminated, and killed, another group of villagers.

Chical howled in rage, raising his *maca* to leap at Cordell. The captain-general slashed at the Eagle Knight. Chical ducked the stroke of Cordell's sword, but the commander reversed his attack quickly and brought the hilt crashing down on the Eagle Knight's skull. Chical collapsed like a stone statue, kicking once and then lying still on the feathered blanket.

Panic compelled Erixitl's reaction, and she darted away from the man, disappearing into the throngs of weeping, screaming Mazticans. Even as she disappeared, Cordell had turned away, stabbing a charging Jaguar Knight through the heart.

The pale flash of light washed the plaza once more, this time flooding around Erix herself. She stared, stunned, as villagers died on all sides of her. Only after the effect had passed did she realize that she herself and several youngsters who had been right beside her had been unaffected by the blast. She sensed her *pluma* token puffing lightly out from her dress, and she realized that somehow her father's magic had saved her from the wizard's spell.

Darien regarded her coldly from the impenetrable depths of that cowled hood. Erix's eyes couldn't penetrate the shadows there, but she saw the elfwoman's eyes, glittering like hard diamonds.

Breaking from her thrall and spinning in panic, Erixitl ran from the wizard. Nearby she heard the stomping and snorting of horses and saw legionnaires swinging into their saddles. The youth with the feathered headband looked up in astonishment as the red-bearded captain of the riders loomed above him. With a cruel sneer, the man slashed savagely with his sword, splitting the youth's body from his forehead to his belly.

Douglas Niles

A woman carrying a baby screamed in front of Erix, falling to the ground, writhing and spitting blood. Erixitl saw one of the deadly steel darts fired by the legionnaires' crossbows. This one had pinned the woman's baby to her own body, and Erix turned away, horrified, as the mother and child perished before her.

More and more of the lethal, steel-tipped arrows flashed past, slaying indiscriminately. The dull *chunk* of the weapons' triggers created a grim cadence of death. The crossbowmen stood in a circle, loading and reloading their weapons, driving their missiles at point-blank range into a solid mass of targets, puncturing bodies of male and female, old and young, with constant, gory slaughter.

Erixitl slipped on blood that washed across the paving stones. Like most of the other Mazticans in the plaza, she thought only of escape. The warriors among them seized their weapons and sprang to battle, desperate to give the women and children time to flee. At the time, it didn't seem odd to Erix that so many spears and *macas* should be available to warriors who had entered the plaza unarmed.

Erix tried to run north, toward her father's house, but the surging crowd carried her west in the stampede to escape the massacre.

She saw the riders charge into the mob. The horse that, moments before, had been contentedly eating and resting, the picture of animal contentment, now became the snorting, stamping creatures of war that had so terrorized the Payit at Ulatos. They had the same effect on the Mazticans at Palul.

The huge war hounds that had once flopped peacefully on the ground now snarled and slavered. They savagely attacked the villagers unfortunate enough to fall before them, tearing with their great fangs and, with their growls, adding to the nightmarish din.

The cavalrymen used their swords to chop about, apparently since the quarters were too confined for their lances. They thundered through a line of warriors that tried to stand before them, breaking the bodies of many brave men. Bodies fell by the dozen, writhing, bleeding, dying.

In moments, the horsemen plowed into the mass of

women and children beyond the warriors. These victims scattered in every direction, but not before the cruel blades and stamping hooves had slain dozens of them.

Above the whirling mass of chaos, Erix saw the black helm, with its trailing streamers, of the captain of the horsemen. He guided his charger with cruel abandon, his face split into a gap-toothed grin. For a moment, once again, his eyes met Erixitl's. She was surprised at the lack of life there—he looked to her every bit as dead as the corpses sprawled around him. She felt certain this time that he recognized her. Then the crowd closed around Erix, sweeping her along with its tidelike rush.

"By the power of almighty Helm, a plague beset you!"

The booming voice of the Bishou thundered over the volume of shrieks and cries, sending powerful tendrils of panic into Erix's heart. She knew, from Hal's descriptions, that the cleric wielded supernatural powers in much the same way as the wizard.

The fleeing mob came to an abrupt halt, and Erix saw people before her suddenly begin to thrash wildly, twisting and crying out in pain. Young children dropped to the ground, wailing, and then, moments later, fell still. At first she could see nothing through the shadows, though she could hear a deep humming sound that filled the air with heavy vibration.

Then Erix saw heavier darkness among her own shadows. At the same time, she felt a burning flash of pain on her wrist. Slapping involuntarily, she saw a huge wasp fall dead, its stinger embedded in her inflamed flesh.

Now the source of the droning became apparent, as more wasps swarmed around the panicked villagers. Before her, all fell into blackness as the savage insects swarmed thickly around every living thing. She saw pathetically twitching bodies, covered all over with stinging, biting bugs. Another jolt of pain, and another, shot through her as stingers plunged into her shoulder and then her neck.

What kind of power was wielded by these men? She realized, with a sense of hopeless awe, that the Bishou had *summoned* these insects, and the creatures had arrived to do his bidding! How could the True World hope to stand against might such as this?

Screaming and crying now, driven by panic and pain, Erix turned with the crowd toward the south. Her own voice melted into the cacophony as, mindless with terror, she sought any path of escape from this hellish place. The mob surged forward in blind terror, trampling those who were too slow or too frail to keep up.

They reached the tree-lined fringe of the square, and here many of the weaker villagers collapsed from exhaustion. Erix saw, with numb surprise, that fights raged among the nearby houses as well. Legionnaire swordsman rushed from building to building, slaying any Matzicans they found. The warriors made valiant attempts at resistance, but divided as they were into small bands, they quickly fell to the savage, sudden onslaught of the steel-toothed strangers.

Across the lane, tongues of fire licked upward from one of the houses. Something seemed to explode there, silently, but with a great eruption of heat and flame. The inferno leaped to the thatched roof of a neighboring dwelling, and quickly the entire block crackled into a tinderbox of fire.

Shadows mixed with smoke everywhere Erix looked, but the combined darkness couldn't block out the sight of blood and death. Her nightmare seemed forgotten, a pale image of true horror.

It seemed to Erix fitting, as she collapsed on the paving stones and gasped for air, that the village should burn.

* * * * *

The terraced pyramid of Zaltec stood, perhaps fifty feet high, near the middle of Palul's plaza in the midst of the feast and, subsequently, the battle. A steep stairway ascended each of the four sides, leading to a square platform on top. In the center of this platform, a small stone building enclosed the sacrificial altar and a statue of the war god, Zaltec.

Brave warriors had gathered below the pyramid at the outbreak of battle, instinctively seeking to protect the sacred image of their god. Equally instinctively, the soldiers of the legion pressed from all sides, attempting to gain the top of the pyramid and shatter the barbarous idol.

The warriors conducted their defense with savage fanaticism, but the tightly packed legionnaires concentrated their attacks. Slowly the defenders fell back, giving up a step at a time, and each with a high price in blood. But the inexorable tide of attack grew ever closer to the bloodstained platform on top.

"Sorcery!" wailed Zilti from before the altar, looking at the massacre below. "How else could they have learned of the trap?"

Shatil, standing beside his high priest, looked around numbly. Accustomed to bloodshed and death—indeed, he had performed over a hundred sacrifices himself—the destruction below nonetheless horrified the young priest.

The legionnaires seemed invincible. The horsemen rode back and forth through the plaza, and only the thinning numbers of Mazticans prevented them from slaying hundreds with each charge. The deadly swords rose and fell, slicing heads from bodies or leaving deep, gashing cuts that sent the blood of the victim pouring in a fatal stream onto the stone pavement of the square.

First they had bottled up the north exit from the plaza, while the sudden horde of insects had closed egress to the west. The cloaked figure with the tiny stick had sealed the eastern side of the square, now marked by hundreds of stiff, frozen corpses. Only to the south could the villagers find escape, and it was from this side that the refugees poured out of the courtyard.

Finally the horses began to slip and stumble on the blood-slicked pavement, and the riders dismounted. There were no more living victims around them, in any event.

Shatil raised his eyes to the surrounding ridges, knowing that thousands of Nexalan warriors were concealed there. From the height of the pyramid, he could see over the houses and trees of the village, gaining a clear view of the surrounding heights. Surely those warriors had seen this treachery.

They had, but the priest saw that the Kultakan allies of the legionnaires had been just as prepared as the strangers themselves. Now the Kultakans fell on these hapless ambushers, and before Shatil's disbelieving eyes, the Nexalan companies were driven away from Palul. The feathered warriors of both sides fought bravely, and showers of spears, arrows, and darts flew back and forth.

The Nexalans tried a desperate charge that was quickly broken and routed by the steady *macas* of the Kultakans. Inexorably, one after another, the attacks separated the thousandmen regiments of Nexal from each other. Each surrounded block of feathered warriors fought desperately as the battle on the ridges degenerated into numerous melees.

But each Nexalan thousandmen fought alone, in isolation and without coordination. The Kultakans, Shatil saw, concentrated their forces against first one, than another block of enemy troops. One by one, the Nexalan regiments broke, pressed from the battlefield by the overwhelming, savage force of the Kultakan ranks.

Around the square, the companies of legionnaire swordsmen attacked the buildings that sheltered the warriors who had been planning to perform their own ambush. Now, faced in small groups, the advantage of surprise taken from them, these warriors fought bravely. The valiant defenders stood firm and died quickly beneath the steel weapons of the legionnaires.

Bolts from legion crossbows raked the pyramid, and in a sudden rush, the attackers pressed upward, three quarters of the way to the top. On all four sides, Shatil observed numbly, the clamor of battle threatened to sweep upward, into the temple and its sacred statue. Grimly, clutching his sacrificial knife, he stood before the door, prepared to give his life in the desperate last stand before the bestial icon.

For now, there was little he could do. The warriors still fought on the narrow stairways, and their *macas* and spears, though outclassed by the invaders' steel, were still more formidable weapons than his obsidian dagger.

A house exploded into flame, and Shatil swore the fire was caused by the woman in the dark robe. She simply raised her hand and pointed. Immediately columns of flame had spurted from the building's doors and windows. Maztican warriors, their bodies blistered and flaming, dove through the windows and doors, only to collapse and die on the street.

Then the disbelieving priest saw the woman turn to another building. This one had started to disgorge warriors from several doors, angry spearmen who rushed forward to exact vengeance for the massacre.

But the woman raised both hands this time. A pale mist suddenly appeared before her and immediately fanned outward into a growing cloud. As the charging warriors met the cloud, they stumbled through it and collapsed, shrieking, gagging, and choking. They fell to the street, writhing in visible agony for several moments before stiffening and growing still. More and more of the warriors succumbed to the cloud as it gained substance and moved on. The victims, wracked by agony, finally dropped and lay still, cast in grotesque postures like so many mayz-husk dolls flung into the street.

The mist grew thicker, seeping through the doors and windows of all the buildings along the street. From some of these, bodies stumbled forth to collapse outside, gasping out their last, wretched breaths. In others, Shatil could see nothing, but he retained no illusions that any villagers remained alive within.

The deadly cloud drifted up the street, and in its wake, the village finally fell into stillness, except around the priests. The warriors fighting on the steps finally fell back to their last position, the top of the pyramid itself.

Companies of swordsmen still smashed into houses, killing whomever they found. More and more, the swordsmen discovered that these buildings had already been abandoned, their residents in flight or perhaps lying dead in the square.

"We are finished here," said Zilti, his voice an agonized grunt. "But one of us must carry word of this betrayal back to Nexal, to Hoxitl."

"We must defend the statue to the death!" objected Shatil. "The invaders must not reach the sacred image of Zaltec!"

"No," Zilti commanded firmly, his voice tempered with gentle compassion for Shatil's devotion. "I will stay here, but you must flee."

"How?" asked Shatil practically, as legionnaires burst onto

the platform, gaining the top of the stairway on two sides. A shrinking ring of warriors, desperately striving to keep the attackers from the sacred altar, surrounded the two priests.

"This way!" Zilti led Shatil into the small temple building itself, past the gruesome statue of Zaltec and its blood-caked maw. Shatil hesitated, shuddering under the image of that statue falling, torn down by the blood-drenched savages from across the sea.

Zilti didn't delay, however. The priest pushed a stone on the back of the statue, and suddenly a hatch fell away in the floor, revealing a steep stairway that vanished into a terribly dark pit.

"This will take you to the bottom of the pyramid," said Zilti. "You will come out beside the temple, but wait until nightfall, until the strangers have gone."

The high priest now pressed a parchment, rolled into a tube, into Shatil's hands. "Take this to Nexal. Give it to Hoxitl, high priest of Zaltec there. It will tell the tale of the treachery here. Now go!"

Shatil took the parchment, knowing that there had been no time for Zilti to compose a message but not questioning the older priest's command. But again he hesitated, not from fear of the dark path but out of loyalty to his teacher. "Come with me," he urged. "We can both get away!"

Zilti looked outside the temple. Already several legionnaires had reached the altar, hacking about themselves with their invincible swords. "No. I have to close the hatch. Begone, and avenge!"

Without another word, Shatil dropped into the hole. He carefully felt his way past the first step. Before he touched the second, Zilti had closed the secret door above him.

* * * * *

The sweet scent of blood tickled Alvarro's nostrils, driving away the fatigue and exhaustion of the long combat. His sword, dripping with gore, remained in his hand, but he saw no victims for its deadly blade. Beside him, his top sergeant, Vane, galloped smoothly. The two horsemen rode far beyond the confines of the small village.

And still they did not rein in their chargers. The horsemen had ridden through the fields, chasing down fleeing natives, but the rest of the cavalry unit scattered in the process. Now the fleeing Mazticans dispersed into the brushy country outside their town. Bands of legionnaire footmen drove through the thickets, often flushing out additional victims.

Alvarro saw a group of swordsmen pull a young woman from a hiding place. With whoops of glee, they dragged her to a grassy clearing. For a moment, the red-bearded captain stared, thinking this might have been the woman who had caught his eye in town. As the footmen threw her to the ground, her panic-stricken face turned toward him, and he saw that he was mistaken.

Why had that woman, the translator, seemed so familiar? A memory tugged at Alvarro's brain, driving him forward even after the other riders turned back. Certainly her beauty was captivating, and the unique feathered cloak she wore had glowed with almost magical color, but his fascination went beyond that. He knew that he had seen her before.

Halloran! Suddenly it came back to him. His old enemy had struck him from his horse at the battle in Payit to save that same woman from Alvarro's lance! The captain's eyes narrowed. The pieces began to fit together. How had she learned the tongue of Faerun, if not from Hal? Shrewdly he wondered if she might know something of the fugitive's present whereabouts.

Alvarro knew of the hatred both Bishou Domincus and Darien harbored for Halloran. If he could apprehend the traitor, he would win the gratitude of these influential leaders of the legion—Cordell's two top lieutenants.

Squinting again, he tried to think. She had fled with the crowd going west, he knew. With a brutal kick at his charger's flanks, Alvarro turned down the road leading west, Vane following closely. The trail lay empty before him, though he saw natives scrambling away to either side. He kept his eyes narrowed, searching the mayzfields along the road, looking for this woman.

They rode at an easy canter. Alvarro laughed every time he flushed panicked villagers from the brush before him, but he no longer cared to ride them down. Now he had specific game in mind.

He saw a flash of movement across a field, a wave of long dark hair above the mayz, and something compelled him to stop. A woman fled the battle, but oddly, unlike the rest of her folk, she seemed to be circling back toward the village. Then he saw the flash of color—that cloak! Still staring, Alvarro saw the girl turn to look at him before she dropped out of sight.

And he recognized his quarry.

* * * * *

Bands of Kultakan warriors roamed the countryside, seizing stragglers as captives. Still, Erixitl knew she couldn't flee with the rest of the villagers, most of whom seemed intent on racing all the way to Nexal. She had to go back and find her father. Surely the invaders would discover his home atop the ridge on the opposite side of the village. She assumed that her brother, trapped atop the pyramid, had fallen during the massacre. Still numb with shock, she began to ache with a foretaste of her pain, for she hadn't yet grasped the full extent of the disaster. Her village had died today.

Erix left the road that ran through the mayzfields lining the valley bottom. She circled to the north of Palul, finally reaching the stream that ran past the town. Here she stopped for a quick look around.

She spotted two silver-plated riders on the road, about a mile away. From the black atop the helm of one of the riders, she recognized him as the captain of the savage horsemen. For a long, hateful moment, she wished she was a warrior, with a powerful bow, so intensely did she want to strike him from his saddle. Then she saw his face turn toward her, and she dropped into the shallow streambed, knowing such a thought for the utterly futile desire that it was.

She splashed through the shallow water, staying low, and started to move along the stream bank on the opposite side. For half a mile, she worked her way back toward the town.

Finally Erix reached a bend in the stream, near the base of

the ridge below her father's house. Here she broke from cover, darting up the bank and through another field of mayz toward the security of the brushy slope before her.

Sudden hoofbeats pounded behind her, and she knew she had been spotted. Without looking back, she guessed the identity of her pursuers, and that knowledge spurred her to deerlike swiftness.

But the horses were swift, too. Before she reached the undergrowth, Erix felt a charger thunder close, and suddenly a brutal weight smashed into her body, sending her crashing to the ground.

With a savage scream, she sprang to her feet and whirled, only to see the red-bearded legionnaire leap from his saddle and crash into her with the full force of his metal-armored frame. Again she smashed into the ground, this time driving the air from her lungs.

The legionnaire's companion pulled up beside him, casting a hungry glance at her. He dismounted, then stood to the side, looking around them.

Erix scratched blindly, hatred driving her fingers, but the horseman only laughed. With one brawny hand, he pinned both of her arms to the ground. She smelled the *octal* on his breath, saw the mad flush in his eyes. His laughter dropped to a menacing chortle.

"You're a pretty one, aren't you!"

She spat at his face, and he sneered.

"Spirited, too! I can see what Halloran liked about you."

At the name, she stiffened reflexively, then cursed to herself as she saw the pleased smile crease his gap-toothed mouth.

"Now," he said, reaching a bloody paw to the bodice of her dress. "Let's have a look at you!"

* * * * *

Lolth tasted the blood, felt the heat of the battle, and began to take a great interest in the faraway realm of Maztica. Her attentions, originally fixed upon the rebellious drow who dared worship another god, began to grow.

Perhaps her vengeance should not be hasty. Measuring in the time scale of godhood, she felt no hurry to punish her

Douglas Niles

wayward children. They would feel the lash of her anger soon enough.

But perhaps, before then, she could enjoy the show of slaughter and butchery presented by the humans.

And in the near future, this land called the True World seemed likely to yield a plentiful harvest of blood.

♣ 9 ♣

FLIGHT AND SANCTUARY

Halloran didn't need to ask Poshtli; he knew the plume of black smoke billowing into the air before them marked the town of Palul. Still miles from the community, they began to meet haggard Mazticans fleeing down the road to Nexal. These refugees invariably scrambled into the brush or mayzfields beside the road at the approach of the two riders on the roan mare.

Sickened with apprehension, Hal felt acute shame at his own appearance, dressed as he was in the uniform of their enemy. Children saw him and shrieked with horror. He saw an old woman with badly injured legs crawling from the roadway, trying pathetically to reach the shelter of the undergrowth.

But Hal's overwhelming fear for Erixitl compelled him to forge ahead.

"We'll never find her!" Hal groaned as they closed to within a mile of the town. They could see the village pyramid, a small, bright blaze marking the temple and its bloody altar. The conflagration had blackened whole rows of houses. They saw few Mazticans this close to Palul. Those they did encounter were badly wounded or numb with shock.

"Do you think she would have recognized us?" asked Poshtli, wondering if they had already passed Erix among the fleeing villagers.

"I don't know," Hal groaned. "I wouldn't blame her if she ran and hid as soon as she saw the horse."

"Perhaps we should separate," said Poshtli. "We can circle Palul in opposite directions and meet beyond the village. If we don't find her, then we can slip into town and see if she's still there."

"Her father's house," said Hal, remembering Erixitl's description. "She said it was on the ridge above Palul, near the top. She might have gone there."

They both saw the looming green slope on the far side of the town.

"Let's meet at the foot of the slope." Poshtli squinted into the distance as he dismounted. "There, near that waterfall." He indicated a bright cascade where a small stream plummeted from a gorge in the side of the ridge.

"All right," Hal agreed. He clasped the warrior's hand. "Keep your eyes open. There'll be legionnaires about."

Poshtli nodded brusquely, then turned and slipped from the right side of the road into a tangle of low trees. Hal reined Storm to the left, starting into a field of mayz. Anxiously he looked around, hoping desperately to catch some sight of Erixitl.

He rode for several minutes, trying to avoid the Mazticans he found—pathetic family groups hiding among the mayz, old couples, speechless and stunned by the events of the day. The most horrifying to Halloran were the lone children, crying waifs, some of whom didn't even know enough to hide at his hoof-pounding approach.

He tried to look past them, to seek Erixitl beyond, on some clean, windswept slope above the fields, but he couldn't. Halloran sensed that, with this battle, something deep and irrevocable had fallen between himself and his former comrades. No longer did he feel like a fugitive, wanting only to avoid the soldiers of the legion. Now he began to feel like their enemy.

Suddenly he squinted, distracted by something he glimpsed through a tree line—a flash of color, nothing more, that reminded him of Erixitl's cloak. Spurring Storm to a gallop, he raced toward the row of greenery. As he suspected, it marked the course of a shallow stream. The mare plowed through the water, throwing a curtain of spray before bounding easily up the far bank.

His eyes flared as he saw Alvarro some distance away, straddling someone on the ground. Another legionnaire, dismounted and held two horses nearby. The latter looked up at Hal with a wicked grin, expecting one of his comrades.

Halloran recognized him as Vane, an unscrupulous bully, one of Alvarro's regular companions.

"Hal!" Erix cried, struggling beneath the red-bearded brute. Alvarro looked up and stared at Halloran in shock, while Vane sneered and leaped into his saddle. Drawing his sword, he thundered toward Hal.

Grimly Halloran turned Storm into Vane's charge, drawing and raising Helmstooth at the same time. He thrust instinctively with the steel blade as the two horses smashed shoulders. The collision threw Hal from the saddle even as the mare moved nimbly to the side.

Vane's horse stumbled and fell, but its rider paid no heed, for Halloran had stabbed him through the heart.

Alvarro, meanwhile, leaped up, leaving Erix gasping on the ground. Blindly Hal sprang to his feet and attacked. His ankle throbbed from his fall, but his limp didn't slow down his hatred or determination.

"I see your treachery is complete!" sneered Alvarro, driving Halloran back with a two-handed blow. "Now you even kill for the savages!"

The blades clashed together, and Hal felt pain shoot through his right arm. Tumbling back, he couldn't twist away from Alvarro's thrust. The man's blade slipped behind his breastplate, slicing into the flesh between his ribs.

Red daggers of pain lanced through Hal's body as he recoiled from the wound. Blood spurted onto his arm and down his flank as he staggered to keep his balance. Grimly he focused his gaze on the beastlike man before him.

Desperately Halloran swung his blade, fighting for his own life because that was the only way he could insure Erix's safety from this madman. Back and forth they stumbled, slashing mightily, each seeking a fatal opening. Sheer agony slowed Hal's arm, but by the force of his will, he kept fighting. Hatred fueled him, and he attacked with renewed strength.

Steel rang as the two blades met, and Hal used every ounce of his strength to drive his weapon toward Alvarro's face. The man's grin twisted in fear at the brutal onslaught. Alvarro's wrist twisted back as he tried to deflect the blow.

With a dull grunt of pain, the horseman suddenly

dropped his sword. Hal stumbled forward, nearly collapsing as Alvarro leaped toward his horse. Sharp tongues of pain lashed across Halloran's eyes, and he couldn't pursue. His enemy got into the saddle and spun his mount away, in seconds disappearing in the direction of Palul.

Climbing weakly from his knees to his feet, Halloran turned to sweep Erixitl into his arms. Finally the dam of shock containing the tumult of her emotions broke. Uncontrolled sobs wracked her body as, for a long while, she finally gave vent to her grief.

* * * * *

"Halloran belongs to the enemy now, without a doubt," said Cordell softly. Beside him, in the bloody plaza of Palul, Alvarro grinned broadly.

"And, my general, he is very near! We can seize him now if we hurry! Give me thirty horsemen, and I will have him in chains by morning!" Alvarro's eyes flashed as he pleaded.

Cordell looked at his captain, and his smile was not pleasant. "It's too bad you and Vane couldn't bring him in. With this much warning and a fast horse, Hal is sure to be gone by now. Besides, the men have fought a battle and will be marching again sooner than they know. I will not tire them out with a fruitless chase by night."

Alvarro scowled. He couldn't miss the rebuke in his commander's words. "I tell you, sir, he was aided by a hundred savages! I was lucky to escape with my life!"

"Nevertheless, I see that you managed to do so," said Cordell wryly. Even Alvarro had sense enough to make no further argument. Still, he seethed inwardly. It almost seemed as if the captain-general didn't desire Halloran's capture or death.

Daggrande clumped up to them, his armor freshly polished. His blade, cleaned and sharpened, hung from his belt. Though the dwarf had shown no stomach for the day's battle, he had commanded his crossbowmen resolutely, following Cordell's command. His disgust he kept, with difficulty, to himself.

"The men have assembled, General. Can I send them to rest now?"

"One moment, Captain." Cordell dismissed Alvarro with a tilt of his head. "I wish to speak to them."

Beyond the pyramid, the legionnaires awaited their commander. Cordell approached the formation, assembled in its trim, neat rows. Then he turned and walked along the rank of swordsmen standing at rigid attention, his heart ready to burst with pride. These brave soldiers had turned a potentially disastrous ambush into a crushing victory, following his orders with speed and resolute determination. He felt certain that the Mazticans would think long and hard before they planned similar treachery.

Part of his mind reflected on the turnabout. Cordell realized that this victory could become a powerful and dramatic asset.

The Golden Legion must strike quickly now, while their enemies were demoralized and confused.

Many of his legionnaires had been wounded, though even most of these now stood at attention, hastily wrapped bandages on heads, arms, or legs. The captain-general knew that at least two of his men had died in the battle, and several more were too badly wounded to move. Bishou Domincus attended to them, however, and Cordell had great faith in the cleric's healing powers.

Normally he would have granted the men several days to rest after a fight such as this. Repairing weapons, refitting equipment, healing minor wounds—all these things would contribute to the welfare and fitness of his troops.

Yet Cordell knew that now, scarce hours after the battle, the Golden Legion stood ready to march. The swordsmen and the crossbowmen, the cavalry, all of them would fight another battle right now if he but gave the command. By Helm, how he loved these men! And knowing this, he understood a little more about the mind-set of his enemies. The great Naltecona would doubtless be shocked and dismayed at the stories from Palul. That advantage would only last for a little while.

The captain-general stopped and faced the trim ranks. For a moment, he couldn't speak, so intense was his emotion. Finally he cleared his throat and began in a clear, strong, voice.

Douglas Niles

"We have won a great victory today—a victory against treachery and betrayal! The vigilance of almighty Helm gave us warning, and you stood ready to act. By Helm, you are the finest fighters on the face of the world! Together, we are *invincible!*

"This town, Palul, has gained an everlasting place in the annals of the Golden Legion for the battle that was fought here today. But aside from that historical footnote, this place is nothing! It means nothing, it is worth nothing, and we have nothing more to do here!"

He paused again, drawing a deep breath and trying to control his surging pride. Several moments passed before he could speak again.

"The real objective of this long march lies within our grasp now. Two more days of marching will take us to Nexal! There, amid mountains of silver and gold—there, in Nexal, will we find the true measure of our worth!"

* * * * *

Shatil awoke suddenly, terrified by the darkness all around him. He bolted upward and cracked his head on the low stone ceiling. Cursing, he sat back down and held his throbbing skull.

At least, with the blow, he remembered that he was still in the secret tunnel below the temple of Zaltec. As soon as Zilti had closed the door behind him, Shatil had followed the steep stairway, in total darkness, to the bottom. There he had felt the outline of a small doorway. While waiting for nightfall, overcome by his tension, forced inactivity, and fear, he had fallen asleep.

Now his mind reeled with horror as he recalled the events that had led him to this place. Palul! Did anything remain of his village? Did any of his neighbors escape the fearful slaughter? It didn't seem possible. Wringing his hands, Shatil felt the wrinkled sheet of parchment given to him by Zilti. With that sensation, his mind returned to his mission: the message. He had to get that message to Hoxitl.

Reasoning that it must be well after dark by now, he pushed at the stone door. Slowly, grudgingly, it slid open.

Shatil emerged from the doorway and crouched beside

the base of the pyramid, looking around the square in shock. A whole row of houses now smoldered, mere heaps of ash and shells of charred adobe. Bodies lay everywhere. At first, in the darkness, he thought that some of them were moving. At closer look, he realized that the moving creatures were vultures and crows that waddled about the square, feasting.

His nerves froze suddenly as he heard a monstrous, rumbling growl. Shatil gasped as one of the strangers' war creatures crept into sight, its hackles raised. The thing growled again, showing its long fangs. It reminded the Maztican of a huge, shaggy coyote.

Then it sprang, and its jaws closed toward his face. The young priest reacted instinctively, drawing his obsidian dagger from his belt. Twisting away, he grunted as the huge body slammed him against the stone wall of the pyramid. The creature's maw clamped shut, barely missing his throat. Shatil desperately flailed with his dagger, scoring a cut in the animal's side as its momentum carried it past.

But the animal turned with startling quickness, attacking once again. Shatil raised a hand and then gasped in agony as the creature's steel jaws clamped onto his wrist. But at the same time, he drove the knife forward, plunging it through the animal's chest. With a shudder, it died.

Shatil fell backward against the pyramid, wrenching his arm from the vicelike jaws. He gasped in pain, struggling to remain conscious as a red haze drifted across his vision. He felt blood flowing into his lap, but only slowly came to realize the danger of his wound.

Shaking his head to ward off the grogginess, Shatil climbed to his feet. Tearing a strip of cloth from his robe, he wrapped it around the bloody flesh of his wrist. Though the bandage quickly became sodden, he hoped it would stem the bleeding enough to allow him to move. He stumbled when he tried to walk, but slowly he managed to stagger out of the square.

He saw that perhaps half the buildings in town had burned. Around him, in the remaining houses, slept the victors of the day's battle.

If you could call it a battle, thought Shatil bitterly. His step grew stronger as he passed the last houses, striking out on the road to Nexal. Thousands of Mazticans had already fled this way, and doubtless Naltecona had been told of the battle. But Shatil had a mission of his own. He had the scroll that he needed to give to Hoxitl, patriarch of Zaltec in the city of Nexal.

His step quickened. As his wrist throbbed, he held it to his chest and fought back the bile of his pain. He began to trot, and somehow he held this pace through the rest of the night.

At dawn, he stopped to drink, but he felt no need for food. Acutely conscious of the parchment he had pledged to carry to Hoxitl, Shatil once again trotted down the road.

His god, he knew, would sustain him.

* * * * *

Poshtli slipped through the darkness, appalled at the extent of the disaster. His route took him past the ruined section of Palul, and he came upon many badly burned survivors. These groaned and pleaded for water; he helped as many as he could, until his own waterskin was empty.

He found no sign of Erixitl, and he began to wonder if he had embarked upon a fool's task. She could have lain, delirious, ten feet away from him and he might have missed her in the gathering darkness.

It was with little hope that Poshtli started toward the rendezvous with Halloran at the base of the ridge. He approached the meeting with a strange sense of revulsion for his friend, simply because Hal was of the people who had done this. Yet he also knew shame for the treacherous ambush, all the more pathetic now for its obvious lack of success.

He heard Storm whinny quietly up ahead, and Poshtli moved toward Hal. He kept his face carefully neutral, so as not to reveal any of his inner emotional torment.

But then he saw Erixitl, and he couldn't hold back the tears of joy. She leaped toward him, then held the warrior tightly as he looked over her shoulder at Halloran. The expression of relief and joy on Hal's face banished Poshtli's earlier pain.

"You are safe!" said Poshtli earnestly. "That is what I feared I would never see."

"Hal's hurt," Erix said, returning to the ex-legionnaire. She had removed his breastplate, revealing a narrow puncture below his left armpit.

"I'll be fine," he grunted, trying to ignore the pain. "It's not serious."

"So many are dead," Erix said quietly, turning back to Poshtli. The warrior could only nod numbly; he had seen the proof. "Such mad butchery!" she blurted, turning back to Hal. "Why? What makes these men go mad with killing?"

Hal lowered his eyes, unable to meet her pain-filled, accusing stare. "The one who seized you is a born killer. His soul is dark and mad. As to the rest . . ." His voice trailed off, shameful.

"The ambush," Poshtli said to Erix. "Who attacked first?"

"The strangers. We presented them with a feast, and the leader, Cordell, murdered Kalnak with one blow. He said things about treachery, and then he killed him."

"He learned about a planned attack, ordered by Naltecona. The feast was a charade," Poshtli said softly, "to lure the invaders into a trap. But the ruse ensnared the trappers, instead."

Erix looked at him in shock. She recalled the weapons, close at hand, used by the warriors in the plaza, and she slowly realized that he spoke the truth. But it was a truth that soothed none of the bitterness of the slaughter.

"Darien, the Bishou—either of them could have learned about the trap through sorcery of one kind or another," Hal explained.

"My father," Erix said finally. "I must go see that he is out of danger."

"I'll go with you, if you'll let me," offered Hal. "Now that it's dark, we can move safely."

"You have to come with me," she said calmly. "Your wound must be tended, and you will need rest before you can travel anywhere."

Poshtli stood up, then looked away from the pair for a moment. When he turned back to them his face was set, though lined with regret.

"There is certain, now, to be war," he said. "And my duty to my nation becomes clear. I must return to Nexal and offer my services to my uncle."

Halloran nodded, understanding. "Take Storm. You'll need to travel fast to reach the city before Cordell. He's certain to march soon."

"But . . ." Poshtli hesitated, looking questioningly from Erix to Halloran.

"Hal needs to rest. His wound runs deep," said Erix. "He will stay in my father's house. He will be easy to hide if you take the horse."

"Very well. I shall leave you together," said Poshtli, "and hope that you may avoid the coming ravages. May . . . Qotal watch over you."

"Good-bye, my friend," said Halloran, ignoring his pain to rise and embrace the warrior. Erix, too, held the Nexalan tightly, but at last broke away to look at him through misty eyes.

"Take good care," she whispered, "that we may see you again."

Poshtli bowed, smiling slightly. Then he turned and mounted the mare. Storm pranced for a moment before wheeling to gallop into the night.

"The house is not far . . . up there," Erix explained, pointing.

Hal nodded, grimacing against the sudden spasm of pain in his chest. She led him onto the lower slope of the great ridge that sheltered Palul. The woman pushed through thickets, slowly working her way higher.

"We're staying off the trail," she explained when they stopped to rest after several minutes. "Can you make it?"

"I'll be all right." Hal managed a weak smile, and she took his hand. The feel of her skin against his gave him strength to rise and start upward again.

"Up here—we're close now," urged Erix, holding back thorny branches as Hal scrambled after her. The inky cloak of night completely surrounded them.

Finally she stopped at a small level shelf in the side of the ridge. "This is my father's house."

Gasping for air after the climb, Halloran raised his eyes to stare at the little structure. "Your home," he said, with unusual gentleness. She looked at him in the darkness, and he wondered if she understood his feelings.

He wanted to take her and hold her close, never to let her out of his sight again. Below, in the village, men of his race and culture made camp. Yet they had become as foreign to him as the scarred priests who practiced their nightly butchery in Nexal. This woman before him had become the only anchor in his life, his only source of purpose and meaning. He wanted to tell her all of this, but the look of pain in her eyes compelled him to silence.

"My daughter! You live!" The voice from the darkened doorway was full of strength and joy. An old man stepped into the yard, and Halloran saw him in the light of the halfmoon that had just risen. The fellow shuffled like the blind man he was, yet he looked up with an alertness that made Hal think he saw more than any of them.

"And Shatil? He is with you?" Lotil's inflection showed that he already knew the answer.

"No, Father. I fear he perished in the temple. The soldiers overran the pyramid, destroying everything there."

The featherworker slumped slightly, stepping back into the hut before turning to face them again. "And who is this who accompanies you?" he asked.

"This is Halloran, the man I told you about, from across the sea. He came from Nexal to—to see if I was safe." Briefly Erix told her father about the events of that bloody afternoon.

"And the shadows, child—are they still there?" asked the old man.

"I . . . I don't know, Father," Erix replied, shaking her head miserably. "I can't see them at night, and I didn't look back at the town before sunset."

"I myself can see very little," said Lotil. Nevertheless he reached out with unerring aim and took one of each of their hands. "But some things it is given me to see, and this I see for the two of you."

Halloran felt the old man's surprisingly strong grip. Lotil's strength was a comfort to him, and he returned the pressure, feeling a deep bond of friendship form between himself and the old man. It was more than the pressure of a handshake, but that clasp seemed to symbolize and define it for him.

"My blind eyes can see that the two of you are linked," Lotil continued. "And part of this link is formed of shadow—a darkness that was not dissipated by the events of this day.

"But another part of the link, and, we can hope, the stronger part, is formed of light. Together the two of you may yet bring light to a darkening world. I know, at least, that you must try."

"Light? Bring it to the world? Father, what do you mean?" asked Erix, looking at Halloran in wonder. He looked back, warmed by the expression in her eyes and by her father's words. Meanwhile, Lotil answered.

"I do not know, child. I wish that I did." The old man turned to Hal. "Now, you are wounded! Come, lie here."

Halloran stared at the blind man in surprise, suddenly sensing again the sharp pain in his chest. Erixitl took his arm and led him toward a straw mat in a corner of the hut.

Before Hal reached it, the world began to spin around him. He groaned, his legs collapsing as he barely sensed Lotil and Erix supporting him. Looking around, he blinked, but everything before his eyes slowly faded to black.

* * * * *

Chical, lord of the Eagle Knights, entered Naltecona's presence for once without donning the rude garments normally required of visitors to the great throne room.

This time there was no need to affect a bedraggled appearance. The scars of battle marked the legs, arms, and face of the warrior. His once proud Eagle cloak was a tattered rag. As he advanced toward the throne, he looked so battered that it seemed a miracle he could even walk. Even so, he had flown, in avian form, from Palul to Nexal.

Now his pride sustained him, holding his head high until he knelt before the great *pluma* litter that was Naltecona's throne.

"Rise and speak!" demanded the Revered Counselor.

"Most Revered One, it is disaster! A thousand times worse than we could have feared!"

"Tell me, man!" Naltecona leaped to his feet. His feathered cloak whirled around him as he stalked toward the groveling warrior. "Where is Kalnak?"

"Dead—slain by the first blow of the battle. My lord, they *knew* of the ambush. They were prepared for it and unleashed their own attack before we could act." Weeping, Chical told the tale of the massacre, and Naltecona sank back into his litter. His face grew slack, his eyes vacant, to the point that it seemed he no longer listened.

"Then they summoned killing smoke, a fog that reached its fingers into the hiding places of our men, slaying them even as they breathed. Revered One, we must make immediate preparations if we hope to stand against men like this—if indeed they are men!"

"No, they are not," said Naltecona with a sigh. "It is clear now that they are not men at all."

He stood and paced slowly along his raised dais. The row of courtiers and attendants behind him stared in universal terror and awe at the tear-streaked face of Chical.

"My lord," said the Eagle Knight, standing at last, "allow me to gather all of our warriors. We can hold them at the causeways. We can keep them out of the city."

Naltecona sighed, a portentous sound in the vast throne room. Evening's shadows drew long across the floor while the ruler paced and thought. Finally he stopped and faced Chical.

"No," he said. "There will be no battle at Nexal. I asked the gods to favor us with a victory at Palul, to show that the invaders are indeed mortal men. That sign was not forthcoming.

"The proof is clear," Naltecona concluded. "The strangers are not men but gods. When they reach Nexal, we must greet them with the respect due their station."

"But, my lord—" Chical stepped forward boldly to object. He stopped suddenly, frozen by the look in the Revered Counsellor's eyes.

"This is my decision. Now leave me to my prayers."

* * * * *

DOUGLAS NILES

From the chronicle of Coton:

Painted in the last bleak weeks of the Waning, as the end draws upon us.

I stand mute as I hear the words of Chical, a tale of grim terror about the slaying in Palul. Again Naltecona orders his courtiers from the throne room, asking only me to remain.

Then, tonight, he rants and paces around me. He accuses me of deceit, and he grovels before the looming presence of these strangers. Thoroughly cowed now, he knows no recourse but abject surrender.

For the first time do I curse my vow. How I want to grasp his shoulders, to shout my knowledge into his face, to awaken him from his blind stupor. Curse him! I want to tell him that he opens the gates of the city to disaster, that he paves the road to make way for his own, and his people's, destruction.

But I can say nothing, and at last he slumbers. It is a fitful dozing, for as he sleeps, he dreams and he cries.

♣ 10 ♣
THE BRAND OF ZALTEC

The smooth-carved blocks of stone fit together with precision, all of them touching snugly, supported by the weight of their neighbors to enclose the dome of the observatory. Here, on the highest hill of Tulom-Itzi, Gultec sat with Zochimaloc and spent the long night staring at the stars.

Holes in the dome of the observatory's ceiling allowed views into precisely selected quadrants of the sky. Now the black sky showed no moon, for this was the period of the black moon, when none could see it in the heavens. And consequently, his teacher had pointed out, this was a splendid night for viewing the stars.

"But we know the moon will return. It waxes tomorrow," explained the teacher, stating the obvious fact. "In a week, it will be half of its self, and in the week following that, it will be full.

"Two weeks from now," Zochimaloc continued with grim finality, "and the moon will be full."

"This I know, my teacher," said Gultec, confused. Zochimaloc crossed the stone floor of the observatory, gesturing upward through several holes toward the west.

"And these stars, these wanderers," the old man went on, as if he had not heard Gultec. "These bright stars hold special portents for the world."

The Jaguar Knight felt it inappropriate to announce that this fact, too, was known to him. Instead, he listened as Zochimaloc explained further.

"In fourteen days, when the full moon rises, it will mask the three wanderers. They will disappear behind it but remain unseen from the world."

"What does this mean, Master?" asked Gultec, intrigued by the description.

Zochimaloc shook his head with a wry chuckle. "What does it mean? I know not for certain. The full moon will shine over the world, as always, and great things will happen—things we cannot predict, or perhaps even explain.

"But when next wanes the moon, the True World will not be the same."

* * * * *

Riding quickly throughout the first night after the battle, Poshtli passed countless refugees. These Mazticans stared in awe at the warrior who galloped along the road atop the snorting monster.

He paused to rest a few hours around dawn, but then he thundered back onto the road. He passed into the valley of Nexal by midmorning, and in a few hours, the lathered mare raced across the causeway, carrying him through the streets of the city, into the sacred plaza, to the doors of Naltecona's palace.

Leaving Storm with a pair of terrified slaves, he ordered them to water and feed the horse. Then he quickly made his way through the palace corridors to the doors before the great throne room itself.

Poshtli placed the ritual rags over his shoulders and entered the throne room. He saw his uncle pacing on the dais, his agitation visible in every abrupt gesture, every dark flash of his eyes.

Naltecona gestured Poshtli forward quickly, before the warrior had performed the three floor-scraping bows normally required of visitors to the throne.

"Where have you been?" demanded the Revered Counselor. "I have sent messengers to search for you over the last two days."

"To Palul," the warrior replied. "I have seen the devastation there myself. Now I come to offer my services in the defense of the city. I will fight wherever you want me, though as you know, I no longer carry the rank of Eagle Knight."

Naltecona brushed the explanation aside as if he had not heard. "You must remain by my side now," the counselor directed his nephew. "You, among all my court, have come to know something about these strangers. I will need you with me when they enter the city, which—according to the Eagles who watch their march—will be very soon!"

"*Enter the city?*" Poshtli stood, stunned. "Don't you mean to fight them?"

"What is the point?" asked Naltecona sadly. "They cannot be beaten, and perhaps they should not be. Perhaps they are destined to claim Nexal, to inherit the feathered throne of my ancestors."

Poshtli couldn't believe what he heard. "Uncle, I advise you to fight them before they reach the city! Pull up the bridges, meet them with a thousand canoes full of warriors! True, the invaders are mighty, but they can be killed! They bleed and die as men!"

Naltecona stared at Poshtli, a hint of the old command in his eyes. The younger man pressed his case. "We outnumber them a hundred to one! If we hold the causeways, they cannot reach us here!"

But Naltecona shook his head slowly, looking at Poshtli as a parent regards a child who simply doesn't grasp the subtleties of adult life. He patted his nephew's shoulder, and the young man's spirit cried silently when he saw the look of dejection and defeat lurking deep within his uncle's eyes.

"Please, Poshtli. You stay by my side," said Naltecona.

His heart breaking, the warrior could only nod and obey.

* * * * *

Shatil crept through the darkened streets of Nexal. He limped on raw and bleeding feet, still clutching his gored wrist to his chest. He had run for the full day following the massacre, but his steps had slowed to a walk by nightfall. Now, eight hours later, he shuffled toward the Great Pyramid in the hours between midnight and dawn.

Still holding the parchment, though the rust-colored stain of his blood marred one edge of it, Shatil thought of the message he carried. He had looked at it earlier in the day and was unable to suppress a gasp of astonishment when he unrolled it. The sheet was blank!

Too devoted a priest to question his patriarch's instructions, he had continued his mission. He knew that there were many mysteries of Zaltec he had yet to understand.

His robe and the ritually inflicted scars on his face and arms distinguished him as a priest of Zaltec, so the Jaguar Knights guarding the gate to the sacred plaza allowed him to enter with no questions. He stumbled toward the pyramid, stopping at the small temple building below the looming massif.

This was a square, stone structure, sunk halfway into the ground. It had sleeping and eating quarters for the priests serving at the Great Pyramid, as well as holding cells for the victims of upcoming rituals.

Shatil passed through the low doorway and staggered down the short stairway into the dark main room. In the darkness, he heard a low growl, and he froze. For a moment, he remembered the great war creature of the strangers, wondering if the beast had somehow risen from the dead and found him here. At the same time, he recognized the delusion for what it was, realizing that his wound and journey were taking a terrible toll. Then the tall figure of a Jaguar Knight stepped into the semidarkness near the door.

"What do you want, priest?" he inquired.

"I must see Hoxitl. It is very urgent!" Shatil gasped, slumping backward to lean against the cool stone wall.

"Urgent enough to wake the patriarch from his sleep?" asked the warrior skeptically.

"Yes!" spat Shatil, pushing himself upward to stand straight. He was the equal of the Jaguar in height.

"What is it? Do you bring word from Palul?" The question came from the darkness within the temple, but Shatil recognized the high priest's voice. "The Eagles have already reported that the battle was a disaster."

"Yes, Patriarch," Shatil said, his voice growing stronger. "The high priest Zilti perished in that fight, as did many of our people. So, too, would I have, but Zilti ordered me to flee that I could bring this to you." Shatil held out the parchment, and Hoxitl quickly took it.

"You have done well," said the patriarch. He unrolled the sheet and held it up so that Shatil and the Jaguar Knight could look over his shoulders at the page.

Shatil gasped as he saw a picture take shape there. "That's

the square!" he said, pointing to the feasting multitudes of Mazticans and legionnaires. "This is what it looked like before the battle."

The sheet resembled a fine painting in its detail and complexity and brightness of color. They looked first at the whole plaza, as it might be seen by a soaring bird. Then the images became more precise, and they saw Cordell speaking pleasantly with Chical and Kalnak.

"How can this happen?" Shatil inquired, amazed at the appearance of the picture at all, not to mention its clarity and accuracy.

"The magic of *hishna*," explained Hoxitl brusquely. "The power of the fang and the talon. The recreation of images is one of its greatest strengths. Now be silent."

As they observed the picture, Shatil's amazement turned to shock. The picture began to move. They saw the black-robed wizard speaking to the warrior behind the houses. The scroll made no sound, but the warrior's meaning was clear.

"The traitor!" spat the Jaguar. "He tells the enemy of our ambush!"

"Through sorcery," observed Hoxitl. "See?" They watched the mage and the warrior disappear behind the house, screened from view. Then the picture shifted, and they saw the scene from a different place, with a clear view of the woman and her victim.

The pale woman touched her cloaked hand to his throat in a gesture that seemed almost tender, but then the warrior's back arched and he fell like a log to the ground. He lay there, stiff, turning blue as his eyes nearly popped from his head. Without a backward look, the woman left as soon as it was clear that he was dead.

Then they watched numbly as the battle unfolded, until at last Shatil had to turn his eyes away. It had been enough to live through that horror once.

Hoxitl and the warrior stood for a long time, engrossed by the scene even as they were appalled. When Shatil looked again, the plaza was a smoking ruin, bodies and blood scattered everywhere.

"So it was in Palul," muttered the Jaguar Knight as Hoxitl

finally rolled up the sheet. "But it will not be in Nexal! We can pull up the bridges on the causeways, mass the warriors on the shore. When the strangers come to the valley, we shall see that they never leave!"

"We shall indeed see that they never leave," agreed Hoxitl. "But not in the way you imagine."

"What do you mean?" asked the warrior.

"Naltecona has decreed that the strangers be welcomed to our city as gods. The causeways will not only remain in place, but they also will be decorated with flowers to honor our 'guests.' "

"How can this be?" demanded Shatil, appalled. "They must be stopped before it is too late!"

"Would that our Revered Counselor was as wise as a young priest," said Hoxitl wryly. "But until that time, we must plan and prepare . . . and wait. The cult of the Viperhand grows daily and will be ready to strike when the time comes.

"But come, Shatil, you are injured. You must now have food and rest. Your message has proven most enlightening, and its delivery shall not go unrewarded."

Shatil bowed his head, warmed by the praise from this, the highest-ranking member of his order. "Patriarch, there is but one reward I could ask."

"Speak your wish," urged Hoxitl. Outside, dawn's purple glow had begun to color the sacred plaza.

"With this dawn's sacrifice, I wish to pledge my life and body to Zaltec—to serve him in war as well as in ritual. Please, Patriarch, grant me the brand of the Viperhand," asked Shatil levelly.

"It shall be as you desire—but not this morning. Tonight," came Hoxitl's reply. "You must rest now. Come here." The cleric took Shatil's wounded hand and led him to one of the sleeping cells. By the time they reached it, Shatil saw with amazement that the savage bite had healed.

* * * * *

"Column, forward!" Daggrande barked the command, and the first company of the legion, the crossbowmen, started on the road to Nexal. In moments, companies of sword and spear fell in after them.

Cordell remained behind, mounted on his prancing charger. Darien, riding a sleek black gelding, waited beside him.

Gradually, like a huge snake uncoiling itself from the confines of Palul, the army began to march. Great ranks of Kultakan warriors joined the procession, raising their spears to the captain-general as they passed. He had led them to a victory greater than any in their history against the hated Nexalans. Even Cordell's decree ordering that none of the captives be sacrificed had failed to dim their loyalty.

Dawn had barely purpled the sky when the first legionnaires set out, but the eastern horizon was pale blue by the time the last of the warriors, the Payit, marched out of the town. These men had played little role in the previous day's fighting, and Cordell sensed that their pride was stung a bit when they saw the great success of the Kultakans. The Payit would be doughty fighters, thought the captain-general—if he needed them.

"The city is well protected by its lakes," explained Darien as Cordell and the elfmage started out, riding through the fields beside the great marching file. "What is your plan of attack?"

Cordell smiled, a narrowing of his already thin mouth. "I don't think an attack will be necessary," he replied. He sensed Darien's surprise in the sudden tilt of her head, but she said nothing.

"I am making a guess about our prospective foe, the great Naltecona," Cordell explained. He was pleased with his deduction, and he thought it sound, but he desired Darien's confirmation of his judgment, so he continued. "I'm guessing that he is very much awed by us now. I shall not be surprised if we are welcomed into his city as guests."

Darien's smile was as tight as the man's. "I hope you're right. It is a gamble."

"So is this march today," countered Cordell. "I know the men need rest, but look at them."

He gestured at the troops, Maztican and legionnaire, that they passed. All the men held their heads high—and marched with a quick, firm step. Many saluted the captain-general as he rode by.

Indeed, the army marched swiftly. Before too many hours had passed, they saw the looming bulk of the twin volcanoes, Zatal and Popol, rising from the horizon ahead. Between them lay the pass leading to Nexal.

Cordell's pulse quickened as the road carried them to they cooler heights. He thrilled to a sense of epic momentum as the approached the pass.

He knew that his destiny lay beyond.

* * * * *

The wound began to fester on the first night, and the next morning Halloran did not awaken. Fever pressed its fiery clasp around him as he lay senseless, unable to eat or drink or speak. Throughout that long day, his temperature climbed and sweat burst from his every pore.

Occasionally, in cruel mockery of the fever, chills wracked Hal's body and convulsions threw him about the straw mat like a child's toy, shaken hard by its owner. Delirium claimed him by evening, and he grunted and cursed through the night.

Erixitl remained by his side, trying to keep him cool, trying to cleanse the infection that seeped from his wound. His mutterings recalled past battles as he spoke of blood and smoke without an apparent pattern.

Just once, when his back arched and his body grew rigid, he uttered a cry like a lost youth. "Erix! My love! Please!" His voice choked, spitting garbled syllables. Then he formed words again: "By Helm, I love you!"

His eyes flashed open, unseeing, and then he collapsed limply on the bed. He seemed to rest for a few minutes before the sickness wracked him again.

By the second dawn, his breath came in rasping bursts, sometimes seeming to cease altogether. His pulse became too faint for detection even by Lotil's sensitive touch.

As the sun climbed all that morning, so did the fever. At high noon, the hot sun blazed against the whitewashed house, though the loose thatch of the roof shielded some of the heat. Within, Hal writhed and Erix administered cool, sponging baths. The water all but sizzled, she thought, as she touched it to his skin.

But as the sun sank and the cool evening breezes arose, the heat wracking Hal's body slowly dissipated. By sunset of the second day, he slept comfortably, even waking once to smile faintly at Erix and gently squeeze her hand.

He was going to live, she knew.

He would live, and he loved her. Unimaginable relief flooded through her at his recovery, and a strange warmth gripped her at the knowledge of his love. Releasing her caged emotions at last, she held him as he slept, rejoicing in the steady, strong rise and fall of his chest beneath her head.

And she knew that she loved him in return.

* * * * *

Shatil joined the other initiates in climbing the steep stairs to the top of the Great Pyramid. A sense of deepest reverence gripped him as he looked below to see the priests leading the file of captives. Each would give his life and his heart for one of the initiates into the cult.

The captives were mostly Kultakans, among the few prisoners taken by the Nexalan warriors outside Palul. Not knowing of Cordell's edict, of course, Shatil assumed that the hundreds of Nexalans taken prisoners there faced a similar fate upon Kultakan altars.

At the top, he looked to the east. High up the slope of the valley, in the saddle between the two great volcanoes, he could see the glittering fires of the legion's camp. They would reach the city tomorrow—and Naltecona would admit them as his guests.

"Kneel!" Hoxitl barked the command as Shatil, first of the initiates, stepped forward.

Shatil knelt, anticipation tingling through his body as Hoxitl sliced open the chest of a captive and pulled forth the slick, bloody heart. The high priest held the flesh toward the setting sun, then tossed it into the heart of the statue.

Turning toward the kneeling figure of Shatil, Hoxitl extended his hand, then paused. Blood dripped unnoticed from his fingers as he fixed Shatil with a penetrating stare.

All the young priest's past failings, he felt, were bared to that gaze.

But so, too, was his passionate devotion to Zaltec, and this was the knowledge Hoxitl sought.

"With this brand, your life belongs to Zaltec, everlasting master of night and war. Your blood, your heart, your very soul itself are his, to be spent as he desires, in the furtherance of his almighty name!"

"I understand and accept," Shatil intoned. He lifted his head and bared his teeth, preparing for the touch of Hoxitl's hand.

"Through this sign, let the might of Zaltec protect you! May it harden your skin, proof against the silver weapons of the enemy. May it sharpen your eye and quicken your wit, that when the killing begins, you shall neither falter nor fail!"

Joy surged through Shatil's body. He was ready now for the brand.

But in truth, nothing could prepare him for the searing agony that hissed into his skin, crackling like lightning through every nerve and fiber of his body. He stiffened reflexively but didn't cry out. Clenching his teeth, Shatil felt sweat break out across his face, trickling unhindered across his skin and onto the ground. Still he kept silent, grimacing. The leering face of the high priest filled Shatil's vision as Hoxitl leaned over him.

The stench of burned flesh wafted upward from the wound, and finally the patriarch pulled his hand away. Shatil swayed drunkenly, but then he felt a new, tingling sense of might surge through his body. He sprang to his feet, the brand still smoking on his chest.

Energy thrummed through his body. A fire blazed hot in his heart, and Shatil knew that he was ready to kill or die for Zaltec. He felt invincible. Numbly, striving to contain his exultation, he stepped to the side and watched.

One by one, a file of a dozen aspirants went through the ritual after Shatil. Several of these were Jaguar Knights, and a pair were priests of Zaltec, but most were common spearmen.

One of the spearmen cried out when the brand was applied, and the apprentices immediately lifted him to the altar, where Hoxitl tore out his heart and offered it to the statue in penance for the man's lack of faith. The remaining initiates accepted the brand, like Shatil, with the silence and stoicism of true fanatics.

At last they all stood in a row before Hoxitl. The high priest addressed them while the apprentices tossed the bodies of the ritual's victims down the back of the pyramid.

"You are brave, true men, and members of a sacred order—the cult of the Viperhand. Our purpose is the destruction of the strangers from across the sea, who threaten not only our land, but also our very gods themselves!" The priest paused, fixing each of them with his passionate gaze.

"Now I must command you to do a very difficult thing, in the name of Zaltec. I must order you to wait! Our numbers grow nightly, and soon we will have the forces we need to overwhelm them. Tomorrow they enter the city, and soon you will receive the command to attack!

"Until then, you must avoid the strangers. If you go near them, the power of Zaltec may compel you to kill!

"But I promise you this: When the time for action arrives, we shall strike, and strike quickly. There will be killing aplenty for each of you.

"And Zaltec will eat well."

* * * * *

At dawn the legion marched, ready for war but hoping for peace. The horsemen, lances ready, trotted in the lead, riding forward and back through the fields to either side of the road. The companies of sword and crossbow marched in loose ranks, ready for speedy deployment. The Kultakans and Payit warriors extended in an elongated column that trailed into the distance behind Cordell's veterans.

Below them lay the great city in its green and fertile valley. The four lakes sparkled in the rising sun, and the lush fields bore crops approaching the fullness of harvest.

And they knew that, at least for now, it would be peace, not war. The road was clear all the way onto a wide causeway that crossed the lake, straight into the city.

Douglas Niles

Leading his column, Cordell caught his breath at the grandeur of Nexal. Its buildings, great and small, gleamed in the sunlight. Among the whiteness of these structures, he saw bedazzling flashes of color from gardens and markets.

"Will the wonders of Helm never cease," murmured the Bishou as he and Darien rode up beside the commander. "Who would have thought these pagan savages could have built a place like this?"

Cordell's awed silence served as ample answer.

"They prepare to welcome us," observed Darien.

Indeed, as the legion quickened its pace into the valley, they saw feathered emissaries waiting for them before the causeway. A cool breeze eased the heat of the march, and the wonders arrayed before them gave the march an eager air of anticipation.

Soon the advance guard of horsemen reached the lakeshore, and by that time, they discerned additional details: The causeway had been strewn with flowers; a great crowd lined the streets of the city; and the emissaries were accompanied by finely wrapped bundles, indicating that Naltecona had sent yet more presents.

When they had reached the shore, they recieved the final proof of welcome. Cordell halted before the emissaries, but didn't dismount. His black eyes locked in a hard stare down the length of the causeway.

He guessed, correctly, that Naltecona came to greet him.

The Revered Counselor of Nexal, lordly master of the Heart of the True World, rode upon a feathered litter that hovered several feet off the ground like a soft, plump mattress. A canopy of *pluma* swung gently over his head, suspended magically to provide Naltecona with shade.

Before him came a procession of richly robed courtiers, spreading additional flowers on the causeway so that that his litter floated over a solid surface of blossoms. Behind the litter came several beautiful maidens, waving great fans over the counselor's head.

The litter floated along the causeway toward Cordell. Behind Naltecona came still more feathered, caped, and colorfully dressed Mazticans, bearing additional bundles of gifts. Nexalans lined both edges of the causeway and prostrated themselves, pressing their faces to the stones as their ruler floated past.

Halting several dozen paces from Cordell, the litter lowered to the ground and adjusted its form so that Naltecona rose smoothly to his feet, through no apparent effort of his own. The ruler stood tall and walked with immense dignity. A towering crown of emerald feathers waved high over his head. A brilliant framework of plumage accentuated and exaggerated the breadth of his shoulders. His handsome face was split by a sharp, aquiline nose, and his eyes observed with intelligence and curiosity, and perhaps a little awe.

Now Cordell dismounted, carefully walking forward so that the two men met exactly halfway between their different conveyances. Several steps behind him, the petite figure of Darien, heavily cloaked against the bright sun, followed to translate.

"My great captain-general," began Naltecona, "I welcome you and your men to my city. I invite you into my father's palace, there to stay as my honored guests."

After Darien translated, Cordell smiled smoothly, offering a slight bow. "This is an invitation I am grateful to receive," he replied. "Our reception to other places in Maztica has not always been so pleasant."

"We greet you with open hands," said Naltecona guilelessly. "But I must ask that your allies—our ancient enemies, the Kultakans—remain encamped on the shore of the lake and do not cross to our island."

"They will accompany us to the city," said Cordell, leveling his black eyes on the Revered Counselor.

"But there is insufficient room in the city," continued the Maztican lord. "And it will be difficult to persuade my people to—"

"They can sleep in the streets if they have to," interrupted the commander, "but the Kultakans enter the city with us."

"Very well." Naltecona dipped his head slightly in involuntary aquiescence.

In another minute, the Golden Legion started across the causeway. Silent, staring crowds of Mazticans stood along the path but gave them plenty of room. Canoes filled the lakes to either side of the roadway. Ahead of the legion loomed the fabulous, exotic city of Nexal, the Heart of the True World.

* * * * *

From the chronicles of Coton:

Before a tangled array of godhood, man awaits his fate.

The followers of Helm enter Nexal, and with them comes their powerful god. Zaltec seethes in resentment, and between the two immortal beings are sown the seeds of terror and confusion.

I feel the presence of the strangers all through the city. Their great beasts have been tethered beyond my temple door. Their stench is everywhere, and their hunger for gold is a palpable thing, a kind of hunger I have never felt before.

But even as the strangers hunger for gold, so does the cult of the Viperhand hunger for war. They have been restrained by the will of Naltecona, though this is a tenuous bond.

It will require but little pressure for the invaders to snap them free.

♣ 11 ♣

A MARRIAGE IN THE SIGHT OF QOTAL

"This was the palace of my father, Axalt," explained Naltecona, ushering Cordell and Darien through a huge doorway into a long, airy corridor. Poshtli followed, uncomfortable and uncertain in his new role as adviser to the counselor. The colorful finery of court hung awkwardly on his shoulders, and he wished for the simple comfort of his Eagle cloak.

But that, of course, he could never wear again.

Naltecona continued. "Now it would honor me if you would make it your home."

The palace, nearly as grand as Naltecona's own, was another of the great buildings in the sacred plaza. The Kultakan and Payit ranks of Cordell's army made camp in the plaza, watched by tense, nervous Nexalan warriors. The legionnaires, however, would occupy this huge edifice.

"You show us a grand welcome," observed Cordell, through Darien as usual. The elfwoman now wore a scarlet silken tunic instead of her robe. The white skin of her legs and arms stood in stark contrast to the material, and a ruby-encrusted hairpin gave a burst of color to her long white hair. She was very beautiful, in an icy and aloof way, thought Poshtli.

"I must disbelieve the tales I have heard—lies, doubtlessly—that it was you who ordered the legion attacked in Palul." Cordell paused to gauge the Revered Counselor's answer.

"Yes, lies," said Naltecona with a downward look. "The chiefs who would practice such treachery will certainly be punished!"

"I believe that they already have been," noted Cordell dryly. "I only hope that their numbers do not grow again, for our reprisals must, at that instance, become truly harsh."

"You have my word on it," replied the Revered Counselor of Nexal.

"Very well." For a while, they talked pleasantries, as Cordell found himself expressing genuine astonishment and delight at the wonders of Axalt's palace. They walked through huge gardens with pleasant, meandering paths, fountains and pools, and brilliant-flowered plants and bushes.

Huge rooms seemed to be nothing more than airy galleries, with splendid tapestries, featherpictures, and paintings on the walls. Other walls were lined with niches, and in these stood small statues of jade and obsidian.

Finally they came to a chamber holding many objects of gold. As they entered, several full-size replicas of human heads, each heavier than a man could lift, stared from niches along the wall.

"The likenesses of the Revered Counselors of Nexal," explained Naltecona. "It is a line that goes back through fifteen men, all of them members of my family."

Poshtli watched Darien's and Cordell's eyes as they walked along the gold-lined wall. The elfwoman's were cold, unaffected by the riches. But Cordell's dark eyes flashed, washing over the golden objects with a lust that the warrior could almost feel.

"It is a grand tradition," said Cordell. "I want to assure you that we have no intention of bringing it to an end."

Naltecona paused and looked at the captain-general after Darien translated this statement. The two men found each others' eyes inscrutable.

"And now I must speak frankly," said Cordell. "I do so, knowing you will see and understand."

As he spoke, he raised his arms and stepped forward, blocking Darien. As soon as she translated his words, she added a quiet phrase of her own, an enchantment, as she cast the spell upon Cordell himself.

Naltecona gasped and stepped backward, awestruck as the captain-general began to grow. Poshtli reached reflexively for his *maca*, forgetting that he was unarmed. He stared in awe, unaware of Darien's spell. Cordell's body, and his clothing and sword, began to increase in size until he quickly attained a height of some twelve feet. His head almost touching the inside of the thatched roof, the commander planted his fists on his hips and stared down at Naltecona.

The Revered Counselor took another backward step, but then stood firm, fighting an almost overwhelming compulsion to flee.

"You are a great man, Naltecona of Nexal," said Cordell, his voice a deep rumble. "But so, you must understand, am I. Let this little demonstration convince you of that."

"Indeed, so it does," whispered the Maztican. As Naltecona and Poshtli stared at Cordell, Darien slipped off to the side. She quickly and silently cast a spell upon the section of wall between two of the golden busts. This time, however, Poshtli observed the gesture. When Cordell spoke again, Darien picked up the translation smoothly, while Poshtli stared at the wall and wondered.

"Know, too, that any treacheries planned against us will be found out! We will learn of such acts through ways you cannot possibly imagine." Cordell turned, addressing the section of wall Darien had worked her magic on moments earlier. "Is this not so?"

The surface of the wall distorted and stretched for a moment, then revealed the clear outline of a giant human mouth. The lips and teeth and tongue were pale, like the wall, but their shape was unmistakable.

Then the mouth spoke. "Indeed, Master, it is so."

Naltecona shook his head in shock while Poshtli narrowed his eyes. Sorcery or not, the warrior knew that surprise would be difficult to attain if his enemy could gain information from the very walls themselves. When he turned back to face the looming commander, the Revered Counselor was in no mood to offer, or order, resistance. "We shall be true to our obligations as your hosts," he pledged.

"Excellent!" A whispered word from Darien, unheard by Naltecona, brought Cordell quickly back to his normal size. Poshtli saw this command as well. "And your hospitality, my lord, is most overwhelming. Such quarters as these surpass our wildest expectations. In truth, we are your humble guests."

A conch-shell horn sounded in the distance, announcing the start of the evening's sacrificial procession.

"You must excuse me," said Naltecona, with a deep bow. "My presence is required at the evening services."

"For the murder of helpless captives?" barked Cordell, knowing all too well the nature of these rituals. "Suppose a greater force compelled you to order that these pagan rites cease?"

Naltecona looked at him with a hint of regret in his eyes. "Should I give such an order, my people would fear that the sun would fail to rise in the morning. My influence over them would cease at that time, for they would know that I was mad.

"It would mean that a new Revered Counselor would take my throne. The rites, of course, would continue."

For a moment longer, Cordell glared at the Revered Counselor, tempted to challenge him on the issue. Something in the Maztican's level gaze convinced him that Naltecona spoke the truth, however. And the practice of sacrifice was far from their most pressing concern, he reminded himself, with a look at the gleaming wall of gold.

"Make yourselves comfortable here. Of course, slaves have been appointed for your use. There will be sufficient room for your men, I trust?"

"Yes, plenty. The Kultakans and Payit will camp outside the palace in that big square," Cordell said breezily.

"I need tell you again that the presence of our enemies among us, camping in the sacred heart of our city, is an affront to all Nexal. The people resent them and will quickly grow restless with restraint." Naltecona repeated the arguments he had made when Cordell's allies had first entered the city.

"We'll keep our eyes on the situation," promised the general. "But for now, they stay."

"As you command," replied the lord and master of Nexal.

* * * * *

Halloran recovered swiftly after his fever broke, though his wound remained a painful reminder of the battle. Still weak, he slept much. He also enjoyed the hot mayzcakes, beans, and fruits that Erixitl brought to him in a steady stream, at least while he remained awake.

Most of his sustenance came from the beans and mayz, though she prepared these with a variety of spices that made each meal a new and exciting experience. He even found himself enjoying the hot burn of the sharp peppers with which she laced his food. And the thin, spiced chocolate she gave him to drink was a rare treat.

They spoke little of the past, or the future. For a while, it seemed enough that they could be together. Indeed, it would be days before Hal's wound healed enough to allow them to think about much else. Although he could rest with little pain, the puncture became very sore when he moved around.

If his waking hours passed pleasantly enough, the same was not so with his sleep. He had vivid, terrifying dreams of the massacre and sometimes awoke tense with fear over Erix's safety. But these concerns he kept to himself.

One dark night he awakened after such a dream, sweating from an image of Erix run down by a charging line of lancers, led by Halloran himself. Hal lay still, staring at the thatched roof of the house, and gradually his terror passed.

Erixitl, he saw, was not in the house. He rose, noticing with mild pleasure that his wound was giving him less pain with each passing day.

"I couldn't sleep," he said, emerging from the house to find Erixitl in the yard. The moon was a half-circle in the east, rising high in the clear, star-speckled sky. A few hours remained before dawn.

The woman sat on the ground, her legs crossed, leaning back on her hands with her eyes skyward. "It's so beautiful up there," she said. "So crisp and clear."

Halloran settled beside her silently. He, too, looked at the night sky and saw its beauty.

"There's the ridge," Erixitl said, lowering her eyes from the heavens slightly. The great shadow of the high slope loomed over them. "It was up there that I was captured and taken into slavery." She turned to look at him. "I haven't gone back up there since I've come home. It's silly, I guess, but I'm frightened."

"You have good cause," offered Hal. He pictured Erix as a young girl, seized by a jaguar-skinned warrior who emerged from the bushes to take her and flee. "Anyone would want to forget." He thought of the battered town in the valley below, and of how much he wanted to forget that.

She looked at him oddly. Suddenly she rose to her feet. Halloran followed her example, also following as she crossed the yard. When she started up the steep slope, he came after, on a narrow trail that they followed without difficulty in the moonlight.

For some time, they climbed in silence. The house, the village, the valley bottom all dropped away behind them. Even the scent of smoke and ash and blood from ruined Palul dissipated with distance. The wind freshened up here, and it was comfortably cool against their skin. It washed around them and seemed to cleanse some of the horror away. Still, Halloran felt the lingering presence of death behind them.

They reached the top and stopped. Erix pointed out the narrow draw where the Kultakan warrior had captured her. She explained that her father's bird snares had, at that time, extended all along the upper slopes of the ridge. Then her eyes drifted upward again.

"It seems almost as if you can touch them," she said. The stars blinked in a great dome around them. The faint illumination of dawn streaked the eastern horizon, promising eventual sunrise. "I wish the sun would wait awhile before he rises . . . just today."

"If I could stop it—him—for you, I would," Hal said. He wanted to tell her that he would do anything she asked. Again the mental pictures of the slaughter at Palul came to him, and he could no longer remain mute. "When I feared that you'd be caught in the battle, my terror was worse than any I have ever known."

She smiled and took his hands. "I think that I knew you'd come for me," she said softly.

"Your father spoke of us together. Shadows and light, he said. What does it mean?"

"Perhaps he means the colors of our skins," she laughed. With the sound of her laughter, Hal knew that he could never again let her go.

"Erixitl, do you know that I . . . I love you?" Hal asked, his voice taut. He feared to look at her face as he spoke.

"Yes, I know," she said. Her brown eyes were wide, and he wanted to fall into them as she looked up at him.

"Do . . . do you . . ." His voice caught. In answer, she reached her hands up around his shoulders, pulling his head down to hers. Halloran crushed his lips to her, and she drew them together with fiery strength. They remained in this embrace for a long time, clinging to each other for love, and strength, and hope. For these moments, Hal was aware only of this warm, loving woman in his arms.

But then the visions of treachery and slaughter returned. Halloran broke away with a tortured groan. "I can't get the pictures out of my mind!" He clasped his hands to his eyes, rubbing them savagely, but still he saw the blood and the death and the crying.

"We can't forget the killing," said Erix. Her voice was thick and her eyes filled with tears. "But neither can we deny our own life."

When her dress fell to the ground, Erixitl's skin glowed in the moonlight with a brilliant copper sheen. Her beauty, and his love for her, drove every other image from Halloran's mind.

* * * * *

"The time draws close," hissed the Ancestor, "and our plan hangs by a thread that can be sliced off by the life of a young woman!" Unprecedented passion blazed in his words.

"I repeat to you all: She must be killed!" The Darkfyre surged upward with his command, swelling around the dark-robed drow gathered in the heart of the Highcave. The seething caldron shook with a deep resonance that caused the very heart of the mountain to rumble. Red coals flared and waned, and the infernal crimson glow rose and fell in a steady pulse.

"The invaders have entered Nexal. The stage is set for Naltecona's death and the cult's preeminence. All our plans, our centuries of preparations, stand in danger because this woman lives!"

The Ancestor trembled, so palpable was his rage. And with him trembled the bedrock of the Highcave.

"She will return to Nexal now—she must. And there we will find her. Alert all the priests, but that is not enough. The bungling of those human clerics has become all too apparent.

"This time, we will go ourselves." The drow around him stood still, in shock. "Yes, my children. We can no longer remain in the sanctity and solitude of our lair. We will enter the city by night and search it from end to end if we must!"

* * * * *

Under Cordell's orders, legionnaires had assembled beams and planks to make tables and benches in the palace. Now Bishou Domincus and Captain Alvarro enjoyed the luxury of a fine meal, served by pretty Maztican slave girls. With a satisifed smacking of lips, the cleric savored the succulent leg of a turkey. The greasy bones of the second leg and a thigh lay on the crude table beside him.

Alvarro cast a sideways glance at the Bishou, noting that they were alone except for the slaves. Kardann had eaten with them, but the assessor had left, declaring his intention to explore the palace that now served as the legion's barracks.

"Halloran was there at Palul," grunted the red-bearded captain of horse.

The Bishou stiffened. "You saw him?" The cleric's brows darkened grimly.

Alvarro nodded.

"And he escaped? He lives?"

The captain cursed and lied. "He fought beside a hundred of those savage warriors. I was alone, except for Vane. We could do nothing!"

"But Cordell—surely you told him!"

Alvarro related the tale of the captain-general's indifference, while the Bishou seethed.

"My daughter's death will not be avenged as long as Halloran lives!" growled Domincus. The fact that Halloran had been powerless to prevent Martine's sacrifice meant nothing to the cleric; the man had been forever branded as one with the savages in his mind.

Suddenly the pudgy form of the assessor burst through the door. His face was flushed with excitement. "Come here—come this way!" Kardann cried.

"What is it, man?" demanded the Bishou, reluctant to leave his repast. Alvarro rose, however, and so the cleric followed.

The assessor from Amn led Bishou Domincus and Captain Alvarro down one of the long corridors in the palace. "It's in here!" Kardan gasped excitedly.

The two men followed him into a small room with multiple columns around its periphery, and many colorful frescoes depicting the mountains and fertile land surrounding the lake and the city. It looked like a passageway, except that the far end was merely a blank wall, not an entrance or hallway.

"Look! I don't know what it is, but it's got to be *something*. Look at this!" Barely containing his excitement, the pudgy assessor held up his lantern and gestured toward the wall at the back of the room.

"What is it?" snapped the Bishou irritably. "You pulled me away from a good meal, dragged me halfway across the palace—"

"Me, too," grumbled Alvarro. "And now we hear that you don't even know what you've found! Couldn't it wait till after dinner?"

But now Bishou Domincus leaned close to the wall, intrigued. Alvarro ceased complaining long enough to investigate whatever it was that had captured the cleric's attention.

"There's definitely some kind of a doorway here," said Domincus, stepping closer to the wall. "Look, here's a crack where you can see the top of it—and here, these are the sides. It's a secret door!"

The Bishou turned to Kardann. "Let's see if we can get it open. There's got to be a catch, a release or something, around here somewhere."

"Look." Alvarro had his dagger out and probed along the

base of the concealed door. He found a slot in the floor, less than a half-inch wide, and the horseman inserted the tip of his weapon there.

They heard a sharp click as Alvarro pressed down with the sword. "Push," he impatiently told the others.

Kardann and the Bishou leaned against the outline of the door and felt the portal swing easily inward. "Quick—get the lamp!" urged the assessor.

As the yellow beams of light spread across the large secret chamber, all three men gasped in astonishment. Alvarro raised the lamp high and stepped into the room, closely followed by the other two.

"It's unbelievable!" whispered the Bishou, staring around in shock.

The others, awestruck, didn't answer. They advanced slowly, stumbling over objects on the floor, stunned. Staring across the expanse of the large room, fully lit by Kardann's lantern, they saw mounds of gold around them. Golden shields, plates and bowls of the metal, box after box filled with dust of purest gold, all of these things scattered across the floor, piled high, and extending from wall to wall.

Around them they saw a fortune in gold, one that put all of their previous treasures to shame.

* * * * *

"You are man and wife, now, in the presence of the god," said Lotil as Halloran and Erix entered the house after daybreak.

The pair stopped in surprise. The old man chuckled and urged them to continue inside.

"If that is the custom of your people, so be it," said Halloran, placing his arms around Erixitl. His reaction surprised even himself with its total conviction, but he realized that a lifetime with Erixitl was the natural extension of the love they shared. "I want you to be my wife—*are* you?"

"Do you make this pledge for our lifetimes?" she asked.

"Yes."

"And I do, as well," replied Erix. "But it is *not* the custom of our people. Why do you say that we are already married, Father?"

"This is not a matter of custom, not the custom of our people nor of any people. It is a matter of destiny. It is in the light and the dark that you see, the light and dark that you *are*.

"Don't you see what has come together in the two of you?" asked Lotil. "Even I, blind as a stone, can tell. This man comes across the great ocean, and then departs his comrades. You are taken from your home into slavery, and led across the True World so that you will be there when he lands!

"Then—" Lotil paused to laugh, ready to lay the clinching seal on his arguments "—then comes the couatl, harbinger of Qotal, and he gives you the gift of the strangers' tongue. Now you come here, to Nexal, where you see not only the shadows of impending disaster, but also the light of potential hope. It is right that the two of you face this light and darkness together, for that is how you can both be truly strong."

"You are right," Erix said softly, taking Hal's hand.

"Now come inside. We must talk." Lotil ushered them to the mats by the kitchen hearth. They sat, and he presented them each with cups of hot, spicy cocoa and mayzcakes wrapped around cooked eggs.

"Man and wife in the presence of *the* god, you said." Halloran raised one eyebrow in question as Lotil sat beside them. "You mean Qotal?"

"Yes, the Plumed One, of course," replied the old man. "The one true god who offers any hope of survival in this age of chaos and doom."

"Yes, I've heard of Qotal. But Erixitl tells me that he left Maztica centuries ago. Even his clerics are bound to silence."

"But do not forget that Qotal promised to return. There were to be several harbingers of his return, and one of them has already occurred."

Erixitl nodded. "True. We saw a couatl. I know that the feathered snake is supposed to be the first sign."

"No one knows about the others, of course," Lotil explained to both of them. "Something about a Cloak of One Plume and the Ice of Summer. Imagine! A feather large enough to make a cloak. Or water, frozen beneath the hot summer sun . . . or moon. But the couatl, that is indeed something.

"And as to you, my son," Lotil continued with true affection, turning to Halloran. "There is, of course, the matter of the dowry."

Hal watched curiously as Lotil got up and went to a box in the corner of his house. He reached inside and began to rummage about.

Halloran looked back at Erixitl and caught her smiling at him. His wife! It began to dawn on him that his wish was coming true. He remembered the promise he had made to himself—that he would never again allow her to be apart from him, and felt only joy at the prospect of its fulfillment.

Erixitl reached out and took his hand, and in the glow of her face, he saw all the hope he needed. The questions of their future, he resolved, would be answered as they were asked.

"Here," said Lotil, returning to the hearthside at last. In his hand he held a pair of small feathered rings. "Hold out your hands."

Halloran did as he was told, and Lotil slid the rings over his hands. They fit, snugly and comfortably, on his wrists. The feathers were tiny tufts of plumage, and the surface of the rings lay smooth against his skin.

"Use them well. They may not look like much, but I think that you will . . . appreciate them." Lotil patted Hal's shoulder affectionately.

"Thank you—thank you very much," he replied sincerely. "But use them *how?* What do they do?"

"In good time, my son, in good time. But now we must celebrate!"

They feasted on one of the ducks that had lived—to no purpose, Hal had thought until now—around the house. Lotil even produced a jug of *octal* he had been saving for some such occasion. As they ate and drank, Halloran and Erix felt a warm sense of well-being. It permeated the air in the room, their conversation, even their bodies themselves.

The armies of Nexal and the legion remained far away. That city, with its sacrifices, its cult of violence, its strident tensions, didn't enter their minds.

Only once, when Erixitl looked at the door, outlined in clear daylight, did she see the shadows lingering.

* * * * *

"It's every bit as fabulous as you claimed," admitted Cordell, clapping Kardann on the shoulder. "This, my good assessor, is a very important discovery!"

Several legionnaires sorted and stacked objects of gold or other treasures in neat piles as the assessor busily inspected the contents of the room. "Millions of pieces, equivalent," he murmured in awe. "The only question is how many millions!"

Cordell watched in amazement as tiny golden figurines were added to a steadily growing pile. Each was no more than the size of a man's hand. They depicted a variety of objects, including male and female humans and grotesque figures that seemed to represent some form of bestial deity.

"And look at this!" exclaimed Kardann. He gestured to a row of large golden bowls. Each of them held a mound of gold dust that reached nearly to the rim. There were a dozen or more of these bowls assembled already, and much of the room remained to be explored.

Cordell, the Bishou, and the assessor supervised the half-dozen legionnaires working to sort the treasures in the room. Several oil lamps illuminated the chamber thoroughly. Another pair of legionnaires stood on guard at the door to the treasure room.

A shrill scream suddenly turned them all toward the door. There they saw a flash of spotted hide and the sharp chop of a weapon—a stone-edged *maca*. One of the guards cried out in pain, and then the orange and black figure sprang through the door into the room.

Kardann shrieked in panic and darted away from the door. Cordell stood firm, drawing his sword and confronting the onrushing Jaguar Knight. The man's face, visible through his gaping-jawed helmet, contorted with hatred.

But then Cordell struck, at the same time as the remaining guard followed the attacker through the door. Transfixed by two thrusts, the Jaguar Knight gasped and fell. Kicking reflexively, he rolled onto his back, fixing them with a hate-filled stare for a few long moments before he died. The experience left them all shaken and not a little alarmed.

"Wh—where did he come from?" babbled Kardann.

"Must be some kind of renegade, hiding out in the palace," the Bishou suggested. "I've warned you, these treacherous savages cannot be trusted!"

Cordell barely heard them. Instead, he knelt down and examined the knight. He felt a vague discomfort, stirred by the expression on the man's face. Never had he seen such fanatical hatred, such an unreasoning bloodlust, in a human face before.

As he pulled the corpse around, the jaguar-skin armor peeled off its chest. "What's this?" he asked, feeling a dull horror.

The man bore a brand on his chest. Scarlet red, angular in shape, it resembled the head of a deadly viper.

Cordell stood and looked at the men around him. "This kind of thing cannot be tolerated. We must teach Naltecona that we are truly a force to be reckoned with." He clapped his fist into his palm, lowering his voice to a whisper.

"It is time for stronger measures!" he growled.

* * * * *

From the chronicles of Coton:

Amid visions of enclosing darkness . . .

The couatl returns to haunt my dreams. The feathered serpent wings about my world, but only where no one else can see. Perhaps the harbinger of hope is a mere delusion, teasing me with anticipation promised, fulfillment denied.

But I must seize that hope, for otherwise all is despair around me. The growing image of the spider goddess, Lolth, draws near. Zaltec, in his arrogance, pays no heed. Indeed, he grows mightier each day.

His priests, spreading the cult of the Viperhand, now provide a mountainous feast of hearts each night as more and more initiates are branded. Zaltec slakes his hunger, while his faithful plot the release of his power against the strangers.

And these men of the Golden Legion—now they dwell within the walls of the sacred plaza itself. Somehow the priests have held the cult away, but the seething hatred of the branded ones builds in pressure, and soon it will burst.

The power of that eruption, coupled with the might of the invaders—as they have shown against Kultaka and Palul—will lead to an explosion from which the city cannot survive.

☙ 12 ❧

EMPIRE IN CHAINS

Naltecona awakened suddenly, blinking in the alien light of a brightly glowing oil lamp. "What is the meaning of this intrusion?" he demanded loudly, sitting up in outrage and surprise.

Squinting into the hot glare, he saw Cordell, Darien, the Bishou, and a half-dozen legionnaires. The men-at-arms brandished longswords, several of the blades bloody. In the room beyond his sleeping chamber, Naltecona saw the still, bleeding figures of his personal slaves.

"We have been attacked in the rooms you gave us!" accused Cordell. "By one of your Jaguar Warriors."

"He acted in disobedience of my orders," objected Naltecona, rising to confront the captain-general.

"That may be, and it may not be. In any event, we must take steps to insure our security. This type of occurrence cannot be tolerated!"

"Your presence in our city is difficult for some of my people to tolerate!"

"We are here as your guests, and our safety is your responsibility. Since you have failed to provide that safety, we shall takes steps of our own!"

"Wait!" The Revered Counselor held up his hand. He was more puzzled than frightened; he even forgot his outrage against this intrusion in his efforts to analyze the problem. "This warrior . . . did you happen to note if he bore the brand of the Viperhand on his chest?"

"So that's what that red . . . Yes, he did," Cordell replied. "What does that mean?"

"They are a legion of priests and warriors," explained the counselor. "They have all taken a vow to defend the name of Zaltec to the last. They seem to interpret that as resisting your forces. I have forbidden this resistance, but there must still be uncontrolled fanatics. I apologize for the breach of faith."

"This will take more than an apology," said Cordell softly, almost with regret.

"What do you mean?" Naltecona drew himself to his full height, showing no trace of fear. "Have you decided to slay me?"

"No," said Cordell. "That would do neither of us any good. Instead, you will gather your personal belongings and move in with us, into the palace of Axalt." Cordell kept his voice level, staring Naltecona in the eyes, as he concluded. "There you will remain as our prisoner."

* * * * *

"What's going on?" demanded Poshtli, trotting through the open doors to the throne room several hours after dawn. The dais was vacant, but he saw a number of spearmen arguing in a small group across the room. Striding over to the warriors, Poshtli commanded their attention with his presence.

"Naltecona has gone to the palace of Axalt to stay with the strangers," said one tall spearman.

"Of his own will?" asked Poshtli, astounded.

"It would seem not," continued the warrior. "His chamber slaves were slain."

"We must rescue him—or die trying!" growled Poshtli. Another thought occurred to him. "The strangers have signed their own death warrants with this outrage!"

"Perhaps, but perhaps not," said the warrior, shaking his head. "Chical was ready to lead a group of warriors after him when Naltecona himself appeared on the roof of Axalt's palace, commanding Chical and his warriors to return to their lodge."

Poshtli stared in disbelief for a moment, then spun on his heel. He raced from the throne room, through the long corridors of the palace of Naltecona, and out into the morning sunlight of the sacred plaza. Slowing his pace to a steady trot, he crossed the courtyard and came to the gates of Axalt's palace.

Douglas Niles

A scowling, mustachioed man stood guard at the gate, holding a long spear with the blade of an axe at its end. Beside him stood one of the short men the strangers called "dwarves," also scowling.

Halting before them, Poshtli tried to remember some of the phrases of common speech he had learned from Halloran and Erixitl.

"I . . . must speak to Naltecona," he said, looking from one to the other.

"No one speaks to 'im without the captain-general's sayso," said the human.

Poshtli stepped forward, and the guard raised his weapon menacingly.

"He is . . . in there?" asked the Maztican.

"Sure. 'Cause he wants to be," said the soldier, with a sly smile.

"You're lying," Poshtli said.

The haft of the man's weapon struck swiftly toward the warrior's chin, but Poshtli stepped backward, out of the way of the blow. The guard swung his weapon around to confront Poshtli with the blade, while the dwarf edged nervously backward, looking into the courtyard behind him, as if he hoped for reinforcements.

Poshtli and the guard stared at each other, neither showing a trace of fear. If anything, the legionnaire's gaze showed a slight measure of respect for Poshtli's quickness and courage. The warrior deeply regretted coming unarmed, though rationally he understood that the presence of a weapon in his hands could do little more than get him killed.

"Wait," came a soft voice that nonetheless had the strength to carry across the palace courtyard. Naltecona emerged from the doors and crossed to the gate, accompanied by several of his courtiers, and also by a half-dozen armed legionnaires. The counselor wore his full regalia—the towering headdress of emerald feathers, a rich, *pluma* cape, and gold plugs in his ears and lip.

"My nephew, you must listen to me," Naltecona urged when he reached the gate. "I am here of my own will. It was the only way!"

"How can you say this," objected the young warrior, "when you are surrounded by armed men? When they won't admit the members of your own court to see you?"

"Poshtli, listen!" Naltecona spoke with more harshness than Poshtli had ever heard him use. "This is the *only* way. You must go back to the warriors and the priests. Tell them that I came here of my own free will. They must not attack the strangers! Such a battle would be disastrous beyond imagination.

"And now it is up to you to prevent it."

* * * * *

Halloran relaxed easily in the sun-drenched yard outside Lotil's house, the wound in his ribs almost fully healed. Below, he could see the slow recovery of Palul as villagers demolished blackened buildings and cleaned away the debris of disaster.

Up on the mountainside, he felt a growing unease about his detachment from the brutal scene in the valley. The lack of activity had begun to grate on him, especially during hours like these when Erixitl labored down in Palul with her neighbors.

He wondered about the legion's fate in Nexal. Word of Cordell's entrance into the city had returned to Palul several days earlier, but no further news had followed.

A woman moved through a field where the Nexalans and Kultakans had clashed. She selected the ears of a mayz that had survived, loading them into a basket on her hip. Men wove new roofs of thatch over some of the lesser-damaged buildings.

Behind him, Lotil hummed in the house. Hal pictured him at his featherloom, dextrously tucking bits of plumage into a mesh of fine cotton, creating pictures of brilliance and splendor. Blind though he was, the old man somehow observed the labor of his craft with keen precision. Apparently he could feel the difference between feathers of different hues.

In the past days, he had seen, from his vantage on the ridge, the pastoral strength of these people. The pyramid stood in disuse. The priests had all been slain in the battle, and without clerical exhortations to faith, people had turned to more pressing concerns.

Hal shuddered as he thought of the dark side of this culture, at the placid resolution with which the folk accepted the bloody hunger of their gods. But he knew of Qotal, too. He knew that these people had not always practiced their gory rituals. Perhaps the day would come when they would no longer do so.

And in his reflections, the hours passed. He saw the graves outside of Palul, and he pictured the legion encamped in Nexal. Amid the wonder and the horror, what catastrophe might ensue? Whatever the fate, he felt that the culture around him deserved better than to be plundered for its gold.

Erixitl returned at sunset. Hal noticed her extreme agitation as soon as she came around the bend in the trail below the house.

"What is it?" He ran to meet her.

"They've taken Naltecona captive!" she gasped, breathless from a hurried climb.

"The legion? Where?"

"In Nexal, the sacred plaza. It was true, what we heard about Naltecona giving Cordell the palace of Axalt. Now Cordell has brought the counselor to the palace and holds him among the legion!" They moved into the house, and Erix looked wildly, in panic, from her husband to her father.

"Why are you so frightened, child?" asked Lotil.

"The shadows! As soon as I heard the news, everything became dark! I could barely see to climb the hill, as if it were the middle of a cloudy night." She took a deep breath, trying to calm down.

"I had a dream, Father, the first time I saw this spreading darkness. It was the night the macaw led us to water in the desert," she told them. The words poured forth, and the men could sense her relief as she unburdened herself of the tale.

"I saw the end of the True World in this dream. It began beneath the glow of a full moon, in Nexal. Naltecona was slain by the strangers—atop a building I didn't know then, but I recognized it when we reached the city. It is Axalt's palace!"

"But surely the warriors have attacked," declared Halloran. "The city must be torn by battle!"

"It sounds very strange," Erixitl admitted. "But there is no fighting. Slaves take food to the legion every day, and Naltecona himself appears—from the palace, from the *roof*—to discuss his contentment. He claims that he is there of his own free will."

"Perhaps he is," said Hal skeptically.

"Even if he is, the danger is still terrible. And in my dream, his death was only the beginning. The devastation that followed spread like nightfall, as if the world itself was destroyed!"

"If you see this, then it can come to pass," said Lotil, "for you are one whom the favor of Qotal has granted special knowledge."

"What do you mean?" asked Erixitl.

Lotil smiled. "Look at your cloak, the one from the featherworker in Nexal. What do you note about it?"

Erix removed the garment and spread it on her lap. Halloran, too, leaned over to look at it closely. "It's even more beautiful than I remembered," she said. She ran her fingers along the brilliant plumage, tracing strands of red, green, white, and blue. Each color formed a long, narrow plume, which overlaid others of the same and different colors.

The whole cloak, unfolded, covered a fan-shaped area some five feet long by an equal width at its full extent. It was several inches thick, with a light, airy mass that nonetheless seemed well-padded.

But Erix was busy following the strands of color together, toward the apex of the cape. Each quill joined its neighbors into a single plume, and these plumes merged again higher up on the cloak. At the top, she noticed as she carefully ran her fingers along the cloak, all of the feathers merged into one strong, supple stem.

"It's a single, giant feather!" she said, astonished. "But from what?"

"What indeed?" asked Lotil, his face creaking into an amused grin.

"What do you mean?" interrupted Hal. "So it's a single feather. So what?"

"The Cloak of One Plume is the gift of Qotal himself, the

second harbinger of his return. I have known since you returned to me," said Lotil softly.

"His gift, like the return of the couatl, is his mark upon you. You are his chosen one. Keep this cloak safe, my dearest. There will be a time when it shall give you the blessing of Qotal."

"But chosen for what?" Erix snapped, frightened. "What do you mean? *Why* do I have this cloak? Just to see disaster before us?"

"Perhaps it has been given that you can do something to avoid that disaster," suggested Lotil quietly.

"But what? How can I?"

"Maybe we *can* do something!" Hal pressed his fists against his forehead, seeing Erixitl's agony, her absolute conviction that she had foreseen catastrophe. He thought for a moment, seeking some sort of a plan, and then spoke impulsively.

"You said that, under the glow of a full moon, Naltecona was killed by the legion atop the palace of Axalt. Well, what if he never goes to the roof? What if he's out of the palace altogether?"

Halloran quickly warmed to his topic, yet he needed to convince himself that his idea was not mere madness. "Perhaps we can rescue Naltecona, and get him to safety. If we can find Poshtli and get his help, we just might have a chance."

"But how? Break into the palace, through the legion's guards?" Erixitl's initial look of hope fell as she considered the obstacles.

"Didn't Poshtli tell us something about secret passages in those palaces? Remember, when we first got to Nexal. Maybe he knows where some of them are!"

Erixitl wondered at the thought, surprised as Lotil spoke. "Go to the door, daughter. Tell me where the moon is now."

"It's low in the east."

"Some time past sunset, correct? I feel the evening chill."

"Yes."

"Well, then," said the featherworker, turning his wrinkled face from Erixitl to Halloran and back again. "It would seem that you have about three days until it is full."

* * * * *

The priests dragged the Kultakan warrior forward, and Shatil saw that the victim was merely a strapping youth, too inexperienced to avoid capture by the retreating Nexalans at Palul. The sun touched the horizon as the scarred, gaunt clerics stretched him across the altar. Shatil's knife fell once, and then he raised the youth's heart to the great warrior statue of Zaltec.

The statue grimaced back, standing tall and broad, with its fanged mouth gaping. Tossing the pulsing flesh into that maw, Shatil turned back to the altar. Priests had already carried the body away, while others brought the next offering.

This one was older, a slave who had been given by his Jaguar Knight master to Zaltec. That warrior, having just received the brand of the Viperhand, had failed to acquire a captive during the recent battle. He made the offering of his lifelong slave in sincere atonement.

The slave didn't quite see it that way, and he struggled helplessly until the last moment. Shatil gave this heart to his god with a vengeance, embarrassed by the man's lack of faith.

And so it went. Hoxitl, Shatil, and a few of the other senior priests of Nexal tried to slake the ravening hunger of their god. Overwhelmed by the honor shown him—he was much younger than any of the other priests performing these desperate rites—Shatil strived to make each sacrifice perfect. Every heart must be another contribution to the strength to Zaltec. Soon now, Hoxitl had promised, would come their call to action.

The cult of the Viperhand flourished in all corners of the city, though its members remained outside the sacred plaza for the most part. The strangers never ventured beyond the walls of the palace of Axalt. Food was supplied daily by the servants of Naltecona, and the Revered Counselor often walked upon the palace roof, apparently happy and serene.

Full darkness settled across the valley before the final sacrifice had been offered. Finally the priests gathered before the altar to hear Hoxitl.

"I have seen the Ancient Ones," explained the high priest. The hearts of his exhausted compatriots pulsed to the news. They awaited his words with awed anticipation.

"Zaltec is pleased with our efforts. When the battle begins, his power will shield us from the metal weapons of the invaders. But we cannot strike yet. This is most important!"

Shatil's heart sank at the news. He sensed the disappointment of the other priests. Impulsively he blurted, "But, Patriarch, why can we not attack while the blood of the cult runs fresh and hot?"

Hoxitl sighed, a patient sound. "This is why it is forbidden: The Ancient Ones have had a warning. There is one who can destroy our plan. She is a young woman selected by the gods, who can by her very existence give victory to the invaders and utter, cataclysmic disaster to us!

"As long as she lives, our uprising would face disaster. Therefore, our entire task, for now, is to find this woman so that her heart can be given to Zaltec and our ultimate victory assured!"

"Where is she? Who is she?" The priests clamored for information, but Hoxitl quieted them with a look. His gaze came to rest on Shantil, and his voice was gentle.

"We are to wait for her to come to Nexal. She may be in the company of the stranger, Halloran." Shatil looked up with a start, to find Hoxitl's eyes squarely upon his own.

"She is your sister, Erixitl of Palul."

* * * * *

Chical, proud captain of the Eagle Warriors, came to see Poshtli in the throne room of Naltecona's palace. Poshtli did not sit atop the dais, but the chamber itself seemed to be the best place for him to conduct the business of the city and nation in the absence of his uncle.

In the presence of Chical and other ranking nobles, Naltecona had entrusted these tasks to his nephew, along with a grim admonishment to maintain peace with the strangers camped in their midst.

Poshtli's primary headache had been relations between the Kultakans and Nexalans in the sacred plaza, surrounding the palaces. The warriors of the city trained in the plaza and frequented the temples and altars there. The Kultakans, and to a lesser extent the Payit, had not yet interfered with these activities, but Poshtli expected a clash at any time.

Now he welcomed the arrival of his old captain, though he already guessed Chical's business.

"When will you order the attack?" demanded the Eagle.

"There will be no attack until Naltecona commands it. You yourself were there when he said this!" Poshtli shot back.

"Surely you could see that he spoke under the threat of the strangers' swords!"

"I saw no such thing. Is it your belief that the Revered Counselor would lie to his people out of fear for his own life?" The question held a grim undertone of challenge, and Chical dropped his eyes.

"No, it is not." When he looked up, deep pain showed in his eyes and in the tight set of his mouth. "But the spirit of Nexal, of all Maztica, is breaking beneath the weight of this outrage," he said quietly. "Our enemies may one day conquer us, but let it be through battle, not as our guests!"

"I am bound by my uncle's word to carry out his wishes, but if the strangers should do him any harm, that bond is broken. And know this, old warrior," Poshtli said, fixing Chical with an aggressive stare. "Before I will submit to conquest, there will be war!"

Privately he wondered if it was not already too late.

* * * * *

They camped in a high meadow, amid a riotous array of alpine blossoms. Staying off the main road, Hal and Erix traversed the shoulder of the northward volcano, Popol, high above the tree line. The only creatures they saw were birds, while far below them, in the valley, lay Nexal. They enjoyed a brilliant sunset while they ate. After dark, the city stood clearly outlined by ten thousand torches and candles.

But for the two lovers, this was a night still to look upward toward the heavens. The torches of the city paled to insignificance against the millions of stars that dotted the great blue-black dome of the sky from one horizon to the next. The moon, past the third quarter in brightness, still couldn't overcome the stars.

The night was just chill enough to make their blankets necessary and comfortable. For a long time, they spoke to each other without words. The terrors of the coming days still loomed, but each became a wellspring of strength for the other, making any horror tolerable so long as they could face it together.

Erixitl suddenly looked away from the city as they sat. Hal wrapped his arms around her, felt her trembling, and understood.

"The shadows come even by night now," she said, burying her face against his chest. "The city goes black. I see the torches and fires blink out one by one. Can't you feel the earth shaking?" she moaned.

He said nothing for a while, just holding her until her turmoil slowly faded. "We will find Poshtli," he declared finally. "With his help in the palace, and my steel—"

"And my *pluma*," Erix added, sitting up again.

"Yes." Hal winced at the thought of Darien, the biggest threat he perceived to their entrance into the palace.

Erixitl's token seemed to offer her, or them, some protection against the wizard's power. How much, they couldn't know, but she had described in intimate detail her experience with the blast of the frost wand.

"Together," Halloran agreed, holding her warm body to his own. There didn't seem to be any other way, and he began to feel grateful for the fact.

They came together then, with abandon, as if they both feared there would be no tomorrow.

* * * * *

From the chronicles of Coton:

A gallery of godhood waits for the contest to begin.

Lolth arises to her full presence and begins to take the measure of the gods, especially Zaltec, who claims the worship of her wayward drow. She studies the others, and she is pleased.

Zaltec feasts, all unknowing of the spider goddess. He is ready for the explosion of the Viperhand across the land,

and he knows the hearts gained by the victory will grant him unchallenged mastery of the True World.

Helm observes as the legion gathers its gold. This warrior god from across the sea remains vigilant. He waits, prepared for anything.

And all across Maztica, the shadows lengthen.

♣ 3 ♣

POINT OF NO RETURN

The Revered Counselor answered the summons from his captor with all the regal dignity of his office. Naltecona didn't walk to Cordell's audience chamber; he rode through the halls of Axalt's palace on his great feathered litter. His cloak of exquisite plumage floated behind him, and an escort of slaves marched before.

A pair of hairy-faced guards halted the slaves at the door. Naltecona rose and stalked between them, entering the chamber to find Cordell and Darien standing impatiently.

"Why have you summoned me?" asked the Maztican ruler.

"Come this way." Darien translated Cordell's directive as the captain-general left the room by a side door. The elfmage and Naltecona followed. Cordell walked for a minute in silence, finally coming around a corner and turning to regard the Revered Counselor.

"Do you have more of these rooms hidden around the palaces?" demanded Cordell. He gestured, indicating to the speechless Naltecona the huge array of gold before them.

The Maztican stared at the vast trove and felt a cold numbness seep into his body. He had never seen this magnificent hoard, but he knew of its existence. Never had he expected the strangers to tear open the very walls of the palace in their search for plunder. But so they had.

"This is the trove of my ancestors. It is a fabled cache, reputedly hidden somewhere in my grandfather's palace. I have never seen it before," explained the Revered Counselor quietly. "I think you have discovered it all."

"I don't believe you." The captain-general's voice, equally soft, challenged him. Darien, however, shook her head slightly. Cordell turned away, angrily stroking his chin. He tried to control his anger, still believing that the Maztican was somehow deceiving him. Yet perhaps Naltecona spoke the truth. In any event, Cordell knew that he couldn't push matters too hard yet.

Nexal had begun adjusting to the delicate state of control. Naltecona remained in Axalt's palace, ostensibly as a voluntary hostage to insure the cooperation of his people. He met with his officials and had a full household of slaves tending him in his customarily luxurious manner.

Meanwhile, the city functioned, on the surface at least, normally. The market was open, and legionnaires—in groups of a dozen or more—wandered there, or explored the other wonders of the city. The attitude of the individual Maztican toward them varied between hesitant interaction and sullen avoidance.

"Very well." Cordell quickly reached a decision. "Perhaps we have discovered the 'trove of your ancestors,' but I know you have more gold than this. I want it gathered before this palace. You must give the order."

Naltecona stared at Cordell, surprised. He had heard of the unquenchable gold-hunger of the bearded strangers, but never had he imagined its directness. He could think of no reason why anyone would care so much for the pliable yellow metal. Did they consume it? Did they worship it, or burn it, or build with it? He could not know.

Yet it was obviously their ultimate desire. When confronted by the ravenous hunger of the gods, Naltecona, all his life, had learned to give them food.

"Very well," he said. "We shall bring you our gold."

* * * * *

Hoxitl gasped as he emerged from his meditation cell and saw the body on the floor. He froze at the door to the central sanctuary of the temple, with its looming statue of beastly Zaltec and its smoking pots of incense.

Kneeling, the high priest saw that one of his apprentices had been slain. The body showed a thin wound over the heart, far too smooth to have been caused by a stone knife.

"A warning, priest." The voice, from the darkened corner of the sanctuary, chilled Hoxitl like a blast of icy wind. Quaking in fear and surprise, he rose.

"*You!*" he whispered, involuntarily stepping backward. His eyes wide, he stared at the black-robed figure that approached.

The Ancient One moved with oily smoothness. The slim body was completely muffled within the robe, except for the hands. These, of dark black skin and long slender fingers, hung free at the figure's sides.

Dully, the high priest became aware that several of the robed figures were in the temple with him. He wasted no time wondering how they had gotten here. He had no doubt that the Ancient Ones could have entered, unnoticed, by any of several means.

"A warning—a warning of what?" he asked.

"The girl who can spell doom for the faith returns to Nexal. Her death is more essential than ever. You *cannot* fail again!"

"No—no, I shall not! Where is she?"

"We do not know. But the wisdom of the Darkfyre—the very will of Zaltec himself—tells us that she arrives here soon. You will have all your priests, all your apprentices, join the search for her. We, too, will be in the city during the hours of darkness. She must be discovered and slain."

"Is she alone?" inquired the priest.

"She was seen with the stranger called Halloran."

"Very well," announced the priest. "I shall assign my priests to search. We will double the guards at all entrances to the city, and also I shall speak to Naltecona. He may know where the man is."

"The Revered Counselor has not long to live," continued the Ancient One. "His death will signal the attack of the cult!"

"Are you going to slay him?" asked Hoxitl, suddenly appalled.

The robed figure remained inscrutable. "Destiny will control its own pace, but that destiny will throw the cult of the Viperhand into battle with a great passion for killing. Zaltec will be pleased.

"But remember," hissed the Ancient One, his voice muffled but menacing through the dark cloth of his robe. The figure gestured to the corpse at Hoxitl's feet. "Do not fail us again."

* * * * *

Staying off the road, Hal and Erix reached the lakeshore, where tall grasses extended from a broad marsh, with open water perhaps half a mile away. Full darkness surrounded them, a low overcast conveniently blotting out the moon. Approaching Nexal, they knew they had tonight and the two following days before the rising of the full moon.

Fishing villages lined the shore of the lake, and the pair chose a path close to one of these, in the hopes of finding a canoe. They came upon a number of the craft pulled onto the shore and quickly slipped one into the water. In moments, they had paddled onto the smooth, dark waters of Lake Zaltec.

Torches winked in the distance, marking the vague outlines of the great city. They both felt relief for the protective darkness, which allowed them a good chance of entering Nexal undetected.

"Let's go to my house first," suggested Hal when they were safely away from shore. "The slaves might know something about Poshtli—where he is, or how we can find him without alerting Cordell."

Erix agreed. They crossed the huge lake swiftly, and soon the city sprawled before and around them. They paddled silently, unnoticed, into a wide canal, and Hal guided the narrow dugout toward his house. The many waterways crisscrossing the city made their passage fast and easy, though confusing.

In fact, Hal wasn't certain they weren't lost until they pulled up to the courtyard itself. He recognized the stone pool and clumps of palms, knowing at last that this was his own garden. The rooms of the house, all opening onto this central yard, spread protectively around them.

How different this crossing was from their first entrance into Nexal, Hal reflected, when Poshtli had boldly taken them into the palace itself. Now they slipped like assassins through the dark of the night, reaching his home without attracting the attention of anyone.

"Master! You live!" Gankak, his venerable slave, cackled with glee and hobbled into the courtyard. "Jaria! Come quick! I told you he'd return!"

"Told me nothing, you old he-goat!" Jaria, white-haired and rounded but remarkably nimble, passed her husband and bowed to Halloran and Erix as they entered the anteroom. "*I* said that you still lived, Master. It was Gankak who was certain that—well, it was otherwise."

Horo, the lithe, pretty one, and Chantil, short and plump beside her fellow slave, came happily out of the kitchen and chattered around them. It was a homecoming that surprised Halloran, and that he found deeply heartwarming.

"This is my wife, Erixitl," he said. The slaves bowed deeply to the woman, obviously pleased for their owner's happiness. For a few minutes, Hal forgot about the bleak view of Erixitl's vision, relaxing in the warm togetherness of his household.

"I'll see you later," Erix said as Horo and Chantil finally swept her away for a tour of the house.

"Master, it is good you return now. These are dangerous times in Nexal," said Gankak ominously.

"I know that my countrymen have entered the sacred square," Hal noted.

"That is not the worst. They have taken Naltecona prisoner, and they keep him with their own troops in the palace of Axalt. And Naltecona forbids his warriors from raising weapons against them!"

"That's something, at least." Hal knew their chances of success would probably vanish entirely if war erupted before they reached Naltecona. "We have much to do. Can you tell me, is there any word of Lord Poshtli?"

"Yes, indeed. He occupies Naltecona's throne room, speaking for his uncle. It is said that the Revered Counselor's captivity weighs heavy upon him."

Halloran imagined his friend's frustration, entrapped by his responsibility to serve his uncle and barred from attacking those who held him hostage.

Perhaps they could reach him. And if they did, perhaps they could offer him some hope.

* * * * *

"You must take charge of an important task, my nephew," said Naltecona. Poshtli stood attentively before him, wondering why the Revered Counselor had summoned him to his quarters in Axalt's palace so early on this bleak and cloudy day.

"I shall follow your commands unto my own death," pledged the warrior.

"You must gather the gold of Nexal, as much of it as you can. Gather it and bring it here." Naltecona stood tall. Only the deep lines around his eyes showed the humiliation he suffered at the request.

For a moment, Poshtli stood speechless. He couldn't imagine the immense arrogance behind such a demand, yet he knew that it must have come from Cordell. Did the man think all Nexal was his conquered serfdom, free for the plundering?

"You must do this, Poshtli, as difficult as I know it will be." Naltecona's pain now carried to his voice, and his nephew's heart broke at the abject surrender so apparent in this great man's bearing. At the same time, the warrior wanted to strike the counselor across the face in his blind anger, to somehow express the rage he felt at the proud nation's debasement.

"My pledge to you stands, my uncle," Poshtli said. "And if this is your sincere wish, so shall it be." His voice deepened, passionate. "But think of what you are saying! We are surrendering our city, our people, our gold, all to this one who comes as a guest to our city, then seeks to treat us as his slaves!"

Poshtli saw that his arguments hurt Naltecona, and he took a savage glee in the knowledge that the Revered Counselor could still be made to feel shame.

"Please, my uncle. Let us attack them and destroy them. We can drive them from Nexal or slay them all! They are not our masters, and you cannot give your people into slavery without the chance to fight for their freedom!"

"What's the use?" Naltecona sighed, a sound that reminded Poshtli of a lifeless desert wind. "We tried to stop them at Palul. You know of that disaster even more than do I. Think of that slaughter, multiplied a hundredfold because it occurs here, in the Heart of the True World."

"But think of what is coming to an end, Uncle. Think of the legacy of Maztica, the True World! And coming to an end for what? Surely you don't believe that the strangers are gods. You have seen their acts, heard their speech!"

Naltecona chuckled, a grim sound. "These are good words, my nephew. But they are mere words, and I must think of lives. I must avoid a conflict that could destroy us utterly."

"But through this, Revered One, we destroy ourselves!" Poshtli forgot himself for a moment, speaking with inappropriate vehemence.

"That is enough," said Naltecona quietly, gently.

"Forgive me, Uncle." Poshtli bowed deeply, torn by conflicting emotions. His overwhelming feeling was a sense of inevitable tragedy, and he stoically accepted this awareness, beginning to understand that his uncle suffered even more than he did.

"It shall be as you command," the warrior said quietly, bowing once again before he left.

* * * * *

The officers of the legion met their captain-general in a chamber that had once sheltered the ruler of all Maztica. Perhaps, thought Daggrande, it did so again.

The throne room of Axalt was as imposing as that of Naltecona. Cordell, however, had ordered his carpenters to build him a large wooden chair, for he didn't trust the floating *pluma* seat of the type used by Naltecona.

Now Daggrande, Kardann, Darien, Bishou Domincus, Alvarro, and the other captains met the general, seeing in the icy cold flash of Cordell's eyes that their leader had important news.

"We must practice the most extreme vigilance over the next few days," he announced. "At the same time, we face the prospect of reaping the ultimate reward."

He briefly related his encounter with Naltecona and the counselor's aquiescence in the matter of his people's gold. "We shall presently be faced with a mountainous trove, a pile of treasure such as few among us have ever imagined."

Cordell's manner turned menacing. "However, we must face the possibility that his people will resist such a demand. This, as you know, could lead to war."

"It *will* lead to war!" Kardann squealed, no longer able to hold his tongue. "Your demands are premature! They will certainly destroy us all!"

Daggrande turned to the pudgy assessor and confronted him, poking a blunt finger into Kardann's ribs. "Seems you still haven't learned to listen when the general's speaking." His finger pushed forward, and the accountant gasped for breath. "Now, shuddup!"

Kardann's eyes bulged, and for a moment, he wavered between terror of the indirect threat of a Nexalan uprising and the direct threat of a further rebuke from the dwarven captain of crossbow. The immediate threat took precedence, and the assessor shut his mouth.

Beside him, Alvarro licked his lips, recalling the pile of gold in the secret storeroom. The picture of many more such piles glowed seductively in his mind. "There's the matter of transport, sir," he said. "How do you intend to get it back to Helmsport?"

"We'll wait to see what kind of amount we're talking about. Then the carpenters will build us sleds. We'll use the Payits to drag them along when we march."

"Do you expect Naltecona to go along with this?" asked the Bishou. He despised everything about these people, but he couldn't believe that they would offer such a complete gesture of submission without a fight.

"Naltecona will go along with it," replied the captain-general. "The question is whether his people will follow."

Darien, unnoticed by any of them, pulled her hood over her face. She made the gesture to hide a rare, and very secret, smile. As the officers dispersed, Darien left the room before Cordell could speak to her.

She returned to her own chamber and pulled the curtains behind her. At the sight of her makeshift spellbook, in which she had collected most—but not all—of her original spells, her hatred for Halloran flashed hot again. One day, soon now, the man would pay for his audacity.

But for the time being, she would make do with the powers she possessed. Seating herself before a low table, she began to study.

Darien was acutely aware that the moment of her destiny drew near.

* * * * *

Halloran slept comfortably in the sleeping chamber of his house, awakening slowly to the light of an overcast, gray day. The rigors of their stealthy journey to Nexal had drained his wife as well, and Erixitl still slumbered beside him.

For a brief moment, between sleep and full awareness, a sense of sublime bliss and contentment swept over him. His love for Erix pushed all other concerns into the background, and the luxurious sense of peace urged him back to sleep. Around his wrists, he felt the smooth, feathered bands that Lotil had given him. He dozed, thinking of Erixitl's father.

But in another instant, full consciousness claimed him, and he remembered the perils that would face them on this day. The sunset after tonight's would bring the rising of the full moon. Today they must enter the palace of Naltecona and find Poshtli.

Erixitl stirred beside him, and he placed an arm around her, delighting in her slow smile as she awakened. Then she, too, felt the full weight of reality, sitting up with an expression of deep seriousness.

"You must let me go to the market," she said, immediately resuming a discussion they had waged before retiring very late the night before. "I can find one of Poshtli's comrades—someone who can help us get in to see him."

"It's too dangerous." He shook his head vehemently. "We have every reason to believe that the priests will still be searching for you."

"How are we going to get through the plaza to the Palace of Naltecona?" she shot back. Gankak had told them about the thousands of Kultakan and Payit warriors encamped there, watched carefully by a host of Nexalan warriors and priests.

"I have an idea," Halloran said, crossing to the saddlebags where he kept his possessions. The night before, he had recovered the bags from the hole where he had concealed them. He rummaged for a moment, then held up a small bottle containing a clear liquid.

"The potion," observed Erix, less than enthusiastically. She vividly remembered her shock when Hal had drunk a similar liquid, one that caused him to immediately grow to a height of some twenty feet. The effect had been temporary, but her memory of the incident still caused her to shiver at the thought of the powerful magic stored in the innocent-looking liquid.

"Invisibility!" Halloran reminded her. "We can each take a drink of this and disappear for an hour or so. It should be long enough for us to slip through the gate and get into the palace."

Erixitl stared, frank skepticism showing clearly on her face.

"Our only hope is to find Poshtli," Hal reminded her. "If we can tell him of your vision and convince him of the danger to Naltecona, he'll help us to rescue his uncle. We've got to get Naltecona out of that palace before the full moon!"

Halloran no longer held any questions about the menace implicit in Erixitl's frightening dream. For both of them, the coming full moon represented a looming presence that could spell the doom of all Maztica.

Erixitl looked at the bottle again and considered the possibilities. She came up with no reasonable alternatives.

"Very well," she finally agreed. "We must try."

* * * * *

From the chronicles of Coton:

Sharing the pain of the True World, I languish in growing despair.

Poshtli visits me again this morning. He wears well the brightly feathered cape and mantle of a lord, yet still he walks with the pride, the commanding bearing of the Eagle Knight. As the load he bears weighs him down, I sense his desire to return to the simple black and white plumes of his old order.

Pain pours from him as he relates the shocking orders of Naltecona. To Poshtli—to all of us—the gold of Nexal is as nothing more than a pretty metal, with uses for simple ornamental tasks.

Yet as the gold is nothing, our pride is everything. I feel for the debasement he senses in its surrender, yet again I can offer him no hope of alternative.

Throughout the city, as word spreads of Cordell's demand, resentment and suspicion grows. There is talk that the Revered Counselor is spellbound, incapable of leadership. Many mutter that Poshtli himself should take the role and lead us in uprising against the stranger.

Poshtli is devoted to the great Naltecona, however, and so he can only obey.

❧ 14 ❧

HOPE AND DESPAIR

"I am ready to see Chical now," Poshtli told the courtier who stood at the door of the throne room. With a deep sigh, he collapsed into the feather litter, having just dismissed the leaders of Nexal's merchant consortium. He did not look forward to this next meeting.

The traders had objected vehemently to his orders to provide their gold to the strangers, but Poshtli had convinced them with a combination of threats and pleas. After all, the merchants—a small group of individuals who controlled, from Nexal, trade across all the realms of the True World—depended on the Revered Counselor and the army for their influence. They couldn't very well dispute those sources of power without risking their station in the society of Nexal.

The Lord of Eagles, Poshtli knew, would be a different matter.

Chical stalked through the door. Unseen hands closed it behind him, leaving the warrior and the nobleman alone in the great chamber. Poshtli saw from the look in his old comrade's eyes that Chical already knew of the orders concerning the nation's gold.

"Thank you for coming to see me," began the nobleman. Despite his break with the order, he found that his affection for this crusty veteran remained undimmed.

Chical, however, seemed anything but affectionate. "How can you order our possessions given to the strangers?" he demanded. "Have you lost your senses? Your pride?"

Poshtli held up a weary hand. A day earlier, such an array of questions would have sent him flying toward Chical, hands clutching for the man's throat. Now, he reflected sadly, it had to be expected.

"My uncle has ordered it. He feels that there is a hope of making peace with the invaders, that if we fulfill their demands, they may leave us."

Chical scowled. "*Why* does he so desire this peace? Are we not a nation that has always gained our ends through war? And have we not emerged victorious from those wars? Why, now, this talk like an old woman?"

Poshtli rose to his feet and stepped toward the unflinching Chical. "You must remember your manners, my old friend. I will bear your insults so long, and no longer. And you shall not degrade my uncle's name!"

The venerable warrior's eyes widened slightly in surprise and perhaps a little pleasure at his former student's show of spirit. "Tell me," Chical repeated, trying to keep his voice reasonable, "*why* has peace become so important?"

"Have you remained unaware of the portents, the signs?" asked Poshtli. Now it was his voice that took on an edge of hardness. "Naltecona has had dreams, visions that showed him the war that would result from a clash with these strangers. I, too, have seen these visions.

"The result, looming before us, is a world gone mad! This is no war such as you and I have known all our lives. This is a war that would wrack the land and leave only death in its wake—a war that cannot be allowed to happen."

Chical glared at Poshtli, and the younger man met his glare with a challenging stare of his own. Finally the Lord of the Eagles sighed.

"The Eagles will obey the wishes of the Revered Counselor and his nephew. But you must know that the priests of Zaltec will resist," Chical said. "Their cult thrives in the city now. It is rumored they have twenty thousand members. Do you think Hoxitl can keep them in check for long?"

"I don't know, my friend," said Poshtli, with another rush of affection for his old teacher. "But knowing that the fate of the world is at stake, we can only try."

* * * * *

Crimson coals flared in their braziers, casting their blood-colored light throughout the darkened temple. Heavy incense fogged the air, adding an unearthly touch to the scene, while the great statue of Zaltec leered, barely visible in the dim glow.

Shatil was profoundly moved by the pervasive atmosphere of the long room as he advanced to greet his high priest. "Praises to Zaltec," he whispered, bowing before Hoxitl.

"Master of night and war," concluded the patriarch. "And I thank you for answering my call."

Shatil bowed, modestly deferring the high priest's gratitude. "It is I who should thank you for the summons, for all the kindnesses you have shown me."

Indeed, the week that Shatil had spent in Nexal had been an enlightening and invigorating time for him, despite the invasive presence of the strangers within the same sacred compound as this temple. He had worked with Hoxitl and other venerable priests, performing rites on the Great Pyramid of Nexal, the living center of worship for Zaltec's faithful across the True World.

The brand of the Viperhand on his chest burned constantly, but it was a spiritual flame, not a physical hurt. The fire grew slowly inside of him, and he lived for the day when it would come bursting forth, a conflagration devoted to the glory of Zaltec!

And all around him were others, kindred souls who also knew the glory of Zaltec and prepared to work his everlasting vengeance. Yet of all these countless members, the thousands who had joined the cult of the Viperhand, Hoxitl had showed great favoritism to this youthful priest from an outlying village.

Shatil had learned some of the reasons for this with the shocking announcement that his sister was considered a great threat to the cult. At first, he had tried to deny this to himself, feeling certain that some mistake had been made.

But as he thought about it, certain things began to suggest otherwise. There was the matter of the stranger, Halloran, of whom Erixitl had spoken so warmly. Then, of course, she had encountered the couatl, and had been granted the gift of the strangers' language. This bespoke of some sort of destiny far beyond her fate as a slave girl or featherworker's daughter.

DOUGLAS NILES

Most pressing was the fact that Shatil had no choice but to accept the decree of the Ancient Ones, since they formed the bedrock of his faith. He could not renounce that, nor did he want to. The matter of Erixitl was a sadness, but a necessity. Raised to respect the wishes of his bloodthirsty god, Shatil knew that he was thoroughly capable of carrying out the killing himself.

Now Shatil cautiously moved toward the altar, watching the crimson radiance of the coals wash over the great statue. Zaltec appeared, in the dim glow, to be a living presence.

"Do you understand that your sister is an enemy of Zaltec and a danger to the faith?" began Hoxitl quietly. Shatil nodded and listened, entranced by the cruel beauty of the statue behind the high priest. He saw movement in the shadowy corners of the room, taking little note of the jaguars slinking there.

"I have asked you to come here this morning because of the matter of Erixitl," Hoxitl continued. "She will return to the city soon, if she has not already. I have this task for you:

"Naltecona has given the man, Halloran, a house. We have learned that this man and Lord Poshtli journeyed to Palul before the battle in order to find Erixitl. We suspect that when she returns, she will go to this house, or will enter the palace to see Poshtli.

"I myself am watching the young lord, which I can do easily. But your task is to go to this house and seek her, or await her, there."

"I have heard her talk of this man," said Shatil grimly.

"You must be careful," cautioned Hoxitl. "He is a very dangerous opponent. But you must not let him prevent you from performing your task." Hoxitl reached into a pouch at his waist, pulling forth a large, curved claw. The thing was shiny black in color and tapered from a wide, blunt end through a long hook, ending in a needle-sharp point. The talon seemed to have come from a very large jaguar.

"This is to aid you in your task," explained the patriarch. "But treat it with care. The slightest scratch from the tip will cause instant death." Shatil leaned closer, seeing that the claw had been hollowed out. A cork sealed the wide end.

"I shall use it well."

"You must," replied the patriarch. "It is called the Talon of Zaltec."

"Now tell me where to find this house," said Shatil, "and I will see that Erixitl never leaves it alive."

* * * * *

"Here, take my hand," urged Halloran.

"Where *is* your hand?" Erix asked. Their fingers touched finally, and they linked grips. "That's better," she admitted. "At least I know where you are now." She reached out a hand and touched his invisible body, as if to convince herself of the fact.

"If you can't see me, we can hope that the guards can't either," he told her, touching the side of her face in order to reassure himself as to Erixitl's location. The two of them stood in the shade of several trees, very close to the gate of the sacred plaza. It was nearly noon, they guessed, though the sun had remained masked by hazy overcast all morning.

"I don't know which I like less, not being able to see *you*, or not even being able to see myself!" Her voice, unusually tentative, underlined her anxiety.

"We'll be in the palace in no time. Are you ready?" asked Hal, and felt Erix squeeze his hand in response. Several slaves hurried along the street beside them, but the avenue was otherwise empty. Moving quietly, they started toward the gate.

Halloran felt a smooth sense of confidence, though he understood full well the risks of their ultimate mission to free Naltecona. Finding Poshtli represented only the first step. Still, he felt excitement and anticipation such as he hadn't known for a long time. Perhaps it was the aura of invisibility. Or maybe he felt simple relief to again know a cause and a challenge. His doubts, the sense of alienness he had felt so strongly, all these things seemed to be behind him now.

Hal had swathed his boots in cotton, and he wore a cloth tunic over his steel plate armor. With his sword drawn and his scabbard lashed to his back, he could move with almost complete silence. The spellbook he carried in his backpack. Wrapped around his waist he brought the *hishna*-magic snakeskin that had bound him, long ago in Payit. The enchanted thing had power, he knew, and though he didn't know how to use it, he saw no purpose in leaving it behind. He knew they would need all of their resources to give their rescue plan a chance of success.

He remembered, too, the other potion bottle. Erixitl had panicked when he tried, once again, to sample it. In fact, she had insisted on carrying it, since he wouldn't leave it behind.

Erixitl, with her moccasins and loose dress, could also move quietly. Yet she currently felt none of Hal's self-assurance. The experience of invisibility she found decidedly unsettling. Her Cloak of One Plume encircled her shoulders, she knew; yet the fact that she could not see it disturbed her. Too, her sight had been full of darkness and shadows. She hadn't told Halloran, but a black sense of futility threatened to claim her, to drive her to despair.

Her dream seemed so real—Naltecona, perishing among the legionnaires atop the palace; the newly risen full moon illuminating the scene—that she wondered if there could be any hope of changing it. But she forced her hopelessness away, if only for Halloran's sake.

A pair of brawny legionnaires, armed with long-hafted weapons with the heads of axes, stood at one side of the single entrance to the sacred plaza. A pair of Jaguar Warriors stood opposite them, on the other side of the gates. This shared duty brought sharply home to Halloran the precarious balance that now existed in the city.

A light breeze circled around them, and one of the Jaguar Warriors sniffed and raised his head. Hal felt a moment of panic, but then the eddy settled and the guard turned back to his task, unalarmed. In another minute, a long file of slaves came down the street, carrying baskets of mayz and gourds of *octal*, the latter having proved quite popular among the strangers. Erix and Hal had no difficulty slipping through the opened gates beside the slaves.

They stopped in astonishment after they passed the long wall. Thousands of warriors, encamped in the sacred plaza, nearly filled the massive square. They clustered in camps around the great temples and palaces, Kultakans and Payits near one great palace, and Nexalan legions gathered around them.

"That must be the palace of Axalt," said Hal. He pointed to the huge, low building before remembering that Erix couldn't see his arm. She, too, had identified the place Cordell had made his headquarters—and Naltecona's prison. The high stone walls, with several balconies along the top edges, formed a solid barrier protecting the legion and its precious hostage.

Erix gasped and shrank backward suddenly as black gouts of smoke seemed to explode from the building, spreading an inky blackness across the plaza. Hal clutched her to him, not knowing the reason for her fear but sensing the terror coursing through her trembling body. Suddenly she shook her head and started forward. They crossed toward the palace of Naltecona, where Gankak had told them that Poshtli now dwelled, taking care to skirt the camps of warriors that lay in their path.

"How long until they can see us again?" asked Erixitl uncertainly.

"I don't know," Hal admitted. "But we have enough time to get inside." *I hope*, he added silently.

The entrance to Naltecona's palace passed through a pair of wide wooden doors, closed and guarded by Eagle Knights. Fortunately they opened frequently for groups of warriors, priests, or slaves. Hal and Erix slipped through behind a file of Maztican women who carried baskets of peppers and beans for the palace kitchens.

Once inside, they saw the familiar grand hallway proceeding straight before them, toward the great doors to Naltecona's—now Poshtli's—throne room. A lone nobleman stood outside. The man wore high sandals, a clean cotton tunic, and a small, shoulder-covering cape of green and red feathers.

Halloran and Erix moved slowly and carefully down the corridor until they stood within a few feet of the great doors. Making no sound, they observed the doors and the listlessly waiting courtier. Was Poshtli inside? They didn't know for certain, but Hal felt that the presence of a nobleman waiting at the door seemed like a good omen.

Abruptly the great portals opened, and a tall Eagle Knight stepped through. The man's posture was rigid, his eyes hard. As he emerged, Halloran was startled to see that the warrior was an old man, though he moved with the fluid ease of a young veteran.

Pulling Erixitl along, Hal darted through the opened door. The courtier followed, after bowing to the departing knight, and the invisible pair barely dodged to the side in time. Indeed, the man turned at the scuffing sound of their feet but faced the great throne when he saw nothing there.

Halloran and Erix saw Poshtli seated on the floating *pluma* throne of his uncle. The first thing striking them both was that their friend looked much older than when they had last seen him, in Palul.

"Shall I summon Hoxitl yet, my Lord Poshtli?" asked the nobleman.

"No!" Poshtli's voice was a harsh chop. Then he sighed, and his tone softened. "Not yet. I will talk to the priests later in the day. Now leave me, please."

With a deep bow, the man turned and departed, closing the great doors behind him. Erixitl and Halloran stood, silent and unseen, in the great throne room of Nexal.

They started forward awkwardly, and as they did, they saw Poshtli lean back in the throne. Tears wet his eyes, though they didn't flow down his cheeks.

Then his face twisted with an expression of utter, soul-wrenching grief.

* * * * *

Shatil found the house of Halloran easily. From the outside, the long, two-story structure seemed to be deserted. Since full daylight would last for several hours yet, he decided to watch the residence for a while. If necessary, he would enter after dark.

Entering a nearby garden, he found a low stone bench and seated himself—a priest at his meditations, a common enough sight in the city. For long hours, he surreptitiously observed the house. Once he saw a plump young slave depart from the front doors, returning an hour later with a basket of fruit. But there was no other sign of life in the place.

Finally dusk, then darkness, settled around Shatil, and he resolved to have a look inside. He left the garden and crossed the street. Silently he slipped into the open antechamber and looked around. He wore a stone knife in his belt and kept the Talon of Zaltec comfortably ready in his right hand.

The central courtyard of the house was empty, but he heard voices coming from the kitchen area near the back. Stealthily he moved through the garden, approaching the open door of the cooking area.

The small room was cheerily lit by a hearthfire and a pair of reed torches. Within, he saw two young women at work. One ground beans in a large clay bowl, while the other patted a paste into circular mayzcakes, using a broad, flat rock as her work surface. He paused for a moment, listening and watching.

"Horo?" asked one of the slaves, the one who had left to get the fruit earlier.

"Yes, Chantil?" replied Horo. She was a very tall and strikingly beautiful slave who appeared to be slightly older than her companion.

"Are the master and mistress in danger, do you believe? Will we see them again?" inquired Chantil, a tremor in her voice.

"Of course! Gankak says so, and he is far wiser than you or I. Surely you do not question his judgment." Horo spoke with an airy sense of confidence. Before they continued, Shatil grew impatient with his eavesdropping. He also felt certain that Erixitl would not be found in the house.

Both slaves looked up with gasps of surprise as the scarred priest of Zaltec stepped into the light. "Who is your master? Who is your mistress?" Shatil demanded.

The two women looked at each other, their eyes widening in terror. Then the tall one, Horo, summoned her courage. "Who are you?" she asked. "What do you want?"

Shatil struck quickly, slapping the slave across the face. In his hand, he held the Talon of Zaltec, and he scraped the tip of the claw across the slave's cheek.

Horo screamed and recoiled, clasping her hand to her face. The tiny wound showed as a thin line of pink. Then her eyes grew even wider, and her mouth worked soundlessly. In seconds, Horo sprawled to her back, her eyes open, staring at the ceiling, but seeing nothing more.

Chantil whimpered and tried to crawl away from the emaciated priest. Shatil raised his hand again but held his blow. "Is your mistress called Erixitl?"

Chantil nodded dumbly.

"And where is she now? Speak or die!"

The slave struggled to overcome her terror enough to speak. "Th—the palace—she has gone to—to see Poshtli!"

"Why?" demanded Shatil, threatening.

"They go—they go to rescue Naltecona!" cried the slave.

Shatil lowered his hand and turned toward the door. "You have done well, slave. Zaltec is pleased to leave you with your life."

But Chantil was not listening. Weeping, she crawled to the body of her friend as the priest of Zaltec disappeared into the darkness.

* * * * *

Gultec learned to fly, in the bodies of hawk and parrot and hummingbird. He swam as a fish. He climbed trees in the form of the howling monkey that commanded the jungle heights of Far Payit. And still he learned from Zochimaloc, studying the ways of the past and future course of the stars.

But now, too, he began to teach. Knowing of the coming of war, he tried to train the men of Tulom-Itzi as warriors. This task he immediately found to be impossible, for these folk were raised with none of the military traditions that played so strong a role in most of the nations of the True World.

The men of Tulom-Itzi thought it foolish to dress in gaudy colors to terrify their foe, and they lacked the individual skill with the *maca* that would allow them to stand and face even one rank of an enemy's army.

The one weapon they had mastered was the bow, and here Gultec found that the men of Tulom-Itzi excelled. Their weapons, made from hard jungle limbs, stretched taut only under a very powerful pull. Their arrows flew swift and true, and the heads—of sharks' teeth or clamshell—were every bit as hard as, and even sharper than, tips of obsidian.

So Gultec adapted his tactics of war to the warriors of Tulom-Itzi. He taught them to skulk through the jungle, to strike from a distance, to retire at the approach of the enemy. In this way, he hoped that they might survive an engagement with an army of Payits or, perhaps, Nexalans. He knew that they could never stand against the foreigners of the Golden Legion. Zochimaloc, unfortunately, could provide him no information on the type of enemy they would have to fight.

As the moon crept toward fullness, Gultec drove himself and his warriors with savage intensity. Tulom-Itzi, with its vast area sprawling through many miles of jungle and clearing, he decided, was indefensible. He formed a plan: If attackers came against the city, the people would melt into the jungle, living there and harassing the enemy.

But all the while he felt a sense of wasted effort. He grew more and more certain that Far Payit, on the distant fringe of the True World, would not be the scene of a cataclysmic war. Finally this certainty led him to decision, and he sought Zochimaloc in the observatory, under the growing light of the moon.

"Teacher," he began, speaking boldly to his wizened mentor, "you have given me knowledge of things I never imagined, provided me judgment I have never possessed. You have told me that this is because Tulom-Itzi needs me to ready your city and land for war."

Zochimaloc nodded, unsmiling. His eyes were soft.

"In using this judgment, I have decided that I must leave Far Payit, leave these lands and learn more about the nature of the threat you perceive."

Now the teacher's head bobbed in a slow, sympathetic nod.

"I will endeavor to return when I am needed, for the learning you have given me is a debt that I can only begin to repay. But until then, I must travel elsewhere to seek the future."

"Where will you go?" asked Zochimaloc finally. Gultec noticed that his teacher showed not the slightest bit of surprise.

"You have given me the powers to fly across the land. I

shall go everywhere, until I find that which I need to know."

Zochimaloc smiled gently. "I have given you precious little, my proud jaguar. All I have done is to help you open doors to powers you have always possessed. But let me give you one last thing before you depart: advice."

The old man chuckled grimly. "Do not try to go everywhere, for that will lead you nowhere. Instead, know that, if you wish to save a life, you must save the heart." Zochimaloc sighed and pressed a hand to the warrior's shoulder.

"And the Heart of the True World is Nexal."

* * * * *

From the chronicles of Coton:

In amusement for the massive vanities of men.

And even the Ancient Ones, the drow elves who live for centuries and consider themselves as gods, even they are caught up in the disaster of their own arrogance.

They believe that the cult of the Viperhand is their tool, used to subvert the humans of Maztica to their own path. Even Zaltec, in the minds of the drow, has been reduced to a plaything and servant.

They forget their own god, Lolth; and the spider queen does not take such neglect kindly. They insult Zaltec with their disdain for his might, while all the while they feed his hunger by pouring hearts into the Darkfyre.

One day, and it will come soon, the gods will grow tired of their pompous vanity. Then they—we all—will have to pay.

♣ 15 ♣
A DARKER NIGHT

"Yes, there is a chance we can do it—a slim chance, but I agree that we must try!" Poshtli grimly clapped his fist into the palm of his other hand. Erix and Halloran, visible for these past few hours, nodded in relief.

The noble warrior had been stunned to speechlessness when they had called to him, invisible, from before his throne. At first, Poshtli had bristled in superstitious fear, but when they touched him, he became convinced of their presence. In any event, the effect of the potion had dissipated shortly after they had begun to speak.

Poshtli showed no surprise at Erixitl's tale of her dreams, and the premonition about Naltecona perishing below the full moon. He agreed that the counselor should be spirited out of Axalt's palace immediately. They had less than twenty-four hours before the rising of the full moon.

"Do you speak directly with Naltecona in his quarters?" asked Halloran. "Can we get to him that way?"

Poshtli shook his head. "I see him alone, but we are always guarded. We could not effect an escape that way."

Halloran's heart fell. They had achieved one objective in reaching Poshtli, but that was only useful if they could proceed to the Revered Counselor himself. "You told us, long ago, about secret passages designed by the rulers and hidden in their palaces. Is there any way you could find these—perhaps use them to get to Naltecona?"

"That might be possible," Poshtli agreed. "It *is* traditional practice for the Revered Counselors to conceal escape routes in their palaces, and a route of exit could certainly be used to gain entrance as well."

"Are there others in the palace of Axalt?" asked Halloran, growing hopeful again.

Douglas Niles

"I do not know for certain, but I would suspect that they exist," Poshtli replied. "The problem will be to locate them. I will visit Naltecona's Lord Architect. He lives here in the palace. He would know about the secrets of this palace, and perhaps the palace of Axalt as well."

They heard a deep rumbling, a powerful throbbing in the air that they could feel in the pits of their stomachs. In moments, the vibration reached the ground, and for several seconds the floor trembled.

All three of them looked at each other in shock. Poshtli, the first to recover, shook his head grimly. "The volcano, Zatal, growls. Wait here, in my private chamber." Their friend ushered them into a smaller gallery leading off one side of the throne room. "I'll see if the Lord Architect can help."

Then, with a swish of the curtain, he was gone.

* * * * *

Shatil hurried to the temple building in the sacred plaza. The bulk of the Great Pyramid towered above him, dark now, hours after sunset. The moon, one night short of full, illuminated the vast square with its thousands of restless warriors. He entered the stone structure, descending through the doorway into the dank coolness of the temple proper. Jaguars skulked in the shadows, and the red brazier cast its glow across the statue of the warrior god Zaltec.

"What is it?" asked Hoxitl, turning from the statue and recognizing the young priest.

"I have been to Halloran's house. Erix was there, but no more," Shatil explained breathlessly. "They are here, in the sacred plaza. They seek Poshtli; they will try to rescue Naltecona from the strangers!"

He spoke in excitement. As Shatil had considered his sister's mission, he had begun to suspect that perhaps Hoxitl had been wrong. Indeed, Erix would be a great heroine if she could bring the Revered Counselor out of the enemy clutches. Surely this was not the act of an enemy of Zaltec!

Hoxitl's reaction surprised him. The high priest's eyes widened in alarm. "She must be stopped!" he cried in sudden panic. Swiftly, angrily, he whirled away and fought for self-control.

Hoxitl remembered vividly the warning of the Ancient One: Naltecona's death, among the strangers, was to be the signal for the uprising. If he were rescued, the signal might not occur. The cult of the Viperhand, coiled and aching for release, might be thwarted of its great explosion.

"Shatil spoke tentatively. "But, Patriarch, is this not good? Would not Naltecona's rescue allow us the freedom to strike at the strangers?"

"No! Can't you see designs of those who would thwart Zaltec?" Hoxitl turned savagely on the young priest. He couldn't tell him of the warning of the Ancient One—that had been *too* private, pertaining to Naltecona's and the high priest's own fates. Yet he needed Shatil's help, his obedience.

"We must go to Poshtli and try to stop your sister. Do you have the Talon of Zaltec?" At Shatil's nod, Hoxitl continued. "We will seek Erixitl in the palace. If we find her, you must be prepared to use it."

"I understand," said Shatil, swallowing a bitter objection. He was a priest of Zaltec. He wore the brand of the Viperhand. He had no choice but to nod humbly and obey.

* * * * *

Helm, patron god of the Golden Legion, was represented by his faithful as the All-seeing Eye. Those who worshiped ever vigilant and watchful Helm would not be surprised by enemy ambush or strategem—or so claimed his clerics. The All-seeing Eye would provide his faithful with warning and alarm.

Now the ever watchful one tickled a cautious nerve in the mind of his devout cleric, Bishou Domincus, awakening him from an early, fitful sleep.

Tingling to a sense of danger he had learned never to ignore, the tall, bearded cleric emerged from his sleeping chamber and started toward the rooms of Cordell and Darien. On the way, he passed the guarded chamber where Naltecona was held.

Here alarm prickled the hair on his neck, and the Bishou hurried to his general. He encountered Alvarro, drinking *octal* with some of his riders in a palace garden.

"Come with me," he said to the captain, then turned to the

men. "Get to Naltecona's chamber! Double the guard! There's treachery about!"

The captain-general, aroused by the tumult, emerged from his chamber with a cotton tunic thrown over his shoulders. Darien, robed, followed moments later.

"What is it?" demanded Cordell.

"I have been warned by Helm," pronounced the Bishou, his voice booming. "There will be an attempt against our prisoner!"

"To kill him?" asked the general, alarmed.

"Perhaps. Or to free him," said the Bishou. "In any event, we must increase the guard."

Cordell acted quickly, having had experience in the past with the Bishou's premonitions of disaster. "Double the men at the gates and in the hallways. Roust the troops from their sleep—now!"

The alarm quickly spread through the palace. Cordell then gestured to Darien, Alvarro, and the Bishou. "Come on—hurry!"

He led them toward Naltecona's chamber.

* * * * *

"*Kirisha*," Hal whispered, and cool white light spilled through the previously dark tunnel. Poshtli looked at him, blinking momentarily in surprise, then turned back to the sheet of paper in his hands.

"That does make map-reading a little easier," he admitted. "Now, this tunnel should take us under the palace of Axalt."

The warrior led the way, with Erixitl behind him and Halloran bringing up the rear, since the dank, stone-lined tunnel offered only enough space for a single-file advance.

The Lord Architect had shown them a passage leading from Naltecona's throne room itself to a network of tunnels passing beneath the palaces, pyramids, and courtyards of the sacred plaza. A courtier had announced the arrival of the priests of Zaltec as the small group was preparing to depart, and Poshtli had instructed him to keep the priests waiting.

The map had been hastily drawn by the architect of Nexal, who had designed the palace of Naltecona. His predecessor, who had created the plans for Axalt's palace some sixty years earlier, no longer lived. Consequently, the architect had warned, the map became less accurate the closer they got to their goal. It didn't show every passage, and the man had told Poshtli that the scale was rough at best.

But it was all they had, and it was far better than nothing.

"I think we're starting to go up," Erix announced after long minutes of walking. The others paused and regarded the tunnel before and behind them, agreeing that she was right.

"The slaves who provide his food tell me that Naltecona is quartered in the old Revered Counselor's chambers. That should make our task a little easier. There's certain to be a secret passage leading there." Poshtli held his steel longsword in one hand now as the climb in the tunnel became more noticeable. "We must be under the palace now."

Abruptly the tunnel met an intersection with another passage crossing at right angles. Poshtli stopped, confronted with three choices of direction.

"That way," said Erix decisively, pointing to the right.

The men looked at her, surprised by her vehemence. She pointed again, and they shrugged. With no more convincing alternative, the warrior led them to the right.

This tunnel proceeded for perhaps two hundred paces and then ended in a steep stone stairway.

"Up there," Erix whispered.

"How can you know where we're going?" asked Halloran, wanting to believe that they were on the right track.

"I don't know," she replied. "But I think we'll find Naltecona up ahead."

Carefully Poshtli led the way up the steep, spiraling steps. After one full circle, the stairway ended at a narrow platform. Before them, fully illuminated in the light of Halloran's spell, stood the outline of a narrow stone door.

"*Kirishone*," Hal whispered, dousing the light. He didn't want any telltale gleam through a crack to give them away to anyone on the other side.

"Let's have a look," Poshtli said, pushing against the portal. With a dull rasp of wooden pivots, the stone door slowly yielded to his pressure.

Soundlessly the warrior slipped through, quickly followed by Erix and Hal. They smelled moist foliage, and grass cushioned their footsteps. For a few moments, they blinked into what seemed like pitch darkness, but gradually their eyes adjusted to the gloom.

They had entered an enclosed garden, Hal saw, one that was open to the sky above. He guessed that they were in the right palace, but he could only hope that somehow they had emerged into the proper area of that palace.

"D'you hear somethin?" The guttural question, spoken from a few feet away, froze them in place. The language was that of the legionnaires.

"I dunno. Here, get a spark for the torch."

"*Slyberius*," hissed Hal, quickly pulling a pinch of sand from his pouch. He had studied the sleep spell but never used it before.

"Hey . . ." The original voice grunted softly in surprise, but then the listeners were rewarded by three soft thuds as bodies fell to the ground.

Erix quickly knelt beside the forms of the slumbering guards. The overcast kept the night very dark, but enough light from the nearly full moon penetrated the clouds to reveal the garden in dim, shadowy detail.

"I thought you killed them," the woman whispered, "but they're only asleep."

"Guards—a good sign," Poshtli added. "It means they have something worth guarding here, and this looks like a royal garden. Naltecona might be in one of these sleeping chambers."

They advanced along a grassy path between ferns and blossoms. Several tall, graceful palms leaned over them, silhouetted against the sky.

"Wait!" Erix warned quietly, her voice taut with alarm.

"What is it?" Hal turned from side to side, peering into the shrubbery around them. Was something moving?

"*Kirisha!*" The command, barked in a woman's voice, suddenly filled the garden with white light. A dozen or more legionnaires leaped from the rooms around them, swords drawn.

"A trap!" cried Poshtli. He raised his longsword and deflected the attack of the first swordsman.

Halloran leaped in front of Erixitl and slashed with Helmstooth at another attacker. He grunted in astonishment as the weapon cleaved his opponent's sword and went on to slash the man's body into two pieces. Never had he struck a blow with such power.

He turned and chopped at another legionnaire who rushed him from the flank, surprising him. Nevertheless, this blow sent another attacker flying across the garden to smash, stunned, against the wall. Halloran hacked again, an overhand chop that once more snapped his opponent's sword and cleaved the man in two.

Poshtli stumbled against Hal, pressed by three attackers, and Halloran whirled. He charged into them, his blade flashing, bone-crushing power behind his attacks. Three savage blows dropped the swordsmen, and Hal rushed ahead, driving a rank of legionnaires back before him.

He saw stark fear in the faces of the men he fought, but, mindful of his companions, he didn't pursue too far. He moved back to Erixitl's side, and saw the awe upon her face. "How did you do that?" she gasped, gesturing to the broken bodies around them.

For the first time, Halloran noticed the tingling in his wrists. He looked down and saw the delicate rings of his feathered wristbands—the dowry given him by Lotil, the featherworker. Could those beautiful objects truly be the source of his sudden, giantlike strength? What had Lotil told him?

". . . they may not look like much, but I think that you will appreciate them."

Indeed he did! Panting slightly, Hal looked around. The swordsmen stood in a rough circle around them, their eyes wide with fear. He saw movement behind the legionnaires, recognizing the dark form of Darien. It was she who had cast the light spell.

She raised her hand, and he saw a dim pebble of light float from her finger—a pebble he had seen in battle before. "Fireball!" he cried, feeling a hopeless sense of panic as that innocent-looking globule of flame drifted toward them.

Erixitl seized his arm and Poshtli's, pulling them both close to her. Spellbound, they watched the dot move closer.

The two or three seconds of its flight passed like hours.

Then the world around them erupted into searing light. Tongues of liquid flame exploded from the pebble, encircling them, hissing with infernal heat. Moist, succulent plants sizzled into ash. The ring of encircling legionnaires stumbled backward, many suffering burns on their faces or hands.

Halloran felt the heat pressing around them, bringing sweat to his forehead. Numb with terror, he awaited the devouring kiss of flame that would end their lives. He sensed Erix's fear beside him as her hand squeezed his arm with viselike pressure.

But then the flames faded away, and they were unharmed! They stood amidst a large, circular patch of blackened, smoldering garden, but Erix's *pluma* had protected them from the spell.

"Take them, you cowards!" He heard Darien's voice, uncharacteristically shrill, commanding the legionnaires. Perhaps two dozen of them still stood, and once again they pressed forward.

"Stay close to me," warned Erix as Hal started to lunge toward the swordsmen. He saw, from the devastated plant life, that the ring of protection around Erix seemed to extend some ten feet away from her.

Feinting toward the men before him, he drove them back. Then he turned and, with Poshtli at his side, attacked those rushing from the rear. In three blows, three more men fell, and the Maztican slayed another. Hal noted that Poshtli readily adapted his skill with a *maca* to the use of the hard steel blade.

Halloran saw Darien raise her hand again. A bolt of magic hissed from her finger, a magic arrow forming in the air. It crackled toward him, and he grunted with pain as it hissed into his hip, leaving a smoking burn.

Again a bolt crackled, and he flinched backward, knowing he couldn't avoid the attack. But then a lithe form stepped before him. The magic arrow struck Erixitl between her breasts, where the *pluma* token lay against her skin, unseen beneath her dress.

The bolt crumbled into sparks and fell harmlessly to the

ground. The swordsmen paused for a moment as Darien's shrill cry of hatred split the air. Bolt after bolt shot forth, each one popping into nothingness against the Maztican woman. Finally Darien dropped her hand, her spell exhausted. The other attackers closed tentatively.

"We've got to get out of here," Poshtli grunted. "They knew we were coming. Naltecona's too well guarded!"

Sensing the truth of his friend's words, Halloran cursed in frustration. He felt he could go anywhere, attack at any odds, with the pulsating might flowing into his muscles from his *pluma* wristbands. But he knew this was an illusion. He might be strong and quick, but he was still mortal.

"Come on!" said Erix, starting back toward the concealed door they had used to enter.

Hal and Poshtli fell back beside her, fighting off the approaches of the attackers. Feeling no remorse in the heat of the battle, Hal struck brutally to the right and left, slaying his former comrades as he would kill any foe in any battle. If anything, the presence of Erixitl beside him and the need to protect her drove him to greater heights of savagery than he had ever known.

The door stood open before them. The three guards still slumbered incongruously as the battle raged around them. One of them began to stir as Hal and Erix turned back to the smoldering garden. The legionaires pursued at a safe distance, giving the bone-crunching sweep of Halloran's sword a wide berth.

"Get through—I'll close the door!" Poshtli leaped into the portal, stepping aside so that Hal and Erix could slip past him.

"Go!" Halloran urged Erix, facing outward to hold back the pursuit.

Neither of them saw the groggy legionnaire sit up near the doorway. The effects of the sleep spell melted away as he saw the fight raging before him.

Swiftly the man sprang to his feet and dove into Erixitl, carrying her heavily to the ground. The two rolled away from the doorway, away from Halloran.

"Erix!" he cried, his voice cracking. He leaped after her, seeing other legionnaires reach down, helping their companion to pull her away.

Dimly he saw Darien raise her hand, her spell a sharp bark of sound amid the chaos in the garden. Erixitl disappeared before Halloran as he crashed into a wall of stone—a hard granite barrier conjured between him and his wife by the elfmage.

"No!" he raged. Legionnaires swarmed around either side of the wall, blocking his passage with their bodies. The stone barrier towered over his head, extending across half the garden to the right and left. Behind him, he sensed Poshtli at the open door.

With a growl of inarticulate rage, Halloran threw back his fist and smashed it into the wall. His knuckles met the granite with stone-crushing force, and the arcane power of his *pluma*, coupled with the berserk rage of his own strength, shattered the barrier. Leaping through the wreckage like a wild beast, Halloran saw Erix, firmly grasped by four swordsmen, disappear into one of the compartments.

Blinded by his own fury, Halloran stumbled forward. Swordsmen fell away from his path, knowing their fate if they came within reach of his blows.

Suddenly a dark reality penetrated his frenzy, and he saw a rank of legionnaires standing between him and the place where Erix had disappeared. No swords for these, however—this was a line of Daggrande's heavy crossbows.

Blinking, halting in a desperate attempt to regain his self-control, Halloran stared at the figure of his old companion. The grizzled dwarf stared back, the set of his mouth firm. Only his eyes showed his pain. With deliberate speed, he ordered the crossbows, their steel-headed missiles glinting in the magical light, raised.

Don't make me do it, lad! Halloran read the message in the old dwarf's eyes and knew beyond a doubt that a volley of those missiles would mean his death.

"Shoot, fools! He's getting away!" Darien's shrill scream followed Hal through the door as he turned and darted into the safety of the secret passage. Tears of frustration and rage choked him, and he didn't even see Poshtli pull the portal shut behind them.

* * * * *

From the chronicles of Coton:

In dreams, may we find the hope and promise that eludes us awake.

Again the feathered snake came to me in my sleep. The golden couatl, brilliant of plume and mighty of power, circles about, taunting with his near presence, frustrating me as he vanishes before daybreak.

And so the couatl remains a dream, a fantasy specter of hope and significance, all the more miserable because of its empty promise. The clouds of doom gather around Nexal, and the city prepares to bathe in blood.

O couatl, harbinger of the Plumed One, we need more than your promise now!

❦ 16 ❦

TO HOLD THE MOON

Three bearded legionnaires threw Erixitl against a wall with enough force to drive the air from her lungs. Gasping, she faced them—not afraid, but bitterly disappointed. One of them pulled her stone knife—her only weapon—from her belt. A fourth walked up to her and scowled into her face.

"What d'you got under them feathers?" he demanded. The Cloak of One Plume covered her shoulders and her back. He reached a hand to its clasp to tear it away. Suddenly a blue spark crackled from the cloak, and he drew his blistered hand away.

"Ouch! Helm's curses, she's a witch!"

Erix was as surprised as the legionnaire. A growing sense of despair seized her, and she took little pleasure in the protection. True, it hid her pouch, but the only thing that contained was the tiny bottle of potion she had insisted Hal let her carry—a potion that frightened her too much to ever allow her to drink it.

"That was Halloran!" she heard one of the men say. "The bastard fought like a demon!"

"Killed Garney, he did," grunted another. Their eyes settled, murderously, back on Erixitl.

Halloran! She struggled to contain her grief. They had failed. Did he live? Had they escaped? Lost in her despair, she didn't notice the captain-general's entrance until the black-bearded leader stood before her, his dark eyes smoldering.

"You were the translator at Palul," Cordell stated, his voice vaguely accusing, confident of its assertion.

"Yes," Erixitl replied, seeing no point in denial. Around her, a menacing ring of legionnaires glowered, brandishing weapons, all but growling for her blood. Cordell stood before her, with the cloaked elfmage at his side.

"Why did you come here?" demanded the general.

"We were lost," Erix answered, forcing her voice to remain calm.

"These questions are a waste of time!" snapped Darien. "Kill the wench now and be done with it."

"Wait!" Cordell raised a hand, mildly reproving. "You sought Naltecona, did you not? To free him, perhaps?"

Erixitl shook her head, but she could see that the man didn't believe her.

Suddenly another figure elbowed his way through the men-at-arms. A grim-faced Alvarro reported to Cordell.

"That son of a whore killed six men, wounded a dozen more!" The man's tones were incredulous. Then his eyes fell upon Erixitl, and a crooked grin twisted Alvarro's mouth. "But I see we have his woman."

The way he said "woman" sent daggers of fear along Erixitl's spine. Darien, too, noticed the inflection, though no one saw her smile within the shadows of her hood.

"His woman?" Cordell repeated in surprise.

Alvarro stopped, thinking fast. He hadn't told Cordell the full story of his encounter with Hal and Erix together, outside of Palul.

"Yeah," he explained quickly. "When he killed Vane, he was trying to get to her. Must have quite a thing for her." The red-bearded man looked at Erixitl's lithe femininity like a hungry animal. "Can't say I blame him!"

Cordell looked at the captain in mild annoyance, then turned back to Erixitl. "If he came for you once, perhaps he'll do so again. We'll keep you here for now. Perhaps you'll bring us bigger game."

"Kill her!" Darien spat. "He'll still come. He won't know she's dead." Her eyes glowed from the depths of her hood, but Erix held her head high and met the elf's fiery gaze. The elven mage had a dozen spells that should be able to strike this woman down, yet she knew that something powerful protected her against magic. This frustration only heightened her fury.

"No!" Cordell said firmly, so that all understood. He gestured to a pair of swordsmen. "Find a secure room and lock her up there."

* * * * *

Halloran and Poshtli tumbled down the stairway, pausing at the bottom to listen for sounds of pursuit. Apparently none of the legionnaires wanted to follow the maddened swordsman into that dark passage, however, for they heard nothing.

"I've got to go back for her!" Hal gasped during the sudden respite in flight.

"Yes, but not now!" Poshtli pressed Hal against the tunnel wall, hissing the words into his face with brutal force. "They're waiting for you up there. You know that! Do you want to throw your life away uselessly, or do you want to have a plan—something that's got a chance to work?"

For a moment, Hal's fists clenched involuntarily. His rage blurred his thoughts, and he almost struck Poshtli a blow that, in his fury, could have killed his friend. Then, with a strangled sob, he brought himself under control.

"What . . . how can we do that?" he grunted, forcing himself to think clearly.

"We still have the map," said Poshtli. "And there's got to be more than one entrance into Axalt's palace. Let's have a look around and see if we can't find some other approach."

Both of them thought of the inexorable sunrise, even now doubtlessly lightening the sky over the city. When next the sun set, the full moon would rise in the east.

"Good idea," said Halloran finally. "Let's get going."

* * * * *

"Is he not back yet?" demanded Hoxitl. He and Shatil had waited long hours outside the throne room used by Poshtli.

The courtier, who had also waited those hours, shook his head sullenly. He had long ago grown tired of the high priest's agitation and complaints. "He will announce his presence."

"This is an outrage!" snarled the high priest. Suddenly he stepped up to the courtier and reached for the door to the throne room. The noble stared at him for a moment, but something in the high priest's impassioned gaze caused his spirits to quail. Meekly the courtier stepped aside.

Hoxitl pushed open the doors and entered the throne room, followed by Shatil. The young priest still clutched the Talon of Zaltec, though he no longer expected to find his sister—his victim—here in the palace.

"Lord Poshtli! My lord, where are you?" Shatil couldn't understand Hoxitl's agitation as the high priest dashed about the room, looking into the corridors that opened from the side opposite the doors.

"This is terrible—disastrous!" declared Hoxitl, turning back to Shatil. "Is it possible they have indeed gone to rescue the Revered Counselor?"

The young priest didn't hear the patriarch, for his attention was distracted by something he had just noticed. "Look!" he cried, crossing the room to point to a dark line along the stone wall of the throne room.

"What is it?" asked Hoxitl. The priest's gaunt face pinched tightly as he scrutinized the faint outline.

"A crack—there's a door concealed here!" Shatil drew his dagger and slipped its stone tip into the crack in the wall. With a slow, steady prying, he forced the stone portal toward him. In moments, it stood open, revealing a darkened passageway to a steep flight of stone steps leading downward.

"They must have gone this way and failed to close it fully behind them!" cried Hoxitl.

The high priest's mind raced through a tumult of concerns. Erixitl must die! For Naltecona's death, promised by the Ancient One, would signal the start of the uprising—and that attack was doomed to failure and disaster if the woman, the chosen daughter of Qotal, was not slain first.

Outside, the cult of the Viperhand grew ever more restless. The other occurrence Hoxitl needed to prevent, at all costs, was a premature attack. The solution came to him naturally.

"I must marshal the cult," Hoxitl told Shatil. "Already they gather in the plaza, and they must be controlled until the proper signal is given. You must go after Erixitl! Your sister will recognize you. She'll be glad to see that you're alive after Palul, will she not?"

Douglas Niles

Shatil nodded. His sister certainly assumed that he had died with all the other priests and warriors on the pyramid. From her perspective, no one had escaped.

Hoxitl continued. "That will let you get close enough to use the talon against her." The patriarch didn't need to conclude the plan, for they both understood that, if Hal or Poshtli accompanied Erixitl, such an attack would almost certainly cost the priest his life.

The young priest nodded. "It shall be as Zaltec commands." Shatil collected several reed torches, igniting one to light his way. He felt numb, detached from the preparations his body made. He watched himself go into a hole in the earth to kill his sister, giving up his own life in the process.

It seemed a proper fate for one who would be a tool of the gods.

* * * * *

Darien summoned Alvarro with a note. She requested his presence at noon, while Cordell inspected the legion's positions around the sprawling palace.

"Yes, my lady wizard?" inquired the red-bearded captain upon entering her darkened chamber in the palace of Axalt. She greeted him seated upon a mat. Awkwardly he sat before her.

"This wench—Halloran's woman, you claim—has angered and affronted me."

Alvarro nodded. Though he hadn't been present, he had heard the stories about how Erixitl had proven invulnerable to Darien's magic. The surviving swordsmen who had attacked the trio told terrible tales of Halloran's prowess, coupled with the failure of the fireball and magic missiles.

"I sensed earlier that your interest in her was something more personal," the elf said coolly, her ivory white skin glowing in the semidarkness of the room. Her eyes seemed huge to Alvarro, huge and beguiling. She wore a red silk dress, a thin sheath tightly outlining the curves of her body, and lust stirred in Alvarro.

"I will get you in to see her and give you time with her to do as you wish. Nothing in her room will be heard beyond those walls. However, in return, when you have finished with her, you must kill her."

"When should I do this?"

"Now. Today." Darien's voice was clipped. "She must die . . ." Her voice trailed away as she appeared to think for a moment. "She must be dead by sunset."

Alvarro blinked, thinking hard. The thought of Erix, alone and in his power, was like a powerful drug. Still, he wasn't an innocent recruit. Cordell had ordered the woman held prisoner. He regarded the elfmage suspiciously.

"What about the general?"

"I will see that he never knows who is to blame," Darien replied confidently.

It just might work, Alvarro told himself. He remembered Erix on the ground at Palul. His mind flamed at the prospect of holding her in his power.

"Why are you so anxious to have her dead?" he demanded.

Darien leaned back, her dress clinging seductively to her skin. "She makes me furious. She stands against my magic; she draws the eyes of men—Cordell's eyes," the albino replied. Her voice was like an icy wind. Alvarro thought briefly that the wizard didn't *look* furious, but then he thought again of Erix, and suddenly the wizard's motive didn't seem to matter.

* * * * *

The black-robed figure awaited Hoxitl in the darkened confines of the temple building below the Great Pyramid. "Greetings, priest," whispered the Ancient One.

The patriarch froze, wondering instinctively if this was an assassin sent to end his days. But the graceful figure advanced, speaking soothingly. "The death of Naltecona will occur tonight, after moonrise," said the Ancient One.

Hoxitl froze, taut with excitement and alarm. He thought of Erixitl, and of Shatil seeking her in the passages below the sacred plaza. Could he find her in time?

"My priest is seeking the girl, Erixitl of Palul, now. He will kill her as soon as he sees her!" Hoxitl blurted the explanation, fearing for his life again. Perhaps the Ancient One had assumed that she was already dead.

"That is fine." The words came from the robed figure dispassionately. The high priest stared in puzzlement, wondering why he didn't detect the heated insistence on Erix's death that had always been the tone of the Ancient Ones previously.

"But—but what if he doesn't find her? Did you not say that disaster would result if the attack began while she still lived?"

Finally the voice grew harsh. "Do not concern yourself, priest. How fares the cult? Will it be ready?"

"Come with me and see for yourself," Hoxitl invited. "I go to address them from the pyramid."

"Answer my question!" hissed the Ancient One. He faced away from the afternoon light spilling through the doorway. Hoxitl remembered other things, of the robed figures searching the city at night, of their subterranean lair. He guessed that, whatever the nature of Ancient Ones, they couldn't bear the light of the sun.

"Very well. The cult gathers within the sacred plaza. We number twenty-five thousand brands now," the patriarch said proudly. "At the sign, we will fall upon the legions of Kultaka and the Payit gathered outside the palace. When their allies have been slain, we attack the strangers themselves. We will be ready tonight."

"Splendid. Do you have sufficient numbers for the task?"

"The rest of the Nexalan army will certainly join our attack," Hoxitl said confidently. He knew that the Jaguar and Eagle Knights chafed at the truce and were eager to fight. They would be incapable of holding themselves aloof once the fighting erupted. "All they require is an initial spark, and the cult of the Viperhand is the spark that will kindle the blaze. Within a few hours, a hundred thousandmen or more will attack.

"And the blaze of their anger will drive the invaders from the True World!"

The Ancient One nodded, apparently pleased. Then, with a suddenness that stunned the high priest, the dark figure disappeared.

* * * * *

VIPERHAND

For long hours, Halloran and Poshtli probed through the darkened confines of the tunnels below the palaces and the sacred plaza. They found corners and niches, connecting passages and dead ends. Working their way around the corridor that had led to their ambush, they investigated every feature that they could find.

Several ladders ascended shafts that led to the sacred plaza itself, rather than the palaces. They could plainly hear the talking or moving about of warriors overhead, and they knew that just beyond the flagstone cap to the shaft, they could find legions of Kultakans or Nexalans.

But they couldn't find another passage that would lead them toward Erixitl.

Halloran's light spell illuminated their path for a while, but finally the power of the spell waned. Then they made do with the dim illumination cast by Helmstooth. The glow of the magic sword did little more than prevent them from tripping over obstacles and walking into walls.

Finally they collapsed, out of breath, discouraged, and apparently lost. Halloran tried to avoid thinking about Erixitl, but with every moment of rest, a new image of her, alone among the likes of Alvarro, Darien, Bishou Domincus, and Cordell himself, formed in his mind. Who knew how enraged the commander might become at one of his former captains, who now attacked in the night and slayed his men?

Wonderingly, Hal thought of the tiny rings of plumage that had given him such powers. They felt soft and comfortable now, exerting no apparent effect on his body. Only when he pressed his own strength to the limit, it seemed, did the *pluma* affect him.

Suddenly they heard a sound, a shuffling of footsteps in the distance. "Look," Hal whispered, discerning the flickering glow of torchlight emerging from a side corridor.

He put his sword behind him to mask its light, noticing that the torch and its bearer came closer. Orange light suddenly flared before them as a man emerged from the side corridor, unaware of their presence.

"Who are you?" challenged Poshtli. They recognized the man as a bloody-scalped priest of Zaltec. The thin figure had a stone dagger. His arms and legs, dirty and scarred, seemed to be mere skin covering the bones of his limbs.

"I—" The priest stopped and turned toward them, surprised but apparently not frightened. "I seek my sister. I fear she is lost in here."

"Are you mad?" demanded Poshtli.

"What's her name—your sister?" Halloran added.

"She is Erixitl of Palul."

"And you are Shatil, then." The young man nodded at Hal's statement. Erix had told Hal much of her brother, whom she had given up for dead atop the pyramid at Palul. The altar and statue had burned with such a conflagration that the identification of bodies had been impossible.

"Where is she?" asked Shatil suddenly. "Is she in danger?"

Halloran studied the priest. Everything about the man brought back memories of Martine's sacrifice and all the other rites of the brutal worship of Zaltec, routines of murder. He couldn't entirely suppress the revulsion he felt for everything this man stood for.

Yet Erix had spoken of Shatil kindly, and Halloran knew she had truly loved her brother. The man must certainly reciprocate the feeling.

"Yes, she is," he replied finally. "We're trying to rescue her. She's been taken by the legion."

Shatil's face twisted with a look of genuine shock and dismay.

"What are you doing down here?" Poshtli demanded. "Why do you seek her?"

Shatil's eyes met the warrior's squarely. Their dark eyes flashed in the torchlight. "Because I feared for her. Because Zaltec has warned me that she is in danger and told me where to look, that I could help her!" The priest held his voice level but urgent.

"Please, let me help you!" he urged. All the while, the Talon of Zaltec lay smooth and deadly in his hand.

* * * * *

"You must believe me! The danger is terrible, and it is tonight!" Erixitl stared into the black eyes of the man before her and he, not unsympathetically, looked back.

"But because you've had a *dream?*" Cordell replied, exhaling sharply in frustration. Some vague feeling made him want to trust this woman, yet all his years of caution warned him against such madness.

"Under the full moon," Erixitl explained again. "Naltecona will be slain by one who is of your legion. And when he dies, the True World dies soon afterward."

She and the captain-general had waged this discussion for nearly an hour. He stalked about the room where they had imprisoned her, clearly agitated. He didn't want to believe her, but he couldn't think of a good reason for her to make up such a story.

Erixitl looked around impatiently. They had placed her in some sort of storage room. She saw jugs of *octal*, baskets of mayz, and a large, locked door. High up on the wall, sunlight streamed into the room, and she could see flashes of clear blue sky, now streaming in from the west.

"How long before sunset—before the full moon rises?" she asked. "Do you really think you can protect the Revered Counselor if the gods have decreed his death?"

"Isn't that what you tried to do?" Cordell shot back. "If his death is ordained, how could your rescue have changed that fate?"

"Perhaps it couldn't," Erixitl murmured, grim defeat staring her in the face.

A sudden knock on the door pulled their attention from each other. "General, you'd better get out here!" The guard's voice, from beyond the portal, carried notes of urgency.

"What is it?" Cordell demanded irritably.

"Warriors, sir. They keep pouring into the plaza. They've got the Kultakans outnumbered already. They haven't attacked yet, but more of 'em keep coming."

Without another word to her, Cordell darted through the door. It slammed again, leaving Erix alone with her thoughts. She looked upward and saw that the sunlight still streamed into the room, but now the beams were black, as if the sun cast nothing but shadows.

Lost in her despair, she didn't hear the door open again. A cool whisper of air against her cheek was her first warning, and she spun to face the leering visage of Captain Alvarro.

Douglas Niles

The expression of animal hunger in his eyes sent chills coursing through her body.

"What do you want?" she demanded.

He opened his mouth and appeared to speak, but no sound came to her. Then Alvarro stepped closer to her, and as if he had passed an unseen barrier of silence, his voice became audible.

". . . think you know what I desire," he said, his thin smile displaying his gap-toothed gums.

Erix saw the sharp dagger in his hand. "Did Cordell order you to do this?" she asked calmly.

Alvarro sneered. "He doesn't know. But you won't be able to warn him, either. Nothing that happens in here will be heard outside."

Her mind whirling, Erixitl tried to think of a plan, a counter to this beast's approach. He advanced smugly. "Hal's wench—and a mighty proud thing you are," he chuckled. He swaggered closer, confident.

No sounds, he had told her. Erix didn't understand how, but she suspected this meant that he had help from the elf wizard. Her mind flashed back to her immediate problem, Alvarro. She remembered the man from the feast at Palul. The man had swilled *octal* as if the drink was the nectar of life itself.

"Why should I make a sound?" she inquired, trying to keep the terror from her voice. Her eyes falling on the jugs along the wall, she lifted one. "Here. First you want a drink, I know."

The captain blinked, surprised at her lack of fear. He snatched the jug and sniffed it suspiciously. "Sure, I'll drink," he grunted, raising the flask and guzzling the fiery stuff. It ran from his lips, soaking his red beard and dripping to the floor.

Overhead, the sunlight on the wall began to fade. Erixitl turned her back on the man, sickened by the sight of him, desperate for escape. She had so little time, but what could she do?

She still had her token, inside of her dress, but while it might stop Darien's mightiest magics, it offered little protection against a crude approach such as Alvarro's. The pouch on her belt chafed her hip as she turned back. Her only other possession, it held only the little glass vial of potion.

The potion she had feared to allow Halloran to drink. She still remembered the shadowy explosion of black terror she had seen when he raised it to his mouth.

Alvarro smacked his lips, lowering the empty jug. "You're a pretty one, d'you know that? I bet you do things for Halloran!"

Her stomach churned as he looked her up and down. He took a step closer.

"Y'know, if you do those things for me, I just might not kill you," he lied. He reached a burly paw to her shoulder, and Erix turned slowly away, forcing herself not to strike him. She knew the stocky horseman could easily overpower her if she gave him cause to attack.

Her hand fell on the pouch, and she slipped the bottle out. She sensed it burning against her hand—a vile and dangerous thing, it was. Roughly he spun her around to face him, his mouth a few inches from her own.

"I—I give him *octal*," she said, trying to be calm through her terror. "He can drink very much. It—it gives him great pleasure!"

With false lightness, she turned away, snatching up another jug. A quick gesture dumped the contents of the vial into the *octal* before she whirled back to Alvarro. "Here—I can do the same for you!"

Her heart pounded as the man brushed the jug aside. "I can have that anytime," he grunted. "I want something a little more special."

Until she felt the wall at her back, Erix was unaware that she had been backing slowly away. Now she stood, trapped by one of Alvarro's arms on either side of her. She still held the jug in her hand and smelled the sweet reek of *octal* on his breath.

"Come. Can we sit?" she said, slowly and carefully. She must not arouse his suspicions!

Scowling, Alvarro nevertheless allowed her to step aside and sink to the floor. Obviously her reaction wasn't the one he had expected. He sat roughly beside her, a curious expression on his face. "Aren't you frightened?" he asked bluntly.

"Yes—I am," she admitted. *Terrified, actually.* "But we are a fatalistic people. Our gods teach us not to fight the inevitable. You are here; we're alone. I know that I am in your power."

Every muscle in her body screamed for her to strike out at this brute, to punch and pummel him. But a violent contest with Alvarro would certainly be futile, so she continued to use her wits. She raised the flask, not offering it to him but insuring that he saw it.

"Give me that," he grunted, snatching it from her hands. He raised the neck to his mouth and once again took a long swallow. Erixitl watched, trembling with fear. Would the potion, diluted by *octal*, have any effect at all? If it did, what would that effect be?

Alvarro set the half-empty container aside, smacking his lips. Suddenly, with shocking violence, he turned on her, pressing her to the floor and climbing on top of her. A mad fire gleamed in his eyes.

Then the man grunted once. His eyes widened and his tongue protruded. His fingers clutched for her neck, and his body shook with convulsions.

Finally he stiffened, gasping inarticulately, and died.

Groaning weakly, Erixitl crawled from beneath him, rolling away from the repulsive form. For long moments, she gasped for breath, nearly gagging. She looked at the little bottle, still in her hand. Reflexively she hurled it against the wall, watching it shatter.

She saw her hopes reflected in the shards of glass that scattered all over the floor, disappearing in the fading light of the sun.

Then she sensed movement beside her, and whirled in shock. Another figure had entered the room, not through any aperture—not through any means she could see. This one looked at her with a trace of humor in his slitted, unblinking eyes. Great feathery wings bent slowly, suspending a twisting, serpentine body in the air. His voice, when he spoke, was a sibilant whisper.

"Greetings," said the feathered snake. "I am Chitikas Couatl, and I have returned."

* * * * *

From the chronicles of Coton:

To the chronicler is given the sight, that afterward the tale of the Waning may be told.

The gods gather in the gallery of their immortal cosmos now to watch the arena floor below. Each is sublime and confident in his, or her, own presence. Each takes little note of the other gods, watching instead the play of the humans below.

This may be their undoing. Helm licks his lips as his men count their gold, an ever-growing pile within the palace of Axalt. The Bishou makes loud thanks, and the god basks in the praise.

Zaltec feasts upon the hearts that are offered, but the massive feeding does not slake his hunger. If anything, it inflames him. Now his sacred cult seethes and strains with warlike fervor. They crave the release of an attack, a chance to feed their god as he has never eaten before.

Neither of them shows awareness of the third immortal presence, the spidery essence of Lolth, slowly taking shape in the cosmic gallery beside them. She has eyes—vengeful eyes—for her wayward children. The drow, committed passionately now to the cause of their adopted god, have forsaken her completely.

And her patience wears thin.

↬17↫

THE LAST SUNSET

"No, by Helm—we *can't* be lost!" Halloran shouted, bashing his fist against the wall of the tunnel. Frustration threatened to tear him apart. His mind burned with countless pictures of Erixitl's fate at the hands of his former comrades-in-arms.

For hours, the three men had pushed themselves frantically through the network of tunnels, backtracking, exploring, desperately seeking a way out. All around them extended connecting passages—apparently identical tunnels, with new intersections, changes in elevation, secret corridors, and hidden chambers every hundred paces. The priest, Erixitl's brother, threw himself into the hunt as diligently as did Poshtli and Hal.

"We'll get out," Poshtli said grimly, pushing himself to his feet following a brief rest. They had paused only for a moment, but he, too, felt the urgency that would not allow them to remain idle.

"I'm sure we've been going down," Hal guessed, frantic at the thought that they had left Erixitl far behind them. "We're underground by now."

"You might be right. Let's look around for some way to climb." Poshtli gestured to the stone ceiling. They had seen several rotting wooden ladders leading upward in various places.

Shatil remained silent, watching Hal and Poshtli growl and bluster. A part of him—the man—admired the passion with which they wanted to rescue his sister; another part—the servant of Zaltec—hoped with equal passion for success, so that he could perform his god-appointed task and slay her.

The priest lit another of his reed torches from the stump

of the last one. "I have only two left," he reported softly. "We will soon find ourselves in darkness."

Halloran whirled on the priest, ready to snarl his anger with this last announcement. Shatil met his gaze coolly, and suddenly Hal felt very foolish. "All the more reason to keep moving," he grunted.

Once again they started along a narrow corridor—a corridor that looked just like a hundred other such passages. "How long have we been down here?" Hal asked, trying to bite back his despair.

"Most of the day, I think," Poshtli replied. "It must be approaching sunset." He didn't elaborate. Both of them fully understood the significance of Erix's premonition. With sunset would come the rising of the full moon, and—if she had seen the truth—shortly afterward would follow the death of Naltecona.

As they plodded along, Halloran turned and saw Shatil studying him, an expression of puzzlement across his features. "What is it?" asked the former legionnaire.

"I am wondering," replied the priest, pointing to Hal's waist, "how it is that you come to carry a band of *hishna*. Talonmagic, so I believed, is used only by the priests of my order. Or are you a master of *hishna* as well?"

"No," Hal replied. He looked at the snakeskin strap wound around him. "This was used to imprison me once, long ago in Payit. When I was freed, I kept it."

"It is a potent token," the priest declared.

"So I learned." Halloran vividly remembered the difficulty he had had with the snakeskin. It had grown into a long, flexible thong that had wrapped around him tightly. When Daggrande tried to cut it with his dagger, the steel edge had dulled without making a mark on the strap.

"Look!" Shatil cried suddenly as the other two marched quickly before him. He pointed to a small alcove beside the corridor that Poshtli and Hal, in their haste, had somehow missed.

"What is it?" grunted Hal, peering into the shadows.

"A ladder," replied Shatil. "Leading up."

* * * * *

Douglas Niles

"Look at them, Captain. They just sit there, watching. What do you make of it?" Cordell turned to Daggrande, waiting for an answer. The dwarf stood beside him on the roof of the palace of Axalt. The broad expanse of planks stretched flat around them, surrounded by a low parapet at the edge of the roof. In the center of the palace, several great peaks of thatch extended high into the sky, marking the throne room and the larger halls. Except for these peaks, the top of the palace consisted of a broad, open platform.

"Makes me damned uneasy, General." The dwarf squinted across the sacred plaza, through the long shadows cast by the lowering sun.

He saw tens of thousands of Nexalan warriors gathered all around the fringes of the plaza and spilling forward in great groups around their temples and pyramids. They wore feathers and carried clubs, *macas*, and spears. Occasionally one group would mutter some kind of chant, not loud enough to be a battle cry but nevertheless a sinister and unsettling sound. All day long the warriors had gathered, their numbers swelling from the apparently inexhaustible populace of the great city.

Below them, arrayed in camps around the palace of Axalt, the ranks of Kultakan and Payit warriors watched nervously, weapons close at hand. The twenty-five thousand men of their allies, appearing so numerous when they marched into the city, now seemed badly outnumbered by the Nexalans. The five hundred men of the Golden Legion, garrisoned within the walls of the palace itself, looked across this formidable array and prayed for peace.

"There's that priest again," grunted Daggrande.

Cordell looked to the highest pyramid, and he saw the black-robed patriarch of Zaltec. Many of the Nexalans gathered around that edifice, and they could see him gesticulating. The harsh bark of his voice carried across the plaza, though even had they known his language, the words would have remained indistinguishable because of the distance.

"It looks ugly," Cordell muttered. "You can feel the hatred and the anger."

"Can't really blame them for that," Daggrande noted. "They have to know Naltecona's not here of his own will."

"And the gold?" challenged the captain-general angrily. "They've stopped bringing it to us." Indeed, the steady deliveries of golden objects and dust had abruptly ceased earlier in the day.

Daggrande looked at his commander with a trace of alarm. The pile of gold they had already collected would be a challenge to transport from Nexal. More importantly, one look at the obviously hostile assemblage around the legionnaires should have warned them all that they had more pressing concerns.

Cordell looked at the sun, about to set over the shoulder of Mount Zatal. A plume of steam marked the summit of the massif, casting a shadow across much of the city. He looked back at the Nexalans, worried.

"Send for Naltecona," he ordered abruptly. "He will speak to his people. He must convince them of the folly of an attack!"

Daggrande nodded and turned away. As he went to the ladder that led down into the palace, he cast a last look at the vast and growing horde around them.

Folly for whom? he wondered.

* * * * *

"Chitikas!" Erixitl gasped in shock, and then delight. "You have returned!"

The couatl hovered in a loose coil, the brilliant down that covered his brightly colored body gleaming in the last rays of the sun. His long, slender form remained airborne, with only the tip of his plumed tail trailing on the floor. His huge golden wings beat very gently, their trailing plumes floating up and down with each leisurely movement.

Flicking his forked tongue in and out of his mouth, the couatl fixed Erixitl with a level stare. His yellow eyes, vertically slitted, did not blink.

"I have returned—that is what I said," hissed the feathered snake with more than a hint of impatience. "When mortals fail to understand and act upon their circumstances, one such as I—"

"*Fail to act!*" Erix held her voice low, but her delight became sudden fury that struck the smug couatl like a blow in the face. "*Who* has failed to act? Where have you been since you disappeared in Payit? What do you mean coming here now, on the very night portrayed in my dream, and telling me I have failed to act?" She gestured at Alvarro's corpse, still warm beside her. "Why couldn't you have come an hour ago? Or a tenday ago?"

"That is enough," said Chitikas, with a trace of his old haughtiness. "Let us act now."

"What do you propose?" Erix, her anger not forgotten, regarded the feathered serpent suspiciously.

The sunlight, streaming in from the west, began to fade. Erixitl pictured the full moon, cresting the horizon to the east.

"Perhaps we should go to the roof." The way Chitikas phrased the words, it sounded almost like a question.

* * * * *

"You must tell them to disperse!" Cordell barked. Darien immediately translated, and Naltecona looked at the general with an expression of utmost fatigue.

"You ask the impossible. Can you not see that they have been summoned by a higher command than my own? You yourselves have robbed my voice of the authority it once had. They will not listen to me."

"Do you want to avoid a war?" demanded Cordell, his voice dropping to a menacing snarl. "Or do you want us to unleash our powers against your city?"

Naltecona sighed, a heartbreaking sound. "The unleashing of power is something neither I nor you can any longer control. No, I do not wish to see this war. My dreams have shown me the inevitable result—a disaster for all."

"Then speak to them, Helm curse you!" Cordell snapped the words and then whirled away, struggling to regain his self-control. The Revered Counselor was a proud man, he knew, and one could push a proud man just so far.

Surprisingly, however, Naltecona started for the edge of the roof overlooking the plaza below. He stopped, clearly visible to all the warriors on this, the eastern side of the palace. Though the sun had set, the full moon before him rose into a sky still blue with the fading light of dusk. Naltecona's voice, when he spoke, thrummed with the vibrant power of rulership.

"Hear me, my people!" A dull silence settled over the assembled masses of warriors, extending slowly, like a ripple across a pond, to the far limits of the plaza.

"My heart knows the pain you feel, and my soul understands the needs of honor! But this is a time when we must swallow our pain. As for honor, my own allows me to dwell here, as the guest of the foreigners. Does that not prove that we are not dishonored?"

A rumble of displeasure rose from the Nexalans. Below them, next to the palace wall, the Kultakans nervously fingered their weapons.

"I must ask you to to show patience—more patience even than you have shown already. I understand the difficulty of restraint."

Howls of indignation, shrieks, and whistles of anger, all these sounds erupted from the multitude of warriors and priests gathered below. Upon many, Naltecona saw the gleaming red scar of the Viperhand. The cult seemed to lead the way, but the counselor knew that all Nexal stood prepared to follow.

"I have seen the future! If we follow the path of war, only disaster can follow—disaster such as our fathers could not have imagined!" Naltecona's voice grew strident as he strived to make himself understood. "My people, *listen* to me!"

But by now it was already too late.

* * * * *

Full darkness settled over the room before the sinuous body of Chitikas Couatl encircled Erixitl. The feathered snake drove his wings with that same leisurely beat. Yet somehow, without visible effort, he propelled himself faster and faster, his rainbow-hued form blurring into a ring of color around her. Sudden light flashed, very bright, in the room.

In the next instant, Erix stood upon the roof of the palace, still encircled by the whirling Chitikas. The Cloak of One

DOUGLAS NILES

Plume billowed outward. The snake quickly floated to a stop, coiled in the air beside her, but she had already forgotten him.

Instead, her eyes locked onto the scene before her—*the exact image of her dream!*

Naltecona stood at the edge of the flat roof, against the rim of wall, perhaps two feet high, that encircled this portion of the palace. The peak of thatch towered behind her, sheltering Chitikas and Erixitl in its shadow.

The rest of the area, of course, stood clearly illuminated in the pale wash of the just-risen full moon. Cordell, Darien, the Bishou, and the dwarven captain, Daggrande, stood around the Revered Counselor in a loose semicircle. Beyond them, filling the plaza like a thick carpet of humanity, seethed the warrior mass of the Nexala.

Erixitl stared as cold, inexorable fear gripped her soul. She felt as though she was observing a play on a stage, a performance aloof and detached from her involvement. She could do nothing as events unfolded.

Then she shook her head, her black hair floating like a cloud around her. She had been brought here for a purpose, she knew. In her determination to act, she had overlooked a thing she had learned before.

The purposes of Chitikas Couatl were not given easily to understand.

* * * * *

"Push! The cursed thing *has* to open!" urged Halloran, below Poshtli on the narrow ladder.

"I—I—can't move it," gasped the warrior, slumping away from the tightly shut trap door above them.

"Let me try!" Hal squeezed to the side as Poshtli dropped several rungs to allow his companion to reach the top.

Hal feared for the destruction of this land, for he believed implicitly in Erixitl's premonition. But mostly he drove himself forward because of fear for her and bitter hatred for those who imprisoned her and threatened all his hopes. He had to reach her!

Feathermagic pulsed around his wrist. His fist crashed upward, and the trap door cracked in two, each piece flying back from the opening. He sprang through the opening, drawing Helmstooth in the same motion, not knowing whether they had reached a palace chamber, courtyard, or garden.

Or roof. He looked around at a broad, flat expanse. He saw a group of legionnaires some distance away and heard a vague rumbling from the vast square around them. The sound had apparently masked the noise of his emergence from the soldiers, for none of the men-at-arms turned toward him. Swiftly Poshtli, and then Shatil, climbed from the trap door.

They were on the roof of a palace, Hal saw—the palace of Naltecona's father, Axalt. They hadn't wandered as far as Hal had feared during their subterranean explorations. He saw the Revered Counselor, apparently addressing the unruly gathering below. Slowly, with shocking awareness, he took in the huge numbers of warriors gathered across the plaza.

"There must be a hundred thousand of them!" he breathed in awe.

"More," Poshtli said quietly, his trained warrior's eye assessing the throng.

"Where is my sister?" Shatil wondered, looking quickly around.

Crouching where they stood, the moon casting their shadows long across the roof, they searched the area with their eyes. They saw dozens of legionnaires and their captains, together with the wizard and the Bishou. All stared at the drama before them, sensing Naltecona's failure to appease the crowd. Most of the roof lay exposed to the cool moonlight, though the thatched peaks left a few areas of deep shadow.

"She's not here," Halloran said, nearing despair.

"Look!" Poshtli whispered, pointing to the crowd below. They saw the Nexalans surging angrily toward the palace, a stormy sea of humanity around their perilous island. Yet the warriors did not attack. "Erixitl's dream—the death of Naltecona among the legion! It could happen now!"

Hal shook his head. "I can't believe Cordell would have him killed. Not now, not like this. Naltecona is the only thing holding them at bay."

"Hey! You over there!"

The harsh bark of a sentry told them that they had been discovered. Halloran whirled to see several crossbowmen, their heavy weapons menacing, advancing from the opposite portion of the roof.

"It's Halloran!" shouted one of the sentries. Instantly the attention of the captains turned toward the trio, clearly illuminated in the bright moonlight. For a moment, Hal thought of diving through the dark trap door beside them. The three of them could easily disappear into those narrow tunnels.

But that course was an admission of failure, and he wasn't ready to admit that they had failed. He saw Darien, her pale face studying them coolly, and he remembered her spellbook in his pack. He seized upon a desperate hope.

"I want to talk to you," he called, meeting Cordell's eyes.

"Come forward," said the captain-general cautiously. "Keep your hands in plain sight." He watched them approach for several moments. "That's close enough."

Hal, flanked by Poshtli and Shatil, stopped about ten paces short of his old commander. Beside Cordell, he saw the albino elfmage, still regarding him with a gaze so devoid of emotion it reminded Halloran of a reptile's.

The crowd beyond the palace surged noisily. Naltecona turned away from them, regarding the confrontation curiously.

"I want to make a trade," Halloran said, looking at Darien. "I have your spellbook—and you have a person who means very much to me . . . to us. I offer you the book in return for the woman."

Cordell looked at Darien, an expression of cool interest on his face. The wizard, to the surprise of all of them, began to laugh. The sound had a cruel, harsh ring to it.

* * * * *

"We must go to them!" whispered Erixitl, her voice straining with urgency. "There is little time!"

"Wait," said Chitikas calmly. They remained in the dark shadow below a peak of the roof, unseen by the others before them.

VIPERHAND

Erix looked at the couatl in surprise, then shook her head vehemently. "I'm going!"

She started forward, sensing the snake sigh heavily beside her. After one step, however, her foot stuck to the planks below her. She tried to turn on Chitikas and found her other foot equally immobilized. She couldn't move.

Twisting her body, she angrily opened her mouth to demand that he free her. But no words came forth. He held her spellbound.

"Wait," ordered the couatl again. "We cannot be seen yet."

And Erix could only turn to watch, as dull horror rose within her soul.

* * * * *

"What is the humor?" the captain-general asked his mistress. "I should think it a sensible exchange—your spellbook for Halloran's woman."

"The humor is in this man's foolish naivete!" Darien barked, her mouth still twisted in grim amusement. Her eyes, however, remained cold and lifeless.

Halloran felt a chill of fear.

"He is in my power now," Darien continued. "Without the wench to protect his body, my magic can tear the secret of the spellbook from his mind!

"But before your soul becomes mine," she added, "there is another thing you should know."

Now Halloran's blood froze in his veins, and he imagined her words before she spoke.

"Your woman is already dead!"

"What?" demanded Cordell. "She was under my protection! How dare you—"

"*Your* protection?" Darien scoffed. "Like the legion is under your protection—the safety of your wisdom, your keen planning?"

"What do you mean? Explain yourself!" Cordell growled. The legionnaires edged nervously back, never having witnessed such an exchange between the general and his elven mistress.

"You have been a useful tool," she sneered, "but that use is finished. The girl is dead. . . ."

The pause that followed seemed to leave room for the sun to rise and set, yet still that bright, full moon hung suspended in the sky.

"And know this," Darien continued, almost conversationally. "There *will* be war."

Suddenly she raised her finger and barked a sharp, magical command. A bolt of hot magic burst like an arrow from her finger, slashing forward to explode in her victim's chest. Another, and a third, and still more magic missiles darted forth. Each struck deep into her target's blistered skin, crackling and sizzling with arcane power, ripping his body apart, driving him backward. Blue sparks hissed while the others stood, shocked and speechless.

As the spell finally waned, Naltecona's torn and bleeding form tottered on the edge of the roof. A sudden hush fell across the mob below. Then, already dead, the mangled figure of the Revered Counselor toppled from the roof to crash to the paving stones of the plaza below.

Magic still sparked across the roof, a residue of the killing power that had slain Naltecona. This power sizzled as light, flaring upward and then falling back, casting everything alternately in brightness and shadows.

As the light pulsed, Halloran stared at Darien, watching her in stunned, disbelieving shock. In the brightness, her skin gleamed with the alabaster whiteness caused by her albinism.

Yet in the shadows, it seemed to be dark, as black as any drow's.

* * * * *

From the chronicles of Coton:

Now the True World stands poised at the brink of chaos. My fingers tremble, and my brushes move unsteadily across the page. I must put them down, and I hold my breath as the fate of the land takes shape.

♣ 18 ♣

BLACK AND WHITE

Erixitl suddenly broke her feet free, and she instantly ran from the shadows into the bright moonlight, toward those clustered at the edge of the roof. Around her, the city seemed frozen, strangely paralyzed. "Hal!" she cried.

Whirling, his face split into a look of disbelief, then disbelieving happiness. He shouted, "Erix! You're alive!" then swept her into his arms. His relief turned to fury, and again he turned to Darien.

He saw the wizard's face then, twisted into a look of shock, dismay . . . and fear.

"No!" Darien gasped, her voice a strangled choke.

"You treasonous witch!" Daggrande howled, looking at the place where Naltecona had stood. "You've killed us all!" From below, howls of outrage erupted from the Nexalan masses. They surged toward the palace, blind rage growing quickly into battle frenzy.

"What—what have you done?" Cordell gaped at her.

"What *are* you?" asked Bishou Domincus, softly, fearfully.

Holding Erixitl at his side, Halloran studied the albino elf. He saw the other legionnaires, with their expressions of shock and anger and disbelief—and, slowly, growing fear as the rage of the Nexalans swelled from the plaza around them.

He alone understood.

"You're one of them, aren't you?" he stated quietly. "An Ancient One. A dark elf. That's why you avoid the sun, not because of your delicate skin. You've planned this for a long time."

The wizard, still gaping at Erixitl, didn't reply. Cordell, however, regarded Hal with confusion that the man found almost pathetic. "What do you mean? What are you saying?"

Douglas Niles

"I'm saying that you have been manipulated—used by the drow who seek to gain control of Maztica. Those who sought to start the war that would tear this land apart and give them ultimate mastery."

The sounds from the plaza below, where Naltecona's death and fall had been plainly visible, indicated that the war had indeed begun.

* * * * *

The sign! Hoxitl, watching from his lofty vantage on the Great Pyramid, saw Naltecona outlined in deadly magic, witnessed the grotesque dance of his assassination, and then observed the limp corpse tumble to the plaza below.

So did thousands of Nexalan warriors. For a prolonged moment, the square fell still from the shock. Then a rumble shook the ground as a burst of smoke billowed upward from Zatal's summit, and finally the high priest lifted his voice in a long, ululating call. Instantly the members of his cult—perhaps one in every five of the assembled warriorhood—understood the order.

The branded ones echoed the call and raised their weapons. Their fury and battle lust spread contagiously, and in another moment, the cult surged forward to attack. As Hoxitl had known they would, the other warriors of Nexal immediately followed.

A great wave of humantide swept across the sacred plaza, converging on the Palace of Axalt. A din of stomping feet, screaming voices, whistles, and wooden-hafted weapons clashing in rhythmic cadence rocked the center of the city. The volume of sound could surely, the priest thought, be heard by the gods themselves.

The Kultakan and Payit warriors allied with the legion suffered the first onslaught of Nexal, quartered as they were outside the palace. The Kultakans guarded the north and east sides of the structure, while the Payit were encamped to the west. This pleased Hoxitl; let the foreigners see the fate of their allies and know what was in store for themselves.

The Kultakans, braced for war, launched volleys of stone-tipped arrows into the approaching mass. Many Nexalan

VIPERHAND

warriors fell, but in seconds, the two forces clashed in melee. Feathered headdresses waved above the fight, marking the line between the two nations, but soon the colors mingled in confused slaughter.

Hoxitl watched the battle, his features flushed with transcendent ecstasy. Zaltec would be well pleased.

Thousands of men whirled through a dance of death, *macas* chopping, stone daggers thrusting, all illuminated by the bright, eerie moonlight. Spears, arrows, and stones flew above the tide of warriors, landing indiscriminately among the packed ranks. Cries of the wounded, shrill howls of triumph, and hoarse shouts of warning all blended into a battlefield cacaphony.

Blood spread slick on the paving stones, glistening like black oil. The bright moon rose higher into the sky, covering the whole gory scene with its mockingly pristine glow.

The five thousand warriors of the Payit, on the west side of the palace, couldn't stand long against the rush. Fragmented by the shock of the attack, these spearmen tried to hold a line but soon found themselves fighting in small islands, surrounded by the hordes of Nexalans.

Desperately the Payit tried to fight their way free of the plaza. Some of them made it and some of them died. Most fell into the hands of their attackers. The Nexalans quickly marched the prisoners toward the Great Pyramid. Even as the battle against the Kultakans raged with increased savagery, the first of the Payit prisoners started the long, one-way climb up to the altar of Zaltec.

* * * * *

Shatil stared, awestruck. Erixitl! His sister still lived! He didn't understand the speech of the foreigners around him, but he sensed their shock, and their anger, directed at the pale woman who had slain Naltecona. Too, he saw the sorcerer's fear when Erixitl arrived.

The young priest looked at his sister with a sense of overwhelming confusion. He couldn't deny the joy he felt at seeing her alive. Yet his mission had been to slay her, so that Naltecona's death could signal the uprising of the cult.

But now the Revered Counselor was dead, and the uprising already raged throughout the plaza below. He could no longer perform his task—it seemed that it was too late. But should he still slay her? What was the will of Zaltec now?

Surely if her death would signal the murder of Naltecona, killing her was no longer necessary. He wished Hoxitl stood beside him to give him advice. In the absence of such instruction, he must decide for himself.

Shatil convinced himself that the use of his venomous talon now did not meet the commands of his god. And so Erix would live.

At least until her brother received another command.

* * * * *

"No!" Cordell barked, suddenly regaining his senses and turning savagely toward Halloran. The attackers surging below seemed to bring him back to some semblance of his former generalship. "You're wrong!"

"He's right," said Darien, finally regaining her own calm demeanor. Suddenly she threw back her head, her white face turned toward the moon. She uttered a strange cry, something like the cry of a hawk, only deeper, more forceful.

Erix clenched Hal's arm, staring at the albino wizard. She sensed Chitikas floating up behind her and derived a vague comfort from the serpent's presence at her other side. Yet she didn't forget that the snake had brought her here, and then held her spellbound while she watched the nightmare begin.

In the next instant, a dozen black-robed figures popped into sight beside Darien, teleporting from some location where she had summoned them.

"The Ancient Ones," Halloran said, pointing. "Do you need more proof?"

"Greetings, sister," said one. He threw back his hood to reveal a tall shock of snow-white hair above a face of deepest midnight black.

"By Helm, it's true!" growled Daggrande. He raised his axe and took a step toward the dark elves.

"There stands the woman. You can see that she still lives!" Darien pointed to Erixitl, and they saw the drows' eyes widen in shock, perhaps fear. "Kill her!" barked the mage.

Instantly the dark elves pulled swords of black steel from their robes, rushing Erix in a pack. Their white eyes reflected milky hatred in the moonlight, but their blades sucked the light from the air and showed only as black, deadly shadow.

But Halloran saw them coming, and he would not lose Erixitl again. And so, too, did Chitikas Couatl.

The feathered snake suddenly glowed with a light like the sun, and many of the drow swordsmen recoiled, shrieking and pulling their robes across their eyes. Dwelling all their lives underground, emerging only at night, their vision was seared by the couatl's sudden brilliance.

Halloran sprang forward, cutting down one with a single hammerlike blow of his sword. Poshtli, too, thrust a blade through the heart of a blinded drow, while Daggrande cut the legs from under a third with a vicious swipe of his axe. The others—Cordell, the Bishou, Shatil—stared in awe at the shocking explosion of violence and magic.

"Strike her down!" shrilled one of the surviving drow, stumbling back to Darien's side. Halloran, Poshtli, and Daggrande advanced menacingly.

"I cannot," the wizard snapped. She would waste none of her precious spells on attacks she knew to be futile.

Halloran rushed forward and hacked a fourth drow in two with a savage sidearm swing. Black blood sprayed the others, and they recoiled, vivid fear marking their features. He leaped toward Darien, murderous hatred propelling his blade.

But he struck only empty air as the blade whistled past the place where Darien had stood. She and the remaining drow blinked out of sight together, teleporting away from the fight on the rooftop.

"She's gone," said Cordell slowly. "What have you done?"

"What have *you* done?" demanded Halloran savagely. "You've led these men into a trap, and now your wizard is gone! You'll have to fight your way out!"

"Shatil!" Erixitl suddenly recognized her brother, standing off to one side. The priest of Zaltec looked at her dazedly. He dropped an object that looked like a small claw into his pouch as she ran to him, and met her embrace with one of his own.

A black-shafted, steel-tipped arrow suddenly cracked against Halloran's breastplate, ricocheting across the roof. "Over there!" he shouted, looking up to see the band of drow on the roof, a hundred paces away. Several of them had dark longbows raised, arrows nocked and ready.

The battle surged with growing intensity below the legion's commanders as the Kultakans fell back to the very shadow of the palace walls. Nexalans pressed all around them, and the howls and shrieks and whistles rang through the night.

"Come," said Chitikas, his whispered tones clearly audible. "*Now* we will strike!"

"*Now?*" Erix demanded. "A few minutes ago, we could have saved Naltecona, and *now* we attack? Are you too late for *everything?*"

Chitikas looked at her inscrutably. Poshtli grunted in pain as a black arrow tore into his shoulder. Pulling the missile free with a grimace, he looked toward the band of drow. Cordell, too, looked at the dark elves, and then at the raging fight below.

"Fight your battle here!" Hal barked at his old commander. "We'll go after them—come on!" He and Poshtli started forward, with Erix and Shatil running after them. Halloran saw the drow preparing for another murderous volley and wondered how many arrows he would endure before he and his companions crossed the distance to the dark elves.

"This way," Chitikas hissed, suddenly driving his wings downward. He settled the coil of his body around the four humans, and again that white light flared on the rooftop. Halloran felt a sickening, whirling sensation as his feet lost contact with the boards beneath them.

But suddenly they stood on the roof again, just a few feet away from the drow—and *behind* them! Chitikas teleported them as swiftly and accurately as the drow themselves! "Get the witch!" Hal grunted, chopping the head from a drow who stood between him and Darien. Poshtli charged beside him as the startled elves whirled to face the sudden attack.

Another drow stepped before Hal, protecting Darien. He raised a blade of midnight black, and Helmstooth clashed against the weapon with a ringing of hard steel. But the power of Hal's *pluma* proved dominant, and the drow howled as the bone in his arm snapped. Halloran stared into Darien's widened eyes, feeling a brutal, angry thrill at the fear he saw there.

Then, once again, the band of Ancient Ones blinked out of sight.

* * * * *

The Nexalan warriors, led by the fanatic bloodlust of the cult of the Viperhand, drove their Kultakan enemies against the walls of the palace. With the Payit already vanquished—slain, routed, or captured—the Kultakans now felt the full brunt of the assault.

Hoxitl watched the battle from the Great Pyramid, knowing that many hearts were coming to Zaltec. The initial flush of his ecstasy did not wane; if anything, it grew as the battle raged throughout the night. He saw his warriors using nets, ropes, and long hooks to drag Kultakan warriors from the ranks of their comrades. A long file of prisoners already stretched around the pyramid, gathering in the temple below.

He awaited only the dawn to commence the feeding of his god.

Down on the blood-slicked stones of the courtyard, Tokol, war chief of the Kultaka, understood the grave peril of his situation. His warriors fought with discipline and savagery, killing even as they died. But the enemy numbered too many, and with the high palace wall behind them, they couldn't fall back any farther. Overhead, bolts fired from legion crossbows showered from the wall into the ranks of the attackers, but there were pitiful few crossbows when compared to the endless thousands of attacking Nexalans.

The son of Takamal wondered if he had led his people into annihilation by placing their trust and their service in the hands of the conquering legion. The battle here was lost, he knew, and all that remained to him was to try to save as many of his warriors as he could.

Douglas Niles

Grimly he spread the word, and the Kultakans tightened their ranks. Upon a whistled signal from their leader—a sound that carried somehow above the din of the battle—the allies of the Golden Legion charged the Nexalan hordes. Their tight formation pushed through the chaotic jumble of the attackers as they drove toward the gate of the sacred plaza.

Soon the Nexalans parted before them, still fighting but making no desperate attempt to prevent the breakout. Tokol led the way, his *maca* dripping with gore, his heart bursting with the tragedy he had brought upon his people. Of the twenty thousand warriors he had brought to Nexal, a little more than half of them escaped—and only because their enemies let them go.

As for Hoxitl and the cult, they knew that the true enemy remained trapped inside the palace of Axalt. Alone now, bereft of allies, the Golden Legion's fate would soon be sealed.

* * * * *

More black arrows arced through the moonlit night, but Chitikas saw them coming and blinked the four humans out of the way before they landed. Once again Halloran and Poshtli pressed home the attack against the drow, and again the dark elves flashed away before their swords could reach Darien.

Another drow lay dead upon the roof, but Poshtli and Halloran bled from several wounds each. Gasping with exhaustion, the companions paused to breathe.

"There!" Erixitl shouted, pointing around a corner of the peaked central roof.

The men, including Shatil, leaped to Erix's side as Chitikas again whisked them into an attack. Again and again, the battle of teleportation raged all around the palace roof, with neither side gaining a clear advantage. The legionnaires took little note of this fight, engrossed as they were in the defense of the building itself.

Throughout the long, bright night, Hal, Poshtli, Erix, and Shatil pursued the dark elves across the rooftop of the palace, while the square around them reeled under the raging battle. Eight or nine of the dark elves perished in the chase, but always Darien escaped.

Finally, as dawn began to color the eastern sky, the Ancient Ones blinked out of sight and did not reappear.

* * * * *

From the chronicles of Coton:

Amid a surging sea of blood, the Temple of Qotal remains a shrinking island of calm.

Around me rages war—total, uncontrolled, hateful battle that can only result in complete annihilation. The priests of Zaltec thrill, now, to their victory, little realizing the future cost of their triumph. The Ancient Ones, serving Zaltec, strive to kill the chosen daughter of Qotal, but now—and they must know this—it is too late to avert disaster.

They remain unaware of Lolth, creeping ever closer, growing ever larger. The spider goddess watches, with pleasure, the bloodshed. She bides her time, not yet ready to add to the killing, when the humans do such a splendid job on their own.

But soon it will be time for her to strike.

♣ 19 ♣

RISING TIDE

Cordell stood on the palace roof with Daggrande and the Bishou, watching the Kultakans fight their way to the gates of the sacred plaza. The commander's sense of discipline wanted to condemn them for their flight and abandoning their allies.

Yet his soldier's spirit admired the courage and precision of their attack. In the pale blue light of dawn, they made their escape, and Cordell couldn't find it in his heart to blame them. The battle around the palace waned as the Kultakans broke from the sacred plaza, and the Nexalans paused to rest. Cordell knew that, despite the momentary calm, the next attack must come soon.

"Captain-General! Captain-General Cordell!" The breathless cry pulled his attention away from the courtyard.

"What is it?" he demanded, seeing Kardann puffing toward him. The pudgy assessor's face was flushed, his eyes wide with fear.

"It's Captain Alvarro, sir! He's been killed—by that woman!"

"Woman?" the general snapped. "Explain yourself!" Even as he spoke, he suspected the answer.

"The wench we captured, the one who came with Halloran! She murdered him!" Kardann gasped out the news as if it was the most important development in this long night of catastrophe.

Cordell sighed, raising a booted foot to the parapet and looking over the plaza. Alvarro. Such a willing tool for Darien's betrayal. It wasn't hard to see what had happened. The fool had disobeyed his commander, for whatever incentive the wizard had offered, and gone into the cell to kill the prisoner.

Only somehow the woman had turned the tables. The general could feel no regret at this news, save for the fact that his own punishment of the impetuous captain was now thwarted. In any event, he had far greater problems confronting him.

"The woman is still here, in the palace!" cried the Bishou, enraged. "She can be caught and punished!"

Cordell looked at the cleric as if he had lost his mind. He knew that Erix, and Halloran, and those two natives—together with that bizarre and frightening snake—had fought through the palace all night, chasing the drow elves that had teleported from one place to another across the roof.

"Thank you for the information," the general said to Kardann. "Now I suggest you go down to the trove. Make a plan for moving the gold, as much as we can. We shall not remain here for long."

The assessor from Amn looked at Cordell in shock. He hadn't considered the possibility of flight, particularly if such flight took them beyond the protecting walls of the palace. Yet something in the captain-general's eyes dissuaded any attempt he might have made at argument.

"Very well, sir," he agreed, with a bow.

"But the witch!" Domincus argued, turning on Cordell. "Surely you want her dead."

"The only witch, I fear, is the one who deceived me—deceived all of us—and is now beyond our reach. As for Halloran's woman, her death would gain us nothing."

"Look, General," said Daggrande grimly. The dwarf pointed across the plaza.

They all stared as the growing light clearly revealed the file of prisoners—Payit and Kultakan—standing on the steps, extending from the lofty temple of Zaltec to the ground, and continuing to wind around the base of the Great Pyramid. As the sun crested the horizon, the line began to move.

* * * * *

Darien stepped forward, passing among the robed figures of the Ancient Ones until she stood at the lip of the great bowl of the Darkfyre. Here she knelt, bowing deeply to the Ancestor as that venerable master of the drow sat back in his throne.

"My Father, I have returned," she whispered.

"And you bring us nearer to success than ever, my daughter," replied the Ancestor, his voice a harsh rasp. He raised his head, his white eyes blazing from his skull-like visage at the other drow gathered around the deep caldron.

"But still that ultimate triumph eludes our grasp," he said. "You tell me that the girl *still* lives, that she eluded the attacks of all of you!"

"She is protected by powerful *pluma*," said a drow, Kizzlok. He still wore the black chain mail and dark steel sword that he had taken to the palace, one of the few survivors of those who had answered Darien's summons there.

"It is true, Father," Darien added. "My strongest spells were useless against her, as long as she wore that token."

"Then we must try again, and keep trying until she dies!" snarled the leader, his voice low but heated. "My visions stressed the importance of slaying her *before* the war began; though we have failed in that, she cannot be allowed to survive any longer! Perhaps there is still time. Destiny shall pivot on the events of the next days. We cannot afford to fail again, when we are so close."

"But what has that destiny unleashed, now that Naltecona has died, and the chosen daughter of Qotal still lives?" asked Kizzlok.

"I cannot say for certain, but the portents are dire. We must cope with events now, as they occur." The Ancestor snapped his commands. "You, Kizzlok, will lead a group into the city as soon as night falls again. There you must, you *will*, find and kill her, or you will not bother to return!"

"Wait," said Darien softly. "Perhaps there is another way."

"What is that?" asked the Ancestor testily.

"I think that the woman will come here of her own free will," she said. "They seek to disrupt our plans for war. After last night, they know where to direct their efforts—toward us, the Ancient Ones. And certainly they will know to find us here."

VIPERHAND

The Ancestor paused for a moment, deep in thought. "Do you really believe this?" he asked, and his daughter nodded firmly. "Very well. We shall gather our strength here and await her arrival.

"And just to be certain that she does not arrive unannounced, we will place guardians outside the cave—those who might even solve our problem for us!" The Ancestor laughed, a sound like the crumpling of brittle parchment.

"Summon the jaguars!" he decreed.

* * * * *

Another chest laid open, another heart ripped forth, tossed into the gorged maw of the god, Zaltec. "Eat well, my master!" croaked Hoxitl, teetering from weariness after the long morning of sacrifice.

More than a thousand of the captive Payit and Kultakans had already given their hearts. Above them, the volcano rumbled its hunger for more, and so the priests worked diligently, killing and feeding, as the dawn lightened into daylight and the legionnaires watched from the walls of the palace that had become their prison.

Finally Hoxitl stepped back, leaving the grisly task to other priests. He barely felt his fatigue, such a powerful stimulant was this, the work of his god. He watched the file of captives march, for the most part placidly, to the altars, and he critically studied the work of his enthusiastic apprentices in completing the rites.

Other priests tumbled the bodies down the rear of the Great Pyramid, where they collected in a huge and bloody pile. As he observed the laboring priests, Hoxitl saw the chief of the Eagle Knights, Chical, ascend the pyramid, together with several Jaguar Knights and other feathered warriors.

"Your battle proceeds splendidly!" exclaimed the patriarch, beaming, as the men reached the upper platform. From the slow, deliberate trudge of their steps up the steep climb, he could see that they were as exhausted as he. "Now you must begin the attack against the foreigners."

Chical looked at him in surprise. "The warriors have fought a battle throughout the night. We have taken many prisoners already—more than in any battle during my lifetime. Now the men must rest. There will be time to attack the foreigners tomorrow."

Hoxitl's eyes flashed. "No! Zaltec craves their hearts! These of the Payit and Kultakans only whet his appetite! We must attack now!"

"Where is Lord Poshtli?" asked Chical, diverting the high priest. "He gives the orders we will obey."

The high priest scowled. He recalled his attempt to find Poshtli, when it seemed that the lord had entered the secret passage below his palace. "I do not know," he replied carefully. "He is nowhere to be found. I suspect that he died among the foreigners, even before his uncle."

Chical's shoulders sagged, but he didn't question Hoxitl's report. "Still, we must rest."

"The foreigners require rest, too!" the patriarch cried, his voice growing shrill. "*Now* is the time to attack, when they are too weary to defend themselves! We must strike them this morning, make them fight through the long day!"

Several of the Jaguar Knights grunted their agreement with Hoxitl's plea. Chical, looking more like a commander who had lost a war than one who had just won a great battle, sighed.

"Zaltec requires their hearts!" raged the priest. "Now! Now!"

"Very well," said the master of Eagles. "Let the banners be raised. The attack will commence at once."

* * * * *

"Halloran? Captain Halloran?" The legionnaire, one of Daggrande's crossbowmen, called to Hal where he sat with his companions, beside one of the great thatched peaks of the roof.

Looking at his companions in puzzlement, Hal rose. "What do you want?"

"The general would like to talk to you, sir. Could you come to see him?"

Halloran shrugged noncommitally. The sun rose into a misty sky, and exhaustion threatened to overwhelm him. Furthering his discouragement, Darien had escaped.

"Come along with me?" he asked the others. Erixitl had arisen, too, but now Poshtli and Shatil climbed wearily to their feet. The feathered serpent Chitikas, apparently tireless, started to float across the rooftop toward Cordell's command post, and the four humans followed.

The general stood with Daggrande and the Bishou, overlooking the sacred plaza—quiet now, though littered with the blood and debris of battle—and the tall pyramid where the legion's allies met their deaths on the altar of Zaltec.

"Welcome, Captain," Cordell said wearily. "How fared your fight?"

Halloran remembered the thrill of that rank, when Cordell had first bestowed it upon him. That had been on a different continent, facing a different enemy. It might as well have been a different life.

"Just Halloran," he replied coldly. "I'm not a legionnaire now—perhaps you'll remember. And as to the fight, the wizard escaped."

Cordell sighed as Erixitl translated the exchange for Poshtli and Shatil's benefit. The general gestured to the plaza, where thousands of Nexalans rested, out of crossbow range but completely surrounding the palace. "It looks bad, doesn't it?"

"Very bad," Hal agreed. "Why did you want to speak to me?"

Studying Erix, wrapped in her bright cloak, and steely-eyed Poshtli, then scrutinizing the coiled form of the feathered snake, Cordell seemed to hesitate. Finally he spoke. "Will you join us in this fight?" he inquired. "Of course, you're pardoned of all charges that might have been brought against you, and I can offer you captaincy of the lancers."

Halloran didn't even laugh, so surprised was he by the offer. But his response was quick and vehement. "I have done nothing that requires a pardon. But I want no part of your 'grand mission'—and I regret the small part I once played. You have come here for nothing more than a massive theft!"

Bishou Domincus had been glowering darkly during the exchange, but now he snorted. "Theft! To steal from barbarous savages who kill each other to feed their gods? Why, they don't even know the value of their gold!"

Hal turned to the cleric, with a meaningful gesture to the warriors in the plaza. "It seems that you are the ones who have placed a mistaken value upon gold. Now you see what it has bought for you.

"And as for savagery, there are good people here as well as bad. When we arrived with the likes of Alvarro and Darien, I wonder who are the savages?"

"You *are* a traitor!" Domincus raged. He stepped closer to Hal and then suddenly recoiled as the sinuous form of Chitikas interposed himself between them. The snake's eyes never wavered from the cleric's, and the Bishou took several steps backward, frightened.

"Darien," said Cordell quietly. "Where do you think she has gone?"

"I don't know," Halloran admitted. "This worries me. She is a great threat to Erixitl."

Suddenly Shatil, who had been following Erix's translation, spoke. "The Highcave," Erix interpreted for the others. "That is the lair of the Ancient Ones."

"Where is that?" Cordell inquired.

"Up there, somewhere near the summit." He pointed to the peak of Zatal, below its rising column of steam. The mountain belched and rumbled, looking every bit the suitable dwelling for a band of drow. "I—we—don't know where, exactly, but it is very high on the mountain."

"She is the enemy of all of us now," said the general.

Halloran thought for a moment. He understood the truth of Cordell's words, and he was surprised to learn that Shatil knew where Darien had gone—or at least, had strong suspicions. In another moment, he made his decision.

"I'll go after her, if my companions are willing." Erix took his arm and Poshtli nodded. Hal may have imagined it, but Chitikas seemed to smile. Shatil stood back, looking at them in confusion, but then he, too, stepped forward.

"I wish you good luck," offered Cordell. "I suspect you'll need it."

Halloran thought for a moment, casting another look around the war-scarred plaza. "Good luck to you, as well," he said.

Then Chitikas surrounded the four humans. Whirling colors formed a bright ring, and they were gone.

* * * * *

The attack began at midmorning, with no warning. Warriors bearing the brand of the Viperhand surged toward the stone-walled palace from all sides, in an explosion of whistling, howling spearmen, archers, slingers, and *maca*-wielding swordsmen.

The stones from the slingers and arrows from the archers drummed onto the palace roof, each volley pounding like a sudden downpour among the ranks of Daggrande's crossbowmen gathered there. The dwarf's doughty company fired back, volley after volley. The steel darts were perhaps a hundred times more lethal than the stone-tipped arrows of the Nexalans, yet the Maztican archers were a thousand times more numerous.

The warriors hacked and bashed the gates of the palace to pieces, then threw themselves into hand-to-hand combat with the legionnaires. Cordell's men fought desperately in the constricted conditions, their discipline and courage enabling them to—just barely—hold each breach.

When the assault began, the legionnaires stood firm at the several wide doorways to the palace. They lined the rooftops, defending against the hordes of attackers who tried to scale the walls and attack from above.

Led by the cult, warriors hurled themselves at the structure throughout the day, their attacks growing in ferocity with each passing hour. Thousands of warriors surged at the ramparts. Crossbows, swords, and spears tore into them, but for each native that fell, two, four—a dozen more advanced to take his place. Urged on by Hoxitl and his fellow priests, the Mazticans attacked with brutal savagery, each man ignoring his own personal safety in the quest to destroy the hated foe.

Once a company of Nexalan warriors burst through the front doorway, driving dozens of feet into the great hallway. Captain Garrant led a furious counterattack by the swordsmen of his company and barely succeeded in driving the attackers back so that the breach could be sealed. More than a hundred Maztican warriors perished in this assault, yet word spread through the native ranks that victory was possible against the foreign devils; they were not invincible!

With Alvarro dead, Cordell personally organized his horsemen for a charge. He appointed a burly sergeant-major, a veteran of many campaigns, to lead them. The riders thundered forth, only to be immediately surrounded by the press of thousands of warriors, packed so tightly together that even the powerful chargers couldn't force their way through the crowd.

Desperately the panic-stricken lancers slashed their way back to the security of the palace compound. Even so, the press of the attack tore three men from their saddles, and screaming warriors quickly spirited them away. Tightly bound and marched into the Temple of Zaltec, these riders despaired while *maca*-wielding warriors chopped their horses to pieces behind them.

Another sortie, attempted by armored troops protected by a bristling barrier of speartips and longswords, made little more progress. The tightly packed legionnaires advanced into the Maztican horde, chopping their way forward, slaying many native warriors for each step gained.

However, by the time the detachment had worked its way free from the palace wall, the precariousness of its position became clear as warriors swept around behind it. Pressed on all sides, it was only with an almost superhuman effort of discipline and courage that the men fought their way back to the palace gates. They left hundreds of Mazticans, and more than a dozen of their own number, dead on the stones of the plaza.

Many of the natives took up torches—dried branches of pine, or clusters of brittle reeds, soaked in pine tar—and then lit and hurled them on top of the palace. The brick and clay walls of the structure resisted the flame, but the roof of wood had spent long decades bleaching in the high Maztican sun.

Frantically the defenders threw these torches back, stomping out the fires that started to crackle among the ancient beams of the roof. Others worked bucket brigades from the palace's lone well, though the level of water in the well grew noticeably lower after less than an hour. Finally Bishou Domincus invoked the water to rise in the name of Helm and it quickly did so, flooding over the rim of its small enclosure and pouring through the palace's central courtyard.

Precious men, ill-spared from the battlements, wielded fresh buckets and large clay jars instead of weapons. The water proved just barely ample to keep the fires at bay. They soaked more and more of the roof, and eventually the torches lost their effect. Late in the day, the Mazticans abandoned the incendiary tactic.

The warriors of the Nexala filled the plaza surrounding the structure. They claimed the high positions, atop the Great Pyramid and lesser pyramids dedicated to the other gods. Even the Pyramid of Qotal, dedicated to the most gentle and unwarlike of the gods, fell to military usage. A hundred warriors armed with slings and stones climbed on top of it, hurling their missiles at the legionnaires on the roof of the palace.

Yet, though the soldiers of Cordell made no headway in their attacks against the Nexalans, neither could the natives advance in their ceaseless assault against the bastion of their enemies. More than a thousand of them paid for the effort with their lives, but the steel-armed, tightly disciplined foreigners held firm against every breach.

In the face of the cautious defense, the Nexalans captured few legionnaires alive. The frustration of the attacking warriors grew, whipped on by Hoxitl's shrill commands. In desperation, warriors hurled themselves in suicidal attacks at the doorways, trying to use long hooks to snatch a legionnaire from the ranks of his comrades. But always they fell dead before they caught a victim.

Suddenly, charging from concealment behind the Great Pyramid, a thousand Nexalans carrying dozens of ladders advanced in a furious assault. All of them warriors of the Viperhand, they had been churned to a frenzy by Hoxitl's exhortations about the hunger of Zaltec, his hunger for the hearts of the invaders. They blew their shrill whistles of wood and bone, racing madly toward the palace wall.

Swarming against a lightly held stretch of the wall, they

quickly raised their scaling ladders, placing them against the wall faster than the legionnaires could knock them down. Even as a ladder touched the wall, fanatic warriors sprang upward, rushing to reach the roof. Desperately the defenders hacked them back down, kicking the ladders away when they could.

But the attackers numbered too many, and some of the warriors inevitably gained a foothold on the ramparts. Immediately they turned to attack the swordsmen beside them. Some succeeded in knocking a legionnaire or two to the ground below, where the press of warriors quickly seized and bound the unfortunate captives.

Cordell rushed a company of reinforcements, led by Daggrande, toward the place. Daggrande assembled two score men and led them in a charge onto the roof. Before they could reach their embattled comrades, however, the attackers swarmed back down their ladders and withdrew from the wall.

They took some dozen legionnaires with them.

* * * * *

All day the companions climbed and traversed the high slopes of Zatal, seeking the entrance to the Highcave. Bitter, sulphurous smoke swirled around them, and sheer cliffs plummeted below. Steep ridges formed most of the mountainside, and they scrambled up and down many of these.

Halloran led the group with fanatical determination, driving himself mercilessly. Poshtli followed watchfully in the rear, while Shatil and Erix struggled to maintain the pace. Chitikas floated about, saying nothing, investigating ledges where the approach was too dangerous for the earthbound climbers.

Shatil noticed, as Hal pressed on, that the snakeskin band around the soldier's waist had begun to drop away, unnoticed. The priest followed the man closely, pulling away from his sister. When the bend of *hishna* finally fell free, he snatched it up and wrapped it around his wrist, under his robe.

The priest continued to follow numbly, terribly confused.

Where once Shatil understood clearly the mission before him, now his mind reeled with haunting questions.

He reminded himself of the vow he had made, the pledge of his life and his soul to Zaltec. That god, the protector of the Nexalans, would reward his faithful. Or so Shatil had always believed.

Before he had scorned as weaklings those, including his sister and his father, who had professed that gods could be gentle and kind. Always he had had the proof of Qotal's disappearance before him, to show that gods like that could not survive in Maztica. They would be driven out by strong, virile gods—gods who feasted upon human hearts.

But now, before his very eyes, here was the couatl, the harbinger of Qotal. The creature had led them against the Ancient Ones, spokesmen of Zaltec, and had prevailed! What did this mean? Could it be that Shatil, that his whole faith, was wrong? He looked at his sister, wrapped in the soft, billowing cloak. She had become very strong, very beautiful.

And Chitikas! How swiftly the couatl had brought them here! Now they searched for the cave, seeking the entrance among the rocky ridges and plummeting gorges of these smoky, steaming heights. And what if they found it?

Angrily the priest shook aside the notion. The couatl was like any other enemy of his faith—a powerful, magical enemy to be sure, but one who could certainly be killed. He watched the colorful creature dart suddenly forward, disappearing around a mountain shoulder before them. Shatil felt the dagger in his belt and touched the Talon of Zaltec in his pouch.

It would be dark soon, he knew. Shatil had a feeling that it would be a long night.

* * * * *

"Bring the first captive forward!" Hoxitl barked the command, the cruel glee plainly audible in his voice. Priests half-dragged, half-carried the hysterically sobbing figure of one of the captured legionnaires to their patriarch, stretching him backward across the altar.

"Praises to Zaltec!" cried the priest, raising the knife over the captive's chest. The man's eyes grew wide, and he babbled something incoherent as the cleric observed him with scorn. These foreigners certainly didn't know how to die! Hoxitl prolonged the moment, enjoying the spectacle, so long desired, of the pale foreigner awaiting the strike of his blade.

Swiftly the stone knife dropped, and with one brutal gesture Hoxitl sliced open his chest and reached inside the man's dying body to tear out his heart.

A great cheer arose from the warriors of the Viperhand, all the surviving members of which were gathered below the pyramid. The cheering continued as the rest of the dozen prisoners were dragged, one at a time, to the altar. There each gave the essence of his life to Zaltec. By the end of the gruesome ceremony, dark night surrounded the pyramid, and a steady rain soaked the city.

After the last of the sacrifices, the shouting, whistling, and stomping in the plaza created a pounding drumbeat of noise throughout the city. The celebration went on and on, and Hoxitl encouraged them. He knew that the enemy, trapped within the palace in the midst of the joyous mass of warriors, would understand what had occurred.

* * * * *

"I *told* you coming here was a terrible idea!" moaned Kardann, wringing his hands. "Now we'll *never* get out of here alive!"

"Shut up!" barked Cordell. "Or I'll send you to join those brave men on the pyramid!"

A grim silence descended over the assembled officers. The scene at sunset had left not one of them untouched, and this, more than their commander's rage cowed them. They met now in one of the rooms that they had used to dine so luxuriously.

"Now," said the captain-general, pacing back and forth before his officers. "We've got to make a plan. I need suggestions!"

Before him sat Daggrande, Garrant, Bishou Domincus, and Kardann. The four squirmed awkwardly, understanding as well as Cordell that their situation was indeed dire.

"Let the horsemen charge them again," declared Daggrande finally. "But back them up with the footmen. We can fight our way out of here!"

"Through that gate? Down these streets? You're mad!" objected Garrant, the Golden Legion's resolute commander of swordsmen.

"What else can we do?" asked Kardann. "You've got to try something!"

Bickering swept through the ranks as Cordell shook his head in dismay. Indeed, what else could they do? Yet without spells, without the magic of Icetongue, without Darien . . .

With a groan, Cordell sat down at the table, placing his head in his hands. How could she have betrayed him? He wallowed in his self-pity for a moment before forcing himself free of the mire, to once again stand and pace before his men.

"They seem to have withdrawn at nightfall, at least to some extent," observed the Bishou. "Perhaps that's our chance, to break out of here in the middle of the night."

"The clouds have moved in," added the dwarf. "It's a dark night—and still raining."

"I have some spells that might prove of some use to us," interjected Bishou Domincus. "An insect plague, perhaps, to clear them from our path. Or wind and water, such as Helm grants me to use."

"Perhaps you're onto something," said Cordell, desperate for any hope. "One thing's for sure—to remain here is death, death for all of us." He made his decision quickly.

"Tonight, then!" said the captain-general, a trace of his old commanding presence returning to his posture and his voice.

"But how many lives will we lose?" squeaked Kardann.

"We know which life you are concerned with, my good assessor," said Cordell dryly. "And rest assured that we shall do our best to get it to safety.

"You, on the other hand," he continued, "must complete the plans to move several tons of gold. You have two hours."

* * * * *

DOUGLAS NILES

From the chronicles of Coton:

A note before I retire, while the city dies around me.

Now at last Qotal sends his sign, as the couatl again strives in his name. Forgive me, Great Wise Master of my faith, that I do not record my gratitude at this event. All my pleas and prayers to this end notwithstanding, hoping—nay, begging—for you to take some action.

But now I must ask why? Why has the couatl come? What purpose is there to any struggles at this hour, in this dark night?

Now, when it is too late for all but the dying?

☙ 20 ☙

THE CRESTING FLOOD

"Are you ready to go?" Cordell asked Sergeant-Major Grimes the question, knowing that there could be only one answer. Grimes, a bluff, profane veteran, had been his choice to replace Alvarro. The sergeant-major was no intellectual giant, but Cordell at least felt he could trust the hearty lancer to follow orders.

The blond horseman stood at the head of the lancers, who were formed in a column of twos in the great corridor of the palace. Never, thought Cordell, had he seen such a collection of wounded, tired men. But he knew they stood ready to march.

Before them, the wooden doors, reconstructed by the legionnaires after the day's battle—remained closed, concealing the escape attempt from the Nexalans. Lookouts on the roof reported that there were only a few dozen warriors pacing restlessly about in the vicinity of the doors.

"Give me the sign," grunted the horseman.

"Another hour. We want to let things settle down out there as much as possible. Remember, when you do go, charge all the way to the gate of the plaza. You have to hold that gate until the rest of the legion gets there." Grimes nodded, scowling in concentration.

"Captain-General?"

"Yes?" Cordell turned in irritation. "What is it, Kardann?"

"It's the gold. We've loaded what we can in saddlebags. But there's still a great pile of it. What do you think we should do?"

The captain-general sighed heavily, regretting the necessity that forced them to abandon much hard-earned treasure. "Let the men have as much as they want to carry. The rest we'll leave behind."

In moments, word spread through the ranks of the legionnaires. The soldiers clustered around the mound of gold, filling pockets, backpacks, pouches, even boots and gloves, with the precious metal, many taking so much they could barely walk. Others such as Daggrande, mindful of the hard fight and long flight ahead, took only a few items of purest gold.

At last darkness and quiet spread through the sacred plaza around the palace. The rain drummed heavily on the roof, splattering on the stone surface of the huge courtyard, deadening sound and restricting vision.

"All right," Cordell hissed to Grimes, after a last reconnaissance. "When the doors open, ride."

Behind the three dozen riders, the other companies of the Golden Legion—swordsmen, crossbowmen, and spears—pressed toward the door. They all understood the necessity for speed if they were to have any chance of escaping this city that had suddenly become their deathtrap.

"Go!" barked Cordell. Two legionnaires immediately pushed the palace doors open, and the horsemen rumbled forth, trampling the few surprised Nexalans in their path. The chargers galloped across the plaza, making it halfway to the gate before any kind of alarm was raised.

But then a volley of whistles and shouts broke from the night. Grimes kicked his trotting lancers into a headlong rush, and they reached the gate to the sacred plaza in a lumbering stampede. Here a hundred warriors stood to bar their way, but the horsemen cut through them like a scythe through straw.

Hooves splashed through puddles of rainwater, and the steady drizzle ran into the riders' eyes, but they nevertheless found many targets for their steel-tipped lances. Through the darkness, their bodies slick with water, they slashed back and forth.

Warriors swarmed into the sacred plaza, scrambling over the walls from the surrounding city, but the column of legionnaires pressed onward to the gate, advancing at a fast march. The men at the front charged with raised shields and a deadly array of speartips before them. The rest of the column followed, maintaining tight formation.

Through the gate, Grimes swept his riders into the street beyond. He saw waves of warriors approaching from both directions, running toward the battle as quickly as possible. He recognized instantly that these were not the well-formed ranks they had faced before, so he gambled.

"Red and Blue wings—with me! Black and Gold, charge to the right!"

He wheeled his horse and lowered his lance. A dozen riders formed a line beside him, and they thundered up the street. Behind him, a similar line charged in the other direction. They met the Mazticans in seconds, lancing them or crushing them under the hooves of the steeds. In another moment, the remaining warriors turned and fled, disrupted and panicked by the sudden, brutal onslaught.

Quickly the sergeant-major wheeled his lancers, racing back to the plaza gate. He found the other wings had done the same, and in another minute, the leading rank of the footmen started into the street from the sacred plaza. The legion poured steadily through the gap in the wall.

"Take half your riders and start toward the causeway." Cordell barked the command to Grimes. "Have the other half bring up the rear. Now, go!"

Instantly the blond rider spurred his mount down the wide avenue toward the southwest causeway, the shortest route to the shore of the lake, with half of his company trailing.

Meanwhile, Cordell wasted no time turning the column of legionnaires after Grimes, leaving the rear guard under Daggrande's steady command. "Double march—move!" he barked. With the captain-general at the head, the invaders trooped toward the hoped-for escape from this city of chaos.

The press of warriors soon spilled from the plaza, and more attackers rushed from side streets and buildings as they passed. The Golden Legion fought its most desperate fight, a running battle through the dark, rainy streets of Nexal. Many men fell, badly wounded, and had to be left behind. Often they begged for a final blow to spare them the horrors of the Nexalan altars. Many a veteran trooper broke down and wept as he delivered this stroke of mercy to an old companion.

Suddenly Cordell, at the front of the footmen, came upon Grimes. The horseman's dozen riders were eight now, halted by a press of Nexalan warriors. Water dripped from their helmets, and their beards and hair were matted from the rain. Grimes shook his head in exhaustion.

"Charge them!" Cordell demanded.

"I did. It cost me four men!" Grimes retorted. "They're packed too thick. It's at the crossing of two of those wide streets."

Cordell recognized the place. It agonized him to know that the causeway lay just beyond.

"Helm may strike us a blow!" said Domincus, coming up behind them through the tightly packed ranks of the legion.

He raised his hand, bearing the gauntlet marked with the all-seeing eye of Helm. Chanting a plea to his god, he raised his other hand and gestured at the mass of warriors in the intersection before them.

Immediately a droning buzz rose above them, and almost as quickly sharp cries of pain and dismay rose from the Nexalans. Visible even in the dim light, a shapeless darkness appeared over the crowd, a darkness that consisted of millions of tiny insects, each of them biting and stinging whatever lay in its path.

Quickly the warriors broke for the shelter of the side streets or nearby buildings as the insect plague gained control of the crucial street crossing. The Bishou raised his hands again, and the buzzing mass began to move out of their path.

Again Grimes's horsemen rushed for the causeway. Cordell led the footmen on a rapid push right behind him. The horses struck a rank of defending Nexalans before the bridge. These warriors, armed with very long spears, knocked several riders from their saddles. Grimes's own horse went down, its belly gashed in a deep, mortal wound.

But a final surge carried the legion forward, and at last they gained the narrow roadway, surrounded on both sides by the deep, black waters of the lake. Grimes and Cordell, heedless of the rain, rushed forward on foot as the men of the legion raised a cheer and followed. They charged headlong down the causeway, meeting no opposition, though gradually they became aware of warriors swimming in the water beside them, in Lake Zaltec to their left and Lake Qotal to their right. Soon they caught sight of canoes—many, *many* canoes—on the dark lake's surface.

And then the advance came to a sudden stop. They had reached the first of the two gaps in the causeway where the waters flowed back and forth between the lakes, beneath the heavy planks of a bridge.

Only now, the bridge had been removed. Rain continued to shower the city, and before the legion stood thirty feet of black, deep, silt-bottomed water.

* * * * *

Heavy clouds swirled around them, and chill winds drove stinging needles of rain into their faces. High on the slope of the mountain, in the dark of impenetrable night, Halloran fought despair, pressing on in the endless search for the Highcave.

He pulled himself up a steep slope, finding a narrow ledge. Reaching down, he helped Erixitl to climb up beside him. She gasped as the mountain rumbled beneath them, and they clung to each other for a panic-filled minute while it seemed that Zaltec tried to shake them loose from his towering volcano.

But then the tremors eased, and finally Shatil and Poshtli reached the ledge as well. Chitikas hovered in the air, swirling slowly while the exhausted humans rested.

"Zaltec's hunger grows," observed Shatil, touching the rock of the peak.

"Hunger!" Erix whirled on him, surprising the three men with her vehemence. "Must a god always feast? Must we always feed him?"

Shatil leaned back, chagrined. "I am sorry to upset you, my sister. But, yes, the gods I know require food. We can do little else but to feed them."

"What of Qotal?" she challenged. "A god who grants food, not demands it? And our ancestors drove him from Maztica for it!"

"Perhaps, if you speak the truth, he will indeed return,"

Shatil said quietly.

She looked at him, half angry that he wouldn't argue, but surprised at his willing aquiescence. She opened her mouth, but then decided not to speak.

"Here," whispered Chitikas Couatl, speaking from the darkness above. "Here I see the mouth of a cave."

* * * * *

Black water stretching before them, Cordell and Grimes turned desperately to the sides, their arms weary from the strain of constant battle. Cordell wielded his sword, Grimes his lance. Rain still drummed the city and the lakes, but they could dimly see the fleets of canoes swarming around the causeway. Behind them, the screams of their comrades told them the battle raged there as well.

The surviving legionnaires couldn't advance along the causeway, since the bridge before them had been removed and the lake to either side swarmed with Nexalan warriors in canoes. At the tail of the column, the press of warriors drove forward savagely, pinching Daggrande's rear guard into a steadily shrinking stretch of the road.

"Below—look out!" Grimes cried, stabbing downward with his blood-and rain-slicked lance.

A warrior fell back into his canoe, toppling the craft. At the same time, Cordell felt strong fingers grab his feet, and he sliced viciously downward with his sword. He was rewarded by the sharp chop of the blade through flesh and bone, though to his horror, the severed hands continued to clutch his ankles until he kicked them free.

The darkness seemed to move, so thick was the press of Nexalan attackers. Cordell stabbed and hacked, unseeing and uncaring of his victims, knowing that everyone in the canoes below them was an enemy.

More of his legionnaires pushed their way to the gaping end of the causeway, hurling themselves into the water in a desperate attempt to swim to safety. Many of these—those who had loaded themselves down with gold—sank beneath the water and disappeared. Others were hauled, screaming and struggling, into canoes, bound, and spirited back to the city, destined for the fate that had become far more fearsome to the legionnaires than death on the battlefield.

Overturned canoes and other craft wrecked during the combat clogged the water before them. Rain alternately pounded them or misted lightly. Many bodies bobbed in the lake now as both Nexalan and legionnaire fighters fell into the water, drowning in the press of chaos.

"We've got to do something!" cried Grimes as more and more of their men jumped or were dragged into the lake. Indeed, before them, the water had virtually disappeared among the mass of wreckage.

"Any ideas?" grunted the captain-general. He heard a cry of pain and a splash behind him, turning to see one of his men struggling with six Mazticans in canoes. The swordsman struggled in the water, slipping on the bodies below him, howling with terror as the natives pulled him into the canoe. With swift strokes of their paddles, three of them steered their craft away while the others turned to the causeway, after more victims.

Cordell heard more screams and the triumphant whistles of the Mazticans, and he knew that, somewhere, still another legionnaire had been dragged to a short, grim captivity.

"Murdering savages!" Bishou Domincus's bellow carried above the din, and Cordell saw the cleric struggling along the edge of the causeway, laying about with a heavy staff.

"Almighty Helm!" cried the Bishou. "Strike the heathens with your vengeance! Deliver your faithful from the jaws of death!"

But the heavens only delivered more rain, in the dull, pounding cadence that had marked the brutal tempo of the night and now, as gray dawn filtered into the valley of Nexal, counted time for the steadily growing illumination.

"Bishou!" The cleric looked up and saw Cordell standing at the lip of the causeway. With a sinking heart, he saw the dark water blocking their path.

"Helm has forsaken us!" groaned Domincus, reaching the commander. "I fear we have angered him, and he turns away from us in our hour of need!"

"Never mind!" snapped the black-bearded commander. "Do you have any magic, anything at all that can help us across this?" Cordell gestured to the strip of water, bristling with enemy canoes. Even the continuation of the causeway across the thirty-foot gap was packed with Maztican warriors who fired arrows or slung stones at the embattled legionnaires.

"No," the cleric said. "My power is exhausted now. It will take many hours of quiet meditation to restore my spells."

Cordell turned away in disgust. He didn't see a hook dart forward from one of the canoes, suddenly sweeping the Bishou from the causeway. Domincus cried out, plunging into the water, and Cordell whirled back to see many natives eagerly pulling the cleric into a canoe.

"No! Leave him, you devils!" cried Cordell, lashing toward them with his sword. The canoes paddled back, out of range, but the captain-general lunged dangerously far in his fury. Only Grimes, reaching out with a brawny hand and pulling him to safety, kept him from following the cleric into captivity.

* * * * *

"Praises to Zaltec!" crowed Hoxitl from his vantage atop the Great Pyramid. The high priest didn't try to suppress his burst of exultation. Though he could see nothing beyond the veil of darkness and rain that shrouded him, he knew of the great victory his warriors won on this black night. "Long live his almighty name!"

Scouts and priests brought him regular reports, and he heard of the many thousands of warriors who fearlessly hurled themselves at the strangers trapped on the causeway. He no longer feared that they would escape him. Already nearly half of the legionnaires had been delivered into his hands.

Still, he hoped to have them all by morning—to march the entire lot of them up the pyramid, offering their hearts to Zaltec in unworthy penance for the wrongs they had inflicted upon Maztica.

Though all Nexal had united and arisen to throw off the yoke of the invaders' presence, it was those men who wore the crimson brand upon their breasts who had ignited the fires of resistance. Warriors of the Viperhand, the most fanatical of attackers, displayed the greatest courage in the battle, and now led the way for their countrymen's greatest victory.

And these were *his* warriors, his to command and control and lead!

"They remain trapped before the bridge," reported Kallict, who had just climbed the long, rain-slicked stairs to the top of the temple. "They shall pass no farther."

"Splendid!" crowed Hoxitl, waving his fist at the sky. "We shall have them all! And Zaltec will feast until he can eat no more!"

* * * * *

Chitikas hovered outside the Highcave as the companions came up to him. The feathered snake floated between the bodies of two jaguars—unmarked by visible wounds, but undeniably dead. Halloran didn't even want to know how the snake had killed them.

"Let's go," he said. He and Chitikas started into the cave, while Erix came right behind them, followed by Shatil. Poshtli brought up the rear.

The entrance led to a smooth, wide passageway, obviously excavated from the soft volcanic rock. Still, no evidence of hammer or pick stroke could be seen in the walls or floor.

A stench of noxious gas burst around them. Hal clapped his hand to his face, squinting. Fortunately a blast of fresher air cleared the hot vapor away.

Chitikas floated out in front as they entered a larger cavern, with a high, domed ceiling. A deep crater filled the center of the room, emitting a dull crimson glow that seemed to pulse in varying intensity. They couldn't see inside the pit, but the surging light frightened them, alternately hot and cold. The feathered snake drew himself into a coil.

They're in here. Halloran sensed the snake's message, though Chitikas had not spoken. *The Ancient Ones. They are invisible.*

The information sent a chill through Halloran's body. He unconsciously tightened his grip on his blade. From the tension in Erixitl's hand, resting on his shoulder, he knew that his wife had received the same news.

Chitikas hovered before them, his tail touching the ground but his twisting neck and head a full ten feet in the air. His great wings beat slowly, supporting him, as the snake turned his head this way and that, looking about the large chamber.

Suddenly a pale white light flashed in the cave. "Icetongue!" shouted Hal, involuntarily flinching backward. At the same time, he noticed that he and Erix weren't even the targets of the attack. Instead, the cone-shaped blast of the wand had struck only one of them.

"Chitikas!" Erix cried. They stared in horror at the feathered snake. Chitikas crashed to the floor before them, his brittle, suddenly frozen wings snapping into many shards of different colors. The wingless couatl writhed there silently.

At the same time, Hal saw Darien appear on the other side of the glowing fire crater. The wizard, her invisibility spell broken by her attack with Icetongue, regarded the intruders with a faint smile that Halloran found more disturbing than a grimace of hate and rage.

She didn't wear her customary robe. Instead, her white skin showed plainly through the tiny, gold-rimmed garments that barely preserved her modesty.

"My spellbook!" she demanded.

"I brought it," Hal answered, sensing that it was foolish to lie. Yet his mind worked desperately, seeking any kind of plan.

They saw other forms blink into sight, then, one by one, until more than a dozen black-skinned elves appeared. They wore tight-fitting armor of fine black chain, and each was armed with a dark longbow. The bows were stretched taut, with arrows nocked and aimed at the small party of intruders.

Another one, a wrinkled, ancient drow, appeared beyond the caldron, seated in a great stone throne. Skeletal of visage, this one sat back, cool and aloof, obviously the leader.

"You will give it to me now," Darien commanded, starting to walk around the caldron toward Halloran.

Desperately seeking a delay, Hal reached into his pack and slowly withdrew the bound, heavy tome. "Wait," he said slowly. He knew that they had been caught in a trap of powerful, deadly cunning. He also understood that once Darien had her spellbook, they would all be killed.

Surprising even Erixitl, who had a hand on his shoulder, Halloran suddenly dove forward, lunging into a headlong slide along the floor. In a split second, he stopped before any of the archers could fire.

Halloran lay still on the floor, the book in his hands extended before him, just over the lip of the smoking crater. Below it flickered and flamed the depths of the Darkfyre. If his grip relaxed even slightly, the book would plunge into the inferno, gone forever.

"Now," Halloran continued, still speaking very slowly, "let's talk."

"Kill him!" urged the Ancestor, rising from his throne and gesturing toward Halloran.

"Wait!" hissed Darien. The pale wizard turned back to Hal. "Speak, then."

Think! Think of something, anything! his mind raced. "The betrayal of the legion—you must have prepared that for years."

Darien smiled again smugly. "For more than ten years, I have been seeking a way back to my people—a way that would bring us closer to our ancient goal. In the legion, I found the perfect vehicle—in Cordell, the perfect tool."

Hal stared at her in growing horror. "This whole expedition, the crossing of the Trackless Sea, conquering the Payit, marching on Nexal? This was all *your* plan?"

"Yes! For generations of human lives, we have strived to gain mastery of this land. With the league of the Viperhand, our numbers grew organized and controlled—humans, branded with the sign of Zaltec, and the priests of Zaltec controlled by us, the Ancient Ones!" She laughed aloud, but her laughter was a dry and empty sound, devoid of humor.

Halloran couldn't see his companions. He was unaware of Shatil, gaping in horror at the woman who had just explained away his life's order as a tool of these manipulative elves. The young priest swayed on his feet, woozy, as it seemed that the world came to pieces around him.

"But we needed an enemy," Darien continued, "a force to

give focus to that hatred, to bring Maztica together under the hands of the cult. The Golden Legion filled that role very well indeed."

Chitikas lay still, his shattered wings in pieces around him. The snake's feathered flanks rose and fell slowly, the only indication that he still lived.

"I am going to my husband," Erixitl announced, stepping forward to kneel at Halloran's side. The bowmen tensed with her movement, but Hal glared at Darien, who raised a hand to restrain them.

None of those before him saw Shatil slowly, carefully unwind the strap of *hishna* from around his wrist. The priest's eyes were locked upon the white-skinned wizard. Only Poshtli, bringing up the rear, saw the movement. The warrior started easing to the side, clenching his sword.

With a sudden gesture, Shatil flung the snakeskin at Darien. "By Zaltec, take her!" he shouted, springing after it.

The scaled strap stretched and twisted in the air, growing into a netlike web. Darien darted to the side, but the growing *hishna* form followed. It struck her arm and instantly, like the lash of enchanted tenctacles, wrapped itself around her, dragging her to the ground and holding her tight.

At the same time, Poshtli charged out of the shadows. The drow archers let fly their missiles, and many of the black-tipped arrows struck the priest of Zaltec, propelling him backward and driving him to the floor. One struck Poshtli's shoulder, while others clattered against the stone walls of the cave.

Then the Ancestor rose from his chair. He raised his hand and started toward Halloran and Erix.

Desperately Hal dropped the spellbook at the edge of the pit and leaped to his feet. He turned toward the archers and saw them swiftly draw additional black arrows from their quivers, nocking them into the bows.

"*Kirisha!*" he cried, suddenly inspired. He cast his light spell directly in the faces of the nocturnal Ancient Ones. The white glow blossomed, illuminating the cavern brightly.

With cries of pain and anguish, many of the drow archers dropped their weapons or turned away from the painful blast of light. In another second, Halloran charged among them, and Helmstooth found the bodies of many of the blinded, stumbling drow.

Poshtli followed, striking a drow with his steel sword, knocking the blow of another aside. The warrior staggered, weakened from the arrow wounds he had suffered just moments before and atop the palace, and one of the dark elves saw his weakness. With a sudden lunge, the drow drove his blade toward the Nexalan.

Twisting away, Poshtli tried to stop the blow, but the black blade knocked his own sword aside. Continuing the lunge, the drow stabbed the warrior in the chest. With a dull moan, Poshtli sprawled onto his back, bleeding.

Erixitl faced the Ancestor as the wizened, decrepit drow hobbled forward, coming around the deep pit of fire. The elf held a wand or some kind of weapon in his hand, a short staff with an evil-looking tip like the outspread claws of a small dragon.

Erix stood, strangely unmoving, before him as he raised the clawlike staff. He was perhaps halfway around the crater when a sudden, searing hiss filled the cave, and red light exploded in tiny beams from the claws on the Ancestor's wand. Each of these rays of light merged with the others into a heavy bolt of solid crimson energy that smashed into Erixitl with crushing force.

Her *pluma* token puffed upward, and the gust of wind that had sheltered her from Darien's magic swiftly swirled around Erix. But the power of the attack blew this protection aside, bashing Erix backward and flattening her to the floor. The Cloak of One Plume billowed behind her.

She lay there, moaning, as the Ancestor took another step and raised the weapon again. He had come nearly all the way around the caldron and soon would loom directly over her. Halloran started for Erixitl, not knowing what he could do. He heard the Ancestor laugh, a harsh, cruel sound.

But neither he nor the aged drow anticipated another reaction. Chitikas—coiled, motionless, and apparently unconscious throughout the battle—suddenly exploded from his coil. The wingless couatl drove like a spear toward the Ancestor.

Chitikas's fangs sought the throat of his victim, but the Ancestor barely managed to knock the snake's head to the side. For a moment, the two of them teetered on the brink of the bubbling caldron. The snake's tail lashed around, striking the spellbook where Hal had left it. Darien, still imprisoned by *hishna*, screamed as the tome toppled into the Darkfyre.

Hal reached Erixitl's side, kneeling to sweep her into his arms. She sobbed against him, helplessly watching the struggle. "Chitikas!" she cried.

Then, locked in their desperate fight, the couatl and the Ancestor fell slowly, following the spellbook into the flaring caldron.

* * * * *

Hoxitl paused for a long, splendid moment, basking in the full scope of his triumph. Below him, the cleric of the strangers' god stared bug-eyed at his poised dagger. The Bishou's lips were flecked with spit, his tongue protruded, and the veins in his face seemed ready to burst.

The priest of Zaltec leered at him, and then began to lower the dagger. With a quick, sharp slash, the stone tip met the skin of the cleric of Helm.

And it pierced that skin, slicing a deep wound into Domincus, though the cleric still lived. Hoxitl thrust his bloody hand into the wound, grasping the Bishou's heart as he had taken thousands of hearts before, ready to pull it forth and offer it to the gaping maw of the statue Zaltec.

But this time, when his hand met the Bishou's flesh, the two gods came together with a force that overwhelmed the cleric's mortal powers.

Behind and far, far above Hoxitl, unseen in the rain but heard by them all, the top of Mount Zatal exploded.

* * * * *

From the chronicles of Coton:

At last the gods converge, and in their meeting, they tear the world asunder.

In the temple of Qotal, I feel the powers come together. Zaltec and Helm clash as the cleric of one tears the heart from the cleric of the other. Such a sacrifice must forever change the face of the land.

And even Qotal, through the harbinger of his couatl, meets Zaltec, as Chitikas gives his life to the Darkfyre. The feathered snake is a meal even hungry Zaltec cannot digest.

Below them all, but rising fast, Lolth seethes now with the passion of her vengeance. She explodes into this world through the Darkfyre, laying her punishment upon her children, the drow.

And the gaming board is swept of its pieces.

♣ 21 ♣
EBB AND FLOW

Gultec wandered far from the jungles of Tulom-Itzi, crossing the lands of the Payit, the Kultakans, the Pezelacs. Always he moved toward Nexal.

Sometimes he walked as a man, visiting the peoples he passed among, learning of their fear. In all these lands, he found a deep foreboding, a great and dire anticipation of terrible things to come.

Other times he soared as a bird, or skulked within the mighty jaguar body that still gave him so much pleasure. He found, in his meandering course, several deep, lush valleys where he had thought lay only desert. Much to his surprise, several of these valleys contained ripe meadows of mayz. No one had planted it there, he knew, for this was deepest wilderness. Yet he remembered this abundance of food, enough for many people, as he pressed onward through the wilds of Maztica.

His course steady, his own courage unfailing, he finally reached the shores of Nexal's lakes.

And here he witnessed the source of the True World's terror.

* * * * *

Halloran sensed Erixitl's arms around him, and he clung to her with all the strength of his mindless terror. Around them the world came to pieces. Chaos reigned.

He didn't wonder why they weren't burned to ashes immediately. He saw fire in the form of red, liquid rock, exploding upward and outward in a wave of certain death. But that wave washed around them, and he knew only that Erix was in his arms, that the two of them were together, and it seemed certain they would die that way.

Squeezing his eyes shut, Hal tried to block out the nightmare around them, but he could not. Still he saw glowing crimson liquid splashing, he saw the summit of the huge mountain as it crumbled and collapsed around them. Rain poured into the cavern, creating a hissing inferno of steam, shattering rock and boiling away the instant it reached the ground.

Slowly the horrors around him seemed to fade, and he knew only that he held the woman he loved. He loved her more than he had ever thought he could love, and he desperately wanted to soothe the trembling he could feel in her body.

"Are you . . . alive?" asked Erix some time later. He wondered at first whether he had dreamed her voice.

"I . . . don't know," he replied honestly. "I think so, but I don't know how."

"I do," she replied, still dreamily nuzzling her face into the hollow of his neck. "It is the will of Qotal."

Halloran looked around them at the inferno of flame and molten rock and explosive gases. For the first time, he realized that they hadn't remained immobile during the eruption. Instead, they floated with the force of the blast, riding gently in the shelter of the . . .

What *did* protect them? He noticed that they watched the fiery chaos through a spiderweb-like grid. Looking closer, he recognized a pattern of feathers and down, creating a globe only large enough to hold the two of them.

"My cloak," explained Erix, still speaking as if she were dazed. "It is truly the gift of Qotal, and so it protects us, holding the fires of Zaltec at bay." Indeed, the Cloak of One Plume encircled them both, protecting them from the inferno yet showing them the full, horrifying devastation wrought by the gods.

"Is this the god—Zaltec?" Hal asked, gesturing to the fiery maelstrom.

"It is Zaltec, and more. This I see now, from a very high place." As Erix spoke, Hal noticed that they had indeed begun to rise above the explosion, floating dreamily in their soft, transparent cocoon, overlooking the god-wracked valley of Nexal so terribly far below.

"I see Zaltec meeting Helm in the struggle for mastery, and

Douglas Niles

both of them threaten to destroy each other. But more, I see a spidery presence, the dark god of the Ancient Ones—"

"Lolth!" interjected Halloran. "Spider queen of darkness! You see her, *too?*"

"Yes. It is her rage that causes the mountain to explode. She is furious with her children, the drow. They have forsaken her in the quest for earthly rewards, turning to the worship of Zaltec."

Erixitl turned to look at Halloran, and the expression in her eyes seemed very far away. "Erix? What's wrong? You're here, with me!" He spoke loudly, with force, and slowly her eyes focused.

"Yes, I know. Hold me." She was quiet for a long time then as they drifted through the sky.

The cocoon of *pluma* seemed to float like a bubble on a light spring breeze. Even through the black of the night, they could see ruin wracked upon the city below. Lava flowed into the cool waters of the lakes, erupting in mountainous pillars of steam. The rain still fell, but it was a black, heavy rain, and it seemed to punish those under its downpour.

Below, in Nexal, they could see many thousands of people fleeing in panic from the confines of the doomed city. They saw the causeway, hours earlier the scene of savage battle, now the avenue for countless thousands of terrified Mazticans. As the two of them watched, drifting safely overhead, a steaming wave rose from the lake. Hissing and bubbling, it swept over one of the causeways, carrying the panicked humans away.

Convulsions wracked the earth upon which the city rested, and most of its great buildings tumbled into ruins. Only the Great Pyramid stood, and as Hal and Erix drifted past, high above it, they saw long, serpentine cracks run up the sides of the structure. The three temples atop the pyramid swayed, finally crumbling.

Then the whole great edifice, mightiest of the centers of the True World, twisted and broke and finally collapsed into rubble.

* * * * *

The palace walls buckled and crumbled around the terrified mare. Storm reared in panic, her hooves kicking the cracked adobe. The courtyard where Poshtil had kept the horse abruptly twisted, a great section sinking away. Wild lake waters surged into the opening.

With a maddened spring, Storm hurled herself across the open water, but her leap fell short. Splashing into the turbulence, she kicked free of the tumbling stone, desperately swimming toward the open waters of the lake.

The city surged, exploded, and died, but the horse pressed forward, uncaring of the surrounding chaos. Pressing through widening canals, snorting and kicking in fear, she finally reached the deep waters of Lake Azul. Deepest of the four lakes and farthest from the exploding mountain, its waters had not yet suffered the worst effects of the convulsions.

With strong strokes, the roan struggled through the waves until she reached the far northern shore. With a toss of her water-soaked head, she scrambled onto the shore and immediately galloped toward the wilds of northern Maztica.

* * * * *

The surviving drow sensed the imminence of disaster and teleported from the Highcave to refuge in caverns deep within the mountain. They escaped seconds before the lair—caldron, Darkfyre, and all—dissolved in an explosive convulsion of heat and pressure.

Zatal erupted, spewing lava, ash, smoke, and volcanic stone into the sky. Sizzling rivers of molten rock flooded down the slopes of the mountain, while chunks of the peak tumbled through the sky, wheeling gracefully before plummeting to earth. Steam billowed upward as a hissing black cloud of ash spread across the valley.

With the release of the volcano, like the popping cork of a bottle, Lolth's power surged into the True World. As the gods of the humans wrestled below, she laid her dark curse across the land.

That curse settled first upon the drow, huddled deep within the bowels of their exploding mountain. Most of them had reached temporary, imagined safety in their subterranean lairs, but even here the curse of Lolth crept toward them. Like a dark fog, her spidery essence slipped into the lairs, punishing her children for their dedication to a god of humans. She cast her curse upon the dark elves, and they changed forever.

Crying out in agony and horror, the drow thrashed and writhed, their bodies wracked by the all-consuming vengeance of their dark goddess. The sleek elven shapes grew grotesque and bloated, trailing great, immobile abdomens as their lower limbs withered and fell away. From these abdomens sprouted legs—eight legs each—that were covered with coarse fur. Dark elven heads and torsos—and minds—remained, so that they could know their disgrace. But the grotesque and hateful bodies would belong to them as long as they lived.

In horror, the drow regarded each other, no longer slim, handsome figures. Lolth had visited upon them the ultimate punishment, and the repulsive, spidery forms of the Ancient Ones would serve as a constant, painful reminder of their deity's vengeance.

For they became driders, outcast spider beasts of the drow.

But Lolth's vengeance was not merely directed at her wayward followers. Her power reached the cult of the Viperhand, since that order had flowed from the bidding of the drow. And its members were marked by the crimson brand.

A great, oppressive cloud lowered from the sky. Across the city, the ash of the volcano mixed with the rain to form a thick sludge that dropped, hissing, to the ground, coating the warriors of Maztica, and the legionaires, and the people of the city. Its corrosive touch burned skin and stung eyes, though they brushed it away without permanent hurt.

But not so with those who wore the brand of the Viperhand. When it struck those warriors, those priests and fanatics, a terrifying transformation occurred.

Once-human faces twisted into bestial expressions of hatred and rage. Bodies distorted, becoming grotesque and misshapen. Some grew into hulking brutes, surrounded by thick sinew. Stooped and hideous, they chomped mouths full of dull fangs and raised rocklike fists to crush any who stood before them.

Others became green and scaly, tall monsters with great, hooked noses and gangly, yet powerful, limbs. Warts burst from their horrid skin, and black eyes, sunk deep into monstrous faces, gleamed wickedly at a world gone mad.

The great masses of warriors who had been branded became orcs. Snuffling through broad snouts, baring wicked tusks, the brutish, evil beasts quickly formed bands and turned upon the humans—Mazticans and legionnaires alike—of the city. Still armed with their stone weapons, they also used savage jaws to tear at the helpless victims of their rage.

The knights, Jaguar and Eagle, who had been branded by Hoxitl became ogres, huge, hulking brutes who cuffed the smaller orcs around them, gruffly commanding their attention and obedience. The giantlike ogres seized beams, trunks, and other huge devices to use as clubs.

And finally, the priests of Zaltec who had been branded into the order grew to twice their height, with a ripping and tearing of skin and sinew. Their appearance distorted most horribly from the human norm, as their skin turned dark green, their features horrible in the extreme.

For they became the trolls. And so the ultimate contortion of war seized the land, while death spread through the city and lava spilled ever closer.

* * * * *

"Run, man! Run for your life!" Cordell gasped at Daggrande. The two legionnaires staggered like drunks along the nightmarishly contorted causeway. Finally they reached the city, even as waves crashed over the narrow roadway and carried it into the black depths of the steaming lake.

"Where?" groaned the dwarf, pausing to fill his straining lungs with air. The ground heaved and buckled underfoot, and they both sprawled to the stones of the street.

"The lakeshore—it's our only chance! We can steal some canoes and get out of here!"

Once again they lumbered forward. A huge beast reared out of the darkness before them. chomping its fang-filled maw. It reached out a wickedly clawed hand, striking for Cordell's face.

"Look, by Helm!" cried the captain-general, stumbling backward in horror.

On the breast of the beast, like a blood-red scar, Cordell saw the diamond-shaped brand of the Viperhand.

Daggrande chopped at the troll with his axe, driving the monster backward and pushing it out of the stream of escaping refugees. Then the men swept past, losing sight of the beast in the swirling advance of the mob.

The fleeing Mazticans, like the few legionnaires among them, hurried toward the lake, trying to escape the crumbling city. Buildings fell, toppling across roadways and crushing hundreds of people at a time. Great cracks opened in the ground, and these swiftly filled with water, forming deep and treacherous moats where moments earlier had stood a pastoral garden or graceful two-story manor.

More and more of the soldiers joined with them as they passed. Cordell saw the weeping form of Kardann huddled beside the road. He roughly pulled the assessor to his feet and dragged him along in their flight.

"Monsters—orcs, ogres! They're everywhere!" wailed the assessor. "I saw them attacking the people, the women, even the little children. They—they simply tore them to pieces!"

"Stop it, man!" Cordell barked. "Just worry about getting away, getting to somewhere safe!"

But this testimony to the savagery of the monsters of the Viperhand made him wonder if there could be anyplace safe left to them. As if to emphasize his fear, bands of orcs, ogres, and trolls snapped at the fringes of the crowd.

Then they reached the shore of the lake. Cordell vaguely recognized the dark, brackish water called Lake Qotal. But now its surface tossed chaotically, too turbulent by far to bear the passage of any canoe.

* * * * *

Hoxitl tossed back his huge, maned head and howled his rage at the skies, his widespread maw revealing long, wickedly curving fangs. He stomped a massive foot, sending cracks shooting outward through the ground. Around him stretched the wreckage of the pyramid.

"You have betrayed me!" he cried, though the words made sense to him alone. All others heard the yapping and snarling of a savage beast. He shrieked his fury at his god, sensing Zaltec's weakness even as he saddled him with blame.

"You, Zaltec! I curse you and your name!" Hoxitl knew dimly that the curse that had wracked him and the members of his league was more than the work of one god, even a god of Zaltec's might. The influence of Helm, the strangers' god, could not be denied. Nor the presence of the dark punisher of the Ancient Ones, the one who had corrupted her followers even as Zaltec had twisted and deformed his own.

With a snarl of animal rage, Hoxitl tore himself from the rubble of the collapsed pyramid, rising to his full height of nearly twenty feet in the courtyard beyond. Around him, snorting and groveling, cavorted the bestial masses of his league, slaying those human warriors who still lived and had not yet fled.

The beast howled again, a shrieking, devastating sound that blasted through the ruins, causing all who heard it to stop and tremble in abject terror. Lurching forward with a rolling, lumbering gait, like an ape's, Hoxitl led his creatures through the ruins.

His eyes saw much, through the smoke and haze of destruction. And on the shore, pinned against Lake Qotal, he saw his victims. Directly, with his monstrous army following at his heels, the huge form of Hoxitl started toward Cordell and his surviving legionnaires.

* * * * *

Poshtli didn't sense consciousness returning as he crawled toward the mouth of the Highcave. Indeed, had he been aware, he would never have left his companions. But motivated by a kind of daze, he crept away.

Then the warrior felt the ground drop away below him. He opened his eyes and saw things with exceptional clarity, a clarity of vision he had not known in many days. He saw a rocky slab falling away, and he dimly realized that he had lain on that slab. When the mountain exploded, that stone bed had carried him high into the sky, and now he looked down upon the death of the peak below him—or was it the death of the True World itself?

He turned to the side, banking easily away from the spume of fire and ash. Poshtli soared in a great arc, slowly descending. Circling the great pillar of destruction, he flew lower and lower.

Slowly he realized the change, yet his body seemed so natural that it took him many minutes of concentration. But then he knew.

He had no fingers now—only feathers. His teeth were gone, replaced by a sharp, curving beak. Keen, bright eyes did his seeing and detected a wealth of detail that would have escaped his human vision. And his arms! His arms were wings, wings of feather and sinew—the wings of a great eagle.

How the change had occurred he couldn't know, nor did he question. It seemed only right and proper now that he should dwell in the body of a bird.

Diving toward the city, Poshtli skimmed above its blackened streets, ruined buildings, and the grotesque, deformed beasts that rampaged through the chaos. He saw it all with a dull sense of familiarity.

This had been his vision of Nexal. The darkness, the monsters, the destruction. He saw the doom of the great city, and from his serene avian detachment, he realized that the city had not been destroyed by the war waged between men.

The city died because the gods tore it apart.

* * * * *

The cocoon of *pluma* carried Hal and Erix inexorably over the dying city, settling slowly toward the earth. They saw a block of houses below them topple forward, falling into a widening canal to sink from sight in black, boiling water. A huge crevasse opened in another area, emitting a steaming column of hot gas. Dozens died before they could escape the explosive effect.

To all the death and destruction below them, the pair in their magical globe remained strangely detached. Perhaps it was because the real extent of the suffering would have driven them mad had they even begun to comprehend the true magnitude of the disaster.

They drifted like a bubble on a light breeze, falling gently toward the dark, choppy surface of a lake. A teeming crowd swarmed below them, people clamoring for safety, trapped between the brackish, marshy waters and the dying city. They saw the horrifying approach of a bestial army, the monsters of the Viperhand.

Halloran clung to Erix, wondering what would happen when their cocoon of protection struck the water. Would they sink? Would the water boil around them?

But as the Cloak of One Plume touched the tops of the waves, the water suddenly ceased its thrashing. Hal and Erix settled onto a solid surface, rough and uneven but unquestionably firm.

"Ice!" Hal exclaimed as the cloak collapsed around them. "The lake's frozen solid!"

Erixitl looked at him with that same dazed expression. "The coming of Summer Ice," she whispered. "The third sign of the return of Qotal."

At the shore, pressed by the horde, the humans started out onto the ice. Many slipped on the treacherous footing. Each one who stood helped another next to him, and slowly, lurchingly, the refugees started across the lake. Legionnaires helped Nexalans, the old helped the young, and in a slow, creeping mass, thousands of people started across to safety.

Erixitl turned to the heavens, suddenly looking at the ruinous convulsions. "The return of Qotal?" she demanded of the skies. "*This* is the sign? The destruction of a city—the deaths of thousands of people? What kind of a god *are* you to torture us so?"

The rain ceased suddenly, and they saw people struggling across the lake, with howling, snapping monsters close behind them. Screams of panic and despair arose from the mass of miserable humanity as they desperately strived to reach safety.

"I ask you, Qotal," Erixitl shouted, still looking up, "what is your purpose? Is *this* how you prepare for your return?"

DOUGLAS NILES

Her rage blistered the air, and Hal stared at her in awe.

"Hear me, Plumed One! We do not need—we do not *want* your return! You have forsaken us too long. Now stay away forever!"

Suddenly Erix started to weep and would have fallen if Hal hadn't caught her.

The monsters lunged onto the ice after the fleeing survivors. Mistrustful of the slick surface, they slipped and fell. Orcs growled and snapped, while the heavier ogres felt the ice cracking underfoot and hastily retreated. Snarling, the beasts watched the humans flee the ruins of their city. They followed too slowly to catch them.

The distance between the pursued and the pursuers lengthened, until finally the humans reached the far shore. There they streamed away from the valley, to seek shelter in the mountains, the forests, or even the desert.

Behind them, the ice began to break apart. Many orcs fell through and were drowned in the lake. Those who fell in shallows scrambled back to the shore of the ruined city. There they stood, waving fists at their escaping quarry. Finally they turned and disappeared into the smoking ruins around them.

* * * * *

A pale gray dawn illuminated the miserable masses huddled along the fringe of the valley. No human lived, any longer, in the city. Those who had not escaped had died in the convulsions, or beneath the talons and fangs of the ravenous beasts of the Viperhand.

Rivers of lava still spilled down the slopes of Zatal, sending hissing columns of steam exploding upward when they contacted the lake waters. The steamy clouds of mist spread like a gray fog, masking visibility, covering despair.

"Perhaps it's a blessing, the clouds and the haze," said Erix quietly. She and Hal sat beneath a withered cedar tree, not far from the lake. "They cannot see what they leave behind."

Halloran looked at the people, thousands of them, slowly trudging away from the lake, upward and out of the doomed valley of Nexal. A few ragged bands of legionnaires stumbled among them, but no one showed any heart for further battle.

"Where will they go? Where *is* there to go?" he wondered aloud. He knew from their own travels that parched desert lay to the south and west, and yet this direction had been the only escape from the city.

"I don't know. Into the House of Tezca, perhaps, to starve or die of thirst." Even the contemplation of this inevitable tragedy, it seemed, could bring Erix no further pain, so shattered was her heart and spirit.

"What about Poshtli?" Hal asked hesitantly. "He must have died on the mountain."

"No!" she replied, somehow finding strength in her voice. "That I cannot believe!"

Halloran looked at her in wonder, and then sighed. He wouldn't argue with her, but quietly and privately he grieved for his friend.

"Erixitl? You are Erixitl of Palul?" The soft voice behind them pulled their attention swiftly around. They rose to their feet in alarm at the sight of the tall Jaguar Knight who stood there.

"What do you want?" Hal demanded harshly.

"Forgive me," replied the warrior, speaking calmly through the open jaws of his helmet. "I am Gultec."

"I remember you," said Erix. Once this knight had helped place her across a sacrificial altar, but strangely now she felt no fear. "What is it?"

"We must gather these people and lead them," said the knight. "They will listen to you. And I know where there is food and water in the desert. Come with me, and I will show you the path to safety."

They looked at him in surprise for a moment. He waited patiently. Finally he turned, and Halloran and Erixitl started after Gultec as the Jaguar Knight headed toward the rim of the valley.

EPILOGUE

Deep below the bowels of the seething volcano, the surviving Ancient Ones waited out the storm. And while they waited, tormented by hatred and rage, they planned their vengeance—a vengeance that would wrack the world for long ages, until the last of them had outlived their shame and their failure.

The conclave no longer consisted of the sleek, handsome figures of the dark elves. Instead, those who lived now turned in revulsion from each other, but everywhere they looked, their eyes were confronted by the inescapable repulsiveness of their new appearance.

The driders huddled in misery, terrified of the trembling mountain but still mighty, still full of rage. Now the spidery forms began to move, creeping from the tunnels of lava and smoke and ash toward the smoldering surface of the world above. Each of them walked upon eight fur-covered legs. A bloated, heavy abdomen suspended from the torso of each, and only the upper body bore a superficial resemblance to the elves they once had been.

One of these, the one that led the way back to the world, had a spider body of purest white, like a bleached insect that had never known the light of the sun.

FOR THE BEST IN PAPERBACKS, LOOK FOR THE 🐧

In every corner of the world, on every subject under the sun, Penguin represents quality and variety – the very best in publishing today.

For complete information about books available from Penguin – including Puffins, Penguin Classics and Arkana – and how to order them, write to us at the appropriate address below. Please note that for copyright reasons the selection of books varies from country to country.

In the United Kingdom: Please write to *Dept E.P., Penguin Books Ltd, Harmondsworth, Middlesex, UB7 0DA.*

If you have any difficulty in obtaining a title, please send your order with the correct money, plus ten per cent for postage and packaging, to *PO Box No 11, West Drayton, Middlesex*

In the United States: Please write to *Dept BA, Penguin, 299 Murray Hill Parkway, East Rutherford, New Jersey 07073*

In Canada: Please write to *Penguin Books Canada Ltd, 2801 John Street, Markham, Ontario L3R 1B4*

In Australia: Please write to the *Marketing Department, Penguin Books Australia Ltd, P.O. Box 257, Ringwood, Victoria 3134*

In New Zealand: Please write to the *Marketing Department, Penguin Books (NZ) Ltd, Private Bag, Takapuna, Auckland 9*

In India: Please write to *Penguin Overseas Ltd, 706 Eros Apartments, 56 Nehru Place, New Delhi, 110019*

In the Netherlands: Please write to *Penguin Books Netherlands B.V., Postbus 195, NL–1380AD Weesp*

In West Germany: Please write to *Penguin Books Ltd, Friedrichstrasse 10–12, D–6000 Frankfurt/Main 1*

In Spain: Please write to *Alhambra Longman S.A., Fernandez de la Hoz 9, E–28010 Madrid*

In Italy: Please write to *Penguin Italia s.r.l., Via Como 4, I-20096 Pioltello (Milano)*

In France: Please write to *Penguin Books Ltd, 39 Rue de Montmorency, F-75003 Paris*

In Japan: Please write to *Longman Penguin Japan Co Ltd, Yamaguchi Building, 2–12–9 Kanda Jimbocho, Chiyoda-Ku, Tokyo 101*

Another stunning fantasy adventure series from the publishers
of the DRAGONLANCE® Saga

FORGOTTEN REALMS®

Travel to a land beyond time ... and join princes and heroes in
the fight against evil forces.

The Moonshae Trilogy

Douglas Niles

Book 1: Darkwalker on Moonshae

Book 2: Black Wizards

Book 3: Darkwell

Enter the Moonshae Isles – a world filled with bizarre creatures,
dire occurrences, wondrous events and bitter struggle – in this
bestselling trilogy.

A deep, dark hole is eating away at the spring sunlight, sapping
its strength. The portents are not good. The evil beast is growing
stronger by the day, and its followers, the Firbolg, are craving
the sight of blood. To halt the spread of darkness, Prince Tristan
Kendrick must rally the Citizens of Moonshae...

Another stunning fantasy adventure series from the
publishers of the DRAGONLANCE® Saga

FORGOTTEN REALMS®

Travel to a land beyond time ... and join princes and heroes
in the fight against evil forces.

already published or in preparation:

The Icewind Dales Trilogy

R. A. Salvatore

Book 1: The Crystal Shard

Book 2: Streams of Silver

and Book 3: Halfling's Gem

Imagine the coldest, most hostile, most desolate place men dare
to live. Imagine battling fantastic creatures and deadly enemies
as the frigid wind bites your flesh, even through the heaviest of
furs and leather. Such is Icewind Dale – the subarctic tundra
wilderness of the Forgotten Realms. Here an unlikely quartet of
heroes must combat assassins, wizards, golems and more in the
struggle to preserve their homes and heritage.

Calling all fantasy fans –

Join the **Penguin/T S R Fantasy Fan Club** for exciting news and fabulous competitions.

For further information write to:

Penguin/T S R Fantasy Fan Club
27 Wrights Lane
London W8 5TZ

Open only to residents of the UK and Republic of Ireland

NOW ON YOUR HOME COMPUTER...

...FANTASY ROLE-PLAYING IN CLASSIC AD&D GAME STYLE!

OFFICIAL Advanced Dungeons & Dragons COMPUTER PRODUCT

POOL OF RADIANCE

A FORGOTTEN REALMS™ Fantasy Role-Playing Epic, Vol. I

SSI
STRATEGIC SIMULATIONS, INC.

AVAILABLE ON AMIGA · ATARI ST CBM 64/128 · MAC APPLE II · IBM PC

ALSO AVAILABLE
CURSE OF THE AZURE BONDS
- **WAR OF THE LANCE** • **DRAGONS OF FLAME**
- **HEROES OF THE LANCE** • **HILLSFAR** •
CHAMPIONS OF KRYNN • **DRAGONSTRIKE**
(CONSULT YOUR DEALER FOR FORMAT AVAILABILITY).

If you have any difficulty obtaining any of these titles contact U.S. Gold Ltd., Units 2/3 Holford Way, Holford, Birmingham B6 7AX. Tel: 021-625-3388.

TSR™ ADVANCED DUNGEONS & DRAGONS, AD&D, DRAGONLANCE and the TSR logo are trademarks owned by TSR, Inc., Lake Geneva, WI, USA and used under license from Strategic Simulations, Inc., Sunnyvale, CA, USA. © 1990 TSR, Inc. © 1990 Strategic Simulations, Inc. All rights reserved.